NEW ARRIVALS AT HEDGEHOG HOLLOW

HEDGEHOG HOLLOW BOOK 2

JESSICA REDLAND

Boldwood

First published in Great Britain in 2020 by Boldwood Books Ltd.

This paperback edition first published in 2021.

1

Copyright © Jessica Redland, 2020

Cover Design by Debbie Clement Design

Cover Photography: Shutterstock

A CIP catalogue record for this book is available from the British Library.

Paperback ISBN: 978-1-80280-361-7

Ebook ISBN: 978-1-83889-228-9

Kindle ISBN: 978-1-83889-107-7

Audio CD ISBN: 978-1-83889-108-4

Digital audio download ISBN: 978-1-83889-105-3

Large Print ISBN: 978-1-80048-837-3

Boldwood Books Ltd.

23 Bowerdean Street, London, SW6 3TN

www.boldwoodbooks.com

MIX
Paper from
responsible sources
FSC® C020471

To my brother-in-law Richard with love
No longer with us but forever in our hearts xx

THE STORY SO FAR...

As bridesmaid at her best friend Hannah's wedding, district nurse Samantha hoped she'd soon be saying 'I do' to boyfriend, James – best man to the groom. James admitted that he wanted to get married too... just not to Samantha. Devastated but desperate not to lose him, she hoped that all he needed was time and then he'd fall in love with her.

James *did* fall in love. Just not with Samantha. At her Gramps's seventieth birthday party that summer, he met Samantha's cousin, Chloe, and the attraction was obvious. Her beloved Gramps saw it too and encouraged Samantha to let James go. Gramps passed away overnight and she fulfilled her final promise to him.

A year later, Samantha was bridesmaid again... at Chloe and James's wedding. Her heart broke watching them say their vows. She hoped a fresh start on the Yorkshire Wolds in a new role as Health and Social Care Tutor at Reddfield TEC would help her get over James and move on.

On the way to the wedding reception, Samantha got lost and stopped at a farm – Hedgehog Hollow – in the hope of finding directions. What she actually found was octogenarian, Thomas Mickleby, collapsed in the farmhouse.

Arriving extremely late to the reception and covered in mud, things went from bad to worse when her vindictive Great-Aunt Agnes outed her for still being in love with James, right in front of Chloe. Chloe was livid and demanded Samantha leave.

A family rift opened up. Samantha had always had a toxic relationship with her mum but now Chloe had turned against her too.

Her fresh start on the Wolds was tinged with sadness as she was ostracised by those she loved but new friends Rich and Dave opened up their home and gave her much-needed friendship and support. Her dad, Jonathan, was there for her as always. And, despite a shaky start, she became good friends with Thomas whose life she'd saved.

Thomas's wife, Gwendoline, had always been passionate about hedgehogs, and her dream had been to run a large-scale rescue operation. They'd bought Hedgehog Hollow for that purpose but she died before they'd been able to get the centre up and running. Thomas then lived a lonely existence for the next two decades while the farm deteriorated around him.

Samantha spent Christmas Day with Thomas but he finally got his wish that afternoon to join his beloved Gwendoline. In his will, Thomas left Hedgehog Hollow to Samantha on the proviso that she finish what he and Gwendoline had started. It was an overwhelming prospect but she was determined to do them proud. Rich, a builder, had also been left instructions and a large budget to develop a barn for the rescue centre and refurbish the farmhouse.

While the building works were underway, Samantha learned about hedgehogs in her spare time. She hoped to engage the services of Alderson & Son Veterinary Practice to provide treatment at cost; an arrangement that Gwendoline had originally established. Her meeting with vet, Josh Alderson, didn't go well. It transpired that Gwendoline's arrangement had been with his father, Paul, who was no longer in Josh's life and never would be again. He had no intention of honouring anything connected to that man.

At the fiftieth birthday party of Lauren – Samantha's boss and also Josh's auntie – Samantha started to see Josh in a new light when he opened up about why he'd cut his dad out of his life. Paul had been in a long-term secret relationship with veterinary practice receptionist, Beth, who'd also been Josh's girlfriend. The affair only came to light when Beth fell pregnant with Paul's baby. Samantha shared her heartbreak over James and the family rift. That night, their relationship shifted from enemies into something pretty special.

A heavily pregnant Chloe asked to see Samantha then accused her of having an affair with James who had started behaving out of character. While angry words were exchanged Chloe went into labour. Samantha accompanied her to hospital where a tentative truce was called after Samantha's swift actions saved baby Samuel's life.

James wasn't having an affair with Samantha or anyone else. He'd been diagnosed with and treated for testicular cancer but had not wanted to worry Chloe who'd experienced a difficult pregnancy and needed to stay stress-free.

Work continued to develop Hedgehog Hollow but the Grimes boys had other ideas. Cousins Brynn and Cody Grimes were Gwendoline's great-nephews. Despite Gwendoline severing ties with her money-grabbing family years before her death, they decided the farm belonged to them. When threats, vandalism and legal action got them nowhere, they torched the barn. Samantha nearly lost her life trying to save their five hedgehog patients. When she came out of her coma, she and Josh admitted they loved each other.

Samantha's newfound happiness was tinged with the sadness that, although the rift with Chloe was healing, there was no hope for her mum. Before the arson attack, Samantha had asked if they could find a way to move forward and the truth came out that her mum never wanted her. Her failure to show at the hospital proved that.

Hedgehog Hollow is now officially open for business…

RECURRING CHARACTERS FROM FINDING LOVE AT HEDGEHOG HOLLOW:

Samantha Wishaw aka Sam or Sammie
Former district nurse turned Health & Social Care Tutor at Reddfield TEC. Owner of Hedgehog Hollow

Jonathan Wishaw
Samantha's dad
Veterinary surgeon at Alderson & Son Veterinary Practice

Debs Wishaw
Samantha's estranged mum
Identical twin to Chloe's mum, Louise

Chloe Turner
Samantha's cousin who married Samantha's ex, James

James Turner
Samantha's ex-boyfriend, now married to her cousin, Chloe

Samuel Turner
Chloe and James's baby

Louise Olsen
Samantha's auntie / Chloe's mum
Identical twin to Samantha's mum

Simon Olsen
Samantha's uncle / Chloe's dad

Josh Alderson
Samantha's boyfriend
Practice owner and veterinary surgeon at Alderson & Son
Veterinary Practice

Paul Alderson
Josh's estranged dad & former business partner

Beth Giddings
Paul's girlfriend / Josh's ex-girlfriend

Connie Harbuckle
Josh's mum
Non-identical twin to Lauren

Lauren Harbuckle
Josh's auntie
Non-identical twin to Connie
Samantha's boss at Reddfield TEC

Thomas Mickleby
Elderly widower befriended by Samantha
Left Hedgehog Hollow to Samantha in his will on the proviso she ran it as a hedgehog rescue centre

Gwendoline Mickleby
Thomas's wife whose dream it was to run the hedgehog rescue centre

Rich Cooper
Ambulance paramedic. Good friend of Samantha / partner of Dave. Samantha stayed with him when she moved to the Wolds

Dave Williams
Builder. Good friend of Samantha / partner of Rich. Samantha stayed with him when she moved to the Wolds

Hannah Spiers
District nurse on maternity leave
Samantha's best friend from university

Toby Spiers
Hannah's husband / James's best friend

Amelia Spiers
Hannah and Toby's baby / Samantha's goddaughter

Harry
Samantha's ex-boyfriend pre-James

Lewis
Josh's best friend from school

1

SAMANTHA

'I can't believe I let you talk me into this.' Josh attempted to plant his hands on his hips but the bulk of his enormous hedgehog costume prevented it.

'The leggings and footwear combo are particularly sexy.' I tried to hide my smirk but failed abysmally. 'I promise you won't have to wear it all afternoon. Just an hour or so.'

There was a knock on the lounge door and my best friend, Hannah, poked her head round it. 'Just checking how you're... Oh my God! Josh! That's hilarious. I need pictures.' She whipped her mobile out of her jeans pocket.

Josh groaned. 'Veterinary surgeon morphs into giant muppet. What a come down!' There was laughter in his tone and I knew he didn't mind really.

After Hannah left, laughing at the photos, Josh turned to me and smiled. 'If at any point in the future, you have even the tiniest doubt about how much I love you, picture me wearing this costume and know that I did it just for you. This right here?' He indicated the outfit. 'This is what true love looks like.'

I stood back, taking in the padded furry costume with curved spines down the back, the brown leggings and long-sleeved T-shirt clinging to his muscular legs and arms, the large paws on his feet and the matching paws for his hands. His face and a tuft of dark hair peeked out from the underside of the hedgehog's head and my heart melted.

'Every day you amaze me and every day I love you even more.' I gently kissed him, laughing as the head from his costume dishevelled my hair. 'Ready to introduce Mickleby the Hedgehog to his public?'

He screwed his face into a mock-mortified expression. 'Ready as I'll ever be.'

* * *

I squinted in the bright sunshine. It was such a beautiful early May day with a cornflower-blue sky and a few wispy clouds floating lazily on the gentlest of breezes. Pulling a bobble out of the pocket of my dress, I scraped my long, dark hair back into a loose ponytail.

Josh stumbled as we crossed the farmyard and I felt a twinge of guilt that he was dressed like a giant football mascot while I was wearing something much more understated and weather-appropriate. He'd given me some hedgehog-themed dresses as a present yesterday and I'd selected a blue short-sleeved one with a red and white hedgehog print for today. I'd combined it with the hedgehog wellies that my good friends Rich and Dave had given me as a housewarming gift when I moved out of their cottage and into the farmhouse a month ago.

As we approached the large stone barn that housed Hedgehog Hollow Rescue Centre, there were several high-pitched squeals and suddenly we were surrounded by children, stroking Mickleby's spines and trying to grasp hold of his paws.

A stream of children followed us, as though Mickleby was the

Pied Piper, as we made our way to the side of the barn. We'd created a meet and greet space there using a woodland backdrop and some wooden red and white spotted toadstools borrowed from the performing arts department at Reddfield TEC – the local college where I'd worked as a Health and Social Care Tutor since September last year. The scene was perfect for parents wishing to take photos of their children with our new mascot in exchange for a small donation towards the running of our charity.

Hannah and her husband Toby had volunteered for 'crowd control' duties. Their eight-month-old daughter, Amelia, was fast asleep in her buggy under the shade of a gazebo. I took a quick peek and smiled at the outfit they'd chosen: a pink cardigan with a hedgehog on each side worn over a pale blue pinafore dress with a giant hedgehog and butterfly on it. She looked so adorable lying there with her fists scrunched up against her cheeks and her lips intermittently smacking together.

Peeling my eyes away from her, I stood back and watched Josh for a while. As a vet, he was understandably superb with animals but this was the first time I'd seen him around children. He was such a natural, getting down on all fours so the smaller ones could stroke his spines and pretending to snuffle for food round the toadstools.

All around me, the sounds of laughter and chatter warmed my heart. We'd really done it. Hedgehog Hollow Rescue Centre was now fully operational, taking in poorly and injured hedgehogs and orphaned hoglets. When we'd officially opened yesterday – a low-key event for the press, local dignitaries and immediate family – we'd had twelve hogs but another two arrived during the evening. I'd been half-expecting someone to thrust one at me today at our Family Fun Day but, so far, there hadn't been any more patients.

Set out in the pasture was a bouncy castle, face painting (hedge-hogs being a popular choice) and various stalls selling locally produced food, drink and crafts. Dad, Uncle Simon, Rich and Dave were in charge of the barbeque. Josh's mum Connie and her twin sister Lauren (who was my manager at the TEC) were running a tombola and raffle while Chloe and my Auntie Louise were supervising some children's crafts.

'I'm off to do another talk,' I told Hannah. 'Look after my favourite hedgehog for me.' I nodded towards Josh.

'I'll make sure I keep him hydrated.'

'Only with water, though, and—'

'Never milk because hedgehogs are lactose intolerant.'

I grinned at her. 'Have I laboured that point too much?'

She shook her head. 'I've learned loads of new things and I'll admit to being completely smitten with hedgehogs now, thanks to you.'

I waved goodbye and made my way to the barn. If Hannah had learned a lot, my learning curve had been of epic proportions. I'd always loved animals – a trait picked up from my dad who, like Josh, was a vet and from my Gramps who'd adored wildlife – but I'd known very little about hedgehogs. Hours spent researching online, reading nature books and poring over pamphlets from The British Hedgehog Preservation Society, plus three days helping at an animal rescue centre, had given me a speedy education although nothing could beat being hands-on with my very own rescue hogs.

* * *

Late that afternoon, I sat forward in my chair in the deserted barn, rested my elbows on the treatment table and closed my eyes. I'd assured everyone I was fully recovered from my time in hospital and ready to face a busy weekend but that had been a big fib. I was still exhausted and ideally needed much more recovery time than I'd allowed myself. If I'd admitted to Josh how drained I was, he'd have insisted on delaying the opening and that was the last thing I wanted. The Grimes boys had already destroyed so much and I couldn't let them destroy our opening plans too. That would be like letting them win.

Although we hadn't officially opened for business when they torched the barn, we already had five hedgehogs. I saved four of them but the barn roof collapsed on me when I returned for the fifth. Josh pulled me to safety but I spent nine days in a coma and was devastated to come round to the discovery that the barn was gone and so was Quilly.

Three of the hedgehogs I'd saved from the fire had since been released but Mr Snuffles was still a patient. With a broken leg, he needed much longer to heal. Even though I tried not to have favourites, I'd always have a soft spot for him after what we'd been through together and I was already dreading having to one day say goodbye to him.

I reluctantly opened my eyes again and stood up. If I stayed there any longer, I was likely to fall asleep. Josh and I had no plans for tomorrow so I'd have a much-needed chance to relax and recover then.

Outside, I found Hannah pulling a rope across the photo scene while Josh simultaneously gulped down a bottle of water and wiped his brow with the back of his hand, his paws abandoned on the ground beside him.

'Aw, Josh! I didn't expect you *still* to be in costume,' I croaked, reaching for a towel and gently mopping his sweaty face. 'You must be melting.'

'I am! They never stopped coming. I've never been so in demand.'

'I can't thank you enough. I owe you big time.'

He winked at me. 'I can think of a few ways you could make it up to me.'

Hannah put her hands over her ears. 'Argh! Stop it! Not listening!'

Laughing, I prised her hands away. 'Sorry. It's gone well, then?'

She nodded. 'I think we've raised quite a lot.'

I flipped open the cashbox lid and whistled at the pile of notes and coins. 'That's way more than I expected.'

'People have been *very* generous with their donations. It was lovely to see so much kindness.'

'The locals have been amazing. I'm so lucky.' While I was incapacitated, the outraged community had pulled together, salvaged the stones and re-built the barn even better and more fit for purpose than it had been before with a proper second floor instead of the mezzanine we'd had installed in the original barn. Today's Family Fun Day was therefore a celebration of Hedgehog Hollow being open for business but also a massive thank you to everyone who had so generously donated their time, resources or money.

'And you've been amazing too,' I added, giving my friend a hug. 'Thank you so much for doing this.'

'Absolute pleasure.' Hannah squeezed me tightly. 'I'm so proud of you and everything you've achieved. You're such an inspiration.'

Tears pricked my eyes. 'Where's Toby and Amelia?' I asked, keen to take the focus away from me. It was a happy day and I didn't want to spend any of it crying.

'She needed changing so he's at the car sorting her out.'

'You look done in,' Josh said, pushing back his hedgehog head and rubbing the towel over his hair. 'And you're losing your voice.'

I rubbed my hand over my throat. 'I didn't think so many people would attend my talks. I've done more than double my estimate but it's nothing some hot blackcurrant won't sort out. Are you ready to get out of Mickleby?'

'Never been more ready.' He picked up the abandoned pair of paws.

'There were way more visitors than we expected,' Josh said as we slowly made our way across the farmyard, me carrying the heavy cashbox in both hands and Josh holding a paw in each of his. 'I'm thinking it's been pretty successful.'

'Definitely. I'm full of ideas for next year already.'

'I knew you would be. And I bet they involve me dressing up as Mickleby again.'

I smiled at the mock-resignation in his voice as I gave him a playful nudge. 'He's your alter-ego now. There's no escaping.'

He laughed. 'I might regret saying this but it's been good fun. Hot and sweaty but definitely fun.'

We'd almost reached the farmhouse when a woman's voice shouted Josh's name. We both turned to face a very pretty pregnant woman with long, pale blonde hair scraped back into a high pony-tail. She looked familiar but I couldn't quite place her. Then my stomach plummeted. I'd only ever seen her in a photo at Josh's cottage but it was definitely her. Beth. The woman who'd broken his heart.

I glanced at Josh, cringing for him coming face-to-face with his ex-girlfriend while dressed as a giant hedgehog. How mortifying must that be? What was she doing here anyway? He'd made it clear that he wanted nothing to do with her and understandably so after what she'd done.

His eyes were narrowed, his jaw tight. With a low snort, he turned his back on her and shuffled towards the farmhouse as fast as his outsized feet would allow.

I didn't want to strike up a conversation with her but it felt rude to completely ignore her so I shrugged my shoulders apologetically and muttered 'sorry' before turning and following Josh.

'Please Josh!' Beth cried.

'I've got nothing to say to you,' he shouted back to her before disappearing into the house.

'Josh!'

Sighing, I stopped and took a couple of steps back towards Beth. I was going to have to say something. 'I'm not sure that turning up here without warning was the best idea.' I hoped I sounded like I was giving her an explanation rather than a lecture.

She stroked her hands over her baby bump. 'I know, but he hasn't left me much choice. He's blocked my calls and emails. You're his girlfriend, right? Samantha, is it?'

I nodded, narrowing my eyes warily, unsure as to how she knew my name or where to find Josh. As though sensing my confusion, she added, 'I've got a friend who still works at Josh's practice. They weren't gossiping about you. I don't want to—'

'It's okay,' I reassured her.

'I'm glad Josh has found someone special,' she said. 'He deserves it. He was an amazing boss and a lovely boyf...' She broke off and shook her head, her pale cheeks colouring. 'I'm sure you already know that. I really do need to speak to him. Could you have a word with him. Please.'

Her ice-blue eyes fixed on mine pleadingly and I felt a wave of compassion for her. She wasn't what I'd expected. Josh had never said much about their relationship. All I knew were the basic facts leading to them splitting up about eighteen months ago. They'd been together for two years and he'd been in love with her but she'd been having a secret affair with his dad, Paul, for the whole of that time and five years prior to that. It all came out when she fell pregnant with Paul's baby – a hell of a shock for Josh and his mum – resulting in Connie filing for divorce and Josh severing all ties with Paul and Beth. I'd therefore built Beth up in my mind to be a horrible person as surely only someone really nasty could deceive him like she had. I'd imagined her to be self-assured and probably a bit arrogant but the woman in front of me looked lost and vulnerable which threw me.

'I'm sorry but it's really nothing to do with me. Josh has made it clear that he doesn't want anything to do with you, his dad or your family, and I have to respect that.' I kept my voice as gentle as I could.

'Please,' she begged again. 'It's really important I speak to him.' Tears glistened in her eyes. 'I know how stubborn he is and I know how much we hurt him but surely you can...'

Her voice tailed off as I shook my head vigorously. 'I'm sorry. I can't. It's Josh's decision and I'm not going to interfere.' I absolutely didn't want to get involved. Relationships between families could be complicated – something I knew first-hand – and I didn't want to say or do anything that might suggest to Josh that I didn't under-stand how he felt, because I absolutely did. I couldn't help feeling sorry for the woman stood before me but she'd made her choices and she had to live with them.

She nodded slowly. 'Okay. Thanks anyway.'

I watched her trudge back across the farmyard, her shoulders slumped and her head low. She opened her car door and my stomach churned as she sat in the driver's seat with the door wide open. The minutes ticked by and I worried she was psyching herself up to coming back and trying again.

'Please go,' I muttered. 'He doesn't need this.' Thankfully she closed the door, reversed out of the space and set off down the track.

I released a deep breath then headed into the farmhouse, shaking my head. Just when things were going really well...

2

JOSH

I slammed the farmhouse door behind me and, with an angry cry, tossed the stupid damn hedgehog paws down the hallway. What the bloody hell was *she* doing here? And how did she even know where to find me? I stomped into the lounge. This was typical Beth. She always had to have things her own way and, every time she was told no, she simply pushed and pushed until she finally got what she wanted, whatever the cost to others. Not that I'd realised that at the time. She'd had me completely under her spell.

I paced up and down in front of the fireplace, clenching and unclenching my fists. What would it be this time? Still trying to persuade me to let them move into Alder Lea – the house at the practice? *My* house. The one they'd driven me from after I discovered they'd been using it for their sordid little affair.

Or would it be yet another request to forgive my father? Yeah, right! *Never* going to happen.

Or perhaps it was the other classic of trying to convince me to meet their baby. 'But he's your half-brother,' she'd whined last time I accepted her call in a lapse of concentration. Half-brother? Biologically, perhaps, but not emotionally. How could they even think I'd be interested in playing happy families after what her pregnancy cost me and, more importantly, what it did to Mum? I'd blocked Beth's calls after that. Not interested. Ever.

And now they had another kid on the way. I'd known she was expecting again – she'd thrown in that little gem during our last conversation – but it was still a shock to actually see her standing there with an obvious baby bump. I shuddered thinking about it. The pair of them could spawn an army for all I cared and there was still no way I was going to step into the role of big brother.

I shuffled towards the sofa and tried to sit but the stupid bulky costume made it impossible. Grimacing as sweat trickled down my back, I attempted to haul the hedgehog over my head but managed to get it halfway up my body before trapping my arms inside the fabric. I couldn't see a thing and cursed loudly as my shins collided with the coffee table. I tried to shift the hedgehog again but I was stuck fast and getting hotter by the second. Where was Sam? Beth had better not be spinning her a one-sided, lie-ridden sob story.

The sound of the farmhouse door closing and Sam calling my name filled me with relief.

'Help!' I called.

Moments later, Sam's lilting laughter filled the lounge. 'Oh my gosh! What happened?'

'I got stuck.'

'I can see that. Can you kneel down?'

I fell forward onto my knees, wincing as they hit the solid wood floor. Sam was still laughing as she gathered the bottom of the costume and yanked it up over my arms then pulled it from the top, finally freeing me.

I gulped in several deep lungfuls of air. 'That was scary. I could hardly breathe in there.'

'You're safe now. I've rescued you.' Her eyes sparkled with mischief. 'Bad Mickleby outfit.' Then she started laughing again.

Her mirth was infectious and I couldn't help smiling as I backed up against the sofa, wiping the sweat trickling down my face. 'I'm shattered.'

'I'm not surprised. It's heavier than I realised. Why don't you get showered and changed while I go back out and help finish things off?' Her voice was hoarse and kept cracking as she spoke.

'I thought you wanted some hot blackcurrant. You sound like you need it.'

'I do but if I sit down in a comfy seat with a drink there's no way I'll manage to get up again. It's not fair of me to leave all the packing away to everyone else. I'll make do with some water for now.'

'Do you need another pair of hands?'

Sam smiled. 'You've done more than your fair share today. There's loads of helpers. We'll be tripping over each other as it is.'

I nodded, relieved that I could be spared.

Much as I didn't want to get into a conversation about Beth right now, I had to ask. 'Has *she* gone?'

'Yes.'

'You were quite a while outside. I hope she wasn't feeding you a sob story.' I tried hard to keep my tone light and not sound like I was accusing her of doing anything wrong but I knew what Beth was like. She was likely to take advantage of Sam's kind nature like she'd taken advantage of mine. Now that I knew what she was really like, I had no qualms about turning my back on her and walking away but Sam didn't know her. She also had a hell of a lot more patience with people than I had. Give me animals instead any day of the week.

'She wanted me to talk you round but I said no so she left. The only reason I was outside for so long was to make sure she actually drove off.'

My tense shoulders relaxed as I scrambled to my feet. 'Hopefully she's got the message but, if she comes back, don't listen to her.

She's a liar and she manipulates people. I don't know what she thinks she's playing at, turning up here like that.' I winced at the bitterness in my voice.

Sam gave my arm a gentle squeeze. 'You get that shower and I'll see you later.' She kissed my damp cheek then headed into the kitchen to get a drink.

The powerful jets of water in the shower a few minutes later did nothing to relax me. All I could hear was Beth's voice. All I could picture was her pleading expression. And that baby bump. Why couldn't she leave me alone? I'd blocked her calls and emails but that clearly wasn't a strong enough message. She'd had to take it a step further and seek me out. She'd infiltrated Sam's special day and, even though Sam didn't seem fazed by it, I was fuming with Beth for doing that. What would it take to get her to back off and accept that I didn't want anything to do with any of them? Ever.

3

SAMANTHA

I closed the farmhouse door behind me, shaking my head. Thank goodness I hadn't agreed to help Beth. From Josh's reaction, pushing him to speak to her definitely wouldn't have gone down well, not that I was surprised by that. I didn't think she'd have dared humiliate Josh or herself by turning up at the veterinary practice after he'd dismissed her from her role as receptionist there but I hoped this wouldn't signal the start of regular visits to the farm now that she knew where to find him.

In the farmyard, Hannah walked towards me holding Amelia. 'Toby's packed everything up and put it in the barn.'

I gave her a grateful smile. 'What a star. Thank you both so much for today. I really appreciate it.'

'It's been great fun. You'll have to let us know how much we've raised later. Oh, moments after you left, a pregnant woman appeared asking after Josh. Did she catch up with you?'

I rolled my eyes ruefully. 'Yes, she found us.'

'You don't look too pleased about that.'

'It was Beth. Josh's ex.'

'That was her?' Hannah grimaced. 'What did she want?'

'I'm not sure. She said she needs to speak to him urgently but Josh wasn't interested. She wanted me to try to talk him round but whether or not Josh re-connects with his dad has got to be *his* decision when and if he's ready to make it.'

She looked surprised. 'I'm impressed. I thought you'd have done whatever you could to fix things.'

I sighed. 'Once upon a time, I would have, but not everything can be fixed. Look at Mum and me.'

Toby appeared and I thanked him for his help while Hannah strapped Amelia into her car seat, then I waved them goodbye.

There weren't many people left now. Most of the cars in the farmyard belonged to friends and family. Ambling into the pasture, I spotted Dad and Uncle Simon who told me I could find Auntie Louise and Chloe in the barn.

I'd been surprised when Chloe volunteered to help today because she wasn't one for helping anyone unless there was something in it for her. I wasn't sure whether Auntie Louise had coaxed her into it or whether Chloe had made the decision herself as another step in trying to repair our damaged relationship. Either way, I was grateful for the assistance.

Things were still tense between Chloe and me but it was unrealistic to expect our friendship to return to normal after everything she'd done. I wasn't going to hold a grudge – that wasn't who I was – but I couldn't simply brush it aside either. She'd hurt me badly and it would take some time and effort for us to re-build our relationship. I still loved my cousin and wanted her in my life, but I couldn't help being cautious.

'Have you had fun?' I asked them both as I stepped into the barn, very conscious that I'd been so busy doing talks that I'd barely had a chance to speak to them all day.

Chloe smiled. 'You know me. Anything crafty and I'm in heaven.'

For someone who was always immaculately dressed – usually in dresses and heels – and never left the house without full make-up and her hair perfectly styled, Chloe's love for glitter, glue and paint flummoxed me. Whenever I saw her dressed for her job as a pre-school assistant in jeans, polo shirt, tabard and trainers, it threw me as it was so un-Chloe.

'I loved every minute,' Auntie Louise said. 'And I'm so proud of this one.' She put her arm round Chloe's shoulders. 'It was a lovely insight into what she's like at work.'

'How has it been without Samuel?' I asked Chloe. She was currently on maternity leave having given birth to Samuel nearly eleven weeks ago but she'd left him at home in Whitsborough Bay with James today.

She scowled. 'Weird. I wanted to bring him with me.'

'And I told her it would do her good to have a break,' Auntie Louise said. 'It's hard work being with a new baby 24/7.'

'Yeah, but James is—'

'Samuel's dad and perfectly capable of looking after his son.' Auntie Louise squeezed Chloe's shoulder. 'And he knows that your Auntie Debs is round the corner if he needs help.'

I nearly snorted with laughter at that one. Mum being helpful in a baby crisis? I couldn't imagine it.

Leaving Auntie Louise and Chloe in the barn, packing away the craft supplies, I helped Dad and Uncle Simon take the gazebos down.

'Are you pleased with how it went?' Dad asked as we stuffed one of the gazebos into its bag.

'Very pleased. I think we might have raised quite a bit.'

'Did you see the donation crates are full?'

'Really? That's brilliant.' I'd put out several large wheeled crates for donations of dog and cat food, disinfectant wipes, fleecy blankets and cleaning products. I genuinely hadn't expected them to get filled.

'I'll help you wheel them inside then I'll head off home,' Dad said.

'You don't want to stop for a drink or something to eat?'

He shook his head. 'I'm sure you and Josh could do with some peace and quiet after being invaded for two days. Besides, I'm going out for dinner with Lauren and Connie.'

'Anywhere nice?'

'We're going to try The Tortoise and Hare in Fimberley now that it's been refurbished.'

It was fabulous to see how settled Dad was, getting to know the area and building friendships. I'd worried about him making so many major life changes in such a short space of time – filing for divorce from Mum, selling the family home in Whitsborough Bay, starting work at Josh's practice, and moving into Lauren's spare room – but I'd never seen him so happy or relaxed. The move to the Yorkshire Wolds had been exactly what we'd both needed.

'Sam! Help!' yelled Chloe from the barn door, panic in her voice.

Heart racing, I dropped the gazebo pole and sprinted over to the barn with Dad right behind me.

'What's wrong?' There were a few people milling around but I couldn't see anything amiss. From Chloe's shrill tone, I'd expected to find someone had keeled over with a heart attack.

'Patient.' She pointed at a tall, silver-haired man, probably in his seventies, holding a cardboard box.

Heartrate slowing as I realised it was case of Chloe being overly dramatic as usual rather than a major crisis, I smiled at the man. 'Hi, I'm Samantha.'

'I'm Terry,' he said, his voice low and gruff. 'I've got a hedgehog for you.'

'Do you want to bring the box over to the table so I can take a look?'

Terry followed me to the treatment table and placed the box down. I pulled on a pair of gloves and peeled back the strips of newspaper inside it.

'What have we got here, then?' I said, lifting out the hog. 'Oh dear. Have we got ourselves tangled?' Thick black netting was wrapped round the hedgehog's spines and front legs.

Chloe joined us. 'Oh no! The poor little thing.'

Terry shook his head. 'Stupid community group fundraised for nets for the goalposts on the playing fields in our village. I told them nets are bad for wildlife but would they listen to me? Told me I was making up problems. I'm out walking our Wilbur this afternoon when he starts bouncing up and down and barking by the goalposts. Then I find this little fella all tangled up in them, just like I warned them. I cut a chunk out the net and managed to get it off his face but some of it's too knotted and I didn't want to hurt him.'

I carefully unfurled the hog to see how deeply the net was wrapped and whether it had cut into the skin.

'Our little friend is a girl.' I lifted some of her spines to check for dehydration but she seemed fine, suggesting she probably hadn't been caught in the net for too long. 'You were right to bring her here. It looks like the netting has cut into her a bit but it isn't wrapped round any vital organs or restricting her breathing. I won't know if there's any damage to her legs until I remove it.'

'She'll live then?' Terry asked, obvious relief in his voice.

'She should be okay.' I'd vowed never to give false hope to anyone bringing a hedgehog in if it was in a bad way, but I was confident that this one would make a full recovery. She was a good size and an initial visual once-over suggested she didn't have any other health problems. 'I'll cut it all off, clean her wounds and keep her here until she's fully healed. Would you like to leave your details so I can contact you when she's ready to be released or would you prefer me to release her here at the farm?'

'I'll take her home when she's better.'

'If you could get me a phone number or email address for the person in charge of the community group, I can let them know that nets like that *do* pose a huge risk to our wildlife, especially hedgehogs, and they need to lift them off the ground on evenings. I'll take photos of our little friend here so they can see the problem for themselves.'

For the first time, Terry smiled. 'You'd do that? That'd be right good.'

'It's the least I can do. We're here to help sick and injured hedgehogs but the best way to help them is to spread the word about how to prevent unnecessary injuries like this.'

I gently placed the hog back in the box so I could prepare the equipment needed to cut her free.

'Chloe, would you mind getting Terry's details for me? It's that clipboard there.' I smiled at Terry. 'Thanks for bringing her in.'

'How much do I owe you?'

'We're a charity so there's no charge but donations are always welcome.'

I wiped down the treatment table, placed a small fleecy blanket on it, added scissors and tweezers on a metal tray, then weighed the hog so that I could prepare the right quantity of painkiller and antibiotics.

'Can I watch?' Terry asked.

'If you'd like.'

Suddenly I was surrounded by a sea of curious faces. There'd been a few people in the barn already but Chloe's cries had obviously brought others running.

'I'll need everyone to step back to give me some space to work.' I looked round the group. 'And can I ask you to stay nice and quiet to avoid stressing the hedgehog any further?'

I handed Chloe my mobile. 'Will you be photographer? If you can get some close-ups of our patient and then some of the treatment, that would be great. And please forgive my croaky voice, everyone. Hopefully it will hold out.' I cleared my throat. 'I'm going to inject our hedgehog with painkillers and antibiotics before I cut the netting away. I've weighed her to see how much I need so I'm going to prepare my syringes now.'

I was used to speaking to groups of people thanks to my teaching role. I was also used to undertaking medical procedures, having been a district nurse for eight years before that. What I wasn't used to was combining the two. Another learning experience.

'We need to give our hedgehog a name.' I placed a smaller tray of syringes on the table. 'We've already gone through all the hedgehog-related names we can think of so Josh and I picked a new theme which is movie and/or book characters. One of last night's patients was a male hog and we named him Frodo from *Lord of the Rings* so can anyone suggest a female character from that series for this little lady? My mind's gone blank.'

'Arwen,' came a few whispered responses.

I smiled. 'Perfect. So, are you ready to meet Arwen?'

* * *

An hour later, Arwen was patched up, fed, watered and nestled in a crate which would be her home until she was fully healed. Outside, all the borrowed gazebos, tables and chairs had been packed away and everyone had gone home.

'Perfect timing,' Josh called from the kitchen when I opened the farmhouse door. 'Kettle's just boiled and there's a hot blackcurrant with your name on it in your favourite hedgehog mug.'

'Ooh, you star.' I eased off my wellies and went into the kitchen to hug him. 'Feeling more human after a shower?'

'Definitely. I'm no longer half-hedgehog, half-perspiration. Has everyone gone now?'

'Yes and we have a new patient.'

We took our drinks through to the lounge and, between grateful sips on soothing hot blackcurrant, I told Josh about Arwen.

He smiled at me when I'd finished, his dark eyes twinkling in that way I loved. 'Check you out, educating your audience with a live case.'

'I know! Not quite what I was expecting but I'm hoping everyone who watched will tell others and they'll think twice about leaving netting out.'

'Hopefully. And I have great news. I counted the money in the cashbox while you were out. Nearly £400.'

'Oh my gosh! That's amazing. With the tombola, raffle and barbeque, I think we might have passed a grand. And the donation crates were full.'

'I'm so proud of you.' He took my hand in his and squeezed it. 'So many people were singing your praises today. You're a local hero.'

'I don't know about that but I do feel like what we're doing here is making a difference already.'

'It definitely is. We've only officially been open for two days but we've already had twenty patients and released four of them.'

'And lost one,' I said, thinking about poor Quilly. I knew I was never going to be able to save all the hedgehogs but Quilly's death would always hurt that bit more with him being the first loss and with it being so unnecessary. Fortunately, they'd caught and charged the Grimes boys. Sentencing would be imminent and then it would all be over.

'Focus on how many you've saved,' he said gently.

I put my empty mug down and Josh lifted his arm up so that I could change position and snuggle up to him. He gently kissed me then pulled me closer and slowly ran his fingers up and down my arm as I relaxed against his chest. He always seemed to say the right things to comfort me and I adored moments like this where we could just be together, holding each other. He made me feel so loved which was refreshing after my previous two relationships. I shuddered at the thought of them.

'Are you cold?' Josh asked, wrapping his arms more tightly round me.

'No. Just thinking about how lovely this is and how it was never like this with James or Harry. I feel a bit stupid for putting up with such rubbish relationships.'

'It's easy to see the bad stuff when you've moved on. Not so easy when you're in the midst of it.'

I wasn't sure if Josh would want to talk about Beth tonight but what he'd just said was clearly referencing her and it was too good a lead-in to ignore. 'Beth turning up earlier was a bit of a surprise.'

His body tensed. 'Yeah, and not a pleasant one.'

I adjusted my position so I could see his face.

'I don't know what part of "not interested" she doesn't understand. She had no right to come here.' He sighed and added in a gentler tone, 'I'm sorry she put a dampener on your special day.'

'*Our* special day. And she didn't put a dampener on it for me. I'm fine. It's you I'm worried about. I can tell she's upset you.'

Josh was quiet for a moment then shook his head. 'I'm not upset. I'm angry. I thought – hoped – the pair of them were out of my life for good.'

'If you're ready to talk about it, I'm listening.'

4

I looked down at Sam's earnest expression and sighed. Bloody Beth. I hadn't wanted to drag Sam into our mess. She'd been through too much crap already with her own dysfunctional family and then the arson attack so she didn't need the burden of my past adding to that. But there was no way Beth would give up. She'd be back and I wouldn't put it past her to try and catch Sam alone so she could manipulate her. She'd turn on the waterworks and plead her case: *I'm so sorry. I was so confused. I didn't realise anyone would get hurt.* Yeah, right. She'd known *exactly* what she was doing and I'd been the sucker who fell for her games.

'Josh...?' Sam gently squeezed my arm.

I shrugged. 'I'm not sure what else there is to tell.' I'd given her the basic facts – how Beth and I got together after her long-term relationship with a married man ended. Except it hadn't really ended. When she fell pregnant, I discovered her married man was actually my dad and the baby was his. Classy. 'What else do you want to know?'

'How you're feeling about it. Cutting a parent out of your life is huge. You know how hard I've found it severing ties with Mum but we always had a toxic relationship. You said you were close to your dad before.'

'Close?' My fists clenched and I could feel the anger welling inside me. 'I idolised that man. He was everything to me. He wasn't just my dad. He was my friend, my business partner and my mentor...'

It was obvious from a young age how lucky I was to have a dad like mine. My best mate Lewis's dad had jumped ship before his brother, Danny, was born. He intermittently turned up over the years demanding to see them then letting them down. Their mum remarried twice. Stepdad number one belittled and yelled at them and stepdad number two used them as his personal punchbags.

My dad became the father-figure they never had and they were like my brothers. They'd join us for family walks, bike rides, camping and fishing trips. When Mum began working weekends, we continued boys-only outings.

Dad always managed to strike what must be a tricky balance between being a father – including to two surrogate sons – and being a friend. Time with him was full of fun and laughter but we were always clear on where the lines were and never took the mickey with our behaviour. I'd had such respect for him back then. Turns out he had none for me or he wouldn't have done what he did.

It was inevitable that I'd follow in Dad's and Granddad's footsteps and become a vet. I'd always loved animals and, when I turned fourteen, I started working on the practice reception every Saturday morning and helping out Dad or Granddad during school holidays. They were such inspiring role models in the way they embraced new thinking and ran an efficient, caring practice. I lapped up every bit of knowledge I could.

Granddad couldn't wait for me to graduate as a vet and join them full-time. He loved the idea of three generations of qualified vets working together at the practice he'd set up but it never happened. The morning after my final exam at university, Mum phoned to tell me that Grandma had died during the night. The heart attack was a hell of a shock to everyone as she'd always been so fit and healthy.

Together since they were sixteen and devoted to each other, Granddad never got over the loss. The day after I graduated, we lost him in exactly the same way. Mum was convinced he'd died from a broken heart and, despite being a man of science, I was inclined to agree.

Granddad's share of the practice passed to me, along with their home, Alder Lea. It didn't feel right accepting such a generous bequest, especially as Granddad's share of the practice was the majority 60 per cent stake. I wanted to swap with Dad or at least make the partnership an equal split but he wouldn't hear of it. He insisted that he could learn as much from me as I could from him. He encouraged me to ask questions and challenge the way things were done and together we expanded the practice. There was never a need for me to play the 'I'm the biggest shareholder' card because our relationship was based on a true partnership.

I shrugged as I looked at Sam. 'I trusted him, I respected him and I loved them both. What did I get in return? They lied to me and nearly destroyed my entire world.'

'I'm so sorry. I still can't believe she was seeing you both. That's not right.'

'It's sick and it's twisted.' I exhaled loudly. 'Eighteen months on and I still cannot get my head round any of it. My parents had a happy marriage so why did he hook up with Beth in the first place? That makes no sense. Then when it ended – if it really did end – why did Beth make a play for me? Who goes out with the dad then moves onto the son? And what about him? He *knew* I was seeing Beth. Not at first because we didn't want anyone at work to know but he knew for well over a year yet he was still carrying on with her. What sort of man does that?'

My voice had risen in volume and pitch. I shook my head. 'I'm sorry. I don't mean to sound so angry but I can't help it. I'm still furious with them both and I can't see that ever going away.'

'Have they ever explained why they did it?' Sam visibly winced. 'Not that I can think of any acceptable excuse for behaving like that.'

'He tried to placate me the day it all came out but I wasn't interested in his excuses. I was more worried about Mum. She needed to know. The affair was bad enough but the baby news was horrendous. Mum and Dad both wanted a big family but it never happened. She miscarried five times, three after having me and twice more after my sister, Kayleigh, was stillborn.'

'Oh my gosh! I'm so sorry.' Sam hugged me tightly. 'That must have been tough for you all.'

'Dad never really talked about it although I think that's why he was so devoted to Lewis and Danny,' I said when she pulled away. 'Mum talked about it quite a lot and was always upbeat and optimistic. Obviously she was devastated but she used to call me her miracle baby and said she was grateful I'd stayed when the others couldn't.' I gave her a weak smile. 'I never really missed out on siblings thanks to Lewis and Danny being my honorary brothers.'

'How did your mum take the news about your dad and Beth?'

'Not good.' My stomach churned and I shuddered as I pictured Mum that evening. 'They'd been together since they were thirteen and they were happy. And then, just like that, it was all over and she discovered that the past seven years had been a lie. Something like that was never going to be easy to deal with.'

Not easy at all. I'd never forgive the pair of them for what happened next.

The hurt that Paul and Beth had caused Josh was obvious from every single word, every frown, every sigh. And no wonder. What they'd done was despicable. He had every right to still feel anger and confusion, especially as it had hurt Connie too so he'd have needed to be there for his mum while reeling from the impact on himself.

'Thanks for telling me. I know it wasn't easy for you to talk about it.'

'I don't want either of them back in my life. I can't do it.'

'Do you think Beth will come back?'

'She's bound to. It's the way she works and she'll try to drag you into it all. I'm really sorry.'

'Hey, don't apologise. It's not your fault. And I can hardly complain about your ex turning up when mine's part of the family.'

Josh smiled ruefully. 'I still think James is a tosser for how he treated you but you'd be proud of me because I had a civil conversation with him at the press launch yesterday. I forgot to mention it.'

I raised my eyebrows, surprised. They'd only seen each other a

few times but hadn't gone beyond awkwardly exchanging pleas-
antries so this was welcome news. Things were uncomfortable
enough in my family without adding bad feeling between Josh and
James into the mix. 'I *am* proud of you. Thank you. What did you
talk about?'

'Football, beer and women.'

I laughed as I lightly nudged him. 'And what did you *really* talk
about?'

'Safe stuff. The hedgehogs, the farm and Samuel.'

'Any mention of the cancer?' James had been diagnosed with
testicular cancer while Chloe was pregnant but the last I'd heard
from her was that the removal of one testicle seemed to have
caught it.

'He said he was tired but I wasn't sure if that was because of the
cancer or Samuel.'

'Probably both. I need to have a proper catch-up with Chloe
about it at some point. I'd ring James direct but she'd probably
accuse me of being after her husband again.' An expression I
couldn't read flickered across Josh's face. Surely not jealousy?
'Please tell me you wouldn't be worried about that.'

He shook his head vigorously. 'God, no! I trust you completely.'

'Then what was that look?'

He grimaced. 'It's was the mention of Chloe. I'm finding it hard
to warm to her and I don't think she likes me either. Urgh. I sound
like a five-year-old.'

I gave him a reassuring smile. 'It's okay. You're not the first to say
that about her. She's guarded around people she doesn't know
which tends to come across as being distant and disinterested.'

'She wasn't very distant or disinterested when she met James,'
he said, his eyes twinkling mischievously. 'Exactly the opposite.'

The fact that I could laugh about it showed how far I'd come.
Even though James had broken my heart by choosing Chloe and

she'd then stamped on it when she cut me off after their wedding, I'd go through it all again if it meant I could have my current life with Josh, the farm and the rescue centre. To find a rainbow, you've got to have some rain and I'd certainly experienced one heck of a storm before I'd found mine.

6

JOSH

Mum used to joke that I could sleep standing up in the middle of a thunderstorm and she was right. Any time, any place. The only time I'd ever struggled was after *the incident*. Until now. I plumped my pillows for what felt like the millionth time and sighed as I lay back down, staring into the darkness. *Another thing you've messed up. Cheers for that, Beth.*

Her appearance this afternoon had stirred up a load of unwelcome memories about our two years together. Our lie of a relationship. So many regrets. So many moments when I could have – and should have – walked away.

This coming August would mark four years since that fateful Friday morning when I found her crying in the staffroom. It wasn't unusual to find a staff member in tears. We saved animals but we had to euthanise too and that could be tough on everyone. I assumed that was the case with Beth and said something to that effect but she blushed, said it wasn't work-related and apologised that she'd been unprofessional by bringing her home-life into work.

She didn't volunteer any details so I could have left it there and things might have been so different but I had to do it. I had to try to be the caring, understanding boss and remind her that my door was open if she ever needed to talk – just like Granddad would have done.

After the weekend, she turned up at my office and said she'd like to take me up on my offer. She claimed to be uncomfortable discussing it at work in case anyone overheard. Another moment where things could have been different if I'd had the sense to close the door and remind her that the walls were extra thick but, instead, I found myself suggesting lunch at The Owl and Pussycat Tearoom in Reddfield – one of Mum's favourite cafés. The tables were well spread out so, if she wanted privacy, she could have it. Even as she returned to the reception, I knew I'd made a mistake, but I didn't change the plan and I knew why. I liked her. A lot. Finding her in tears had cranked that attraction up a notch. I wanted to be the one to comfort her and tell her things would be all right. I wanted to be the one to make them all right.

In the tearoom, the waitress taking our order had barely stepped away from the table before Beth blurted out the reason for her distress.

'It's a man. You'd probably already guessed that. He's a bit older than me and we've been together for five years. The problem is that he keeps lying to me.'

'About anything in particular?'

She fixed her eyes on mine. 'About leaving his wife.'

'He's married?' I was disappointed. Beth seemed so sweet and kind. I'd never have had her pinned as 'the other woman'. She mustn't have known he was married and was in too deep by the time she found out.

Beth twiddled with the end of her plait. 'I knew he was married when I met him...'

More disappointment. Why hadn't she walked away?

'... but I was only seventeen at the time,' she continued. 'It was just meant to be a bit of harmless fun.'

Her eyes were big and sad and my disappointment faded. It hadn't been her fault. She'd been young and flattered by the attention of an older man. He'd no doubt fed her some bullshit about his wife not understanding him or the marriage being on the rocks. I knew the sort. Wanker.

'You can't control who you fall in love with, can you?' she asked, her voice pleading with me to understand.

'I suppose not.' I hadn't a clue. I'd never actually fallen in love. Not even close. I wasn't going to admit to Beth that my longest-lasting relationship had been four months.

'Anyway, he kept promising me he'd leave his wife for me. Said they didn't get on anymore and the marriage had been over for a long time. So I waited and waited and waited some more. Five years is a long time to keep stringing someone along, isn't it?'

I wasn't sure how to respond to that. I wouldn't have waited five days, let alone five years. Although I wouldn't have gone out with someone married in the first place, even for a bit of 'harmless fun' as she called it because it wasn't harmless, was it? Someone always got hurt.

'I'd had enough so I gave him an ultimatum – one week to end it with his wife or we were over for good. That took us to the end of last week and he...' Her voice broke and tears ran down her cheeks.

'He didn't leave his wife?' I suggested gently, offering her a paper napkin.

She nodded as she dabbed her eyes. 'He says he loves us both but that doesn't make sense. How can you love two people at the same time? And how can he possibly still love *her*? They live separate lives. They barely speak to each other.'

I shrugged, aware that I was being no help whatsoever. I had no experience of the situation, no platitudes I could offer her.

'I think it's because of his son,' she wailed.

'He has kids too?' Another flicker of disappointment.

'Just the one although he's adamant that the son isn't the reason he's never ended it.'

'I suppose it's an added complication,' I offered feebly.

'You probably think I'm a horrible person,' she said, her voice full of defeat as her shoulders slumped. 'And you'd be right. I *am* a horrible person. I did a bad thing by getting involved with him and this is my punishment. I deserve it. I should have walked away as soon as he told me he was married and not believed all the crap he fed me about it being over.'

The need to make it better for her took hold. 'It's not your fault. As you said, you were only seventeen at the time and you weren't the one who was married so you weren't doing anything wrong. It's *his* fault. He should have known better and he shouldn't have strung you along for five years if he had no intention of leaving his wife.'

She placed her hand over mine and my pulse raced.

'You'd never treat anyone like that, would you?' She gently stroked her thumb across the back of my hand, sending a zip of electricity up my arm.

'Erm... I'm not a convincing liar. It's much easier to stick to the truth. If I was seeing someone then met someone else I liked, I'd take that as a signal that my current relationship wasn't working and I'd end that first.'

She still didn't move her hand. 'And is your current relationship working?' she asked, her voice low and seductive.

'I'm not in one.'

Her eyes widened. 'I'd have thought a hottie like you would have been snapped up ages ago.'

Had she really just called me a 'hottie'? Did she seriously think of me that way? It was flattering. She was gorgeous and sweet but anything happening between us was out of the question. Rebound relationships were never a good idea and I was her boss. We had to work together and how awkward would that be if she returned to her married man or my initial attraction faded as usual and I walked away when I realised it wasn't going anywhere?

So I shrugged, trying not to focus on her compliment or the feel of her hand over mine. 'I've not met the right person yet. Maybe one day.'

Beth gazed at me through lowered lashes. 'Maybe one day soon. You never know, you could already have met the right person and just not realised it yet.'

The air crackled with sexual tension and, for the first time ever, I felt out of my depth, not knowing what to say or do.

Our lunch arrived, she removed her hand, the conversation shifted onto 'safe' subjects like the food and work, and I returned to my comfort zone. Beth was chatty but not flirty and she kept her hands to herself for the rest of lunch. I felt a frisson of disappointment.

We'd travelled in separate cars to avoid any speculation as to why we were heading out for lunch together.

'I'll give you a couple of minutes' head start,' I said as she unlocked her car.

She smiled. 'Thanks for listening. And thanks for not judging me.'

'It's not my place to judge. What you do outside of work is your business.'

She stood on her tiptoes and placed a light kiss on my cheek. 'You could always make it your business,' she whispered into my ear. Then she got in her car and drove off, leaving me standing in the market square, still feeling her lips against my skin and her warm breath on my neck and imagining her taking it further. Bad idea. Very bad.

I should have kept my distance but, across the week, I found excuses to venture into reception more often than usual and was rewarded each time with a suggestive look or a flirtatious smile. It felt exciting. Risky. Dangerous even.

At home time on Friday, she knocked on my office door. 'Have you got much more work to do?' she asked, eyeing the overflowing in-tray on my desk.

'A couple of hours. I'm behind with my paperwork.' Because I'd spent too much time thinking about her instead of focusing. 'At least I don't have a long commute.'

She laughed. 'Thirty seconds?'

'If that. You off home, then?'

'Yeah, not that there's anything to rush home for. Boring weekend all alone.' She gave me a meaningful look and it would have been so easy to ask if she wanted to catch a film or go for a drink but I couldn't go there. Too messy.

I should have returned to my work but instead asked the question that had been prodding me all week. 'Your married man hasn't left his wife then?'

Tears glistened in her eyes. 'No. Still with her so still finished with me.'

'I'm sorry.' I genuinely was – not because it was over but because I didn't like to think of her being upset.

'My fault for believing his lies.' She sighed. 'I'd better leave you to it. I just wanted to say thanks for listening on Monday.'

'That's okay. Any time.'

'Monday lunchtime again? Same place?'

'Yeah, great.' I'd walked into that one.

I couldn't stop thinking about Beth all weekend, despite working on the Saturday, despite being called out several times over the weekend. I could try to convince myself that we were merely two colleagues grabbing lunch together but that was bollocks. I knew exactly where that second trip to The Owl and Pussycat Tearoom was leading. And I knew I wanted that.

Monday lunchtimes at the tearoom became a weekly thing. The more I got to know her, the deeper I fell – something that had never happened before. She was great to talk to – witty, smart, interesting. I tried to find faults but, back then, I couldn't. My protest voice became weaker. So what if she was on the rebound? Wasn't everyone? So what if I had a relationship with one of my staff? It wasn't ideal but it wasn't illegal or unethical.

Lunchtimes were too short and I longed for more time with Beth. I'd never struggled to ask women out before but I couldn't seem to find the words to ask her. Why was it so different? Probably because I hadn't been bothered about the answer in the past but, with her, I cared. Too much. Insecurities gripped me. Was she only being friendly because I was her boss? Was she only being tactile because I'd been nice to her when she'd needed a friend? Was I no better than her married creep for wanting more than friendship?

After four Monday lunches, she suggested meeting at the tearoom on Friday evening so we could talk for longer. She said it so casually, as though we were merely friends meeting for drinks. It didn't sound like a date. I'd misread the signs. I'd imagined the chemistry. I'd created something that wasn't there. Yet from the outset, it felt like a date. She'd changed her clothes, applied darker make-up, released her hair from its usual plait so it tumbled down her back in soft waves. She was stunning.

The ambiance in the tearoom was completely different with subdued lighting, candles on the tables, mood music. Beth shuffled her chair closer and my breath caught as her leg pressed against mine. She ramped up the flirting, was more tactile than before, peppered the conversation with compliments. Friends didn't do that. She had to want more.

Nerves gripped me as the meal drew to a close. I imagined

asking her out and pictured that dazzling smile of hers as she said yes. I imagined kissing her goodnight. I imagined a hell of a lot more and was thankful the bill arrived to re-focus my mind.

The evening was chilly when we stepped outside so I helped her into her coat. She turned and kissed me on the cheek and whispered, 'Thank you'. She kissed me again, a bit nearer my mouth. There was a moment of electricity between us before our lips met. The kiss was hot and full of pent-up longing. My hands were in her hair, hers running down my back as she pulled me closer. Suddenly she pulled away and stepped back, breathing rapidly.

Bathed in the golden glow of the streetlight, she looked so beautiful but her brow was creased with confusion. My stomach sank. I *had* misread the signs after all. I'd gone too far. Better recover it. 'I'm sorry. I shouldn't have d—'

She pressed her fingers to my lips, silencing the words. 'It's me. I'm sorry. It's just that I was with him for five years. It's strange kissing someone else.' She stroked her hand across my cheek, frowning. 'Good strange, though.' She kissed me again and this time she didn't suddenly pull away.

She said she wanted to take things slowly, worried about the impact on us both of her coming out of a long-term relationship: *I really loved him and I'm scared of getting hurt again / What if I'm on the rebound and end up hurting you? / If he finally gets his act together and leaves his wife, I don't know if I'm strong enough to resist him.* I told her I understood. That was true. I told her I liked her but it was early days and I'd get over it if she went back to him. Not so true.

She was worried about people finding out at work: *What if they accuse me of getting favourable treatment from the boss? / What if they think I'm trying to sleep my way into a promotion?* The second excuse was laughable because we weren't sleeping together and she'd made it clear that sex was off the cards for a long time. But I understood her point and, as I didn't want any speculation or gossip either, I was more than happy to keep our relationship under wraps.

'When I say I don't want anyone at work to know, I mean your dad too,' she said. There was no reason for that to ring alarm bells. He was my business partner and her joint boss. If she wanted nobody at work to know about us, it was logical that 'nobody' included him. It made no odds to me. I wasn't in the habit of taking women home to meet my parents. Over the years, they'd met a few girlfriends who I'd been seeing around my birthday or a family event but most were never introduced. I saw no point in them meeting someone I wasn't serious about. Hiding Beth was not unusual.

Beth and I didn't go out for lunch together again in case anyone became suspicious but The Owl and Pussycat Tearoom remained *our* place. Every Friday night we booked the same table and every Friday night, I fell a little more deeply in love with her. I didn't tell her in case I scared her off but I was sure she had to know from the way I held her and kissed her.

In early November, six weeks after that first kiss, we added Tuesdays at the cinema to our routine. Every evening together ended in the same way – lingering, passionate kisses which left us both breathless – but there was never any suggestion of taking things further.

One evening after we left the cinema, I suggested I make her a meal at Alder Lea the following Tuesday for a change.

She smiled sweetly while shaking her head. 'We agreed to take things slowly and, if I come back to yours or have you over to mine, that's not going to happen.'

'I promise I'd never pressure you into doing anything you don't want to do.'

'That's the problem. I *do* want to take things further but I can't. I'm not ready.'

'I know that. But it's only a meal. I'm not expecting anything else.'

She lightly traced her finger across my lips. 'Have you any idea how irresistible you are, Josh? *I'd* be the problem. Not you. I'd want you for dessert. And I can't cross that line. Not yet.'

Not yet – which translated as 'but it will happen in the future.' So we stuck to our routine. It didn't matter that sex wasn't on the agenda – yet – because everything about our relationship was different to anything I'd experienced before. I loved her and was sure she loved me. We were taking it slowly but, for the first time ever, I was in a relationship that felt like it was going somewhere.

Then two weeks before Christmas – after nearly three months together – she ended it.

Her married man was back on the scene. He knew she was seeing someone else and he couldn't bear it. He loved her, missed her, wanted her back.

'He's finally left his wife then?' I asked.

She lowered her eyes. 'He's going to.'

'Jesus, Beth! So nothing's changed?'

'It has. He's realised he made a mistake and he's definitely going to end it after New Year.'

'New Year? Why not now?'

'He can hardly leave his wife just before Christmas, can he?'

'No, of course not. Not when he can have his cake and eat it,' I snapped.

'What's that supposed to mean?'

'He's jealous of you for being with another man so he gets you to dump me yet he gets to spend Christmas and New Year with his wife and kid while you're all alone waiting for him to grow a pair. Again.'

'It's not like that.'

'It's *exactly* like it. Why would you let him do that to you?'

'I can't help it. I love him!'

'And I love you!'

I'm not sure who gasped the loudest. I certainly hadn't meant to say it and Beth clearly hadn't expected to hear it. She muttered that she was sorry and ran to her car, leaving me standing in the rain outside the cinema, scrunching up two wasted tickets to a Christmas romcom.

That Christmas was bleak. New Year was no better. At work, I could have won an Oscar for my performance as the brilliant boss rather than the broken boyfriend. But that's what I was. Broken. So that was how it felt to be dumped? Being in love sucked.

By the end of January, I was no closer to getting over Beth than I'd been that night outside the cinema. Putting on an act all day at work was knackering so I spent evenings welded to the sofa, staring numbly at the TV, nursing a single bottle of lager. I hated what I'd become, resented what she'd done to me, and I constantly berated myself for getting involved in the first place when I'd known the risks.

Lewis and I usually went out to the pub on a Wednesday – his night off from his job as bar manager at Aversford Manor – but I couldn't face it. The only company I craved was Beth's.

After too many cancellations in a row, Lewis turned up at Alder Lea and plied me with drink until I spilled my guts. He wasn't impressed that I hadn't told him about Beth, but how could I? The connection between Lewis and Dad was too strong. Something would have slipped out and I'd promised Beth that nobody at work would ever hear it from me.

'I can't stand this. I want her back,' I told Lewis. 'I'd even be the other bloke if it meant I could be with her.'

'That's the drink talking, mate. You don't want that.'

* * *

A few days later, I sprinted across to Alder Lea after work in torrential rain and stopped dead as a figure rose from my doorstep. 'Beth?'

She was bedraggled, her hair plastered to her face, her clothes clinging to her body.

My pulse raced. 'What are you doing here?'

'I messed up.'

My legs seemed to have lost their ability to move so I stood there, staring at her, my rain-sodden shirt clinging to me.

She took a step closer. 'We never got back together. He wouldn't leave his wife.'

'I'm sorry.' I wasn't.

'I've missed you.' Another step closer. 'Did you mean what you said before Christmas?'

I nodded numbly.

A couple more steps. 'And now?'

'The same.'

She was within touching distance and the air crackled between us.

'I love you too.'

She threw herself at me and we kissed in the downpour then stumbled, locked together, towards the house, down the hall and into the lounge. I had questions but I didn't want to ask them. I had worries but I didn't want to voice them. I just wanted Beth.

In total, we were together for nearly two years on and off. Two turbulent years during which she confused the hell out of me by being all over me one week then pushing me away the next. I'd never have considered myself as someone who responded to games yet every pushback weirdly made me want her more. Had I enjoyed the chase? Had I seen her as a challenge? I must have done otherwise why would I have put up with all her crap?

* * *

Sam murmured something in her sleep, bringing me back to the present. I turned onto my side and the tension ebbed away as I lightly placed my hand over hers.

My phone ringing was a welcome interruption to fretting about Beth's reappearance. I whispered to Sam that I'd been called out. She mumbled something about missing me then turned over and fell straight back to sleep. I lightly kissed her cheek then pulled on some clothes and headed out into the darkness.

Beth wasn't welcome in my life or in my head and if she had the audacity to show up again, I'd tell her that and make sure she understood it this time. I didn't care how many tears she cried or how much she pleaded. I wasn't falling for that again. I had a new life, a new love and a new future and Beth, my dad and their family would never be part of it. They meant nothing to me.

7

SAMANTHA

Bank holiday Monday arrived with a chorus of birds chirping in the trees out the front and sunlight filtering through a gap where I hadn't closed the curtains properly.

I smiled as I opened my eyes and stretched. It had been one heck of a weekend so far – emotional yet exciting, exhausting yet exhilarating – and now I was looking forward to a quiet, drama-free day with my amazing boyfriend.

I turned onto my side to look at Josh but he was in a deep sleep, his chest steadily rising and falling, his dark hair all mussed up. His soft lips, slightly parted, looked so kissable but I had to resist. He'd been called out in the early hours and hadn't returned until after 5.30 a.m. so it wouldn't be fair to disturb him.

Rolling onto my back, I snuggled into my pillows and cast my gaze round the bedroom. I'd moved into the farmhouse exactly a month ago today and I'd loved it instantly. Before now, the only time I'd properly felt at home anywhere was when I'd stayed at Meadowcroft – Nanna and Gramps's bungalow – but I got that same feeling of belonging at Hedgehog Hollow. It was as though the farm had been destined to be my home.

With three storeys and seven bedrooms, the farmhouse was enormous but it never felt that way, especially when Josh was with me. It felt cosy. It felt complete. *I* felt complete and as though something was missing when he wasn't here.

I glanced at Josh again. Was it too soon to suggest he officially move in? He'd only spent three nights at Wisteria Cottage over the past month so he'd practically moved in anyway. He had his own key. He had his own wardrobe and chest of drawers in the bedroom which were steadily filling with his clothes. He'd even moved his desk from the cottage into one of the spare bedrooms so he could catch up on paperwork at home instead of staying late at the practice. It would be amazing waking up next to him every day in *our* home.

I crept out of bed, pulled on a hoodie over my PJs and went downstairs to feed Thomas's cat, Misty-Blue, who had thankfully adopted Josh and me as her new owners. She was a beautiful, affectionate, grey-striped tabby cat with a fondness for sprawling across my knee or clambering up onto my shoulders.

I made a coffee in my hedgehog mug and took it outside. Misty-Blue followed me and jumped up beside me as I sat on Thomas's bench – a sturdy wooden one overlooking the garden and the stunning wildflower meadow beyond it which he and Gwendoline had sowed before she took ill. It was my favourite place at Hedgehog Hollow and I always felt close to Thomas when I sat there.

'Yesterday was a huge success,' I said, raising my mug towards the meadow. 'And we had another new arrival. Arwen's our twentieth. Can you believe that? You were so right to have this vision. Thank you for trusting me with it.'

It was so peaceful sitting there, stroking Misty-Blue while I sipped on my coffee, watching the birds and butterflies flitting across a rainbow canvas of flowers and listening to the chirps and the low buzz of insects.

'I have a question. Do you think I should ask Josh to move in with me?'

My heart raced and goose bumps broke out on my arms as a pair of rabbits emerged from the meadow. They chased each other round the garden for a minute or so before disappearing back into the wildflowers.

'I'll take that as a yes,' I whispered to Misty-Blue who gave a loud purr. 'I know it's quick but it doesn't feel like it, not after everything we've been through. It just feels right.'

When I'd finished my drink, I leaned back with my head tilted towards the blue sky and let the morning sun warm my cheeks.

A crunch of gravel a few minutes later made me open my eyes. I smiled as Josh approached.

'I thought I might find you out here.' He leaned forward and his lips met mine for a soft, lingering kiss, making my heart race once more.

He picked up Misty-Blue then sat down beside me with the cat on his knee. 'Have you been talking to Thomas?'

'I know it's probably daft but I think he'd have liked it.'

Josh put his arm round me. 'Not daft at all. I think it's sweet that you still talk to him. Did you tell him about yesterday?'

I nodded. 'And I asked him a very important question.'

'Did he answer?'

I pictured the rabbits bounding across the lawn. 'He did. So now I have a very important question for you.' I placed my empty mug down on the gravel and adjusted position to face him better. Butterflies swooped and soared in my stomach but I knew it was excitement rather than nerves. Nothing about my future with Josh made me feel nervous.

'You know how you sometimes drive home via Wisteria Cottage to collect clothes or paperwork?'

'Yes...?'

'What if you didn't have to do that anymore because everything you needed was here?'

The wide smile and twinkly eyes suggested he'd just realised where this was heading and he liked the idea. 'That would be pretty great.'

'Hedgehog Hollow has always felt like *our* home rather than mine. It never feels right when you're not here so the hedgehogs and I were wondering whether you'd like to give notice on Wisteria Cottage and move in here permanently.'

Josh gently cupped my face in his hands and gave me the most tender, loving, heart-melting kiss. He lightly ran his thumbs across my cheeks as he pulled away, smiling. 'I'd love to. Thank you.' He lifted up Misty-Blue and scratched her behind her ears. 'And are you happy for me to officially move in?' She gave a gentle mew in response. 'Looks like the boss approves.'

He put his arm round me again and I cuddled against him as Misty-Blue stretched across both our laps. 'It's been a pretty special weekend all round,' he said. 'If we ignore the Beth-shaped blip and me getting stuck inside Mickleby, I'd say it's been pretty much perfect.'

Gazing at the meadow, stroking our cat, feeling so loved and in love, that moment was pretty perfect too and I liked to think that, after all the heartache I'd experienced in my life so far, this was Thomas and Gwendoline, Nanna and Gramps finally sending me some peace and happiness.

* * *

I spent the morning in the barn, finishing clearing away after the Family Fun Day and checking on the hedgehogs while Josh went to Wisteria Cottage to start packing.

Arwen's cuts were already showing signs of healing and our

other patients were all making good progress. I couldn't stop smiling at the thought of Josh moving in permanently. The three nights he'd stayed at Wisteria Cottage instead of Hedgehog Hollow, I'd missed him so much. Misty-Blue had been restless and so had I. Josh was part of our family and we needed him with us.

Around late morning, I heard the crunch of gravel in the farmyard. It was too soon for Josh to be back so I put down Frodo's medical chart, picked up a pair of gloves and made my way towards the barn door, expecting a new arrival.

A car raced towards the farm track and soon disappeared from view, leaving behind a cloud of dust.

'That's weird,' I muttered to myself. I was about to turn back to the barn when I spotted a cardboard box in the middle of the farmyard. I wandered over to it, opened the flaps and leapt back squealing.

Heart thumping, palms sweating, I took a few deep calming breaths then pulled on my gloves, crouched down and tentatively flicked open the flaps once more. A few flies escaped while others remained inside the box, buzzing round the hedgehogs' carcasses. As I carefully moved each aside, it became clear they were all victims of roadkill. Seven of them. My heart broke.

Blinking back the tears, I closed the flaps with shaking hands and carried the box over to the barn where I gently placed it down a little way from the entrance. Those poor little mites would need to go to Josh's veterinary practice for cremation.

Who'd do something like that? It was sick – which meant it had to be the Grimes boys or, if they'd already been locked up, it had to be one of their relatives. I hoped they hadn't been the cause of the deaths although I wouldn't put it past them to deliberately drive at hedgehogs or other wildlife 'for fun'.

Ten minutes later, I heard another vehicle outside and my heart started racing once more. *Please don't let it be them.* Thankfully, it was a man probably in his forties wearing a suit, who stepped out of a shiny car. He waved at me before opening the back door.

'Morning,' I said, striding over to him. 'Do you have a hedgehog for me?'

'I have a pair of them. My mum found them in her garden this morning or rather her Yorkshire Terrier did. They don't look so good.'

'Did the dog bite them?'

'No. He's all bark and no bite. Far too scared to go close to them.' He thrust a cardboard box towards me. 'I'm meant to be at a wedding right now but Mum was bordering on hysteria when she phoned me, worried they'd die if they weren't treated immediately.' He rolled his eyes at me. 'Do you need me to stay?' The expression on his face suggested he was hoping for a no.

'No. You get back to the wedding but can I take your number or your mum's?' I placed the box on the ground, dropped my gloves on top of it and whipped my phone out.

'Why do you need that?'

'To see if your mum would like them releasing back into her garden.'

'No thanks. You can release them here. If they survive.'

Before I had a chance to say another word, he jumped back in his car and sped away.

It wasn't ideal having no contact details. We were approaching babies' season and if a mum was taken away from her hoglets, I needed to make sure there wasn't a nest of little ones nearby who'd have no chance of survival on their own.

'Let's see what we have here.' I took the box into the barn, placed it on the treatment table and peeked inside. 'Oh, you poor things.'

Two adult hedgehogs were curled up next to each other, surrounded by urine and faeces. Neither the man nor his mum had thought to put anything in the box like newspapers or towels to keep them warm and provide a safe space to hide under. Both hedgehogs had mange and one case was particularly severe.

I grabbed a fresh plastic crate, lined it with a puppy training pad then added in a mixture of newspaper and fleece strips before placing the hog with the less severe condition inside.

They were my first hedgehogs with mange but likely the first of many. Triggered by parasite mites burrowing through the skin then laying eggs, it was a common and extremely painful disease for hogs. Restricted by their spines, they were unable to scratch so the pain would steadily become more intense. Spines could fall out and a hedgehog with a severe case could be covered in dead caked-on skin to the point where they could barely move, meaning they couldn't eat or drink and they couldn't protect themselves from predators.

I lifted the other hedgehog out of the cardboard box. As I turned it round for a closer inspection, I could see that the dead and damaged skin was preventing it from fully unfurling which meant it was extremely dehydrated and likely starving.

I took photos of them as I was keen to build a gallery on our website and social media – when I found time to set them up – to show the plight of the hogs and the difference we could make when they were brought in quickly enough.

An injection of painkillers and antibiotics for each hedgehog was the starting point and then I pulled up a chair and set to work removing some of the dead skin from the worst-affected one. Some of it came off easily with a rub of my gloved fingers and other bits came off with tweezers. Baby oil massaged into the tougher parts softened the skin and made removal easier.

Although I was gentle, the treatment would have been very stressful for the hedgehog so I kept giving it breaks, refreshing my gloves, and moving onto the other one. The hog with the less severe case was a girl so, in keeping with the movie character theme, I named her Ripley from the *Alien* films as the pair of them did look a little like aliens in their damaged state.

'A boy,' I observed when the worst-affected one was finally free of enough skin to unfurl. 'Would it be mean to continue with *Lord of the Rings* characters and call you Gollum?' With clumps of fur and spines missing, he did have a look of Tolkien's creature about him. 'Hang on in there, little one, we'll make you better. When Josh gets back, he'll be able to give you both some special medicine to kill off all those nasty parasites.'

As I worked, I tried not to think about the gruesome contents in the box outside and focus instead on the excitement of Josh moving in. But every so often, the image popped into my head and I shuddered.

* * *

Josh returned a couple of hours later. I'd done as much as I could to remove the dead skin from Gollum and was finishing with Ripley.

'Another new patient?' he asked, joining me at the table.

'Two of them, both with mange, so I'll need you to get your magic medicine out.' I placed Ripley back in her crate then looked up at Josh, my mouth set in a straight line. 'They weren't the only arrivals today. I need to show you something.'

Keeping my gloves on, I indicated that Josh should follow me outside.

'It's not pretty.' I crouched down and winced as I lifted the flaps on the cardboard box of squashed hedgehogs.

He peered inside. 'That's grim. The Grimes boys?'

I shrugged. 'Presumably. Or someone connected to them. Can't think of anyone else who'd want to do anything so horrible.' I closed the flaps again.

'Have you phoned the police? Checked the CCTV?'

'Both. The police are sending someone round later and the CCTV picked up the licence plate but it'll probably be stolen again. Only the passenger got out and he had a hoodie up so, like before, no faces.' I sighed and shook my head. 'I thought it was over.'

'So did I.' He held me close, his warmth and strength providing instant comfort and a feeling of being safe. 'I'm sure it will be soon. Maybe they're getting sentenced tomorrow and this was their sick idea of a goodbye.'

'I hope you're right.' But a nagging feeling in the pit of my stomach told me this wasn't over yet.

8

The following morning, Josh and I were both up early to check on the hedgehogs before going to work.

Oh my goodness, look at you,' I gushed, carefully picking up Gollum. 'Look, Josh! He can already curl into a ball.'

'He's looking great. Unrecognisable from your photos.'

I felt a stab of pride as I smiled at Josh. I'd spent eight years as a nurse and had helped thousands of patients and saved lives during that time but there was such a special feeling that came with helping the hedgehogs.

I glanced up at the large whiteboard on the wall – my 'Happy Hog Board' – showing the names of our current patients, the number of hogs we'd treated so far and the number of successful releases. *I'd* done that. I'd helped those poor little creatures who'd have probably perished otherwise. Could there be anything more rewarding and satisfying, especially when hedgehogs were vulnerable to extinction?

We cleaned the crates, put out fresh food and water and dished out medicine to those who needed it before returning to the farmhouse to get ready for work.

'How are you feeling about the first day back?' Josh asked while I dressed.

I was returning to my teaching role for the first time since the arson attack. 'Looking forward to seeing my students.'

'I sense a but,' Josh prompted.

I shrugged as I sat down on the side of the bed to pull on my socks. 'It feels like there is one but I can't quite put my finger on what it is. I'm probably just a bit tired after the weekend's excitement.'

He sat beside me. 'You know Auntie Lauren would give you more time off if you're not ready to return just yet.'

'I know she would. She's been amazing but I'm sure I'll be fine when I get there and settle into a routine again.'

He put his arm round me and hugged me to his side. 'Promise you'll tell her if it's too much.'

'Yes, Nurse Alderson,' I joked. 'I promise.'

Laughing, he kissed me goodbye then left for the veterinary practice. I stayed on the bed and gazed round the room, my eyes resting on the canvas I'd commissioned for Thomas of the meadow he and Gwendoline created.

'You know what I think the but is, Thomas?' I said to the picture. 'I'd rather stay here.'

I finished getting ready and, as I drove down the farm track, looking back at the barn in the rear-view mirror, a wave of sadness swept over me. Like my previous career as a district nurse, I found my teaching job both rewarding and challenging and I didn't regret the change in career direction. The problem was, I now had another pull on my time and I couldn't deny that I loved the time spent at Hedgehog Hollow more than that at college. The twenty-two patients we'd treated so far had captured my heart in a way I'd never anticipated. Checking on the hogs this morning and seeing the huge improvements overnight in Ripley and Gollum had made me quite teary and I didn't like the idea of being away from them all day.

* * *

Lauren was already in the department office when I arrived, scowling at something on her screen. She looked up and replaced her scowl with a warm smile.

'Morning, Sam,' she chirped. 'How is my lovely niece-in-law to be?'

I smiled and rolled my eyes at her. 'Do you never let up? Is it not enough that he's officially moved in?'

She gasped. 'Yes! That's amazing news. I'm so thrilled for you both.' She started whistling 'Here Comes the Bride'.

'Behave!' I shook my head at her as I sat down at my desk.

She flashed me a mischievous grin across the office. 'I've told you before, I've given up on relationships so I have to meddle in other people's instead.'

'I was worried you might think moving in was too quick but, seeing as you're already onto us getting married...' I raised my eyebrows at her and she laughed.

'Not everyone is lucky enough to find their perfect match. When two people do – like you and Josh – what's the point in going slowly? You both already know it's right so what difference would waiting a few more months make?'

She looked wistful for a moment and I felt for her. Twice divorced and, from what I could gather, stung badly by the second experience, I often wondered if the bravado about swearing off men was a defence mechanism to stop her from getting hurt again.

'So, are you fit and well and ready to face your students again?' she asked.

'I am indeed.' I hoped I sounded more confident than I felt.

'You have to tell me if it's too much too soon.'

'I'm sure I'll be fine.' My voice wobbled and I suddenly felt quite tearful. I busied myself taking folders out of my bag, willing the tears to stay put.

Lauren wandered over and perched herself on my desk. 'You've been through a lot, Sam, so don't push yourself too far too soon. You're hardworking and dedicated so I know you'll have felt guilty about having your classes covered even though being off sick was hardly your fault.'

I looked up and smiled at her weakly. 'Am I that transparent?'

'No, but your work ethic matches mine so I recognise the traits. It's not a sign of weakness or failure to ask for help or to say you need more time to recover.'

'Thank you. I appreciate it. I'm ready, though. Don't worry about me.'

'You're family now. It's my job to worry about you.'

The tears threatened to fall again. How blessed was I to have met this wonderful woman? In the eight months I'd known her, she'd been more like a mum to me than my own mother had been in twenty-nine years.

A couple of colleagues burst through the door. Lauren patted my hand and returned to her desk while I fought to compose myself. Before long, we'd dispersed to classes and the first lesson of the day was underway.

* * *

My first day back ran smoothly but I found myself clock-watching and counting down the hours until I could get home to the hedgehogs. I hoped I was only feeling like that because I'd become used to being at the farm each day and that I'd soon settle into the routine I'd had before the arson attack. Back then, there hadn't been as many hedgehogs, though. Back then, the rescue centre hadn't officially opened. Back then, I hadn't nearly died trying to save one of our patients.

As soon as the last class of the day was over, I raced home as fast as I safely could to check on my hedgehogs. The moment I entered the barn, I could feel the tension easing. Hedgehog Hollow was officially my happy place. Even though I loved my job at Reddfield TEC, I'd felt on edge there all day. But that feeling would pass after a few days... wouldn't it?

9

JOSH

Knowing she'd had the nerve to show up at the farm, I wouldn't have put it past Beth to turn up at the practice but by Wednesday lunchtime, there hadn't been a peep out of her. Either she hadn't been that desperate to speak to me or she'd finally got the message. Good riddance. I wasn't going to waste another minute dwelling on her.

My landlord at Wisteria Cottage had accepted my notice. He had another tenant desperate to move into the village so had agreed no penalty for ending my lease early provided I move out over the weekend. Sam's friend Dave, a builder with a van, had offered to help on Saturday afternoon, saving me several trips with the jeep. When we'd made arrangements, he'd asked if there was anything from Alder Lea that needed moving while we were at it. Was there? I hadn't been inside the house for so long. Was it time to lay the demons to rest?

I tentatively opened the top drawer on my desk and stared at the set of keys resting in the pen tidy. Sod it. I could do this! Eighteen months had passed and there was so much good stuff going on in

my life. I needed to focus on my future with Sam and stop letting
the crap from the past bring me down.

Snatching up the keys, I strode purposefully out of the practice
and over to the house. I thrust the front door key into the lock and
pushed the door open with such force that it slammed against the
hall wall but my confidence vanished. My heart thumped and I
gulped as memories of that night rushed into my head. Shit! I still
couldn't do it. I yanked the door shut and stormed back to my office.
They'd done that to me. *They'd* turned my grandparents' happy
family home into a place I hated and I'd never forgive them for it.
Never.

* * *

'You've got to let it go, mate.' Lewis took a sip on his pint in the pub
that evening. 'It must have been about a year now.'

'Eighteen months.'

'No way! And you seriously haven't been inside the house for all
that time?'

'That's right.'

'And you haven't spoken to your dad either?'

'I've got nothing to say to *him*.'

Lewis shook his head, frowning. 'Mate. That's crazy.'

'Why?'

'Because he's your dad.'

'And when did you last speak to your dad?' I cringed as the
words left my mouth. Completely uncalled for.

Lewis narrowed his eyes at me. 'You are such an arse
sometimes.'

'I know. Sorry.'

He took another sip of his drink. 'What your dad did was an
epic shit-fest and I'm not trying to lessen the impact because it was

huge and you have every right to be fuming with him. But he's your dad and, before it all came out, he was a decent bloke. The best. Look at everything he did for me and our Danny. And look at everything he did for you afterwards. He handed over his share of the practice to you and he gave your mum the house. He'd have had to start again with nothing.'

'A house and a business can't repair the damage.'

'Maybe not but can't you see how big a gesture it was, particularly handing over the practice? We both know how much it meant to him. Doesn't that show how sorry he was?'

'I get what you're saying—'

'But you disagree?' Lewis sighed. 'I can't make you pick up the phone but I wish you would.'

'It's not that simple.'

'It is. Watch this.' Lewis picked up my phone and held it up to his ear while staring at me meaningfully. 'Hi Dad, it's your stubborn son. Long-time no speak. You're a stupid twat and I hate what you did but I can't be angry forever so how about a drink one night?' He put the phone down and raised his eyebrows at me. 'Simple. So go in the house and get your dad called.'

I couldn't help smiling at him. He'd always taken a pragmatic approach to life whereas I tended to be more influenced by emotions. I could see exactly why he viewed it that way but he didn't know the full story. If he did, I could guarantee he'd see things differently. It wasn't so simple after all.

10

SAMANTHA

By Thursday – my third day back at work – the tension was still there. My head thumped, my eyes burned and I intermittently felt waves of nausea. At lunchtime, I sat at my desk in the department office and dug my sandwich out of my bag.

'I hope you're not planning on working through lunch again,' Lauren said, looking up from her computer.

I shrugged. 'Maybe.'

She stood up and grabbed her bag. 'Right, that's it. We're going to the canteen. You need a proper break and I won't take no for an answer.'

There was no point in protesting so I stood up and smiled as I saluted her. 'Yes, boss.' I left my sandwich on my desk thinking a bowl of soup might slip down more easily.

* * *

'Any new hedgehogs?' she asked as we sat down in the canteen.

'Not since the two with mange on Monday.' I swallowed a spoonful of soup. 'I was thinking last night that I could offer work experience during the summer holidays for some of the students on the animal care course. What do you think?'

'Great idea,' she said between mouthfuls of jacket potato. 'I bet you'd get loads of volunteers. What about an accountancy student doing your bookkeeping? I'm sure they'd love the chance to keep a real set of accounts and it would free you up to focus on the bits you love. Unless you love doing the accounts.' She raised her eyebrows doubtfully.

I grimaced. 'Definitely *not* my favourite task and that's a brilliant idea although maybe it can wait until after half-term. It's not my top priority at the moment.'

'When you're ready, I can do the intros. The accounts tutor is called Adam. Nice bloke. He's married to Briony, the new Art and Design tutor.'

'I met her at my induction. She's nice. Oh my gosh, that's prompted another idea. I haven't got around to getting a sign made for Hedgehog Hollow because I need a logo designing first. I could run a competition for the art students.' I smiled as I felt a surge of excitement.

Lauren wagged her salad-filled fork at me. 'That's better. I was beginning to think you'd forgotten how to smile.'

'Have I been that bad?'

'No, but you haven't been your usual self this week.'

'Sorry. It's been harder than expected to get back into the hang of concentrating all day.'

'Do you need more time?'

'I'll be fine. All I need right now is more sleep.' *And forty-eight hours in each day. And two pairs of hands. And a never-ending income stream so I can work at Hedgehog Hollow full-time.*

* * *

As per the previous two days, I raced home after work to be in my happy place. I'd spoken to Briony who'd loved my logo competition idea so my priority this evening was to pull together some details for her students.

I headed straight for the barn and came to a halt, heart thumping, as I spotted a cardboard box next to the door.

'Not more dead hogs,' I whispered. 'Please.'

Gulping, I cautiously opened the flaps but this box contained scrumpled up sheets of kitchen towel. Pushing them aside revealed a hedgehog curled into a ball in one corner and I winced at the open wound on its back. I hoped it hadn't been there long. Poor thing had to be in agony.

* * *

'I knew I'd find you in here.' Josh walked towards the treatment table and kissed me. 'You're still in your work clothes.'

'I haven't made it into the house yet. New arrival. I've named her Katniss from *The Hunger Games*. She was in a box outside and I was worried it was another roadkill delivery.'

'What's wrong with her?'

'Strimmer injury by the looks of it. It was fresh so I suspect the person who dropped her off was the one with the strimmer. She's all patched up and pumped full of painkillers and antibiotics so she should make a full recovery. Can you update the Happy Hog Board for me while I put her in her crate?'

'Patient twenty-three,' he said. 'And we only officially opened four days ago.'

I loved that he used 'we'. I saw Hedgehog Hollow – both the farm and the rescue centre – as ours and was touched that he felt part of it too.

'I want to get some more mange off Ripley and Gollum before I start on dinner.' We took it in turns to cook and sometimes prepared a meal together but Josh had been the chef for the last few nights and it was only fair that I took my turn. I didn't relish it, though. The thought of cooking made my stomach churn.

'How about I make dinner while you finish off here?' Josh suggested.

I smiled gratefully. 'You're sure? Because that would be amazing.'

'I'm hungry and you're busy so it's logical that way.'

'Thank you. I really appreciate it.'

* * *

Josh was taking his last mouthful of dinner when his phone rang with an emergency callout.

'Hopefully I won't be too long,' he said, pushing his chair back from the kitchen table. He frowned at my barely touched meal. 'Are you okay? You've hardly eaten anything.'

My head was still thumping and I could feel my cheeks burning. 'Sorry. I'm just a bit tired after a few days of solid concentration so I'm on a go-slow. I *will* eat some more, though. It's really tasty.'

'Why don't you put your feet up afterwards and watch a film?'

That sounded really good. 'I've got about an hour's prep to do for tomorrow and I need to do some flyers for Briony but I'll maybe do those while watching a film.'

'Good.' He gave me a gentle kiss then left.

I put the kettle on and stood by the window while it boiled, watching Josh's jeep disappearing down the farm track. Some fresh air might do me good.

The temperature had dropped so I wrapped up warm and took my mug of tea outside. I wanted to tell Thomas and Gwendoline about Katniss and the great progress that Gollum had made.

As I approached Thomas's bench, spots started swimming before my eyes and the ground felt like it was about to jump up at me. My pulse raced and I felt sweat prickle my forehead and upper lip. *Don't faint. Not while you're alone.* My mug slipped from my hand and smashed on the gravel, soaking my canvas shoes and scalding my bare ankles. I swayed and grabbed onto the wall, taking deep breaths, willing myself to stay conscious. I stumbled towards the bench and managed to lie down with my feet up on the arm rest. More deep breaths. The sensation was unsettling – like the feeling you get when you've been on a boat but still feel like you're bobbing once you return to dry land. I held the back of my shaky hand against my burning forehead and shuddered as a wave of heat swept over my body from head to toe.

And then it stopped.

I lay there for several minutes as my heartrate slowed, my skin cooled, my stomach settled. Where had that come from? I'd never fainted before. I bit my lip, feeling completely unnerved by it. What if I'd hit my head as I fell? I didn't like to dwell on the thought of being all alone and unconscious. Shivering now, I pulled my cardigan round me and ever so slowly lowered my feet onto the bench, then onto the ground, then gently eased myself into a seated position making sure my head was the last thing I raised.

My ankles throbbed and I looked down at the angry red streaks across them from my spilt tea. Fortunately, my shoes had taken the brunt of it.

Misty-Blue jumped up beside me. 'Hello you,' I said, stroking her back. 'I was wondering where you'd got to. Have you come to make sure I'm okay?'

She nudged my arm, purring. 'That was a scary moment,' I told her. 'Don't tell Josh. He'll tell Lauren and they'll make me take some more time off.'

I closed my eyes for a moment. Would that be such a bad thing?

I'd be able to spend my days with the hedgehogs. Opening my eyes once more, I looked down at my cat.

'The problem is,' I told her, 'if I take some more time off, I'll *never* want to return. And if I don't return, I'll be letting Lauren down and my colleagues down and, most of all, I'll be letting Thomas and Gwendoline down because I need my teaching salary to keep the rescue centre running.'

I shivered again. Time to retreat indoors and tend to my scalds. Maybe I'd relax with a film after that and do my prep later.

Rising slowly from the bench, I took a few tentative steps towards the farmhouse. Pieces of smashed mug were scattered across the gravel. My favourite mug. How typical was that? It was tempting to leave it for now but I didn't want Misty-Blue to step on any sharp edges so I bent down to pick up the pieces, praying the effort wouldn't make me dizzy again.

Misty-Blue followed me into the farmhouse and watched as I placed the remnants of my mug in the kitchen bin. She nudged my legs and mewed. 'Yes, yes, I'll feed you but you have to promise not to tell Josh. It's not like I actually fainted. I just had a one-off dizzy spell. That's all.'

I hoped.

The following day, I felt a little brighter although I couldn't help but wonder if that was because the weekend was approaching, which meant more time with Josh and the hedgehogs.

I had watched a film last night although I hadn't fully relaxed as I'd prepared the flyers for Briony which I placed in her pigeonhole first thing. Hopefully I'd get plenty of entries.

During afternoon break, I checked my phone as I walked back to the department office and was surprised to see five missed calls from a local number, although no voicemail messages had been left. I stepped outside to return the call.

'Hi there. My name's Samantha Wishaw. I've got five missed calls from this number.'

'Are you the hedgehog rescuer?' The woman on the end of the phone sounded angry.

I sat down on a low wall in front of the building. 'Yes. I run Hedgehog Hollow.'

'About time! I've been trying you all afternoon. Don't you ever answer your phone?'

I flinched at her harsh tone but chose to ignore her comments. 'How can I help?'

'I need you to collect a hedgehog from Fimberley.'

'Can I ask what's wrong with it?'

'How the bloody hell should I know? I'm not a vet.'

I took a deep breath so I could keep my response calm. 'I appreciate that. I just mean what prompted you to call? Is the hedgehog bleeding, for example?'

'No. So can you be here in the next fifteen minutes?'

Further details about what was wrong with the hedgehog were clearly not forthcoming. It was 2.45 p.m. now and college didn't finish till four. 'I can be with you between quarter past and half past four.'

'That's no good. I'm leaving for my holidays in half an hour.'

'I'm really sorry but I can't get there sooner. Is there any—'

She cut me short. 'I'll shove it in a box on my doorstep. It's 11 Finton Row. I've done my bit now so it'll be your fault if it dies.' Then she hung up.

My stomach churned as I quickly typed the address into the Notes app on my phone before it slipped my mind. I hated confrontations. Why were some people like that? Maybe she was one of those people who got stressed and nervous before going on holiday. There was no need to take it out on me, though. I was none the wiser as to what had prompted her to call me and that made me nervous. No blood was a good thing but that didn't mean there wasn't cause for concern.

* * *

I pulled up outside a row of small whitewashed cottages in Fimberley ninety minutes later. None of them had front gardens, the doors opening straight out onto the lane. I spotted number eleven before I clocked the house number thanks to a multipack crisps box on the doorstep.

Opening the car door, I turned and looked up at the sun shining directly onto the front of the house. Not good. I pulled on a pair of gloves and crouched down beside the box. The top flaps had been folded inside, meaning the hedgehog had no protection from the sun or predators. My breath caught. There was a trail of blood across the base of the box and the hedgehog was on its side. I sank back onto the path, tears welling in my eyes. I didn't need to lift the poor thing out of the box to know it had already gone.

'What happened to you, little one? I asked, gently picking it up and turning it over to reveal several large puncture wounds and a lot of blood. Dog attack. I glanced up at the cottage. Taped inside the window was a yellow warning sign with a photo of a large dog breed and the words 'BEWARE! I LIVE HERE' against it. Why couldn't the woman have been honest? Even if she didn't want to admit that her dog had attacked the hedgehog – a female – I'd specifically asked her if there'd been blood and she'd said no. I could have phoned Josh and seen if one of his team could collect the hog if I'd had any inkling she was in such a state.

'I'm so sorry,' I whispered. I ran my finger along her belly and my breath caught. *She was pregnant!* I stared at her swollen stomach, my own churning. Surely there was no way any of the babies could still be alive... but I had to be absolutely certain. I sped back to Hedgehog Hollow.

* * *

My hands were shaking as I picked up the scalpel back home in the barn. I dropped it back into the tray and took several deep calming breaths until they steadied. I picked up the scalpel again and bit my lip. *It's medically impossible for them to have survived. Leave it! Don't torture yourself with how many more precious creatures died today.* But a tiny miniscule hope for a miracle drove me on and I made my incision.

The Fimberley hedgehog had been expecting a litter of five. All gone. I slumped back in my chair, fighting back the tears. I was too late. I'd failed this beautiful creature and her five babies and I'd failed the Micklebys. Thomas and Gwendoline would have been on hand to respond to an emergency callout instead of making a day job their priority and squeezing in their responsibilities to the hogs round that. I thought about Katniss yesterday. She'd been dropped off goodness knows when during the day and she could have come to further harm left there all alone in a cardboard box. Flies could have got inside the box and infected her wound or curious wildlife could have got to her. Misty-Blue could even have been a threat. I held my head in my hands. This wasn't going to work. Even with a relatively small number of patients, running the rescue centre was a full-time job. What had I been thinking?

I swallowed down the lump in my throat as I opened out a puppy pad and gently placed the mum on one half with her five babies nestled round her. I folded the other half over the top. 'Rest in peace, little ones.'

Peeling off my gloves, I washed my hands. I needed to focus on something positive. Gollum. I'd remove some more mange and give him a baby oil massage.

Half an hour later, free of more dead skin, Gollum curled up on a towel as I massaged baby oil into his back. He had very few spines left and I suspected he'd be completely bald within the next couple of days. I turned him over. He definitely loved lying on his back and having his tummy tickled and I liked to think he was smiling or even giggling as he spread his paws wide for me to get more coverage.

The massage would have done him the world of good and it had certainly eased the tension from me. I hadn't been able to help the Fimberley family but I was definitely helping Gollum.

With Gollum back in his crate and the table wiped down, I opened the door to Ripley's quarters. I gently moved the shredded paper and fleece aside.

'Are you hiding right at the back?' I wrapped my gloved hands round her, lifted her out and placed her on the scales.

She didn't move.

'Ripley?' My stomach tightened. 'No, Ripley. You can't be.'

I grabbed her and lay her on her back on a fleecy blanket, massaging her heart. 'Please, Ripley,' I pleaded, tears splashing onto the fleece. 'Please come back.'

But it was too late. There was no saving Ripley either. I gave her belly one final stroke before lying her next to the Fimberley family. I covered her with a piece of grey fleece then sank onto the chair, anguished sobs racking my body.

Lewis's words were still preying on my mind as I locked up the practice on Friday evening. Let it go? If only. Every other aspect of my life was going so well. The practice was going from strength to strength now that we had a full quota of vets, Hedgehog Hollow was officially my home, and Sam had shown me how amazing being in a proper, genuine, monogamous relationship could be. I should be on cloud nine yet one memory of that fateful day was always there at the back of my mind, haunting me. If Lewis knew the whole truth, he'd know why I couldn't let go.

As I got into my jeep, I had an urge to see Mum. I'd phoned her with the news that I was moving into Hedgehog Hollow and she'd sounded genuinely delighted, but I was conscious that I'd normally have told her something big like that face to face. Uncomfortable as it would be, she had a right to know that Beth had turned up at the farm just in case she decided to seek out Mum. I'd like to think she'd draw the line there but I wouldn't put it past Beth. The woman had no morals.

I fired off a quick text to Sam to say I was going home via Mum's and would be a bit late, then set off towards Little Tilbury.

Ten minutes later, I pulled up against the churchyard wall opposite Primrose Cottage. Mum's new home was a pretty two-bedroom stone cottage painted in a light yellowy-cream with a pale green door, window frames and matching shutters. It was such a contrast to the airy, modern family home I'd grown up in yet it couldn't have been more perfect for her. She seemed so relaxed and content since she'd moved. Village life definitely agreed with her. Or perhaps it was being away from a house full of memories of her life with *him* that agreed with her.

Just about the only thing my father hadn't screwed up was the divorce. He didn't contest it and he let Mum have the house which, as far as I was concerned, was the only decent thing to do.

'This is an unexpected surprise,' Mum said, crossing the cobbled lane and giving me a warm hug. 'I'd just got up to make a cup of tea when I spotted you pulling up so your timing's perfect.'

She sent me into the lounge while she went to make drinks. I sat in a high-backed armchair, placed my phone on the arm rest and gazed round the room. The furniture and décor, like the cottage, were such a contrast to our family home but everything about Mum had changed since *the incident.* She'd packed in her job as a clothes shop manager to retrain as a counsellor. She'd had her long, blonde hair cut into a highlighted bob, started wearing contacts instead of glasses and even dressed differently. Weirdly, despite changing everything, she seemed more like my mum than ever before.

'Here you go.' She handed me a mug of tea. 'Let's pretend it's something stronger to toast your good news. Happy new home!'

I smiled at her and clinked my mug against hers. 'Thank you. I should probably have told you in person.'

She sat down on the sofa and shook her head. 'The phone was absolutely fine so don't you fret about that. I'm so thrilled for you both. Samantha's lovely.'

We chatted about me giving notice on Wisteria Cottage and my plans to move everything across tomorrow with Dave's help.

'Are you going to move your stuff out of Alder Lea too?' she asked.

I sighed. I knew I might as well be honest about that. 'Dave offered but I'm not sure. I haven't been inside Alder Lea for quite a while.'

She narrowed her eyes at me. 'Define "quite a while".'

'Erm... since I first moved out.'

She pressed her fingers against her lips. 'Oh, Josh! Why ever not?'

'For the same reason I moved out in the first place. Because it reminds me of *them* and what they did.' I kept imagining them together in *my* house. Had they shagged on my bed? The sofa? Anger coursed through my veins every time I was in Alder Lea. I took out a year's rental contract on the first property I found – a pokey flat above a village shop. It was cold and dated but it was quiet, close to work, and held no painful memories. I was a little less impulsive about my next move – Wisteria Cottage – making sure I found somewhere decent that felt a lot more like home.

'But that was eighteen months ago,' Mum said, frowning. 'You really haven't been inside for that long? It must be filthy for a start.'

'Our cleaner goes in every fortnight to stop the dust and cobwebs building up.'

'That's good. But you haven't been inside yourself?'

'I can't seem to do it. It's not just about them being there together. It's about everything else.'

She studied my face for a moment then nodded. 'I'm so sorry. I never meant—'

'No, Mum. *He's* the one who should be sorry. *He* caused all this. And her.'

'Even so...'

'Lewis thinks I'm being stupid and should just let it go but he doesn't know what really happened. I don't think...' I tailed off as a text from Sam flashed up on my phone:

✉ From Sam
Can you come home asap? I need you xx

I jumped to my feet, heart thumping, and rang Sam's mobile but there was no answer. Mum watched me, her forehead creased with concern.

'It's Sam,' I said as I disconnected the call. 'I've got to go.' I quickly tapped in a response.

✉ To Sam
On my way xx

Mum stood up. 'Is she okay?'

'I'm not sure. I'm hoping it isn't the Grimes boys again.'

'Can you text me when you get home to let me know she's okay? Or I'm going to worry.'

'I will. Hopefully it's nothing.' But Sam never sent cryptic messages like that. That was more her cousin Chloe's style. Something bad must have happened.

* * *

There were no lights on in the barn or the farmhouse when I arrived home but Sam's car was in the farmyard. The darkness unnerved me.

'I'm home,' I called, unlocking the farmhouse door and switching on the hallway light.

No response.

'Sam?'

'I'm in the lounge.' Her words were quiet and slow.

I pushed open the door and flicked on the light. She was lying on the sofa with a folded flannel across her forehead and a box of tissues resting on her stomach. She squinted in the brightness.

I felt sick with relief to find her safe. 'What's happened?' I asked anxiously, perching on the sofa beside her. Her eyes were red and puffy, her cheeks were flushed and she was surrounded by scrunched up tissues.

'Ripley's dead,' she wailed, releasing a fresh torrent of tears.

I gasped. 'When? How?'

'I don't know.' She gave a loud sniff and grabbed at a tissue from the box. 'I don't get it. Gollum's mange was far more severe and he's doing really well. I was never worried about Ripley. She always seemed fine. It's my fault for not being here full-time. I could have spotted something else wrong if I had been.'

'You can't think like that,' I said, hugging her tightly and stroking her hair. 'You'd treated Ripley's mange and there was nothing else obviously wrong with her.'

She pulled away and shook her head. 'I could have missed something. What if I do that again? I had years of training to make me competent as a nurse and what have I done to get qualified for this? A bit of reading and some work experience? I'm not a vet. What made me think I could do it?' Her voice kept breaking with sobs.

I took both her hands in mine and looked her in the eyes. 'Listen to me carefully, Samantha Wishaw, hedgehog lady.' The nickname drew the weakest of smiles. 'You are brilliant at what you do and you are more than qualified and capable of running Hedgehog Hollow and saving thousands of hedgehogs. You know exactly what you're doing and you defer to me and your dad for the more complex stuff which is exactly what happens in rescue centres the length and breadth of the country. You didn't miss anything because there was nothing to miss. I couldn't see anything wrong with Ripley other than the mange. Animals die. It's sad. It hurts. But it happens. Ripley could simply have been old. It could have been her time.'

Tears rained silently down Sam's cheeks but the agonised sobs had ceased. I released one of her hands, grabbed a tissue and gently wiped her cheeks. It was heartbreaking seeing her like this. The last time I'd seen her in so much pain was when she'd returned from Whitsborough Bay after her mum chose to sever all ties with her. I hugged her again.

'There's something else,' she whispered, pulling away. 'I went to collect a hedgehog in Fimberley after work. This woman had been trying to get hold of me all afternoon and she had a right go at me because I hadn't answered the phone—'

'That's unfair,' I interrupted, feeling incensed for her. 'You've got to ignore people like that.'

'That's not the worst part. She made out she didn't know what had happened to the hedgehog and she said it wasn't bleeding so I assumed it wasn't too serious. She was going on holiday so she left it on her doorstep for me to collect but when I...'

Her voice broke with a huge shuddering sob and I held her once more until she was able to control her breathing.

'When I collected her, she was already dead. The woman had lied. She was covered in blood and puncture wounds.'

'Dog?'

Sam nodded. 'The woman's dog, I think.' She wiped her wet cheeks and took a deep breath. 'I noticed that she was pregnant. I didn't think there was any chance of the hoglets being alive if she was but...'

Tears streamed down her face again and she clung onto me.

'You found babies?' I asked gently.

'Five. All gone.'

'Oh, Sam. I'm so sorry.' I'd be lying if I said that animals dying never affected me but it was a regular part of my job and I'd found ways of coping with even the most traumatic or senseless deaths over the years, but seeing the pain through Sam's eyes, I found myself welling up too.

'I was too late. What if I'd been able to pick up that first call and go to Fimberley immediately? I might have saved them all.'

'And you might not. You can't deal in what ifs? And you can't blame yourself for every hedgehog who doesn't make it.'

We sat there, arms round each other, as the minutes ticked by. Ever so gradually the tension eased from Sam's body and she eventually released her hold on me.

She gazed at the collection of dirty tissues and sighed. 'Sorry. Major meltdown.'

I gave her a reassuring smile. 'Everyone's entitled to one of those every so often. But will you do something for me?'

'Pick up the snotty tissues?'

I laughed. 'Well, yeah, but that wasn't what I was going to suggest.'

'Okay. What do you want me to do?'

'Repeat after me: I, Samantha Wishaw, am a badass hedgehog saviour.'

She smiled and rolled her eyes at me. 'I'm *not* saying that.'

'You have to. It's what Ripley would have wanted.'

'Josh!'

'Seriously. It is. How can you deny a hedgehog's final wish?'

'Oh my gosh. Go on, then. I, Samantha Wishaw, am a badass hedgehog saviour.'

I frowned and looked round the lounge then back at her. 'Did you hear something? I thought I heard some whispering but I couldn't quite make it out.'

She smiled again and repeated the words more loudly and confidently this time.

'Much better. And now say: I am the best thing that ever happened to hedgehogs in Yorkshire.'

She rolled her eyes once more but repeated the words with conviction. 'Thanks, Josh. I don't know what I'd do without you.'

'You'll never be without me.' I cupped her face and gently kissed her. 'You look done in. Why don't you have a bath?'

'I can't. I haven't fed the hedgehogs and I haven't made anything to eat.'

'I'll sort the hedgehogs then go out for a takeaway. You have a relax.'

Sam squeezed my hand. 'Ripley's on the table under a fleece and the mum and babies are under...' She sobbed again.

'It's okay. I'll sort it.'

* * *

I waited until I heard the bath running then headed over to the barn. I shook my head as I reached the treatment table and clocked the grey fleece and the puppy pad covering the bodies. Poor Sam. What a shitty evening she'd had.

Pulling on a pair of gloves, I removed the fleece and picked up Ripley's stiff body. Sam had done such an amazing job of clearing up the mange. There was no sign of flystrike or other parasites and I stood by what I'd said earlier; it had probably been Ripley's time. The fact that she hadn't been pregnant when she came in suggested she was an older hedgehog.

I placed her in a carry crate then lifted the puppy pad and swallowed the lump in my throat as I imagined Sam gently laying each baby round the mother hedgehog so they'd remain close even in death. It was such a Sam thing to do and one of the many reasons I loved her so much: she cared about everyone and everything.

After examining them, I transferred the family into the carry case beside Ripley, lying them together like Sam had done. She'd questioned whether she could have saved the hoglets if she'd got to Fimberley sooner but three of the five had puncture wounds and the other two had likely been crushed in the attack. She couldn't have saved the mum either. The dog's teeth had caught her heart and intestines. I wouldn't be surprised if the hedgehog wasn't already dead by the time the dog released its hold. The news wouldn't provide Sam with much comfort but it would hopefully ease the guilt she was clearly feeling for not responding to the call immediately.

I placed the crate by the door alongside the blood-covered card-board box to take to work for incineration then checked on the rest of the hedgehogs, administering any treatment they needed and putting out fresh food and water. As I worked, I couldn't shake my own feeling of guilt that I hadn't been back sooner to help her. She'd had to text to beg me to come home. How bad was that? If it hadn't been for me going to Mum's to talk to her about Beth, I'd have been there for her. Jesus! That bloody woman again, causing problems. And I'd never even had a chance to mention her visit to Mum. That delight would have to wait for another day.

13

SAMANTHA

I hadn't expected to sleep after the upset over Ripley and the Fimberley hedgehog family but the lavender bubble bath, the camomile tea and the sheer exhaustion did the trick. I slept longer and deeper than I'd done since returning from hospital, waking up shortly before nine.

The bedroom door swung open and Josh stepped inside. 'Thought you might like breakfast in bed,' he announced, placing a tray on the bed beside me and sitting down. 'I nipped out to get some croissants from the bakery in Great Tilbury. They're still warm.'

'They smell delicious.' I felt hungry for the first time in a week.

He passed me a mug of coffee. 'You'll have to make do with rabbits today. I couldn't find your hedgehog mug.'

'Erm... it got broken.'

'Oh no! How?'

I couldn't bring myself to look at him. I reached for a croissant and busied myself adding some butter and jam to it. 'I... erm...' Misty-Blue entered the room and jumped onto the bed. 'It was

Misty-Blue. She got under my feet and I dropped it outside after you were called out on Thursday. I was gutted.'

'We'll have to see if we can replace it.'

I took a bite of croissant and my mouth watered at the taste of the soft, warm, buttery pastry. Delicious. The first one went down quickly and I even managed most of a second.

'How are you feeling this morning?' Josh asked as we settled back against the pillows with our drinks.

'Sad but better after a good sleep. I'd probably have been okay if it had been Ripley *or* the Fimberley family but it was a bit much having both together.'

'It was a tough day but it's rare to get days like that. You know that, don't you?'

I nodded. 'Thank goodness because I don't know if I could cope with many of them.'

'You could and do you know why? Because you're a badass hedgehog saviour.' He held his hand up for me to high five. 'I think you should get that put on your business cards and flyers.'

'Better than hedgehog lady,' I said, laughing. 'But maybe not one for the kids.'

'You know what I think you should do today?'

'Help you move in?'

'No. I think you should go across to Whitsborough Bay and have a proper catch-up with Chloe and your Auntie Louise. You said you felt bad for not getting to speak to them much last weekend so this could be your chance.'

'That's a really good idea.'

'Stick with me and you'll find I'm a goldmine of ideas.'

'Goldmine or not, I'm more than happy to stick with you.' I cuddled up against him, feeling so lucky to have found him.

* * *

When I rang Chloe, apologising that it was last-minute, she said she'd love to see me. Auntie Louise had gone to York for the day with some work friends and James was playing golf with Toby so the company would be welcome and we could have an undisturbed catch-up.

A sunny drive across to Whitsborough Bay was just what I needed. I turned up my music and sang along to some cheesy pop classics, feeling cheerier with each song. I drove along the seafront, where the tide was out and South Bay beach was busy with families enjoying a sunny Saturday on the golden sands. I saw people eating fish and chips or ice-creams and children squealing with delight on the small rides outside the arcades.

I continued past the harbour, over the River Abbleby via the swing bridge, round the headland and towards the quieter North Bay. The wide pathway next to the sea wall was busy with tourists and locals out walking, jogging or cycling. With my window down, I breathed in the salty air and smiled at the squawk of gulls. It was busy, loud and vibrant – a contrast to the tranquillity of Hedgehog Hollow. I would always love Whitsborough Bay and be thrilled to visit but it wasn't my home anymore. I belonged on the Wolds now with Josh and my hedgehogs.

I pulled up outside Chloe and James's house feeling calm and relaxed and looking forward to a long overdue catch-up. We hadn't had any quality time together, just the two of us, since before the wedding and it would be another significant step in moving forward.

The lounge window was open and, as soon as I exited my car, I could hear Samuel's cries. The door flew open to reveal a frazzled-looking Chloe with Samuel in her arms, red-faced, fists balled. 'He's just woken up,' she said by way of a greeting. 'Make yourself a drink and I'll be down soon.'

I felt uncomfortable pottering round Chloe's kitchen while she was upstairs. The words 'I love you Chloe' were spelt out in magnetic letters on the fridge door and there was a collage on the wall of photos of them together. Although I had absolutely no feelings for James anymore, I still couldn't help feeling uneasy looking at so many indicators of how happy they were together when that's what I'd longed for with James. Once. Not now. How I felt about Josh eclipsed what I'd felt for James.

I'd finished my coffee by the time Chloe came back down. 'Do you want him?' She thrust Samuel at me before I had a chance to respond.

'Hello, gorgeous,' I said to him. 'Have you been a good boy for your mummy?'

'He's very loud,' Chloe responded, sounding weary.

'Babies generally are. How are you finding motherhood?'

She shrugged. 'The lack of sleep is a shock to the system but I'm sure I'll get used to it.' She scraped her messy long, blonde hair back into a ponytail and I couldn't help noticing that she was wearing sweatpants and a stained T-shirt. Very un-Chloe.

'Can we talk about something other than babies?' She rolled her eyes at me. 'It's all anyone seems to be capable of talking about these days. What's new with you?'

'Josh is moving in with me.'

Chloe frowned. 'That's not new. He already lives with you.'

'He doesn't.'

'He does.'

Why was she arguing with me on something she knew nothing about? I fought to keep the frustration out of my voice. 'I can see why you'd think that because he has stayed over most nights but it was never official that Hedgehog Hollow was his home and I wanted it to be. I asked him on Sunday and he said yes.'

The frown was still there. 'Oh. Congratulations on continuing to do what you were already doing. I'm very happy for you both.'

I winced at the lack of enthusiasm in her voice. When I'd Face-Timed Hannah with the news, she'd squealed with excitement and wanted to know all the details about what I'd said and how Josh had reacted. I'd been sure that Chloe's response would be the same. Once upon a time it would have been.

It would have probably made sense to shut up and change subject but I kept going. 'He's moving his stuff across today so coming to see you was the perfect excuse to avoid lugging boxes.'

Chloe's eyes widened. 'So that's why it was a last-minute thing. You wouldn't have bothered otherwise. Thanks for that, Samantha.'

She only ever used my full name when she was mad with me although her tone of voice already made that clear. 'That's not how it was.'

'It's fine. I get it. I traipsed across to the farm two days in a row last weekend to be there for you but you can only be bothered to visit me when you want to avoid being the removals service. Good to know where I stand.' She smiled sweetly at me while every word dripped with sarcasm.

'Do you want me to go?' I asked, now unable to keep the frustration out of my voice. This wasn't how I'd imagined spending the afternoon.

'Do you want to go?'

'Of course not! I came across to spend time with you and I was really looking forward to it because I've had a horrendous couple of weeks but if you're—'

'What's happened?' Chloe suddenly looked all interested.

'What?'

'You said you've had a horrendous couple of weeks. I thought life on the farm was perfect. What's being going on?'

I couldn't decide if she was being genuine or sarcastic. 'You really want to know?'

She nodded vigorously. 'I'm all ears.'

'For starters, there've been a couple more incidents with the Grimes boys...'

I told Chloe about the delivery of dead hedgehogs and yesterday's traumatic losses. I also confessed to my near-fainting incident and how I had no idea how I was going to be able to balance my teaching role with running the rescue centre. With the recent distance between us, I hadn't expected Chloe to be the first person I opened up to.

The more problems I described, the more animated she seemed to get, asking questions and sympathising. I was conscious that I was doing all the talking but she didn't seem to mind. Clearly, she found this way more exciting than the news about Josh moving in although that unnerved me. Why was she so anxious to hear about the bad stuff and so dismissive of the good things?

The doorbell rang and Chloe frowned. 'Back in a second.' She closed the lounge door behind her.

Moments later, it opened again and Chloe looked at me uncertainly. 'Surprise visitor.'

My stomach churned as Mum followed her into the lounge. I hadn't seen her since that hideous day a couple of months ago when she'd told me she'd never wanted me then chose to sever ties completely instead of trying to draw a line and move our relationship forward.

She stopped dead when she clocked me. 'I didn't realise *you* were here.'

I gulped, my pulse racing with nerves. 'Hi, Mum.'

'I'll come back later, Chloe.'

She turned towards the door but Chloe grabbed her arm. 'You'll do no such thing. Didn't the two of you make an agreement to be civil if you saw each other? Well, now's your chance. Sit down.'

I was surprised by Chloe's forceful tone but it worked because Mum sat down in the other armchair.

'I can't stay long,' she said. 'I only came round to drop those clothes off and have a cuddle with my great-nephew.'

There was no mistaking the sly look in my direction so I stood up and handed over Samuel. 'All yours.'

Her face broke into a huge smile as she gazed down at him and stroked his soft cheeks. 'Hello, sweetheart. I've missed you.'

Sitting back down, I swallowed the lump in my throat as I watched her cooing over Samuel. It was obvious she adored him and was capable of giving so much love to him, to Chloe and to Auntie Louise. Just not to Dad or me.

'Are you all settled into your new home?' I asked Mum.

'Yes. You?'

'Yes, thank you.'

Silence.

'Sammie was just telling me that she's still having trouble with the Grimes boys,' Chloe said.

Mum didn't look up from Samuel. 'Who?'

'The ones who burned down the barn.' I watched her carefully but she didn't flinch, even when I added. 'The ones who nearly killed me.'

'Yes, well, you're still alive to tell the tale, aren't you?' The sarcasm was clear but I couldn't decide if there was regret in there too. No. Wishful thinking on my part. She'd never come to see me in hospital so apparently she hadn't been bothered about almost losing her only daughter.

'Sammie's boyfriend, Josh, has moved in with her,' Chloe said.

Mum finally looked up and sighed. 'At least it's your house this time so you won't be inflicting your presence on one of us when it all goes wrong.'

'Why would it go wrong?' I snapped.

She smirked. 'Because it's you, Samantha. Your track record's shocking.'

'That's not my fault. Harry was seeing someone else and—' I looked pointedly at Chloe '—so was James.'

'I'm sure this one will last longer,' Mum said gently. Had she just been nice to me? Then she smirked again. 'Huge house, land, no mortgage, no rent. He's onto a winner there.'

'Auntie Debs!'

She turned to Chloe, her face a picture of innocence. 'What? I'm just pointing out the facts.'

'You promised to be nice.'

'I promised to be civil.'

Chloe sighed and turned to me, picking up where we'd left off when the doorbell rang. 'What are you going to do about work? Are you going to resign?'

'Leaving another job already?' Mum asked, dragging out the last word for emphasis.

My jaw clenched. 'No. All I'd said to Chloe was that the rescue centre is getting busier and it's a challenge to fit it round my teaching role.'

'So you're going to pack in running the rescue centre instead?'

'I'm not going to pack anything in.'

'Oh. So you're going to give a half-baked effort at both of them?'

'No, but—'

'They're both full-time jobs, Samantha. What did you expect was going to happen?'

'I don't know,' I snapped. 'I didn't think it through properly.'

'That's your problem. You never think things through.'

'That's not fair! I do.'

'Oh, please. When have you ever thought something through? Name me one thing.'

I thought as hard as I could but nothing sprang to mind. I'd always thought that Chloe was the impulsive one yet every big decision I'd made over the past five years had been reactive. I'd moved in with Harry to escape from Mum and tried to kid myself that it was love. I'd moved back home the moment that ended without considering the impact of that on my parents. I'd kept seeing James, hoping he'd grow to love me, when he'd made it clear that he didn't see me as a future wife. I'd made a rash decision to hand in my notice at work and move to the Wolds – even changing my career in the process – to get away from James and Chloe starting their married life in Whitsborough Bay. And I'd accepted the gift of Hedgehog Hollow when I knew nothing about hedgehogs and didn't have the time or finances to fully commit to it. She was absolutely right but it didn't stop the words hurting any less.

'Struggling, aren't you?' Mum shook her head at me. 'Honestly, Samantha, is there anything in your whole life that you've ever stuck at?'

My stomach churned. There was one thing. One thing I'd stupidly stuck with my whole life. 'You,' I spat, my fists curling into balls. 'My whole life, I've stuck with trying to get you to love me. Heck, even liking me would have been good. Waste of time, that was.' I rose to my feet and looked at Chloe. 'I think I'd better head back to the farm now.'

'I thought we were going to have a proper catch-up.'

'I'm sorry but I need to check on the hedgehogs.' I didn't need to rush back at all but I had no energy to stay and fight with Mum again. I stared at her, hoping she'd insist on leaving instead, especially after her declaration that she couldn't stay long, but then I realised that had been her exit strategy if I hadn't broken first. It didn't matter. Even before she'd arrived, the afternoon hadn't been how I'd imagined it and I felt quite relieved to be leaving.

Chloe walked me to the door. 'I didn't invite her,' she snapped. 'I wasn't trying to interfere again so don't you go blaming me for this.'

'I'm *not* blaming you but surely you understand why I can't do this.'

She shrugged petulantly: a typical Chloe-ism.

I opened the door, stepped outside and gave her a weak smile. 'We'll catch up properly soon, yeah?'

'If you can be bothered.'

I flinched at the sarcasm but said nothing. I'd normally have hugged her but she had her arms crossed tightly across her chest and was leaning against the doorframe with a face like thunder. 'See you, then.'

'Bye.'

She slammed the door behind her before I'd even unlocked the car. I sighed and shook my head, wondering if I should go back but what was the point? Chloe hadn't exactly been welcoming, she'd been dismissive of Josh moving in, and she'd only perked up when I'd told her about everything going wrong with my life, as though she was revelling in my misery.

Why had she invited Mum in when I was there and then insisted she stay? She could have told her I was there and asked her to come back when I'd gone. It wasn't like Mum had made a long journey. She lived less than a ten-minute walk away. And how rude had Chloe been at the door just now? She *knew* how much altercations with Mum hurt me yet she was acting as if it was all about her. Living in Chloe-world as usual.

The stress had brought my headache back with a vengeance so I drove to North Bay and parked along the seafront. Some fresh air would hopefully clear it before I headed home.

I bought a takeaway tea then ambled along the promenade with it. The beach was busy but not quite as packed as the one at South Bay had been. Many of the colourful orange, yellow, red, sky-blue and lime-green beach huts were in use and the smell of barbeques filled the air. Each step made me feel a little calmer.

At the far end of the promenade, past the beach huts, I leaned on the sea wall and sipped on my tea. Why had Chloe been like that today? Sarcastic, distant, argumentative. As for Mum, where could I start? Her comments, as always, had been cruel but the worst was her comment about me still being here to tell the tale after the arson attack. Was that really all she had to say about it? Why had I ever expected anything different? I swallowed down the lump in my throat. Enough. I'd wasted too much time and energy on wishing things could be different. They couldn't be. I had to let go.

14

'Looks like Sam's back,' I said to Rich and Dave, spotting her car as we approached the farmyard with a van full from Wisteria Cottage. 'That was quicker than expected.'

'Another bust-up with Chloe?' Dave suggested.

I shrugged. 'If it is, it's no great loss.'

'Not a fan either?' Rich asked.

'To be fair to her, I've only met her a handful of times but I'm not impressed with how she treated Sam.'

'We're not either,' Dave said. 'Sam was in a pretty bad place last year thanks to Chloe yet she still idolises her. We don't get it.'

He reversed the van along the front of the house and we all clambered out. I unlocked the front door and called out Sam's name but was met with silence.

'Do you two want to make yourselves a drink before we unpack? I'd better go and find Sam and see why she's back so early.'

I left them in the kitchen and found Sam in the barn massaging Gollum. She looked up and smiled as I approached. There was no sign of tears so it couldn't be all bad.

'How was Whitsborough Bay?'

'Whitsborough Bay was lovely.' Then her smile slipped. 'It was the people that were the problem.'

I sat down. 'What happened?'

'Chloe was in a strange mood, almost hostile, and then Mum turned up and was her usual delightful self.'

'Your mum was there? Was that part of Chloe's plan?'

'No. I genuinely think it was a coincidence but it wasn't a happy one. Long story short is that I left early, had a walk along the seafront then drove home. I'm okay. Just fed up with the whole thing. I'll tell you the full sorry tale later. Where's Rich and Dave?'

'In the kitchen.'

'Give me ten minutes to finish up here then I'll come over to say hi and help.'

I gave her a quick hug then walked back to the farmhouse, cursing Chloe under my breath and also kicking myself for suggesting she drive over there. I thought the company would do her good but it sounded as though she'd have been better off staying here.

* * *

'Your mum should not have said any of those things,' I said after Rich and Dave left and Sam had given me the full lowdown on her afternoon.

She shrugged. 'I think it's become her default setting. It's impossible for her to say anything nice in my presence.'

'And I can't believe Chloe let you leave. It should have been your mum going home.'

'You'd think so, but I've given up trying to understand Chloe's logic. It was pretty much a disaster from start to finish.'

'I'm sorry.'

'Yeah, me too. It'll be interesting to see whether Chloe reaches out to say sorry.'

'Do you think she will?'

'No. Chloe doesn't do apologies.' Sam sighed. 'It'll fester and then she'll make out that I said or did something to upset her and I'm the one who was in the wrong and should be apologising. It's a recurring pattern.'

I bit my tongue. The more I heard about Chloe, the more I disliked her. She sounded just like Beth, playing the victim and manipulating people. And I knew how easy it was to get sucked in by someone like that.

'Why don't you take a shower while I unpack my clothes, then I'll take you out for dinner to celebrate me moving in? I don't care what your cousin thinks, I say it's a big thing and it's cause for celebration.'

Sam smiled. 'That would be lovely. Thank you.'

* * *

I'd finished unpacking my clothes and was in my office putting some papers in my desk drawers when I heard Sam crying out my name.

I dashed across the hall, panic gripping me. 'Are you okay?' She was wrapped in a towel, her long dark hair dripping down her back, clinging onto the open en-suite door.

'Dizzy.'

'Do you need to lie down?'

'Floor.'

I placed my left arm round her waist from the front and my right round her shoulders and took her weight as I gently lowered her to the floor.

'Pillows. Feet,' she mumbled.

I grabbed a couple of pillows from the bed and raised her feet onto them. She was white as a sheet as she rapidly breathed in and out, her eyelids flickering. I dashed into the en-suite and ran a flannel under the cold tap then rested it across her forehead.

'Anything else I can do?'

'No.' The word was barely audible.

I sat beside her and held her clammy hand. I had questions but they could wait until she was feeling better. She shivered. 'Are you cold?'

'A bit.'

I grabbed her fluffy dressing gown from the back of the en-suite door and lay it across her arms and shoulders then returned to the sink to rinse out the flannel.

'Thanks,' she whispered as I placed it back on her forehead.

'Anything else you need?'

'Not yet.'

We stayed there for several minutes and slowly the colour returned to her face. 'Can you help me up?'

After I'd eased her to her feet, she sat down on the edge of the bed. 'Sorry.'

I sat beside her. 'No need to apologise. Are you sure you're okay?'

'I am now. The room just started spinning. I must have had the shower too hot or something.'

'It hasn't happened before, then?'

She hesitated then her shoulders slumped. 'Once.'

'Recently?'

'On Thursday when you were out on call. I went outside to have my tea on Thomas's bench and the same thing happened. I dropped my mug.'

I frowned. 'The hedgehog mug?'

She nodded.

'Did you scald your feet? Was that what those red marks were?' I'd noticed them but she said she'd had an allergic reaction to her new shower gel, which sounded plausible.

She nodded again. 'Sorry.'

'Why didn't you tell me?' I asked, keeping my voice gentle so she'd know I was concerned rather than annoyed.

'I didn't want you to worry. You'd have told me to take more time off and—'

'And I'm going to tell you that now. Come on, Sam. You've nearly fainted twice in the space of a few days, you're barely eating, and I know you're not sleeping properly. I know you think you're letting Auntie Lauren down but you're not. Your health's more important. I really think you need to phone in sick next week and give yourself more time to recover.'

I expected Sam to protest but she hung her head, suggesting my worries weren't ill-founded. 'I'm not trying to order you about,' I added gently.

She sighed. 'I know. How about I make a promise to take it easy tomorrow and see how I feel on Monday morning?'

I hugged her to my side. 'Okay. And maybe we'll go out next weekend instead. How does macaroni cheese and a film sound tonight?'

'It sounds good. Thank you.'

While Sam dressed and dried her hair, I continued to unpack in the office but I felt uneasy. Two dizzy spells since returning to work. That wasn't good.

Sam went to bed after we'd watched a film. It was only 9 p.m. but she obviously needed the sleep as she was spark out when I went upstairs a couple of hours later. She seemed a lot livelier when we woke up on Sunday morning but promised me she'd take it easy.

It was another bright sunny day so we ate breakfast on Thomas's bench, watching Misty-Blue chasing butterflies in the meadow. Afterwards, Sam checked on the hedgehogs then returned to Thomas's bench with a book while I continued to unpack. I wasn't particularly productive because I kept checking out of the window to make sure she was resting and that she was okay.

We were in the kitchen together around mid-morning making a drink when I spotted a car coming down the farm track.

'Looks like we might have another patient,' I said to Sam. My stomach lurched as the car pulled into the farmyard. 'I should have known.' I tossed the teaspoon into the sink with a clatter and strode towards the door.

'Who is it?' asked Sam, chasing after me.

'Who do you think?'

Beth was walking across the yard as we stepped outside.

'Was I not clear enough last week?' I called to her. 'I'm *not* interested. Leave us alone.'

She took a few steps towards the house. 'I need to talk to you.'

'And I don't need to talk to you.'

'But it's important.' Cradling her stomach protectively, she moved even closer.

'To you, perhaps. Not to me. Nothing you say could possibly be important to me.' Shaking with rage that she'd dared to turn up at our home again, especially after the horrendous weekend Sam had faced, I marched back towards the house. 'Go away, Beth! You're not welcome here.'

'Josh! Stop! I have to talk to you.'

'I'm sorry,' I whispered to Sam as I passed her. 'She makes me so mad. Why won't she listen?'

Her fingers lightly touched mine. 'I'll speak to her. I'll sort it.'

I nodded gratefully and stepped into the hall.

'Josh!' Beth screamed. 'Please! Josh!'

Silence.

'Josh! Help!' Sam yelled moments later.

I was halfway up the stairs and stopped dead, a shiver running down my spine at Sam's cry. That didn't sound good.

I dashed back outside and my pulse raced. 'Shit! What happened?' Beth was lying on her right side on the gravel path in front of the house with Sam bent over her. Beth's face was deathly white and she was eerily still. Bile rose in my throat and I swallowed hard. 'She's not…?'

'It's okay, Josh. She's breathing. We need to try to bring her round.' Sam sounded so calm – the exact opposite of how I felt.

'What do you need me to do?' I tried to keep the panic out of my voice but I don't think I managed. Sick animals I could deal with but sick humans? Especially sick humans I couldn't bear the sight of.

Sam stood up. 'Can you talk to her?'

She ran into the house and I crouched down beside Beth. Talk to her? What the hell was I supposed to say? I'd just told her I never wanted to speak to her again and now she was unconscious outside my home. I had no idea how to feel about that. The anger still raged inside of me but how could I not feel sympathy? I wasn't a monster.

'Erm, Beth, can you hear me? It's Josh.' I gave her shoulder a nudge but she didn't stir. I cleared my throat and increased the volume, trying to sound confident and in control. 'Can you open your eyes, Beth? Hello? Beth? Wake up!' I reached out towards her hand then changed my mind and nudged her shoulder again instead.

'Any change?' Sam asked, re-appearing with a throw from the lounge draped over one arm, a couple of cushions, her medical bag and a golf brolly.

'No.'

'Damn. It's been longer than a minute.' She opened out the brolly and thrust it at me. 'Can you hold this over her and phone for an ambulance?'

Shading Beth from the afternoon sun, my hands shook as I dialled 999. While I gave the details to the emergency services operator, Sam worked calmly and quickly. She placed the cushions under Beth's legs to elevate them and dug her stethoscope out of her bag. I felt so proud of her but also so ashamed of my own behaviour. I'd shouted at and walked away from a pregnant woman twice. Yes, she was my ex and she'd behaved deplorably but had my behaviour really been any better?

'Baby sounds good but Beth's pulse is racing,' Sam told me, which I relayed to the operator.

'There'll be a first responder with us in about ten minutes,' I said, disconnecting the call. 'An ambulance could be up to half an hour.'

'Thanks. We'll need it. Even if she comes round soon, she'll need checking over in hospital after her fall.'

She put her stethoscope back in her bag. 'Can you keep talking to her? She knows your voice so she's more likely to respond to yours than mine.'

I crouched down beside her. 'Beth? It's Josh. Can you hear me? We need you to wake up.'

Beth released a soft moan and her eyes started to flicker.

'Keep going,' Sam encouraged.

'That's great, Beth. Try again. You collapsed but you're okay. Can you hear me?' It felt so alien to be speaking to her in gentle tones when all our recent exchanges had been full of anger and bitterness.

Beth murmured something as her eyes flickered open but it wasn't coherent.

'It's Samantha and Josh,' Sam said, loud and clear. 'You're at the farm and you fainted. There's an ambulance on its way.'

She murmured again.

'We can't hear you,' I said. 'Does somewhere hurt? Is it the baby?'

Beth's eyes flickered once more. 'Archie?'

Sam looked at me questioningly. My dad's name was Paul and I had no idea who... 'Oh shit! The baby!' I dropped the brolly and pelted towards the farmyard. *Please don't say he's trapped in the car in this heat.*

My heart pounded as I neared Beth's car and spotted the Eeyore 'baby on board' sign displayed in the back window. There he was – a sleeping baby lolling in his car seat. Or at least I hoped he was sleeping.

I grabbed at the back door handle and then the front one. 'It's locked,' I yelled in Sam's direction as I raced round the car, trying the other two doors and the boot.

I frantically scanned for something with which to smash the window but there was nothing. I was about to run into the rescue centre, my mind racing as to what I could use when Sam ran towards me, arm outstretched.

'I've got the keys,' she called. Seconds later, the locks clicked open and I flung the back door open, recoiling at the heat. I swiftly unclipped the straps, grabbed Archie and stepped back clutching him protectively against my chest.

Sam reached the car.

'It's boiling inside,' I told her, lifting Archie away from my chest. His eyes were closed and his face was red but he was breathing.

'We need to get him cool and hydrated,' she said, reaching for him. 'Look for a changing bag. I need a bottle or a sippy cup. I'll be in the kitchen.'

'Do you think he'll be okay?'

Her eyes widened. 'I honestly don't know but I hope so.'

16

I ran back towards the farmhouse with Archie in my arms.

'I've got him,' I called as I rushed past Beth.

In the kitchen, I opened a drawer containing hand towels and tea towels, scooped up the entire pile and dumped them on the table. With one hand, I lay out one of the towels, placed Archie on it and swiftly removed his T-shirt and trousers.

'The first responder's coming down the track,' Josh said, bursting through the door with a changing bag. 'Do you need me or should I be with Beth?'

'Me first. Can you wet one of those towels with cold water and bring it to me? Then fill the washing up bowl with cold water and bring me that.'

Moments later, I gently lay the wet towel across Archie's body. He kicked out his arms and legs in protest and released a loud wail. A good sign.

Josh turned off the tap and placed the bowl on the table beside me. 'Did we get to him in time?' he asked, his voice shaky.

'I think so. Can you see if there's a cup in the bag?' I dunked another towel in the water.

Josh produced a sippy cup from one of the bag's side pockets. 'It feels hot.'

'Tip it out and fill it with the cooled down water from the kettle.'

I wrung the second towel out and dabbed Archie's face with it before placing it across his legs. Josh handed me the cup.

'Thanks. How old is he?'

Josh's brow furrowed, suggesting he was calculating it. 'Nearly eleven months I think.'

I propped Archie up and held the cup to his lips. After he'd taken a couple of eager glugs I looked up at Josh. 'Can you check on Beth now and tell the first responder what's happened?'

With one more anxious look at his half-brother, he left the kitchen and I released a long breath.

'I know, sweetheart,' I said as Archie scrunched up his eyes, balled his fists and started to howl. 'You're going to be okay. And so is your mummy.'

As I swapped over the towels, I lightly stroked the side of Archie's cooling face and hoped I wasn't lying on either count.

* * *

Josh and I stood shoulder to shoulder as Beth was wheeled into the back of the ambulance. Archie, cooled down and now in his baby carrier, was secured in place.

I slipped my hand into Josh's. 'Give me a call and I'll pick you up when you're ready.'

He didn't say anything but he squeezed my hand. I could only imagine the turmoil he was going through right now. An ambulance journey with the ex-girlfriend he despised and the half-brother he'd never wanted to meet wasn't how he'd have wanted to spend the afternoon.

Beth hadn't had to ask him to accompany her and I hadn't

needed to suggest it; he'd stepped up and offered which couldn't have been easy.

He sighed. 'I'm going to have to phone *him*, aren't I?'

'He needs to know. Do you want me to do it?'

'No. It's not fair on you. I'll ring him from the ambulance.'

'All ready if you want to clamber in,' said one of the paramedics.

Josh kissed the top of my head. 'I'll see you later.'

The pained expression in his eyes was the last thing I saw before the doors were closed and the ambulance pulled away.

17

I hated leaving Sam on her own after everything she'd been through this weekend but even I knew it would be wrong to abandon Beth no matter how much I despised her. Having her collapse had been bad enough but the situation with Archie had been terrifying. For a brief moment, anger had surged through me at her careless ineptitude leaving a baby in the car like that – like those thoughtless imbeciles who left their dogs to cook while nipping to the pub or the supermarket – and I'd had to remind myself that she'd never have done that intentionally. Dropping to the ground unconscious wouldn't have been part of her plan.

'Paul,' Beth murmured.

I clenched my teeth as I removed my phone from my jeans pocket. The last person I wanted to speak to right now was *him*, but it had to be done and I was the only one who could do it.

'There's no service,' I told her.

'Keep trying.' Her eyes pleaded with me.

I kept checking my phone all the way to the hospital but the signal was too weak. The thought of speaking to *him* after all this time was seriously grim and I was unwilling to prolong the experience with a horrendous I-can't-hear-you broken-up conversation. It would have to wait until we got to Reddfield Hospital. Except, when we arrived, it made more sense to me to find out where they were taking Beth first. Procrastination at its best.

'Promise you won't leave,' Beth whispered as the back door to the ambulance opened. She grabbed for my hand but missed. I told myself I'd be in the way if I reached out and took her hand but that was a lie. I could have done. If I'd wanted to.

'Please,' she pleaded, her voice stronger as they wheeled out her stretcher. 'I'm scared.'

'Okay,' I agreed. With a sigh, I picked up the baby carrier. Archie was fast asleep, his cheeks red, his rosebud lips pouting. I swept his dark hair back from his forehead then followed the stretcher in a daze, gazing down at my sleeping half-brother. Around me, information was being passed between medical staff and, when an auburn-haired nurse reached for the baby carrier, I had to force myself to release my tight grip on the handle.

'You'll look after him?' It was such a stupid thing to say. Of course they would.

The nurse gave me a gentle smile. 'I'm Anna and he's in good hands. Are you Dad?'

I shook my head. 'No. I'm his...' I couldn't bring myself to say the words out loud. 'I'm not related.'

'Then why don't you make yourself comfortable in the waiting room down there and to the right?'

A set of double doors to the left automatically opened and, moments later, they disappeared out of sight leaving me standing in the corridor, alone.

Not related to Archie. I'd told myself that lie so many times that I'd almost believed it.

I had felt some sort of momentary connection towards him but it wasn't because of who he was. It was only because we'd been through something traumatic together. He could have been a random stranger and I'd have felt something if I'd been the one to help save him.

I ran my hands through my hair and sighed. I couldn't keep putting off the inevitable. I made my way out of the main entrance and past a couple of patients wearing hospital gowns, drawing greedily on cigarettes right under the enormous 'No Smoking' sign.

As I made the call, I willed it to go to voicemail, yet knew I wasn't going to be that fortunate.

'Josh? Is that you?' He sounded uncertain.

'Yes.' It was more of a sound than a fully formed word.

'It's so great to hear from you. How are you?' He sounded genuinely delighted and I couldn't do it. I couldn't have an everyday friendly conversation with him. I couldn't ask him how he was because I didn't care. I couldn't feign interest or compassion, especially after the experience I'd just had.

'Beth collapsed and she's on ward two at Reddfield Hospital with your kid,' I said, my voice completely devoid of any sort of emotion. And then I hung up. I leaned back against the brick wall and released a slow, shaky breath.

My phone started ringing, the caller ID of 'TWAT' flashing up. It was childish of me to have done that to his number but I'd been livid with him at the time and it was tame compared to what I could have called him.

'What?' I snapped as I reluctantly accepted the call.

'What the hell are you playing at, saying something like that then hanging up?'

My jaw clenched. How dare he be angry with me after what he'd done. 'What the hell am I playing at?' I cried. 'Do you *really* want to play that game?'

He sighed. 'Are they okay?' he asked in a softer voice.

'I believe so.'

'What's that supposed to mean?'

'It means I believe so. They're being checked out.'

'Reddfield Hospital, you say?'

'Yes.'

'I'll be there as soon as I can.'

And now I had a dilemma. Stay and face *him* or go? I'd hated that man for a year and a half. As far as I was concerned, he was out of my life and I wasn't ready for him to be catapulted right back into it but Beth had made me promise to stay. And there was Archie. I needed to know he was okay... but only because Sam would want to know.

Back inside the hospital, I bought a coffee then headed into the waiting room and did the only thing I could. Waited.

* * *

About an hour later, there was still no sign of *him*. Anna – the nurse who'd taken Archie from me – appeared with the baby carrier and the changing bag slung over her shoulder. Archie was wide awake, kicking his legs and chewing on a brightly coloured, caterpillar-shaped teething toy.

'Beth tells me you're this little man's half-brother,' she announced, placing the carrier on the empty chair beside me. I could hear the unspoken question: *Why didn't you say so earlier?*

'It's complicated,' I muttered.

She smiled. 'Isn't it always?' She placed the bag on the floor by my feet. 'The good news is that young Archie here is absolutely fine. His temperature's normal, his fluids are topped up and there's no need for us to do any further observation. Mum's going for a scan and she was keen for him to be with his family in the meantime. So are you okay if I leave him with you?' It was obvious from her tone that it was a statement rather than a question so I nodded.

'Good,' she said. 'He's had a change too so all he needs from his big brother is plenty of cuddles.'

She'd smiled at me and been friendly enough but I felt well and truly chastised. Probably my own guilt at refusing to have anything to do with an innocent baby who'd had no influence over his parentage.

Aware that the handful of other people in the waiting room were watching me, most not even trying to disguise it, I unclipped the straps and lifted Archie out of his carrier. I wasn't used to handling babies and was probably doing it all wrong but hoped that I was giving off 'back-off' vibes. There was a time and a place for 'helpful' advice from strangers and this was definitely not it.

I sat Archie on my lap and turned him towards me so I could study his face. He kept pulling the caterpillar out of his mouth, showering me with slobber as he waved it around, then shoving it back in his mouth for another chew.

He'd inherited the Alderson colouring with his dark hair and brown eyes. I could visualise baby photos of me and the resemblance was striking. Uncanny, in fact. *Oh no! No way!* My shoulders tensed for a moment and I held my breath ... then slowly released it and relaxed. No, he *definitely* wasn't mine. Beth would have had to have been pregnant for about eleven months for there to be any possibility of that. At least that part of our situation wasn't complicated. The resemblance was simply down to us sharing the same father.

I held out my index finger towards him. Archie grabbed it with a slobbery hand and I felt a warm feeling in the pit of my stomach as he fixed his dark eyes on mine, smiled, and waggled my finger.

After a while, he started grizzling so I wandered over to the window with him. The hospital was built in a quad and the waiting room overlooked the gardens in the middle where patients and visitors were sitting on benches or ambling along the pathways.

'What can you see?' I self-consciously asked him in the sort of sing-song voice adults seemed to use when talking to babies. 'Can you see that little girl over there?' I pointed towards a toddler pushing a toy pushchair. 'She's got a penguin in her buggy. Do you like penguins?' Something about the word 'penguin' seemed to amuse him. His eyes sparkled and he jiggled with excitement in my arms, so I continued, emphasising the word each time. 'I love *penguins* but I've never treated one at the practice. We don't get many *penguins* round here. Do you know where *penguins* live? They live in—'

'Josh?'

My whole body tensed as I slowly turned to face my estranged father. He looked absolutely knackered and I couldn't help feeling it served him right for starting over with babies in his fifties. He'd always been slim but he'd lost weight – sleepless nights no doubt taking their toll. His dark hair was cropped short and peppered with grey. Presumably that was Beth's influence, trying to make him look younger and trendier, although he must have drawn the line at having it dyed. I bet she repeatedly nagged him about it. She'd no doubt get her own way eventually. As always.

He glanced down at the baby in my arms then narrowed his eyes at me. 'Why have you got Archie? And why was Beth with you?' He might as well have asked me if I was sleeping with her because the sharp edge to his voice and the suspicious expression on his face suggested that was what he meant.

Biting back a tirade of verbal abuse, I straightened up and fixed him with a hard stare. 'Your girlfriend seems to be okay and should be back from her scan shortly and your son is in good health too. I think that's what you meant to ask.' I'd managed to keep my voice low but bitterness clung to every word.

A vein pulsed in his forehead which I knew to be his tell-tale sign that he was livid. He had no right to be. *I* was the innocent party in the mess he'd created.

'That would have been my next question,' he snapped.

'If I was in your situation, it would have been my f—'

'Paul Alderson?' Anna cut me short as she looked expectantly in our direction.

He whipped round. 'Yes.'

'Beth's asking for you. Do you want to come with me?' She smiled at us both then turned and left the room.

Without another glance in my direction, he walked towards the door. I don't know what possessed me. It was so juvenile and unnecessary but I shouted after him, 'So I'll just continue to look after your son, should I, while you check on my ex-girlfriend?'

He marched back to me, grabbed Archie and gave me such a filthy look. 'She was *my* girlfriend first,' he hissed then snatched up the baby carrier and bag and stormed out of the waiting room.

I should have left it there. I should have made my escape, dignity almost intact but I couldn't quell the urge to have the last word. I ran to the door and shouted down the corridor, 'Yeah and Mum was your wife and I was your son first, not that you gave a shit about that while you were out pulling seventeen-year-olds.'

He paused for a moment, body rigid, then continued after Anna and out of sight. I heard murmurs and giggles from the waiting room. Thank God I didn't have to go back in there to collect anything.

After storming outside, I leaned against the wall and rubbed my hands down my face. That hadn't been one of my finest moments but I was so disgusted at him for not enquiring after Beth and Archie, for his clear insinuation that something was going on between us, and for not immediately reaching for his son. Surely a man who'd been so desperate for more kids would have shown more concern than he had just now. Could there be trouble in paradise already? He'd caused so much pain to others that, if their relationship was on the rocks, it was karma. Ha!

I glanced across to the taxi rank where a car was waiting for a fare and started towards it but I kept seeing Beth's face as she'd begged me to stay. I shook my head as I reluctantly retraced my steps. Much as I wanted to flee back to Hedgehog Hollow, I knew I had to stick around to make sure Beth and the new baby were okay. I definitely had no feelings for her anymore but I wasn't completely heartless. Besides, Sam would ask and telling her, 'I had words with the twat and stormed out before finding out about Beth and the baby,' was hardly an acceptable response. I didn't need to see Beth again, though. I could ask that nurse. That would be enough.

I heard a key turn in the front door shortly after 7.30 p.m. and went into the hall to investigate. 'You're back! I thought you were going to call me when you were ready for a lift home.'

Josh kicked off his Converse, the strain from the day's events evident in the hunch of his shoulders. 'I needed to get out of there so I got a taxi.'

'How was it?' I asked tentatively.

He straightened up and shook his head. 'Awful. *He* came to the hospital and we had words.' His tone was flat but the expression on his face told of the pain of that encounter.

'Oh, Josh. Come here.' I reached out my arms and held him close. 'I'm so sorry.'

When he released me, I sent him into the lounge to put his feet up while I made us both a mug of tea.

'Are Beth and Archie okay?' I asked, curling up on the opposite end of the sofa to him.

'Yes. The nurse confirmed that Archie had some more fluids but you'd done a brilliant job of getting his body temperature down so he was fine. Beth's bruised and shaken. She's got low blood pressure so they're keeping her in for observation but she had a scan and the new baby shows no sign of stress.' He presented it all in a very monotone way, as though he could just about manage to relay the facts as long as he kept all the emotion out of it. It was too early to push on how he'd felt seeing his half-brother for the first time, especially in such dramatic circumstances.

'That's good news. And what about your dad?'

He relayed the phone call and the confrontation at the hospital. His voice rose in pitch and volume as it all tumbled out, then he exhaled and shook his head. 'I'm sorry. I didn't mean to sound off.'

'Don't worry about that. You have every right to be livid with him after what he did.'

'I shouldn't have said those things to him but I saw red. If he'd just turned up, hugged Archie and asked after him and Beth, it could have remained civil but he had to be in there with the insinuations first. How's that his first priority? I don't get it.'

I shrugged. 'Stress and worry can make people behave strangely. Imagine it from his perspective. You haven't spoken to each other in eighteen months and then, out of the blue, he gets a call from you to say his girlfriend and baby son are at hospital and you're with them. Yes, he's going to be worried about them but he's also going to be wondering why they're with you. He obviously had no idea she was coming to the farm so Beth must have lied about where she was going. If I was your dad, my mind would be working overtime. When he walked into the waiting room and saw you cuddling his son I'd suggest that those unanswered questions toppled out first. We're all guilty of speaking first, thinking later when under pressure.'

Josh scrunched his eyes for a moment and ran his fingers through his hair. 'You're so right.' He looked at me. 'How do you do it? How do you always see the best in people?'

'A lifetime of practice with my mum but also with Chloe to a certain extent. If either of them said anything cutting or did anything questionable, I'd try to find a positive reason for it. It helped ease some of the hurt.'

He bit his lip, grimacing. 'I *never* used to be like this. I always saw the best in people. I didn't even know I had a temper until *the incident.*'

'And I didn't know I had one either until Chloe told me the truth about when she and James got together. I yelled at her big time when that came out. I think even the most patient, reasonable person has a breaking point. Chloe found mine and your dad found yours.'

'I can't imagine you losing your temper,' he said.

'Hopefully you'll never see it. It wasn't pretty.'

We sat in silence for a couple of minutes. His discomfort was obvious and I wished there was something I could say or do to take the pain away but only time could do that.

'The first time seeing your dad was always going to be difficult,' I said eventually. 'Besides, it sounds like he threw the first verbal punch.'

'I know, but I went for the jugular.'

'It's hard not to lash out when you're hurting but I bet he regrets what he said too. I know you're not going to be able to forget about it but try not to dwell on it too much. The important thing is that Beth and Archie are okay.'

A buzzer sounded from the kitchen. 'I made a shepherd's pie,' I said. 'Hungry?'

'Starving.' He smiled for the first time since coming home. 'Have I got time to get changed first? When I come back down, will you promise me something? Can we talk about anything but *him* and Beth?'

'I promise.'

Josh went upstairs and I went into the kitchen to switch off the

Aga, breathing in the rich aroma. It was the perfect comfort food for our current situation.

As I lay out the cutlery and plates, it struck me that I still didn't know why Beth was so desperate to speak to Josh that she'd turned up at the farm twice. Would she have said anything in the ambulance? I was dying to ask but a promise was a promise. It could wait until another day.

I kissed Sam goodbye the following morning and set off to the practice feeling tense. She'd been adamant that she felt well, there'd been no more dizziness, and she didn't need to call in sick. I wasn't convinced. Thanks to Beth, yesterday had been far from relaxing for any of us. What could I do? Sam was a nurse so if she said she was well enough to work, she was well enough to work.

Back-to-back appointments all morning should have kept my mind occupied but, between clients, I couldn't let go of yesterday. I kept seeing Beth inert on the ground. For a few seconds, I'd feared the worst and it was confusing. I still hated her but I was worried about her too. As for *him*, he'd done sod all to redeem himself. Who did he think he was?

When I returned to my office at lunchtime, there were two missed calls from *him* on my mobile but no voicemail. Good. I didn't want to hear his whining apology.

I missed another call while I was in afternoon surgery but, that time, he left a message. I sat at my desk staring at my phone. Picked it up, put it down, picked it up again. Shoved it in my drawer. Took it out. Dialled into voicemail and ended the call before it connected.

'Bloody hell!' I cried at the phone. 'Leave me alone!'

Everyone had left and the silence in the practice amplified my troubled thoughts. I needed to go home and be with Sam. She'd tell me to listen to the message. She'd say, 'It's only a voicemail. What's the worst that could happen? And what's the best?' I sat in reception and contemplated that. There was nothing he could say that would make me think any worse of him than I already did and an apology might make me feel a little better. Might. Shaking my head, I dialled into the message.

'Hi Josh, it's your dad.' Pause. 'I'm really sorry about yesterday. I should never have... I don't know what I was thinking. Beth said you and your girlfriend saved Archie yesterday. I can't thank you enough.' Pause. 'Look, I know what I did to you and your mum was unforgiveable and I understand why you've wanted nothing to do with me since then but I miss you. I wish you were still in my life and I'm sure Archie and his sister would love to have a big brother as they grow up.' Pause. 'I won't bombard you with calls but if there's any chance of me repairing even a tiny bit of the damage I've caused, I'd jump at it.' Pause. 'You know where I am, son. Bye.'

His voice was heavy with emotion and I could hear the sadness and regret but I wasn't going to let it weaken me.

'Should have thought about that sooner,' I muttered. 'You knew what you were doing and you knew there'd be repercussions.' I was about to delete the message but decided to save it instead. Only so Sam could hear it. No way was I interested in listening to it again.

* * *

Back at Hedgehog Hollow, Sam and I sat on Thomas's bench with mugs of tea.

'What do you make of it?' I asked after she'd listened to the voicemail.

'It's weird hearing your dad's voice. He sounds so much like you. As for the message itself, I don't know. It certainly sounds heartfelt. How do you feel?'

'I honestly don't know. He does sound genuinely sorry but there's this niggle. I still don't know what Beth was desperate to talk to me about. Last time I spoke to her – the day I met you – she was on a mission to convince me to let them live in Alder Lea because it was too cramped in their flat for two adults and a baby. The new baby's due in a couple of months' time so I can't help thinking that's what they're both after and they're on the charm offensive to get what they want.'

'You might be right about them wanting the house. The timing would fit. Your dad sounds pretty genuine to me but I'm conscious I've never met him. Is he good at putting on an act?'

I shrugged. 'I'd have said not but he put on an act for seven years, pretending he was a caring dad and husband and, all the while, he was seeing Beth. I don't know what to believe anymore and I can't stand the thought of the pair of them manipulating me like that just to get my house. I have such fond memories of being there with my grandparents when I was younger and I loved living there, feeling close to them. Or I did before *they* tainted things.'

We sat in silence for a moment, sipping on our drinks.

'So Beth's expecting a girl?' Sam said after a while.

'It would appear so.'

'And how was it holding Archie yesterday?'

I pondered for a moment. 'Weird.'

'Good weird or bad weird?'

'Just weird. I'm thirty years old and he's not even one yet and we're half-brothers. That's a hell of an age gap. It just didn't feel like we could be related.'

'Did you feel anything?'

'I felt something but... I don't know. I think it was just an urge to protect him after what happened.' I didn't know how to feel about him. I'd been adamant I didn't want Archie in my life so I'd expected to feel some sort of animosity or resentment towards him. But I didn't.

'Are you going to call your dad back?'

'I've no idea. As far as I was concerned, he was out of my life. Dead to me. I was so angry with him but now...'

'But now...?' Sam prompted.

I smiled and took her hand in mine. 'But now I've got you and I feel happy every day instead of angry. After I nearly lost you, my priorities are different.'

'So you want to give him a chance to fix things?'

She sounded excited and I felt terrible. I should have been clearer. That wasn't where my head was at. Not even close. I grimaced. 'Not with *him*. He destroyed my mum, he destroyed me and he could have destroyed the practice. I have no intention of ever letting *him* back in my life.' I heard the bitterness and added in a lighter tone. 'It's the kids I was thinking of. None of this is their fault. I'm thinking I—'

My phone rang.

'I've got to go,' I said to Sam when I'd taken the details of the emergency callout. 'Don't wait up for me.' We both stood up and I drew her into a hug but she felt stiff in my arms. 'Have I upset you by saying that?'

She stepped back and looked me in the eyes. 'No. It's just that, if my mum had ever reached out to me like that, I'd have bitten her hand off for a reconciliation.'

'Before you had that big bust-up?'

Sam shrugged. 'Yes, but maybe even now, crazy as that sounds. She's still my mum. Life with her has always been tough but you were close to your dad. That makes me sad.' She shook her head. 'Ignore me. It's your choice and I honestly do understand why you feel the way you do and I'll support you whatever happens.'

She looked so hopeful and I knew I had to tell her. Not now but soon. Then she'd think differently.

20

I awoke with a start at the sound of a car door slamming. Was that Josh back? But a soft snuffle indicated he was in bed beside me. Fear gripped me and my pulse raced as I flicked on the bedside light.

'Are you okay?' Josh murmured as I raced to the window and peered out into the darkness.

The sight of a vehicle's taillights disappearing down the farm track transported me back to the night of the fire and my whole body shuddered.

'I think they're back. The Grimes boys.'

'Shit!'

We raced down the stairs together. I thrust my feet into my wellies by the front door while Josh pulled on his Converse and we both grabbed torches.

Outside, I sniffed the cool night air but it was fresh – no smoke – although the Grimes boys would have had to be even more stupid than we believed to have gone for arson again. The security lights illuminated the yard as we ran towards the barn.

'The lock's intact,' Josh called, reaching it first.

'What about the windows? You take the back, I'll take the front.'

I ran along the front of the barn, directing the beam of my torch at the windows but the glass wasn't smashed.

'All clear,' Josh called from the other end.

'Then I don't know what they—' I stopped dead, my heart thumping. 'Josh!'

'What is it?' He ran to my side.

'Look!' I shone the torch along the stonework. Daubed in red paint – still dripping so that it looked like blood trickling down the wall – were the words 'GOLD DIGGER'.

Josh ran his beam along the graffiti too and I squealed as it caught something I'd missed: a squashed hedgehog nailed into the cement.

He put his arm out and turned me away from the sickening vision. I slumped against him, head buried into his shoulder, and sobbed. 'When's it going to end?'

'I wish I could answer that.' He sighed. 'Come on, the hogs are safe so let's get back inside and call the police again.'

My legs felt like jelly and my stomach was churning as I let him lead me across the farmyard and back into the house.

Inside, I curled up on the sofa, wrapped in a throw, while Josh relayed the latest incident over the phone. It had to end soon. They'd be sentenced and put away and if it was other family members instead, surely they'd get bored. Or caught. Because I couldn't do this anymore.

The following day Dad must have finished work early because his car was in the farmyard when I arrived home from college. Beth's car had gone so presumably someone had been to collect it.

'I'm so sorry, poppet.' Dad strode towards me with his arms outstretched. 'It's awful.'

Hugs from my dad always made me feel safe and protected. When I was younger and Mum would yell at me, he'd hold me close, covering my ears with his strong arms, trying to block out the sound. He couldn't block out the sting, though.

I stepped back and nodded towards the barn. 'Guess what I'll be doing tonight?' The graffiti remained but Josh had removed the gruesome attachment first thing and taken it to the practice this morning for cremation. I'd been terrified that the Grimes boys might have deliberately impaled an innocent creature but he'd confirmed it had definitely been a victim of roadkill first.

Dad shook his head. 'No you won't. Rich and Dave will be here around six and the three of us will sort it out. Dave's got some stuff he says will clear the paint off the stones.'

I hugged him again, a lump forming in my throat at such a kind gesture. 'Thanks for sorting that out, Dad. I wasn't looking forward to it.' Rich and Dave were such good friends. I'd rented their spare bedroom when I first relocated from Whitsborough Bay to the Wolds and Thomas had adored them. When he'd left Hedgehog Hollow to me, he'd also left instructions and a sizeable budget with Dave to organise a team to help him sort out the barn and restore the farm back to its former glory. There was still money left in the pot but I hadn't had time to think about where to direct it yet. Another thing for my mounting to-do list.

'It was Josh's idea,' Dad said. 'He's caught up in surgery, by the way.'

'Thanks. I thought that might be the case.' I took one more look at the graffiti and shuddered. The sooner that was gone, the better. Time to focus on more pleasant things. 'Do you want to meet Gollum and Katniss?'

'I'd love to.' Dad followed me to the barn. 'You look shattered,' he said as I unlocked the door, his voice full of concern.

I felt it. Although I'd had no more dizzy spells, my head had been pounding all day and a couple of doses of paracetamol hadn't touched it. My stomach felt like it was on a permanent spin cycle and I was off my food yet again.

'I am,' I admitted. 'I've been awake since two thanks to our visiting artists.'

'Do you think you might have returned to work too soon?' he asked as we stepped into the barn.

I tried hard to sound convincing. 'No. I'll admit that last week was tiring but I got some rest over the weekend and I'd have been fine if I'd got a full night's sleep last night.' I filled the kettle in the kitchen area and put it on to boil.

'I thought the Grimes boys had been sentenced.'

'They've definitely been charged but I don't know if sentencing has actually happened. Nobody's ever confirmed that so they're either still at large or they've sent someone else to do their dirty work. Who else would call me a gold digger?'

'I'm worried about you, Sammie,' he said softly. 'Especially when Josh is on call and you're here alone.'

I gave him what I hoped looked like a confident smile. 'It's a bit of pointless vandalism. Everything will be fine.'

'If you're ever here on your own and you're scared or worried, you *must* call me, no matter how late it is. I can be here in under twenty minutes.'

'Thanks, Dad. I appreciate it. Hedgehogs?'

* * *

Rich and Dave arrived shortly after six and, after hugs and a quick catch-up, the pair of them set to work scrubbing off the graffiti, insisting on Dad staying in the barn to help me.

The extra pair of hands were very welcome, especially as I felt like everything was taking me twice as long as normal to do at the moment. At first I thought I was subconsciously moving more slowly to avoid bringing on any further dizzy spells but then it struck me that I couldn't move quickly even if I wanted to. I felt like I was constantly in a dream-like state, wading against the tide, clumsy, cumbersome. My writing was messy, my fingers were heavy-handed on my laptop or phone, and I'd developed a severe case of butterfingers so had to concentrate extra hard.

When I heard a car pull into the farmyard twenty minutes later, I assumed it would be Josh returning from work but Rich poked his head through the barn door. 'More patients for you,' he said.

'Be right there.'

Dad followed me out of the barn. Rich, Dave, a man and two young boys dressed in cub scout uniforms were crowded round the boot of a car.

'Hi, I'm Samantha,' I said as I approached the vehicle. 'What have we got here?

The man turned round and I did a double-take. Wearing a scouting leader uniform, he looked like an older, slimmer version of Dave but with greying rather than dark hair.

'Are you two related?' I asked, looking from one to the other.

'Yes. I'm Alex Williams.' The man thrust out his hand and shook mine enthusiastically. 'I'm Dave's uncle. And what we have here are some baby hedgehogs.'

'Granddad! They're called hoglets,' declared the older of the boys.

'You made that up,' the younger one said, giving him a shove.

'Oscar!' Alex scolded, gently. 'We don't shove people. What do you say to Charlie?'

'Sorry, Charlie.' He looked up at me, eyes wide. 'He's wrong, isn't he?'

I grimaced. 'I'm afraid your brother's right, Oscar. Baby hedgehogs *are* called hoglets. It's a cute name, isn't it?'

'Hoglets,' he said, giggling. 'Hoglets, hoglets, hoglets.'

'Can I see them please?' I asked.

'Mind out the way, boys,' Dave said, leading them to one side. 'Let the hedgehog lady look at them.'

I peered into the box in the boot. Five tiny pink hoglets were nestled among the folds of a towel. Their eyes and ears were tightly closed and a spattering of pigmented spines could be seen among a covering of white ones suggesting they were only a few days old.

'Where did you find them?' I asked Alex.

'I saw them at the end of my garden last night and, when I got home from work tonight, they were still there.' He lowered his voice. 'There was a sixth one but it was already dead.'

'No sign of the mum?'

He glanced towards his grandsons and kept his voice low. 'There was a squashed hedgehog in the lane near my house. Could be coincidence but...'

I nodded. 'Mums do sometimes abandon their litters but it's rare so I suspect it was her. I need to get them inside, warmed up and some fluids into them. Thanks for bringing them in.' I lifted the box out of the boot.

'Do you need me for anything?' Alex asked, glancing at Oscar and Charlie.

'No.' I turned to the boys. 'Are you on your way to cubs?'

They both nodded.

'You'll have to ask the other cubs if they know what baby hedgehogs are called and impress them with your knowledge if they don't know.'

I'd tried to sound cheerful but this wasn't good. If the hoglets had been without their mum for at least twenty-four hours at such a young age, it was incredible that only one had already died. I had to be a realist about this. The odds were stacked against them and if one of the five made it, it would be a miracle. They were early too. June was usually babies' month but March had been unseasonably warm this year, possibly putting a premature end to hibernation and bringing forward mating season.

As soon as Alex set off, I enlisted Rich and Dave's help and, five minutes later, had heat pads plugged in covered with small fleecy blankets. The four of us massaged the five hoglets – one each with Dad working on the two slightly larger ones.

'They desperately need some formula and to get rehydrated,' I explained, 'but they have no energy to take it at the moment so forcing it into them could actually kill them. If they were with their mum, she'd be cleaning them and shoving them around, being quite rough with them so we need to emulate that by massaging them. She'd also be licking their genitals to stimulate their bowels as they can't go to the toilet on their own.'

'Please tell us you're not going to make us do that,' Rich begged, injecting welcome light relief into the tense atmosphere.

'I'll let you off on that one.' I smiled gratefully at him. 'I'll do the stimulating. And not by licking, I'll just add. I would like you to do this, though.' I lifted my hoglet towards my mouth and released my warm breath over its face. 'If you can do a bit of alternating between breathing on them, holding them in your hands and massaging them, that's the best we can do for now and then we'll hopefully give them enough energy to take some formula.' I was very conscious that Rich, as an ambulance paramedic, had some transferrable skills but nothing in Dave's building career would have prepared him for this. I watched him closely, prepared to step in if he appeared to be struggling, but was so proud of him for throwing himself into something that had to be completely out of his comfort zone.

One of Dad's hoglets started squeaking – a high-pitched noise like a baby bird – which meant he was hungry. I passed mine to Rich while I mixed up some special infant wildlife formula and loaded a syringe, which it would hopefully accept.

'Hedgehog party?' Josh asked, wandering into the barn.

'Orphan hoglets.' I released a drop of formula onto the mouth of the hoglet in Dad's hands. To my relief, a tiny tongue flicked out and lapped it up.

'How many?' Josh asked as he washed his hands.

'Five,' Rich said. 'You can take one of mine.'

'Oh crap!' Dave cried. 'I think mine's stopped breathing.'

Josh took Dave's instead and released a long breath over it then dashed round to my side of the table and lay it on the heat pad, massaging round its heart.

'Come on,' he muttered. 'You can do it. Fight for it.'

I swallowed hard and focused on giving Dad's hoglet some more formula.

'It's back!' Josh cried.

'And one of mine's squeaking for food,' Rich said.

A feeling of euphoria surged through me and I could have cheered but we certainly weren't out of the woods yet. It was going to be a long night.

* * *

Dad and Rich made a stir-fry for everyone and we took it in turns to go over to the farmhouse for a bowl of food. I only managed a couple of mouthfuls and they lay heavily in my stomach although I told everyone I'd eaten a full bowl. We had more important things to worry about than my lack of appetite.

Shortly after 9 p.m., the moment I'd been dreading arrived. The hoglet Dad had been working on had gradually become more and more listless. It wasn't responding to his attempts to get it moving, it hadn't been to the toilet and it hadn't squeaked for formula.

My heart pounded as I watched Dad scoop it up and blow frantically on it, then massage its heart like Josh had done to Dave's hoglet earlier, but to no avail.

With a sigh, Dad lay it down on the table. 'Sorry, Sammie. We can't save this one. It was too weak.'

I blinked back the tears. 'Thanks for trying.'

A subdued silence settled on us.

'How do you guys deal with this every day?' Dave asked, shaking his head. 'It's brutal.'

'We focus on the ones we save,' Dad responded.

'Same for me,' Rich said softly.

'Why don't you get some fresh air for a moment?' I suggested.

Dave nodded solemnly and left the barn.

'I'm so sorry,' I said to Rich. 'I shouldn't have put this on him. Will he be okay?'

Rich gave me a reassuring smile. 'He'll quickly bounce back and don't feel guilty for one second. He'll have loved being helpful but, if you could spare us in about half an hour, that might be good.'

'Definitely.' Five people to four hoglets was more than enough. 'I really appreciate what you've both done tonight.'

Dave returned five minutes later and was eager to be hands-on straightaway but, as agreed, I suggested they head off half an hour later. Dave protested but it was obvious that the hoglet's death had taken its toll on him. I hated that helping me out had upset my friend.

I insisted Dad go home shortly afterwards too and that Josh and I could manage two each. He reluctantly agreed, saying he'd be back in the early hours to relieve us.

About half an hour later, a text came through from Rich reassuring me that Dave was fine, that he'd found the experience 'heartbreaking but enriching' and that he 'wouldn't have missed it for the world'. I felt so much better for reading that.

* * *

'Shift change,' I announced to Josh, pulling my hair into a low ponytail as I made my way through the dimly lit barn at 3 a.m. 'Any news?'

'We've lost another.'

'No!' Tears pricked my eyes but I held them back. I could grieve for the little one later. For now, I needed to focus on the three who were still fighting for their lives and let Josh get some sleep. If he could. I'd barely managed any myself so was surprised at how wide awake I felt now – probably adrenaline. I could tell Josh was flagging, his eyes bloodshot and his lids droopy as he propped his head up with one arm.

'Did you get much sleep?' he asked wrapping his arms round my waist and resting his head against me as I stood beside him.

'Some. It's your turn now.'

He looked up at me, obvious worry etched across his face. 'I don't like to leave you. Not after last night.'

'They won't come back so soon. I'll be fine. Go on. Besides, Dad will be back shortly.'

Josh's lack of further protest told me how drained he actually was. It was easy to forget the toll my hospitalisation had taken on him. While I'd been in a coma for nine days, he'd spent the time flitting between work, checking on the farmhouse, treating the four hogs I'd rescued from the fire and sitting by my bedside. He likely hadn't come close to recovering from all that lost sleep.

Dad returned about forty minutes later, looking a lot more refreshed than I felt.

'How's progress?' he asked, sitting down beside me.

'We lost another.'

'Damn! Not unexpected, though. What a shame.'

I nodded. 'Hardest part of the job and I don't imagine it will get any easier.'

'Loss is never easy but we find ways to deal with it and your Happy Hog Board is a great way of remembering all those who do make it. That release number *will* grow and you'll feel so proud each time you hit a milestone but remember that hoglets are different to adults. Even one in a litter of five is one more than would have survived if you hadn't set this place up. Every small step makes a huge difference.'

Dad always knew the right thing to say and I did cry at that point, thinking about how thrilled Thomas and Gwendoline would have been to see their dream fulfilled.

One of the hoglets started squeaking which seemed to set the other two off so we did another round of feeds.

'I've named them,' I said to Dad. 'Luke, Leia and Solo.'

He smiled. '*Star Wars*? Let's hope the force is strong with these ones and they make it through the night.'

* * *

The force was strong and, to my surprise and delight, all three of them were still with us when it was time to leave for work. Josh had returned to the barn shortly after 6 a.m. and the three of us rotated between hoglets, adult hedgehog patients and showers/breakfast.

There was no way the hoglets could be left alone all day so Josh took them to the veterinary practice with him. Both Josh and Dad assured me it was no problem and there were plenty of staff who'd be able to take care of them but guilt weighed heavily on me as I drove to college. Hedgehog Hollow hadn't even been open a fortnight but we already had seventeen adult patients and three hoglets all needing differing levels of care and attention, the hoglets obviously being the most demanding. We were right at the start of an early babies' season and I could have a steady stream of hoglets across the rest of May and June. What was going to happen with them? Dad and Josh couldn't take them all into work. They had paying clients to attend to.

I bashed the steering wheel with the palm of my hand as I waited at a junction for a tractor to pass. 'Stupid woman,' I muttered. 'Mum was right. You did *not* think this through.' And I really hadn't. For all my extensive research into hedgehogs, I had swept the biggest issue under the carpet. Time. There'd always been a niggle at the back of my mind about whether I could physically fit this in alongside a full-time day job and I'd pushed it aside, convinced it would just work out. How? How could something like this 'just work out'?

The tractor passed and I continued driving towards Reddfield.

As well as the first hoglets who needed round-the-clock attention, there'd been Katniss dumped outside the barn, severely injured, when nobody was home and the Fimberley hedgehog I couldn't save because I was working. Josh had told me that I'd never have saved her even if I'd been living right next door to that angry woman, but it didn't mean there wouldn't be other incidents where I needed to respond quicker.

As we grew, there'd be more occasions where collections were needed. What if the person finding the hedgehog had no transport? What if they were too afraid to touch it or didn't have the time to bring it to me? Or what if the hedgehog was trapped and the caller couldn't get to it? I'd definitely need to make house visits, especially when I got set up on social media and spread the word about us being open. When rescue calls came, they'd be during the day because that's when people were out and about and that's when ill or injured hogs were likely to be found. And where was I during the day? In lessons with my phone switched off.

A huge yawn signalled yet another problem. I could have a couple of months of all-nighters ahead of me as we cared for hoglets. Dad and Josh would help where they could but they had to factor in being on call so I'd need to take responsibility for most of the all-night care. How was it fair on my students or on Lauren if I wasn't at my most alert during lessons because I'd been up most of the night?

'What about marking and lesson prep?' I muttered. 'Where am I going to fit all of that in?'

And what if the Grimes boys continued their hate campaign? I dreaded to think what they'd do next. I was already at breaking point.

I was normally a calm and rational person but, by the time I pulled into the car park, I felt panicky. Sweat prickled my forehead and I couldn't seem to catch my breath. I had to sit in the car and take several deep calming breaths but, even with my breathing regulated, I felt unsteady on my feet as I tentatively made my way towards the entrance. It was going to be a difficult day.

* * *

At lunchtime, I was in the department office on my own. A sandwich with a couple of nibbles out of it lay abandoned beside me and I'd moved onto a yoghurt which I was only just managing to force down, half a teaspoon at a time. My phone beeped with the text I'd been dreading:

✉ From Dad
Really sorry but Luke didn't make it. Leia and Solo are feeding well. Stay strong xx

I stared numbly at my phone. Luke was the one who'd stopped breathing in Dave's hands last night so he'd perhaps been the weaker of the three. Even with the odds stacked against them, I'd clung onto the hope that they'd all make it.

'What are you doing hiding in here on your own?' Lauren asked, bursting through the door. She plonked her bag on her desk then turned to face me and her smile disappeared. 'That is *not* a happy face.'

'Another of the hoglets has died.'

'Oh no. I'm so sorry. Your dad showed me some photos of them last night. I've never seen the babies before.'

'Most people haven't. They're adorable.'

She perched on the desk opposite mine. 'Are you okay?'

Looking at her concerned expression, I hesitated. Should I share my worries about balancing teaching and hedgehogs? There seemed little point when I didn't have an alternative solution to the one we'd already explored. Before the fire, I'd sounded out the idea of working part-time but Lauren had said it wasn't an option; it simply wouldn't work for the role. Not that it would really have worked for Hedgehog Hollow either. Ideally the hedgehogs needed me full-time which meant resigning from teaching. The problem was I needed my full-time salary to continue to run the farm and, after Thomas's money ran out, the rescue centre too. Why hadn't I given this more consideration?

'Just a bit tired.' I gave her a weak smile. 'Which is why I'm hiding in here. I needed some quiet time.'

Lauren nodded and stood up. 'Let me know if you need anything.'

'Thanks. I appreciate it.'

I tapped in a response to Dad's text:

✉ To Dad
Thanks for letting me know. Keeping everything crossed for Leia and Solo. Hope Solo doesn't end up being solo! May not have been the best name choice xx

✉ From Dad
Hopefully he won't. They're both doing great xx

I still felt shaky as I pulled into the farmyard after college. My head hadn't ceased pounding and I'd moved swiftly between the shivers and the sweats all day. If a patient of mine described my symptoms – especially after the two near-fainting episodes – I'd have given them a stern look and prescribed fluids, a good meal and plenty of rest. However, there's a big difference between handing out advice and taking it yourself. Fluids I could manage, food was debatable and there was zero chance of rest.

My stomach did somersaults and I stopped dead in the middle of the farmyard as I spotted a note taped to the barn door. I pressed my hand against my mouth and shook my head. *Please no! Not more threats from the Grimes boys or their minions.* Gulping back my fear, I shuffled towards the barn. I removed a tissue from my bag in case the police needed to check for prints and carefully removed the note, my heart racing as I read the words:

LEFT SOMETHING IN THE OTHER BARN FOR YOU.

What now? More roadkill?

The farm had three additional stone barns of varying sizes, all in need of work, an enormous dairy shed and some stables. Palms sweating, I thrust back the bolt on the nearest barn and pulled open the wide wooden door. Natural light flooded in from the side windows. I braced myself then released a shrill laugh. No roadkill. Just a pallet of cardboard boxes with the branding of a pet food manufacturer on the side.

There was a delivery note taped to one of the boxes and I removed it. Inside was a letter from a local primary school.

Dear Hedgehog Hollow

We were very sorry to hear about the fire. Our topic for this term is British Wildlife and the children were eager for half our profits from our Easter Fair to go to the hedgehogs.

Millbury Ministores have kindly matched the funds and provided their stock at cost. We've learned that hedgehogs eat dog and cat food and we hope this large supply of biscuits and wet food will help see them through a few months.

We know you've only just opened but, if you feel ready for visitors before the summer holidays, the children would love to come to the rescue centre. Small groups, of course!

My contact details are below but please be assured that the food will not be reclaimed if you'd rather not have a schoolchildren invasion at any point!

Wishing you and the hedgehogs all the best on behalf of the children and staff at Bentonbray Primary School.

Ellen Sampson,

Headteacher

I clutched the letter against my chest, a swell of pride making me stand taller. To think I'd been scared to step into the barn. People like the Grimes boys were in the minority and I wasn't going to let them make me fearful on my own property. In the past few months, the kindness of strangers in rebuilding the main barn and getting the rescue centre up and running had been astonishing and I was so lucky to be part of a community that cared, as this delivery had just proved once more.

* * *

After I'd quickly checked on the hedgehogs, I changed clothes then made myself a mug of tea and took it to the back of the farmhouse to Thomas's bench. I felt the need to cling onto the feeling of positivity from the school's generous gift for as long as possible and this was the best place to do it.

Now halfway through May, the wildflower meadow was alive with colour. Red field poppies towered over golden buttercups, corn marigolds and pale primroses. Cornflowers and columbine added in blue and purple tones, complimented by the white clover and campion. Peacock butterflies, red admirals, painted ladies and cabbage whites flitted from plant to plant and the buzz of insects provided a low accompaniment to the chirp of birds in the trees and hedgerows.

From the midst of the meadow, Misty-Blue leapt into the air then bounded towards me, sending grass seeds scattering.

'Have you missed me?' I asked as she jumped up beside me.

I lay back against the bench, closed my eyes, and stroked her back as I soaked in the peace and tranquillity. But the image of the hedgehog nailed to the side of the barn kept nudging its way into my mind. The box of roadkill. The Fimberley hedgehog. Ripley. Before long, my cheeks were drenched with tears.

* * *

When Josh arrived back with the remaining two hoglets, I'd managed to just about compose myself by returning to the barn and focusing on massaging baby oil into Gollum's back. I'd managed to scrape the last bits of mange off him but he was now completely bald and, if I hadn't known he was a hedgehog, I'd never have identified him as one.

'Baldness aside, he's looking great.' Josh planted a gentle kiss on my lips. 'You've done an amazing job with him.'

I smiled. 'I'm so pleased with his progress.' I nodded towards the carry crate Josh had placed on the table. 'I'm hoping there are still two in there.'

'There are. I'm sorry about Luke.'

'Thanks. Me too.' I rubbed the last drops of oil into Gollum's skin then picked him up and returned him to his crate. Swapping into a fresh pair of gloves, I switched the heat pad on then removed Leia and Solo from the carry crate. 'They've grown since this morning.'

'It's all the formula they've been having. They're greedy little hoglets, that pair.' He sat down beside me. 'How are you holding up?'

'I'm sad about Luke but trying to stay strong. I'm tired. And I'm anxious about how I'm going to fit this in alongside teaching full-time. I'm worried I've taken on too much.' Tears stung my eyes and I squeezed them tightly shut. I didn't want to cry again. If I started, I might not stop and there was far too much to do.

'Here's an idea,' Josh said, giving Leia a few gentle prods to get her moving round the pad. 'What if you gave up teaching and did this full-time?'

If only... 'I can't afford to do that,' I responded, defeat in my voice.

'Let's look at this another way. If money wasn't an issue, what would you rather do full-time? Continue teaching, return to nursing or run Hedgehog Hollow?'

'Hedgehog Hollow,' I answered without hesitation, the surge of passion I felt for it taking me by surprise.

'Then we'll make that happen.'

I widened my eyes at him. 'How? I can't draw a salary from the rescue centre. Thomas left some money but that's needed to keep this place running and it won't last forever.' Hedgehog Hollow had been chosen by the staff at Josh's veterinary practice as their charity of the year which meant investment too but every penny would be needed. Food alone was a massive expense.

'Serious question,' Josh said, looking at me earnestly as he skilfully massaged Leia. 'What do you need a salary for?'

I rolled my eyes at him. 'You said it was a serious question.'

'It is,' he insisted. 'You own the farm outright and it's fully refurbished. You have a few rooms to finish but you still have some of your inheritance from Thomas put by for that. So what else do you need a salary for?'

I stopped massaging Solo for a moment and counted off on my fingers. 'Gas, electricity, water, council tax, food, fuel, insurance, the car and...' I shrugged. 'I'm sure there are other bills I'm forgetting. And that's not even thinking about the occasional night out or Christmas and birthdays. Clothes. I might need some new knickers at some point. They don't last forever you know. I'm not wandering around in holey pants.'

'If your pants don't have holes in them, how do you get your legs in them?' Josh asked, his expression deadly serious.

We both started laughing and it felt good to do that after a stressful week.

'Here's another idea,' Josh said when we'd both calmed down. 'I know I've never lived with a girlfriend before but surely living together means sharing the financial burdens. I can't contribute to the mortgage because there isn't one so I'd be happy to pay *all* the bills, food included. I'll even buy you some new pants... but only if you're getting desperate.'

I gasped. 'I couldn't ask you to pay *all* the bills. That's not fair.'

'Not fair?' He shook his head. 'I get to live in that gorgeous farmhouse in this stunning setting with my beautiful badass hedgehog saviour. I think that's worth far more than a few bills and groceries.'

'You'd really do that?' I asked, feeling quite choked up.

'Of course I would. I meant to say something sooner but it's been so busy lately.'

Solo started squeaking which set Leia off so I mixed some fresh formula. We busied ourselves feeding them and then let them settle for a nap on the heat pad.

'What do you say?' Josh asked, taking my hand across the table. 'Can I pay the bills and buy the food?'

I looked into his warm hazel eyes and smiled. 'Yes, you can. Thank you.'

'Don't forget you have rent coming in from the fields so you could call that your salary.'

I smacked my palm against my forehead. 'Where's my head at? I hadn't even thought about that.' The farm had sixty acres and Thomas had rented a significant part of that out to a local farmer, an arrangement I'd been happy to continue. 'I still have some money from Gramps too.' I'd always intended to put it towards a house deposit but, now that I had the farmhouse, it could be re-purposed.

'Then I think we can safely say you don't need to worry about money, can't we? We can afford for you to do this full-time.' He gently tilted my chin towards him and kissed me tenderly. My heart raced and I felt lightheaded again, but for a different reason this time.

'So are you going to hand your notice in tomorrow?' he asked. 'The sooner it's done, the sooner you'll be able to leave.'

I sighed. 'There's a problem. To avoid disruption to students, teachers are meant to hand in their notice before the end of the previous term and then work a term's notice.'

'Just as well we're on really good terms with your boss.'

I grimaced. 'I don't want to let her down. She's been so good to me.'

'She'll understand. She's probably been expecting it since you inherited this place, especially as you've already had a discussion about going part-time. If I know my Auntie Lauren, she'll already have put feelers out.'

I held my head in my hands, the momentary elation I'd felt at being able to run Hedgehog Hollow full-time being replaced by guilt at letting Lauren and my students down. Lauren had been right about how guilty I'd felt about having cover while I was off sick. I couldn't bear the thought of causing further inconvenience.

'I don't know if I can do it, Josh. I need to think some more.'

'Whatever you decide, I'll stand by you. If you want to continue teaching, we'll find a way to cover the work here but I'd like to remind you of your reaction when I said teaching, nursing or here. You know where your heart is.'

At lunchtime on Thursday, I sat in my office mulling over the situation at home. I was worried about Sam. She'd barely touched her dinner last night and I'd only dished up a small portion. Every time I asked her if she was okay, she simply smiled and said she was tired. Hardly surprising after the disturbance in the early hours of Monday morning then two nights on hoglet-watch.

There was an air of sadness about her that I hadn't seen before. I knew she was upset about the hedgehogs and hoglets we'd lost over the past week but, as a nurse raised by a vet, she was pragmatic about death so that wasn't it.

Could it be the run-in with Chloe and her mum? I wasn't convinced. She seemed more resigned and disappointed than upset about that.

Which only left the work situation. Her passion for working with the hedgehogs was obvious so why hadn't she jumped at the opportunity to resign and do it full-time? Financially, it was absolutely possible and I kicked myself for not bringing up money sooner because I could easily have alleviated her anxiety about that. She was kind-hearted and a people-pleaser and, while I loved that about her, it was potentially her undoing. She *always* put others first but ended up losing out on what she wanted. I couldn't help wondering if this was going to be one of those occasions where she tried to do 'the right thing' by the college when it wasn't 'the right thing' for her. I couldn't make her resign and I wasn't going to interfere with her career by having a word with Auntie Lauren, but I'd do my best to convince her it was the way forward and that, sometimes, you had to put yourself first.

My mobile started ringing and my pulse raced as soon as I saw Auntie Lauren's name flash up on the screen. She never rang me at work which could only mean one thing.

'Is Sam okay?' I asked as soon as I answered.

'Yes and no. She fainted but don't panic. She's okay now.'

Don't panic? Even though Auntie Lauren didn't sound the slightest bit concerned, how could I not panic? 'She actually fainted? Not just a dizzy spell?'

'Went down like a sack of spuds in the middle of a lesson according to one of her students.'

'Did she hit her head?'

'No, but she's got a cracker of a bruise developing on her arm where she collided with a filing cabinet.'

I slumped back in my chair, relieved that she hadn't hit her head but still worried about her fainting. 'Give me twenty minutes to sort some cover and I'll be over to get her.'

'No need. Your mum's just arrived and she's going to take Sam back to the farmhouse and stay with her until you finish work. Sam says you're not to rush home because there's nothing you can do and she feels bad enough abandoning her students and doesn't want to feel also guilty about you abandoning your clients.'

That was very Sam. 'Okay. Can you thank Mum for me and give Sam my love? Tell them both that I won't rush home now but I will be home as soon as I can.'

We said our goodbyes and I held my head in my hands while I took a few calming breaths. I should have known this would happen. Should I have put my foot down and insisted on her phoning in sick on Monday? Would she have listened if I had? I'd better let her dad know.

I crossed the corridor to Jonathan's office. The door was propped open and he was eating a bowl of pasta salad while reading a news article online. I lightly knocked on the door. 'Have you got a second?'

He nodded and beckoned me in while he finished his mouthful. I closed the door behind me. 'Sam fainted at work today.'

His eyes widened. 'Fainted?'

Taking a seat, I filled him in on the conversation I'd just had with Auntie Lauren, Sam's previous dizzy spells, and my worries about her lack of food and sleep.

Jonathan sighed. 'I was worried about her when I saw her on Tuesday night. She looked shattered but she said it was because of the vandalism so I didn't think anything more about it.'

'She says she's never fainted before. Is that true?'

'As far as I'm aware, it is. She does have a history of not eating, though. I think it's stress-related. She was off her food after her Nanna died and when she moved back in after splitting up with Harry. She was skin and bones after losing her Gramps because she split up with James then too. Do you think it could be stress over the Grimes boys?'

'I think there's a lot that's stressing her at the moment and the biggest problem is that the rescue centre needs her full-time attention and she can't give it that while she's working.'

'I think you could be right.'

'Then I need you to help me convince her to resign.'

* * *

The reception team did a brilliant job in shuffling around appointments and managed to re-allocate my clients so I could finish at 4 p.m. and get home to Sam. Jonathan said he'd call round after he'd finished work and do whatever he could to coax Sam into handing in her notice.

Mum was in the kitchen when I got back to Hedgehog Hollow. She held her finger to her lips and whispered, 'Samantha's asleep.'

'Is she okay?'

'She's very tired and a bit embarrassed although I told her there was no need to be. She had some soup but she went to bed about an hour ago and was sound asleep when I looked in ten minutes ago.'

I was dying to see her but didn't want to risk waking her. 'Thanks for collecting her.'

'No bother at all. How does a coffee outside sound?'

A few minutes later, we sat on Thomas's bench and had pretty much the same discussion I'd had with Jonathan.

'It could be stress,' Mum agreed. 'There's something else it could be, though.'

'Her coma? I thought about it being connected but I don't think it can be. She came out of it a month ago and the dizzy spells only started last week. If it was coma-related, she'd surely have had one sooner.'

'I agree. What I was wondering is whether there's any possibility that Samantha could be pregnant.'

My stomach did a massive loop-the-loop. Pregnant? The thought had never even entered my head. What if she was? The timing wasn't ideal but I loved Sam and definitely saw marriage and kids at some point in our future. This was a more immediate future than I'd have anticipated but our whole relationship had been fast and exciting and the thought of a baby so soon didn't fill me with dread. Exactly the opposite.

24

SAMANTHA

My eyes flickered open and had a moment of disorientation trying to work out why I was in my bed during daylight hours. Then it came back to me. I shut my eyes again, cringing. Why did I have to faint in front of my students? Why did I have to faint at all? Why had so many bad things happened lately?

Opening my eyes once more, I shivered as a feeling of hopelessness clawed at me. Never in my life had I felt like such a failure: the continuing vendetta of hate against me, the disastrous visit to Whitsborough Bay at the weekend, losing Chloe's friendship, never having Mum's love... it was all too much and I couldn't cope anymore. But most of all was the overwhelming worry that I'd let Thomas and Gwendoline down. I should have instructed Mr Jeffreys to sell the farm and give the proceeds to the hedgehog charity Thomas had named instead of thinking I could save the world one hedgehog at a time.

A solitary tear trailed from the corner of my eye, across my cheekbone and towards my ear as I gazed at the meadow canvas.

'I've failed,' I whispered. 'I've let you both down. I can't do this. It's too big.'

It wasn't the same talking to the canvas. I needed to be by the actual meadow and let Thomas know what a mess I'd made of everything.

When I stood up, I still felt lightheaded. Stairs would not be a good idea. My desk looked out over the garden and meadow. Maybe I could talk to Thomas from my office window instead.

I'd felt really hot when I came upstairs earlier so I'd opened several windows. The coolness of the through-draft was both soothing and reviving as I lowered myself onto my desk chair and took a deep breath.

Voices drifted up to me from below and I leaned forward to peek out of the window. Josh was back, sitting on Thomas's bench and talking to his mum. I hoped I hadn't caused him too much worry. He'd already had more than his fair share to deal with while I was in hospital.

I didn't mean to listen but their voices were really clear.

'...and the dizzy spells only started last week,' Josh said. 'If it was coma-related, she'd surely have had one sooner.'

'I agree,' Connie replied. 'What I was wondering is whether there's any possibility that Samantha could be pregnant.'

My stomach somersaulted. *What?!*

'I don't think so.' Josh said the words slowly, as though trying to work out whether it was feasible.

'I'm only asking because I had dizzy spells with you and with Kayleigh during my first trimester. I even fainted a couple of times with you.'

'I never knew that.'

'It's not something that crops up in everyday conversation but it's fairly common. Sorry. I don't mean to pry.'

'No, it's fine.' Josh paused for a moment. 'I suppose it's always a possibility.'

I clapped my hand across my mouth, my heart thumping. Oh

my gosh! I couldn't be, could I? I'd gone on the pill shortly after getting together with Josh but I'd never questioned what had happened while I was in hospital. On returning home, I'd taken two packets in a row to avoid a period over opening weekend but not taking the pill while in a coma could have compromised my protection.

I stood up and leaned across my desk to hear better, butterflies swirling in my stomach.

'...feel about being a dad?' Connie asked.

I held my breath, heart thudding, as I waited for Josh's response. Our relationship had moved forward at pace and we'd talked about being together forever but we hadn't had a serious conversation about marriage or children. Should we have?

'It would be amazing,' he said eventually, warmth in his voice. 'A lot sooner than I'd have liked but we love each other, we've got the perfect family home and Sam would be such an amazing mum.'

Panic gripped me. I couldn't listen to any more. But in my haste to scramble back from the window, I knocked over a pen pot.

'Did you hear something?' Josh asked.

I didn't dare look out of the window in case they were looking up. Silently backing out of the office, I hurried across the hall and dived under the duvet.

A couple of minutes later, I heard footsteps and the bedroom door opened. 'Sam?' Josh whispered. 'Are you awake?'

I stayed still, thankful my breathing had regulated. The seconds ticked past as I willed him to leave. After the door closed and I heard his footsteps on the stairs, I turned over and opened my eyes. What just happened? Why had I panicked like that and why hadn't I been able to admit to Josh that I'd overheard his conversation? I had no idea.

* * *

A knock on the bedroom door awoke me and I reached for my phone. 5.43 p.m. I must have dozed off again.

'Hello?' I said.

The door opened and Lauren poked her head round it. 'Couldn't resist stopping by and checking you were okay. We thought you might like a cuppa.'

I rubbed the sleep out of my eyes. 'That would be great, thanks.'

'Am I okay to come in?'

'Yes.' I sat up against my pillows as Lauren handed me a mug then sat on the end of the bed.

'How are you feeling?'

'A bit woozy still. Mortified. Are my students alright?'

'They're fine. Worried about you like we all are. What's going on, Sam?' Her voice was so gentle and she looked at me with such concern that tears rushed to my eyes. Mum had never looked at me like that.

'I can't do it.' My words were barely a whisper.

'What can't you do?'

'Run Hedgehog Hollow.' Saying the words out loud sent the tears tumbling down my cheeks as an overwhelming sense of loss enveloped me.

'Run Hedgehog Hollow or run Hedgehog Hollow while holding down a full-time teaching post?'

I swiped at my cheeks. 'Bit of both. Mainly the second one.'

'Then I accept your resignation with immediate effect, no notice required.'

'What?' I gawped at her.

'Josh told me about your conversation earlier this week and please don't be mad with him because I prised it out of him. Thomas left you money and the practice is sponsoring you so you're financially stable for a long time yet. After that, there are grants available for charities and we can all help to fundraise.'

'What about my students?'

'They'll get a new tutor. You were the stand-out candidate at interview but there was another strong contender. When you inherited the farm, I had a feeling we wouldn't be able to keep you so I put feelers out to see if Alice was still interested and she was. She can start after half-term and I can cover your classes in the meantime.'

'But I'd be—'

'Don't you dare say you'd be letting anyone down. If anyone has done that, it's me letting you down.'

'How?'

'You asked me if you could work part-time. I said no because it's not a part-time job but I could have looked into a job share. I should have realised the impossible position you were in with two jobs.'

I shook my head. 'I should have spoken up sooner.'

'Can I ring Alice and tell her she's got the job?'

For the first time in days, the tight knots in my stomach started to unravel. 'Yes please. That would be amazing.'

'Yeah, well, that's because I'm amazing.' She flicked her hair over her shoulders and grinned at me. 'Best boss ever. But do you know what I'm even better at?'

'I've no idea,' I said, smiling.

'Being an auntie. Or auntie-in-law.'

I started laughing. 'You never stop, do you?'

'Nope. Just think, most people who resign get to walk out of my life but not you. You're family. Not officially at the moment but you will be one day soon. You can't escape.' She threw her head back and gave a Disney-villain-style cackle.

'I think I can live with that.' And I could. Josh had been right. Lauren was never going to take it badly because she wasn't that sort of person. It was me who'd worked it up into a big thing because I couldn't bear to let anyone down. I'd always been a people-pleaser and I needed to accept that, sometimes, decisions had to be made that couldn't please everyone but were best for me.

Lauren stood up. 'I'll let you have your tea in peace and make that call.' She leaned over and gave me a hug then wandered over to the door. She stopped and turned back to me. 'If you've got any doubts about your ability to run this place, get rid of them. Look at all the amazing things you've managed so far while you've been trying to fit this round your teaching. When you're doing this full-time, you'll be on fire.' She clapped her hand over her mouth. 'Really bad choice of words. Sorry.'

I laughed. 'Forgiven. Thank you. I owe you so much.'

'You can repay me by marrying that fabulous nephew of mine and having a brood of gorgeous babies.' She left the room laughing but that momentary feeling of relief was swiftly replaced by panic again at the mention of babies. Why? What was going on?

25

When Auntie Lauren came downstairs and confirmed that Sam was no longer an employee of Reddfield TEC, I couldn't have been more relieved. I ran straight upstairs.

Sam was pulling on her dressing gown when I entered the bedroom.

'How are you feeling?' I asked, wrapping my arms round her.

She snuggled against me. 'Better after some sleep. Sorry about worrying everyone. You were all right about me returning to work too soon. I knew I wasn't ready but I didn't want to admit it, despite the dizzy spells being my body's way of telling me to slow down. I always told my patients to listen to what their body was saying. Should probably have heeded my own advice.'

Not pregnant then. I wasn't sure whether I felt relieved or disappointed.

She retrieved her slippers from beside the bed then looked up and smiled. 'All sorted now, though, if you're sure about paying all the bills.'

'Definitely.'

'I bet that's my dad,' she said when the doorbell sounded. 'Can you answer it? I'll be down in a minute.'

* * *

Sam didn't like the idea of her car being in the college car park all night so I left her with Jonathan and Auntie Lauren while Mum drove me to Reddfield to collect it.

'I'm glad we've got some more alone-time,' I said as we pulled out of the farmyard. 'Sam's not pregnant. It was the stress of returning to work too soon. But there's something baby-related that I do need to tell you.'

Mum glanced at me. 'Oh yes?'

'I met Archie on Sunday. *His* baby.'

I noticed her grip tighten on the wheel. 'Oh my goodness. Really? I didn't think you wanted to see him.'

'I didn't. It wasn't planned...' I brought her up to speed on what had happened.

'How did you feel seeing him?' she asked.

'Depends which him you mean. Seeing my father was as grim as expected but seeing Archie was...' I shook my head, struggling to articulate my feelings. 'I didn't hate him or resent him. He was quite cute, actually. He grabbed hold of my finger at one point and, even though his hand was covered in slobber, I didn't mind.' As I spoke, I pictured his face and felt an unexpected yearning to hold him once more. I recalled a feeling of warmth as I gazed into his dark eyes, so much like my own. I visualised his smile each time I'd said 'penguin'.

We'd stopped at a junction and Mum studied my face, a gentle smile on her lips. 'I think your little half-brother might have done more than grabbed hold of your finger this week. I think he might have grabbed hold of your heart.'

I frowned as I shook my head at her. 'No. He's not done that. He can't have. He's the cause of all the problems.'

'No he isn't!' she cried. 'And I know you know that.' Her voice softened. 'He's an innocent baby with no control over his heritage and you're a lovely, caring, generous person who would be the most amazing big brother that any child could wish for.' She pulled away from the junction.

'You think I should see him again?'

'It's not about what I think. It's about what feels right to you. I know you're still hurting but you've come so far, especially since meeting Samantha. Maybe getting to know your half-brother and their new baby when it arrives is part of that continued healing process.'

'You wouldn't be upset if I did see Archie and the new baby?'

'Oh, sweetheart, of course not. I've found my peace with the situation. I'd be more upset if you didn't see them, especially if the reason was some misplaced loyalty towards me.'

We'd reached the outskirts of Reddfield and I stared out of the window at the buildings, mulling over what she'd said. Could she be right about my feelings towards Archie? Was it bullshit when I'd told Sam I was just feeling protective towards him for helping save his life? Had it really been brotherly love?

I turned back to Mum. 'Can I ask you something? After I met Sam, you said it was okay to tell her what happened. Are you still comfortable for me to do that?'

She glanced at me, her expression solemn. 'She's family, Josh. I think it's best she knows. And I don't mind you telling Lewis and Danny either. Just…'

'Just what?' I asked when she fell silent.

'Just don't be too harsh on your father. He wasn't to know what would happen.'

We pulled into the car park. Sam's was the only vehicle in there.

Mum stepped out of her car and gave me a hug. 'Thanks for the update. Please never feel there's anything about your dad and his new family that you can't tell me. I'd rather hear it from you than anyone else.' She gave me another squeeze, then released me.

'You're sure you're okay?' I asked.

'Eighteen months ago, maybe even a year ago, what you've told me tonight would have floored me but now it makes me happy. You *should* have your half-siblings in your life. I wonder if the new baby will be a boy or girl.'

'It's a girl.'

Tears glistened in Mum's eyes, filling me with panic. She must have seen the worried expression on my face because she gave me a reassuring smile.

'I'm absolutely fine. I know you might find it hard to believe but I'm happy for your dad. I was never bothered about gender but your dad's dream was always for at least one of each. After you were born, he was so desperate for a girl next. I feel quite emotional for him that he's getting what he always wanted, especially after we lost Kayleigh.'

I shook my head, marvelling again at her attitude. 'How can you be so understanding?'

'Time, space and counselling. I've said it before and I'll say it again – retraining to be a counsellor is the best thing I could ever have done to come to terms with my past or, as my mentor says, "sort my shit out".'

'Maybe I should book a proper counselling session with you to "sort my shit out".'

She gave a gentle laugh. 'I'm not fully qualified yet and it would be a serious conflict of interest to be your counsellor but you know I'm always here as your mum if you want to talk about anything.'

'Thanks, Mum.' I gave her a quick hug again then climbed into Sam's car.

She knocked on the window so I wound it down and looked at her expectantly. She leaned forward and rested her hands on the window frame. 'I genuinely think it would be good for you if you let Archie and the new baby into your life but do you know what else I think would be even better for you?'

'Enlighten me.'

'Making peace with your dad.'

My stomach sank. 'Mum! You can't be serious.'

'I *am* serious. You two had such a strong bond before all this kicked off and it breaks my heart that you're now enemies and that Lewis and Danny have lost touch with him too.'

My jaw clenched. 'That's hardly my fault, is it? He's the one who created the mess.'

'I know he did, but—'

'There are no buts in this, Mum. You might be able to forgive and forget but I can't.'

'It's not about forgiving or forgetting,' she pleaded. 'It's about moving on.'

'And I've done that,' I snapped. 'Without *him* in my life.'

'Josh! Don't say that.'

Mum looked so hurt. Damn him! He wasn't even here but he was still messing things up.

She took a deep breath. 'None of us can undo what happened and we can't change how any of us reacted to it but we *can* control how we let it affect our future. Do you *really* want to spend the rest of your life without your father in it, feeling all this anger and pain? Because it isn't you, Josh. I don't recognise you when you lash out like that.'

I started the engine. 'I need to get back to Sam.' I tried to keep the frustration out of my voice but I could hear that it had an edge.

'Promise me you're not mad with me.'

My shoulders relaxed as I turned to her. '*He's* the only one I'm mad with.' I gave her a gentle smile. 'Look, I'm dead chuffed you've dealt with your demons but, the thing is, you can move on without ever seeing him again. I'm not saying it's easier for you than it is for me but moving forward is different for us both. Nobody's asking you to be friends again and spend time with him but that's what I'd have to do and it's a huge ask. Do you see where I'm coming from?'

She sighed and nodded slowly. 'I do. But...' Tears sparkled in her eyes and I hated that I was hurting her and hated *him* even more for being the cause of it. 'Will you at least think about it? I'm not saying next week or next month but maybe one day in the not too distant future.'

I wasn't going to lie to her. 'I'll think about it but I can't make any promises because I can't see me ever changing my mind.'

'What if you have children? Wouldn't you want them to know their granddad?'

'That's not fair, Mum.'

'All I can ask is that you think about it, Josh. Please.' She straightened up and got back into her car and drove off waving but she wasn't smiling. I hoped she wasn't going to cry. I wanted so much for her to be happy but I didn't have it in me to do what she wanted. She'd come out of the other side as a strong, powerful, inspiring woman who never ceased to amaze me. But it could have been so much different and that was the part that I couldn't let go.

Lauren left shortly after Josh returned from collecting my car from college. Dad went over to the barn to feed the hedgehogs and insisted on taking the first shift with the hoglets which was very kind of him as there was no way I could have done it.

I managed to eat a bowl of soup and a soft bread bun then retired to the lounge with a mug of tea.

'So how was your day other than my fainting drama?' I asked Josh.

'Busy as usual. I had a couple of missed calls from Beth but no message so I still don't know what she wants.'

'Are you going to call her back?'

He shook his head. 'I know it sounds bad after what happened on Sunday but I don't have the energy to deal with her at the moment. I told Mum what happened.'

'How did she react?'

'She was surprisingly positive about it,' he said slowly, as though trying to make sense of Connie's reaction. 'She thinks I *should* play big brother to Archie and the new baby when she arrives.'

'Really? I'd have thought that would have been difficult for her.'

'So did I but she didn't seem fazed. She also thinks I should let my dad back in. Like that's ever going to happen.'

I hesitated. While I wholeheartedly agreed with Connie, I was conscious that I was projecting my relationship with Mum into that thought process. 'You haven't had a fallout with your mum over it, have you?'

'Nothing like that. She understands.'

We sat in silence for a few moments, sipping on our drinks. I couldn't let it go. I hated the thought of him staying angry with his dad then regretting the years wasted somewhere down the line.

'Do you think you ever could see a way of letting him back in?' I asked eventually.

'No.'

'But he's your dad and you were really close to him before. I know it's unrealistic that things can ever go back to exactly how they were. Look at Chloe and me. But we found a way forward and we're taking it a step at a time.' I rolled my eyes at him. 'Or we were. Not sure where things stand after Saturday. Do you *really* not see a way of trying again with your dad?' I hoped I sounded concerned rather than like I was nagging.

'I know that I'm stubborn but I'm also a reasonable person. If this was just about me being stubborn, I could probably get over it.'

'Then what is it about?' I asked gently. 'Is there something I don't know about what happened?'

His shoulders stiffened and his expression darkened as he nodded slowly. 'But I'll tell you about it another time.'

I squeezed his leg. 'Fainting didn't damage my ability to listen. I'm all ears now.'

'If you're sure...?' He paused and took a deep breath. 'When I discovered what had been going on between *him* and Beth, it was a hell of a shock. I told her to fetch her bag and leave then I marched *him* across to Alder Lea. That's when it all came out – when he met her, how he kept promising he'd leave Mum for her but couldn't bring himself to do it because he loved them both, blah, blah, blah.'

He ran his fingers through his hair, shook his head and sighed. 'I felt like I was in this surreal living nightmare where someone would jump out and cry "April Fool" at any moment. He kept saying he was sorry and he never meant for anyone to get hurt, as though he'd thought there was some possibility we were ever going to come through something like that unscathed. The worst thing was that he didn't look remotely sorry and I knew why. *My* girlfriend had just delivered him the news he'd longed for since I was born – another child – and he couldn't hide how excited he was.'

'That must have been awful.'

'It was but there was worse to come. I didn't need to ask him whether he was going to choose Beth or Mum because it was obvious that Beth had just played her trump card. I told him he had to tell Mum but he said he couldn't do it. He thought it would sound better coming from me.'

I gasped. 'What? Oh, Josh, that wasn't fair of him.'

'Tell me about it. Of course, I refused. Told him it was his mess and up to him to sort it out. We had a huge argument about it but he eventually accepted that I was right and it was the decent thing to do. It was Mum's day off so he'd have caught her at home if he'd done it immediately but he wanted to go to Beth's first and think about the best way to deliver the news. As if there was a *best* way to tell his wife of thirty years that he'd been seeing a woman half her age for the past seven years and, by the way, she's pregnant. That big family could be coming his way after all.'

The rawness was clearly still there in the shake of Josh's voice and the glisten in his eyes. I leaned forward and took hold of his hand. My throat tightened with emotion and I could have cried for him and for Connie but I needed to stay strong.

Josh squeezed my hand and looked down as he ran his thumb

back and forth over mine. 'When he left that day, I hated him so much for what he'd done. I hated Beth too but we'd had such a weird on-off relationship, I wasn't that shocked to discover she'd been seeing her married man all that time. The shock was who the married man was. I couldn't believe my dad would do that to me or to Mum.'

He looked up, his eyes full of sadness. 'You've asked if I could ever let him back in my life because of how close we were before it happened. I don't know. Maybe, with time, I could have found a way to forgive him. If it wasn't for what happened next...'

When he closed his eyes and shuddered, goose bumps pricked my arms and my pulse began to race. I hardly dared ask. 'What happened next?'

I took in Sam's pale cheeks, the dark circles beneath her eyes, the gleam of tears and shook my head. I shouldn't have gone down this path tonight. I should have let her rest and told her another time.

As though sensing my hesitation, she squeezed my hand. 'I'm listening.'

Always so full of kindness and always thinking of others before herself. I cupped her face and gently kissed her. 'Okay. I'll tell you the rest...'

* * *

Dad left and I paced up and down in the lounge, cursing them both. The last thing I wanted to do was go back to work and pretend everything was normal but I had a life-saving operation scheduled for a dog that afternoon. I couldn't cancel and the only other person who could have performed the operation was *him*. Bloody typical.

The op kept me occupied for the next few hours but I returned to my office and couldn't stop thinking about Mum. I hated the thought of *him* breaking the news out of the blue then packing a bag and leaving Mum on her own to try to come to terms with it. She'd be absolutely devastated.

I rang him but it went to voicemail. I left a message telling him that I wanted to be there for Mum when he made his confession but he needed to be clear that I would be there to support Mum only and would not be doing any smoothing over of things on his behalf because I was disgusted with him.

As the end of the day approached, I felt uneasy. He hadn't called back and I suddenly felt compelled to drive to their home.

I was halfway there when he rang. 'I got your message but I've already told her.'

I slapped my hand on the steering wheel. 'Shit! How did she take it?'

'Surprisingly well. She was shocked and upset but very calm.'

'Seriously?'

'Why would I lie?'

I emitted a derisive snort. 'Oh, I don't know. Why would you?' He deserved every ounce of sarcasm.

'Josh! Anyway, she made herself a cuppa while I packed a case and she told me to return for the rest on Saturday while she's at work.'

I thought about my reaction, marching him across to Alder Lea and yelling at him compared to Mum's. It must have taken a hell of a lot of self-restraint not to let rip. Unless it was the shock. She might let go later.

'Why didn't you wait for me?' I asked.

'Because I didn't know you wanted to be there.'

'I only thought about it later and you said you were going to tell her this evening.'

'Beth wouldn't let me into the flat until I'd ended it. She said it was better to get it over with, like ripping off a plaster. She thought—'

'I don't give a shit about what Beth says or thinks. The only person I care about right now is Mum.'

'She was fine. I swear.'

'She was probably trying to maintain some sort of dignity after you humiliated the hell out of her.'

'I'm sorry. I hate myself for—'

'Save it for someone who's interested.' I cut off the call and swore a few times.

I pulled onto the drive of my childhood home shortly afterwards and rang the bell. No answer. Mum's car was on the drive so she hadn't gone out. I rang the bell again and tried the door but it was locked. And suddenly I was worried. I kept a spare key in my glove box and grabbed it.

The house was eerily silent which sent alarm bells ringing. Mum loved to sing and always had music on.

'Mum?'

No response.

I checked downstairs. A full mug of tea stood beside the kettle. I held my hand against it. Cold.

Heart racing, I took the stairs two at a time. 'Mum? Where are you?'

In her bedroom, the doors of Dad's wardrobe were open, the hangers empty, the shelves bare, a pile of his clothes heaped on the floor.

I could hear the fan going in the en-suite and yanked open the door. No-one there. But in the sink there was an empty box of codeine.

'Shit!' I raced out of the en-suite yelling for her. The bathroom was empty. The spare bedroom was empty. Then I pushed open the door to my old bedroom and there she was, slumped face-down on my bed.

'Mum! No!' It felt like I was in a dream, swimming through heavy air as I tried to get to her. Her face was pale, her long, blonde hair hanging in limp locks across her forehead, her lips tinged with blue. But she was breathing – a shallow, gurgling sound.

Adrenaline kicking in, I removed the pillows and pushed her hair back from her face. I manoeuvred her into the recovery position with one hand as I dialled 999.

* * *

'Oh, Josh!' Sam steepled her hands against her mouth. 'I don't know what to say. Your poor mum. Poor you. That must have been terrifying.'

I gulped. 'I really thought I'd lost her that day, just like I thought I'd lost you that night in the barn.'

She shuffled closer and wrapped her arms round me. She didn't say anything but I felt every unspoken word emanating from her. She'd found her Gramps and Thomas dead so she knew the anguish, shared the pain.

'She'd never had any mental health problems before, even when she lost Kayleigh,' I said eventually. 'She doesn't know what made her do it but it wasn't a calculated decision to end her life. She told me that the shock of it all helped her to hold it together while he was there but, as soon as he left, she was furious. She stormed upstairs, yanked his clothes off hangers in a frenzy, unsure whether to cut them up, burn them, throw them out the window or give them away. Next minute she was slumped to the floor in floods of tears. Crying gave her a headache so she went into the en-suite to take a couple of paracetamol but she'd run out so she grabbed some codeine instead and, without pausing to think, she swallowed the rest of the packet.'

'I'm so sorry,' Sam whispered. 'No wonder you don't want anything to do with him.'

'I can't. Not after that. If I hadn't driven over when I did...' I shuddered at the thought. 'Mum's fine now. She's moved on. There was no lasting damage and I'm not worried it's something that will ever happen again but I can't bury the fact that I nearly lost her. Since then, she's been amazing. Moving and retraining have been the making of her and she's in a really good place now. She got tearful when I told her earlier that they're expecting a girl but it wasn't because she was upset about him having another baby. It was because she's thrilled that he's having the daughter he always longed for. He put her through hell and she still somehow manages to feel happy for him.'

'That takes some strength of character.'

'You know who Mum reminds me of?' I shifted position so I could face Sam. 'You.'

'Me?'

'You've both got that same quiet determination and resilience and you're both able to see the best in people, including those who hurt you the most. You're both amazing.'

'Thank you. And thanks for telling me about your mum. I always understood the hurt but this adds another dimension to it. I'm sorry I ever questioned you about cutting your dad out of your life.'

'And I'm sorry I didn't tell you sooner. It's not easy to talk about.'

Sam cuddled in close again and we lay there, our breathing in time with each other until she drifted off to sleep. I eased out from under her and covered her with a throw and sat on the coffee table watching her. Would I tell Lewis and Danny too? It had been painful to relive it just now but it wouldn't quite be so hard saying it again. Sam snuffled in her sleep and I thought about what she'd say to that: who would it benefit? And she was right. Who *would* it benefit? Nobody. Not even me. Surprisingly, the thought of turning them even more against *him* didn't make me happy.

I sighed as I stood up. She knew everything now. Almost.

28

SAMANTHA

How bad was it that I'd fallen asleep on Josh after he'd poured his heart out about his mum? I'd tried to fight it but my eyelids had felt so heavy and I'd been so comfortable lying against his chest that fatigue had overcome me. I've no idea how he managed to move off the sofa without disturbing me and only had a vague recollection of it being dark and him helping me up the stairs and into bed.

I woke up on Friday morning a little after nine, feeling so much better for sleeping round the clock. Josh had left a note on my bedside drawers:

To my gorgeous badass hedgehog saviour
Sorry for leaving without saying goodbye but you needed the sleep.
The hogs are fed & watered. Your dad and I shared hoglet duty last night and I've taken them to work.
Mum's downstairs. We know there's no chance you'll rest up completely – especially now you're a full-time badass hedgehog saviour – so she's your PA for the day to share the burden.
Missing you

Josh xx

After using the bathroom – and grimacing at the angry purple and black bruises down my right arm – I padded downstairs in search of Connie. She was at the kitchen table, flicking through a textbook and tapping something into a laptop.

'I see Josh has roped you into babysitting duty,' I joked.

She looked up and smiled. 'I volunteered. I know you're more than capable of looking after yourself but I thought you might like the company and the help. I'd certainly appreciate some company for a change. Hope that's okay.'

I smiled back. 'More than okay. I have a million and one things I haven't got around to, like setting up on social media. It would be great to have some help.'

* * *

By lunchtime, Connie had set up an email address, secured a website domain name, and created profiles for Hedgehog Hollow on Facebook, Twitter and Instagram. I began a blog, adding in some photos of our current patients and explaining why they'd been brought in and the treatment they'd received.

I'd emailed the head teacher at Bentonbray Primary School after their generous delivery arrived but rang her now to confirm a date for the children to visit after half-term. Terry – the man who'd brought Arwen in a fortnight ago after she'd got tangled in the goalpost netting – had texted me with the name and contact details of the community leader for his village, Jeanette Kingston, so I emailed her asking if there was a good time to meet over the next couple of weeks. I'd originally planned on sending her the pictures of the damage to Arwen but decided the images could be distressing. The softly-softly approach was more likely to generate the results. I wanted to get the community onside, not alienate them.

It was lovely spending time with Connie. I'd warmed to her the moment we met and had always enjoyed her company but we'd never spent time alone until now. While we worked, she regaled me with amusing stories from Josh's childhood and some of the pranks Josh, Lewis and Danny used to play on each other. When she spoke about Paul, I couldn't help noticing the warmth in her voice and the wistful expression.

'Sounds like Josh had a great childhood.'

'Oh, he did. It was wonderful that he had Lewis and Danny to play with and it meant a lot to Paul and me to have them in our lives too.'

I closed my laptop lid. 'I'm really sorry about what happened.'

She gave me a gentle smile. 'Thank you. Josh said he'd told you. It was a dark time for us both but I'm so much happier and fulfilled with life as it is now so, weird as it sounds, I'd go through it all again to be where I am today. I have moments, of course, where I miss my marriage but counselling helped me realise it was more about missing the companionship than missing the marriage itself because, quite honestly, we didn't have the most successful one and...' She paused and frowned at me. 'You look surprised.'

I realised my mouth was wide open and quickly closed it. 'Sorry. It's just that I always got the impression from Josh that things were great between you and Paul. He said there were ups and downs like in most marriages but it was predominantly good which made it all the more shocking that his dad had strayed.'

'The first ten years of our marriage were pretty amazing. We had our moments. What relationship doesn't? But we were really happy together and so perfect together. At first.'

'So what went wrong?' I ventured when she fell silent.

'Oh gosh, Samantha, everything and nothing. We hit our thirties and things started to unravel. Looking back, I think we might have married too young, before we'd developed into the people we were meant to become. I could list a hundred things that we felt differently about and none of them in isolation were significant but, add them all together, and it was a big issue. Two best friends suddenly had nothing in common except their son and that wasn't enough to make our marriage work.'

'I'm so sorry. It must have been hard realising that.'

'The problem was that I didn't realise it at the time and if Paul did, he never voiced it. We argued a lot, although never in front of Josh, then we started doing our own thing. He'd go out to pubs with his friends and I'd go out for meals or to the theatre with my friends or Lauren. We even sometimes holidayed separately. Having so much time apart stopped the bickering and I thought we'd found the secret to a happy marriage. The reality was that I'd made it really easy for my husband to have an affair without me suspecting a thing. I can't be mad with him for finding the missing part of our relationship with someone else. Our marriage was over before he ever met Beth but neither of us wanted to admit it.'

'This might sound cheeky but would you mind sharing that with Josh? He's so angry with his dad and I completely understand why, especially after what he told me about what happened to you. I'm just wondering if he might feel a tiny bit less hurt if he knew that your marriage wasn't as good as he thought.'

Connie nodded eagerly. 'More than happy to do that. It's hard seeing how much he resents his dad, especially when it was my moment of darkness that deepened his anger. If you think it might help, I'm all for trying it.'

29

Saturday was a big day at Hedgehog Hollow with nine of our seventeen adult hogs leaving us. Four were being collected to be released where they'd originally been found and the other five would be let go on the farm which, with the woods, pastures and hedgerows providing food and nesting opportunities, couldn't be more ideal for them.

'What time's the first collection due?' Josh asked. It was mid-morning and I was giving the barn windows a wash, enjoying the warmth of the sun on my bare arms.

'Any time now.' I glanced towards the farm track. 'And that's probably them.'

But it wasn't.

A pale-faced woman exited the car and thrust a large shoebox at me. 'My stupid bloody husband did this,' she said, her voice shaking. 'It might already be too late to save him. Damn strimmer.'

She ran back to her car and, with a spin of her wheels on the gravel, she disappeared down the track.

'I hardly dare look,' I said to Josh, my pulse racing.

In the barn, I lifted the lid and winced at the blood-soaked kitchen towel inside. I peeled the layers back but there was nothing I could do. The poor hedgehog had already long gone, a deep welt across both its back and stomach.

I sank onto the chair, sadness engulfing me. Why was everyone in such a rush these days? Why couldn't people take five minutes to check there was no wildlife resting among tall grass or weeds before wielding their strimmers or starting their mowers? Too many poor creatures lost their lives in this way and it was so unnecessary.

'Rest in peace, little one,' I whispered. I was determined not to cry. In the space of two days, I was already feeling so much stronger and more relaxed but my resolve broke as soon as Josh wrapped his arms round me.

'All you can do is educate people, Sammie,' he said, his voice soft and understanding. 'But you'll never be able to save them all.' He kissed the top of my head. 'Why don't you get some air and I'll deal with this?'

I wiped my eyes, nodded, and stepped out of the barn. Another vehicle was on its way down the track so I took a deep calming breath and readied myself to deal with whatever it contained – hopefully not another dead, mutilated hedgehog. I smiled with relief when I recognised the man who got out of the car as someone picking up a hedgehog for release – something positive instead.

It was only later that I realised Josh had called me Sammie for the first time ever. Only Dad, Gramps, Thomas and Chloe – pre-rift – had ever called me that. I loved hearing Josh use it. Somehow it made me feel even more loved.

* * *

The rest of the day was non-stop comings and goings. The other three release hogs were picked up but were replaced by three more arrivals. It struck me that they were the first new adults we'd had all week. The breathing space had been welcome.

I chose *Harry Potter* characters for our new arrivals but couldn't bring myself to name one Harry because of my ex. Potter had a dog bite which was thankfully not too deep, Hermione was severely hydrated and had a bad flystrike infestation and Ron had been found in a pond, desperately scrabbling to get out. Hedgehogs can swim but get into trouble when there's no means of easily exiting the water – another thing to educate the community about. I decided to ask Dave whether one of his joiner friends could knock together some hedgehog ramps that I could sell and hopefully save a few more lives while raising vital funds.

'You called me Sammie earlier,' I said when Josh and I took a well-earned break on Thomas's bench shortly before 6 p.m.

'It slipped out. I wasn't sure whether you'd noticed or whether you'd like it.'

'I didn't register until later but I loved you calling me that.'

'Sammie it is, then.' He kissed me tenderly. As we snuggled on the bench, listening to birdsong, everything finally felt right in my world.

I pricked up my ears at the sound of several vehicles pulling into the farmyard. 'Sounds like more visitors.'

Josh smiled. 'Not ones needing treatment this time, though.'

'What have you been up to?' I asked, moving to the edge of the farmhouse for a clear view of the farmyard. I grinned as I recognised all three cars.

'You've perked up so much over the past couple of days that I thought you might like a congratulations-on-your-new-career barbeque,' he said, putting his arm round my shoulders.

I cuddled to his side. 'That's a lovely idea. But we don't actually have a barbeque or any food to cook on one.'

'It's all in hand.'

We wandered over to the cars to welcome Rich and Dave, Dad, Lauren and Connie, and Hannah and Toby.

'No Amelia?' I asked Hannah and Toby after I'd given out hugs.

'Toby's sister offered to babysit so we're baby-free this evening and I can't wait to have a drink. This will be my first glass of wine since I discovered I was pregnant.'

'She nearly opened the bottle in the car,' Toby said.

'Can you blame me? It's been a long haul.'

Fifteen minutes later, an eclectic mix of deck chairs and camping chairs were spread across the back garden, several take-away barbeques were lit and everyone was mingling with drinks. Connie and Lauren had arrived with potato salad, homemade coleslaw and a large wooden bowl full of chopped salad, Hannah had marinated kebabs, Rich and Dave had made burgers from scratch and there was a mountain of other food and drink spread across a couple of makeshift tables constructed from planks of wood resting on two breezeblock stacks.

Lauren raised her voice. 'Now that everyone's got a drink, I'd like to propose a toast.' She lifted her drink in the air. 'She's been a superb tutor and I know from her previous boss that she was an amazing nurse so I have no doubt she's going to excel in her new role as hedgehog whisperer. To Sam!'

Everyone echoed her toast and clinked their drinks against mine.

'Thank you,' I said, grinning at them all. 'And thank you for this amazing spread. It's been a manic day with hedgehog releases, new arrivals and, sadly, one we couldn't save, and this couldn't have been a more perfect way to end it.'

Dave took me aside a couple of minutes later. 'My Uncle Alex was asking after the hoglets. His cub pack are doing a badge and he wants to get some photos to show them how they've changed since Tuesday. I hope you don't mind but I told him I'd be here tonight and he said he might swing by at about seven. Is that okay?'

'He's welcome anytime. Why don't you invite him for food? There's loads so he might as well join us if he hasn't already eaten.'

'Nice one. I'll give him a call.'

'Before you do, can I just check you're okay after the tough night on Tuesday?'

He smiled and nodded. 'I'm good. Cheers. I'm not sure what came over me. A mixture of sadness he'd died but also amazement at watching you in action. I'm so proud of you, kiddo.'

'Aw, Dave. That's so sweet.' I gave him a big hug.

* * *

Dave and I met Alex in the farmyard a little later.

'I love barbeques,' Alex said. 'I have gifts to say thanks for the invite.' He opened the back door and handed me a bag which, from the clinking, presumably contained bottles. 'Dave, can you get the bag out of the other side? I've brought some food for the hedgehogs too.'

'Thank you. That's much appreciated. Did Dave tell you we lost three of them?'

'Yes. I wasn't sure if you'd manage to save any so it's brilliant that there are still two. Not that I don't think you're capable of saving them. I didn't mean it that way.'

I gave him a reassuring smile. 'Don't worry. I know exactly what you meant. Unfortunately, the odds were stacked against them the minute their mum left them.'

We stepped into the barn.

'Do you think more would have survived if I'd brought them in sooner?' Alex asked, obvious concern in his voice.

'There's no way of knowing so please don't dwell on it. If you'd brought them in the day before then mum reappeared looking for her babies, that wouldn't have been good. It's really hard to know what to do for the best. The way to look at it is that your actions saved two and that's amazing. Are you ready to see how much they've grown?'

It was lovely watching the expression on Alex's face as I took Solo out of his crate and placed him in Alex's hands.

'Are you welling up, Uncle Alex?' Dave asked, winking at me.

'I can't help it,' Alex said, sniffing. 'I feel like a proud father seeing how much my baby's grown.'

I handed Leia to Dave. 'I'm going to mix some formula so you can both have a go at feeding them, if you'd like.' I thought it might be especially good for Dave to feed one of them so his lasting memory was a more positive one.

Watching two huge bearded men handling my two little hoglets with such tenderness gave me a warm and fuzzy feeling. They struggled with the feeding at first, squirting more of it over their gloves and the fleecy blankets than the hoglets consumed but they soon found their stride. Alex handed me his phone and I took several photos of him feeding them and some close-ups of Leia and Solo.

'Did your grandsons enjoy telling the other cubs about the hoglets?' I asked Alex.

'They were in their element but I'm apparently a bad granddad because my other grandchildren haven't seen them so I've had to promise they'll get to see these pictures before Charlie and Oscar.'

'How many grandchildren have you got?'

'Six and a seventh on the way.' His eyes twinkled as he ran through their names and ages. It was obvious that he adored being a grandfather.

'I bet they keep you busy.'

'They certainly do but I wouldn't have it any other way. I've always adored kids.'

'Probably wouldn't be a good idea to be a cub leader if you didn't.'

He laughed. 'Fair point. They were desperate for leaders when my son joined. I said I'd help out temporarily. Twenty-six years later, I'm still there.'

I smiled at him. 'It's great that there are people like you willing to give up their time like that.'

He talked about how rewarding he found it and how his two daughters ran the younger group – beavers – and his son led the scouts pack.

'My wife used to run cubs with me too so it was a proper family set-up.'

'She doesn't run it anymore?' I asked.

'We're divorced. It was amicable but she had other interests and it made sense for her to step down as leader to pursue those. I'm still a leader short if you know anyone who'd be interested.'

'I'll keep my ears peeled.'

There was something about the way Alex spoke and the wistful expression on his face that reminded me so much of Thomas. When I'd stumbled into his life, Thomas had eked out a heart-breakingly lonely existence for twenty years without his beloved wife, Gwendoline, by his side. I felt that same loneliness emanating from Alex. He clearly had a large family whom he adored and a busy life but he presumably went home alone.

'Hello?' a voice called from the doorway. 'Are you in here, Samantha?'

'Come in, Connie,' I called. 'We're down the end.'

'I've been sent with a ten-minute warning for food,' she said, approaching the table. 'Oh my goodness, are these the hoglets?'

Alex held his hand out. 'Do you want to hold one?'

'Do I need gloves on?' she asked, looking at me.

'Yes please, and can I get you to wash your hands first?'

All sorted, Connie returned to the table and slipped into the chair next to Alex. 'It just shows how deceptive photos can be. They didn't look this small from the pictures Josh showed me.'

'Alex, this is Connie, my boyfriend Josh's mum. Connie, this is Alex, Dave's uncle who brought the hoglets to us.'

'And this is Solo,' he said placing the hoglet in Connie's outstretched hand.

They looked up and smiled at each other, then both frowned as a flicker of recognition moved over their faces.

'Have we met before?' Alex asked.

'I was just thinking the same,' Connie responded.

Dave and I exchanged amused glances as they ran through a list of possibilities – where they lived, worked, schools and clubs their children had attended – but couldn't seem to find a connection.

'How funny,' Connie said. 'We must both have one of those faces.' She turned her attention to Solo. 'I absolutely adore babies – animal or human – so I'm in my element here. I could gaze at this little beauty all evening.'

'Anytime you fancy pulling an all-nighter, you give me a shout,' I joked.

* * *

An hour later, I'd scoffed more than I'd eaten in the whole of the past week. I plonked myself down next to Josh on Thomas's bench and rubbed my full stomach.

'Thank you for tonight. It's been perfect.'

He put his arm round me and I rested my head on his shoulder. 'It's been good fun, hasn't it? It's the perfect venue for an evening outdoors. Lots of space and no neighbours to disturb.'

'We'll have to make it a regular thing, then.'

'Sounds good. But I'm thinking we might need some outdoor furniture and a barbeque. How about I order some furniture in the same design as Thomas's bench? We'll call it my moving in gift to us both. I'll get a barbeque too.'

I snuggled closer to him. 'I'd love that. Thank you.'

My eyes were drawn towards Dad and Lauren, clinging onto each other as they laughed hysterically at something that Rich had said. 'I still can't decide about those two. Dad swears it's platonic but they're very touchy-feely and he was never like that with Mum.' I sighed. 'Maybe he was in the early days before I came along and ruined their happy marriage.'

Josh tightened his hold and kissed the top of my head. 'I'm sure them falling apart wasn't your fault.'

'It is the way Mum tells it.' I shook my head. 'I don't want to talk about her. So what do you think about my dad and your Auntie Lauren?'

He watched them for a few more moments. 'I think it might be wishful thinking. I honestly think they're just really comfortable together and great friends.'

'You're probably right.'

My gaze shifted to Connie and Alex, deep in conversation, big smiles on their faces. 'They think they've met before but they can't place it. I hate it when that happens.'

'Me too. If the recognition's mutual, they'll probably work it out eventually.'

I smiled as Alex laughed loudly at something Connie said and she placed her hand on his forearm. Could that be the start of something? I hoped so. If her relationship with Paul had run its course long before it actually ended, she was way overdue some attention and, from what I'd seen of him so far, she could do a lot worse than Alex.

30

The sound of a phone ringing on Sunday morning interrupted my dreams and by the time I'd stirred enough to register that it was my phone, it had stopped. I turned over and reached for it. One missed call from CHEAT. Also childish but, as with *him*, mild compared to what I could have put.

I could pretty much guarantee that Beth would give it two minutes then try again so there was no point going back to sleep and no point switching it to silent as I'd not be able to settle. So much for a lie in after several nights up with the hoglets.

I lay there looking at the canvas of Thomas's meadow on the wall opposite the bed, waiting. Sure enough, my phone rang a couple of minutes later.

'Hi, Beth,' I said, my tone flat. I didn't want her to think I was pleased to hear from her because I definitely wasn't.

'I was beginning to think I was never going to catch you,' she said, relief apparent in her voice. 'Can we talk?'

I sighed. 'Isn't that what we're doing now?'

'No. Not on the phone. I need to see you. Are you free this afternoon?'

No way was I giving up an afternoon at the farm with Sammie to be with Beth. 'I've got stuff to do.'

'Please, Josh. It's really important.'

'If it's about you and *him* moving into Alder Lea again, you can f—'

'It isn't that. Can you meet me in The Owl and Pussycat Tearoom at two?'

'No.'

'Josh! I need to speak to you.'

'And I don't need to speak to you. What part of "I'm not interested" don't you understand?'

'It's important so I'm not going to stop calling or turning up until we've spoken in person. It's your choice. Drag it out or hear me out.'

It absolutely wasn't how I wanted to spend my afternoon but I knew it wasn't a casual threat. She'd definitely keep bugging me. I didn't need it and there was no way I was going to subject Sammie to it. 'Okay,' I snapped. 'I'll meet you but I won't have long. I genuinely do have things to do in the rescue centre.'

'Thank you. I really appreciate it.'

'Will Archie be with you?' I asked, the words spilling out before I could stop them.

'Do you want him to be?' I recognised the teasing tone in her voice and kicked myself for saying anything. I wasn't ready to give her any indication of wanting my half-brother in my life, especially when I didn't know what it was she was so desperate to speak to me about.

'I was just being practical in case I got there first. I wondered whether we'd need space for a buggy.'

'Oh. Yeah, that's a good point.' She sounded disappointed. 'Yes, Archie will be with me. See you at two.' And then she hung up.

I slumped back against the pillows for a moment then reluctantly rolled out of bed. I'd better get a shower then find Sammie in the barn and let her know I was going to have to abandon her for the afternoon.

* * *

My palms were sweating as I reversed into a parking space in the market square in Reddfield. I kept having to wipe them down my jeans. Why was I so nervous? I certainly wasn't anxious about seeing Beth again. Any feelings I'd had for her had disappeared after *the incident* along with my trust and respect. I was more curious than apprehensive about whatever it was she desperately wanted to talk to me about, especially when she was adamant it wasn't about living at Alder Lea. Which only left Archie. Was I nervous about seeing my half-brother again?

I switched off the ignition and undid my seatbelt but stayed in the car for a couple more minutes. Mum was convinced Archie had found a way into my heart already. Was she right? If so, that was definitely reasonable cause for nerves because letting Archie into my life meant maintaining contact with the two people I'd hoped never to have to see again.

* * *

The Owl and Pussycat Tearoom. Crap. I'd come close to suggesting an alternative venue but to do so would imply that the place still meant something to me and it didn't. Not for a long time.

Sighing, I reached for the door. Best get this over with and then I could get back to Sammie, the woman I loved more than anything in the world. She couldn't have been more different to Beth. Selfless, honest and kind versus selfish and deceitful. Right now, I had no idea why I'd ever fallen for Beth but there wasn't time to dwell on that.

I could see her at what had become our regular table with her hands clasped round a mug of tea. Archie was asleep in a buggy beside her. I realised with a jolt that I'd hoped he'd be awake.

She spotted me and gave a half-hearted wave.

'I ordered tea for two.' She pointed to a large owl-shaped teapot in the middle of the table when I sat down. 'But you can order something different if you prefer. You don't have to have tea.'

'Tea's fine. Has everything been okay since Sunday?' I asked.

'Yes. Archie's been fine and I'm fine and baby's fine.' She smiled weakly. 'That's a lot of fines. Sorry. Thank you for everything you did. And Samantha. I'm so grateful.'

'But that's not what you want to speak to me about,' I prompted, eager to get whatever it was onto the table.

'Wow! Straight to the point.'

'What did you expect?'

She shrugged. 'It's been eighteen months. I thought we could have a catch-up first.'

My jaw clenched and I fought to keep the anger out of my voice. 'You do realise that me coming to the hospital with you hasn't changed anything? We're not friends, Beth, and we never will be. I'm sorry if that sounds harsh but I once told you, right at this very table, that I'm not a convincing liar so I tend to stick to the truth.'

'Unlike me,' she said bitterly.

'If the cap fits...' I felt mean saying it but it was accurate.

'You've changed,' she snapped, narrowing her eyes at me. 'And not for the better.'

'Really? And who do you think might have caused that change?'

'This was a bad idea.' She pushed her chair back and reached for her bag.

I tutted. 'You cannot be serious. You turn up at the farm twice, bombard me with calls and beg me to meet you today and then you walk out the minute it isn't going your way?'

She opened her purse and slapped a ten-pound note on the table. 'It was eighteen months ago, Josh. Stop holding a grudge, grow up and move on.'

'I'm *not* holding a grudge.'

'Really? What was that bullshit you just said? "I'm not a convincing liar so I tend to stick to the truth".' She adopted a cartoon-like macho voice in an attempt to mimic me, making me cringe.

'Okay, I *do* hold a grudge and who can blame me after what you both did? But I *have* moved on and life was bloody good until you reappeared and tried to ruin it all.'

'That's not what I was trying to do.' Her voice had risen and we were drawing curious looks from the other diners.

Realising we were in danger of being asked to leave, I lowered my voice. 'I didn't come here for an argument and I don't think it's in either of our interests to rake over what happened. You asked me to meet you and I'm here so what's so urgent?'

She tossed her purse back in her bag with a sigh then pulled her chair back up to the table. 'If I tell you why I wanted to see you, will you promise to hear me out?'

'I promise.'

'I mean it, Josh. Don't get mad with me until you've heard the full explanation.'

'Yes, fine, I get it. I promise.' I held my hands up in a surrender gesture.

'It's your dad. I want you to see him.'

'Beth! You know that's *not* going to happen.'

'Hello? Earth calling Joshua? What did you just promise me literally twenty seconds ago?'

'Okay. Whatever. I'll hear you out but I can guess how it goes. He's sorry. He never meant to hurt me or Mum or the business. He misses me. He knows things can't go back to how they used to be but he wants to try to move on.' I inwardly cringed at how childish and stroppy I sounded.

Beth folded her arms and stared at me, her expression unreadable. 'Have you quite finished?'

'I'm only paraphrasing the voicemail he left. He didn't need to send you to repeat what he'd already said.'

'He didn't send me. He doesn't know I'm here.'

I narrowed my eyes at her. 'He didn't know you were at the farm on Sunday either.'

'No, he didn't, because he specifically told me not to tell you what I'm going to tell you. Yes, he's sorry. Yes, he never meant to hurt anyone. Yes to everything else you said. The only thing he didn't tell you is that, if there's any chance of you two having any sort of relationship again, you'd best not leave it too long.' Her voice cracked and tears glistened in her eyes.

The chatter around us seemed to quieten and my pulse started racing. 'Meaning...?' But I knew exactly what it had to mean. The thought had popped into my head when she'd turned up at Hedgehog Hollow after the Family Fun Day. It was the reason I'd unblocked her number on my phone after I left hospital last weekend. I'd pushed it away, though, because if I'd acknowledged it, I'd have started thinking differently towards him and I didn't want to do that. After what he'd done, he didn't deserve my compassion so I'd refused to go there.

Beth's expression softened as she said the words. 'Meaning he might be dying, Josh.'

I reached for that one word like a life-raft. '*Might* be?'

'He's got stage four Hodgkin lymphoma. He's already had a full cycle of chemo and it hasn't worked. He could need a stem cell transplant and if that doesn't work...' Tears ran down her cheeks and dripped onto the table.

31

SAMANTHA

When I heard a vehicle pull into the farmyard shortly after four, I stepped out of the barn, hoping it was Josh. I'd been looking forward to an afternoon together but it was right that he met Beth and finally discovered what she wanted. I hadn't relished the idea of her turning up unannounced again so it was better to deal with it.

It wasn't Josh. It was Terry again.

'Another hedgehog delivery for you,' he said, taking a box out of the front passenger side footwell and handing it to me. 'Also tangled but not in goalpost netting this time.'

'What's it tangled in?' I asked.

'Bloody rubber band. Look at this lot.' He opened up a carrier bag revealing dozens of elastic bands. 'I picked these up in one week.'

'One week? Oh my goodness! Where from?'

'Postal workers. They wander round the village with their letters bundled together in bands then they drop them instead of taking them back to the depot. On people's drives and doorsteps and in the middle of the street. They're a double menace. Litter *and* a danger to our wildlife as you can see.'

'Do you want to watch while I treat this one?' I asked. 'It won't be quite so busy today.'

'I would but I've got family at mine and I abandoned them when I spotted this little fella so I'd best be getting back.'

'Can I ask you what you're going to do with the elastic bands?'

'Send them back to the Post Office like I usually do.'

'Would you mind if I hang onto them? If postal workers are dropping that many bands in your village, they're likely doing the same in all the surrounding villages. I think there's potential for a campaign involving local schools here and this bag of bands could be a starting point to illustrate how big a problem it is.'

He handed over the bag and smiled at me. 'I like you, lass. You get things done.'

'I try my best.'

I waved him off and went into the barn to check out my newest patient.

'Aw, you poor thing. That's got to hurt.' The elastic band was wrapped tightly round the hog's middle and I suspected it had wriggled into it when it was an infant and the band had become gradually tighter as it grew. 'We'll have that off in no time and clean up any damage.'

As I washed my hands, I hoped the damage would be external only and that the band hadn't been pressing on any organs or it could be a very different outcome.

An hour later, Dumbledore was settled in his new crate. The wound thankfully hadn't been too deep so, like Arwen, he shouldn't take too long to heal. I heard another vehicle on the gravel outside, peeked out the window and spotted Josh's jeep.

Ten minutes later, I'd wiped down the table and cleared everything away but he hadn't appeared in the barn. I figured he must have gone straight into the farmhouse but it was empty.

'Josh?' I called, going back outside.

Silence.

The only other place I could think of was Thomas's bench. I rounded the corner of the farmhouse and there he was, slumped against the back of the bench with his head back and his eyes closed.

'Josh? Are you okay?'

He looked up at me. His face was pale and his eyes were red and puffy as though he'd been crying. 'Not really.'

I sat down beside him. 'What happened?'

'My dad's got cancer.'

'Oh my goodness, Josh. I'm so sorry.' I put my arms out and drew him into my embrace. No wonder Beth was so desperate to see him face to face. That definitely wasn't news to give over the phone or by email.

'Do you want to talk about it?'

He nodded. 'I don't know what to do next.'

'Would a coffee or a beer be helpful?'

'A beer would be *very* helpful. Maybe a whole keg.' He managed a weak smile.

'We'll start with one bottle, eh? Back soon.'

When I returned a few minutes later with three bottles – one each and a spare for Josh as I suspected his first might go down very quickly – he was giving Misty-Blue a scratch behind her ears.

He took a drink from me, giving me a grateful smile, and took a long swig. 'Just what I needed.'

I sat down beside him and waited.

32

JOSH

I had the strangest sensation as though I was in a dream but all my senses were on high alert. I could see the vibrant colours of the meadow, hear the birds chirping, taste the fizzy tang of the lime wedged in the neck of my bottle, feel the chill of the alcohol slipping down my throat and smell Sammie's pink grapefruit perfume as she sat by my side. Yet none of it felt real. None of it felt right. I'd spent the past eighteen months hating my father and doing my utmost to obliterate him from every part of my life.

When I'd returned from hospital the night I nearly lost Mum, I'd raced round Alder Lea like a man possessed, filling binbag after binbag with reminders of *him*. Photos were the obvious items but it didn't stop there. I hurled in gifts he'd given me, books he'd loaned me, a shirt I'd worn to celebrate his birthday, a T-shirt I'd once loaned him. I didn't care what I smashed or damaged because I didn't care about *him*. After all, he clearly didn't care about me, Mum or the business. Pouring with sweat and out of breath, I'd tossed the binbags into the attic and slammed the hatch closed.

But now he was ill and how could you hate a man who had

cancer? The man I'd vehemently proclaimed was dead to me literally could be dead soon.

Sammie's hand slipped into mine and I squeezed it gratefully. *Best just say it. Maybe saying it aloud will make it seem real.*

'Dad's got Hodgkin lymphoma.' The words came out flat and factual. Easier that way. 'He's had a round of chemo already. Beth said they'd hoped that would be all he needed because most patients respond well to treatment, even when it's caught late.'

'They caught it late, then?' Sammie asked.

I nodded. 'Beth said he was permanently exhausted last summer but they thought nothing of it. Why would they? Archie arrived in June and they were both sleep-deprived. When Dad did manage to sleep, he had bad night sweats. He lost weight but it was only when Beth noticed a lump under his arm that they thought to see a doctor. Turned out it was all connected and pointing to the same thing.'

Sammie squeezed my hand again. 'I'm so sorry. So what's next?'

'They're talking about a stem cell transplant.'

She looked surprised. 'Oh. Is that definite?'

'I'm not sure. Beth got upset and then Archie woke up and started crying so the details were a bit sketchy.'

'Do you know anything about Hodgkin lymphoma?' she asked.

'Not really. I know it's a type of blood cancer but that's about it. Do you know much about it?'

She shrugged. 'A basic knowledge but only because I had a patient who was in remission from it. It develops when a certain type of white blood cells stops behaving how it should by either multiplying too quickly or not dying off. I think it's the fourth or fifth most common type of cancer and, as you said, patients with it do usually respond well to chemotherapy.'

I sighed. 'Trust my dad to be the exception. He's apparently in the wrong age bracket too. Beth said the variation he's got is most common in people under thirty-five or over sixty but he's fifty, like Mum.'

'I'm surprised nobody told you about the original diagnosis last year.'

I slumped forward with my head in my hands. 'I'm not.' I cringed as I recalled my furious rant. Packing up every reminder of him hadn't been enough. Anger still surging through my veins, I'd wanted to unleash my feelings on him but his phone repeatedly went straight to voicemail. A voice in my head kept telling me to wait until I'd calmed down but I quashed it. He needed to know the damage he'd done – they both did – and I wanted to be the one to tell them. I'd sped over to Beth's flat. He had to be there. Where else could he be? Someone was coming out of the building so I went in without buzzing them and pounded on the door until he answered. I shoved him aside, stormed into their lounge and exploded.

'Are you okay?' Sammie asked, bringing me back to the present and instantly calming me, like she always did.

I lifted my head and gazed at the meadow. 'The night it happened, I stormed round to Beth's flat in the early hours. I told him exactly what I thought of him and, when she appeared out of the bedroom, I laid into her too. But mainly him. I told him where Mum was and why. I told him how I'd found her and pulled no punches about what would have happened if I hadn't finished work early and gone straight there. He went white and sank down onto the sofa, shaking, but I didn't care about him. All I cared about was what he'd done to Mum. Beth was in tears. Kept saying it was her fault because she'd given him an ultimatum of Mum or the baby and wouldn't let Dad into the flat until he'd ended it. Hearing her wittering on about new life when my mum could have lost hers tipped me over the edge and my parting shot was...' My voice cracked and I hung my head.

'You can tell me,' Sammie urged, gently nudging my arm.

'I told him I wished it was him who'd taken the pills but that nobody had found him because, as far as I was concerned, I had no father, he was dead to me and he would never be welcome in my life ever again.'

I felt so ashamed saying it out loud now. It sounded so cold and completely unlike me. I'd never been the sort of person who got angry, raised their voice, argued or said cruel things. And to have held onto that hate for so long, even when Mum had been able to move on... what did that say about me? When Sammie and I got together, I'd told her my dad was dead to me but I hadn't told her I'd actually said those words to him. It felt a hundred times worse to admit that I'd vocalised rather than internalised my feelings.

Sammie slipped her arm round my waist and rested her head against my shoulder. 'You only said those things because you were hurt and angry and, after what he did and the repercussions of it, you had every right to be.'

'I'm *not* that person,' I said. 'You know that, don't you?'

She kissed my shoulder. 'Of course I do. Your dad knows that too.'

I turned to look up at her. 'Does he? He took me at my word and didn't get in touch when he was diagnosed with cancer.'

'But he's reached out now and—'

'He hasn't, Sammie. He told Beth that I'd made my feelings clear and he was going to respect my request to stay away. He didn't think it was fair to "play the cancer card" as Beth put it and expect me to forgive and forget.'

'He didn't know she was meeting you today?'

'He thought she was taking Archie on a playdate.'

We sat in silence for a few minutes.

'What's your gut reaction about what to do,' Sammie said eventually.

'I wasn't sure but, now I've said it all aloud, I think there's only one thing I *can* do. I need to go and see him.'

'I agree. When?'

'I'll go after work one night next week. I need some time to think first.'

'Can I make a suggestion? Before you see your dad again, I think you should speak to your mum.'

'To tell her about the cancer?'

'I do think she'd want to know about that but I was thinking more about her telling you something that I don't think you're aware of.' She wrinkled her nose. 'I'm sorry if that sounds a bit cryptic but it's your mum you need to hear it from, not me, because I can't answer any questions you might have.'

I raised my eyebrows at her. 'That does sound *very* cryptic.' I lifted my bottle. I hadn't even had half. 'Would you mind if I drove across to Mum's now?'

'Not at all.'

We stood up and I hugged her. 'Thanks for listening.'

'Please never worry that I won't understand or won't accept anything you've said or done in the past because I will. I know how it feels when a parent lets you down and, believe me, I've prepared hundreds of speeches for my mum where I've told her exactly what I think of her behaviour.'

'The difference is you never delivered them.'

'No. The difference is that my mum wouldn't have cared if I had. She'd have turned my words back on me and called me stupid for trying to flog a dead horse. She'd have laughed. She'd have made me feel worthless. Your dad on the other hand cared enough about you to respect what you'd asked of him. He knew he'd done wrong and that he didn't deserve your instant forgiveness. Your dad and my mum are very, very different scenarios.'

I hugged Sammie tightly. 'If I ever cross paths with your mum, I'll happily tell her what I think of her for how she's treated you.'

'Thanks. But you'll never cross paths with her. She made her choice and that's a life without me in it. Just how she always wanted it.'

33

SAMANTHA

After Josh set off to his mum's, I went into the barn and gazed round the enormous space.

'There's nowhere comfortable to sit,' I muttered to myself. I opened my laptop and started searching for sofa beds and hedgehog-themed bedding for the barn so that whoever was on hoglet-duty could try to get some sleep between feeds. A relatively small financial outlay could make such a big difference and I felt relieved once I'd placed the order.

I was watering the hanging baskets outside the farmhouse a little later when I spotted a vehicle approaching along the farm track. I put my watering can down and made my way over to the farmyard.

The driver – a woman of about my age dressed in a nurse's uniform – wound down her window as soon as she'd parked. 'Is this where I bring poorly hedgehogs?'

'Yes. I'm Samantha.'

'That's a relief. I spotted a hedgehog in the middle of the road. I couldn't leave him there or he'd have got squashed but I'm on my way to work so I'm in a rush.'

She opened the back door and lifted out a bucket with a large hedgehog curled into a ball in the bottom.

'Do you want to come into the barn with me and I can transfer him into a crate and give you the bucket straight back? It'll only take a minute.'

'I can just about spare that. I hope you don't mind but a brilliant name popped into my head for him. Can he keep it?'

I smiled. 'Hit me with it.'

'It's Snoop Hoggy Hog.'

I stared at her for a moment as the name sank in, then I burst out laughing. 'Oh my gosh. That has to be the best name ever! We thought we'd exhausted all the hedgehog-themed names but that one never entered our heads. Love it! Right, Snoop Hoggy Hog, let's get you out of that bucket.'

I walked as fast as I could, conscious I didn't want to jostle my new patient too much. He appeared to be tangled in some green twine. This afternoon, I'd made up a couple of crates ready for new arrivals so I grabbed one, pulled on my thick gloves and lifted the hedgehog out of the bucket. A quick check established that it was a male so I didn't need to delay the nurse by taking her contact details as there was no risk of abandoned hoglets. Which was just as well because the minute I returned her bucket, she dashed out of the barn calling, 'Thank you, must run.'

'Let me get my scissors and tweezers organised than I'll untangle you,' I said to our new arrival after the barn door closed. 'We'll make it all better.'

Snoop Hoggy Hog wasn't in a bad state at all. The twine – like the sort a gardener would use – wasn't tight round his torso but it had become knotted between his front paws. Thankfully there didn't appear to be any damage so I suspected he might have only just got tangled in it before he crossed the road and the movement had snagged his feet, stopping him from going any further at the point the nurse found him. Thank goodness she had or he'd have either tried to continue across the road and done some serious damage to his limbs or he'd have been hit by a car. I gave a little shudder at the thought.

The hoglets started squeaking as I was finishing up with Snoop Hoggy Hog so I had their feeds to sort. It was amazing how quickly they were growing. Their eyes and ears were now open and loads more pigmented spines had come through.

Being kept so busy didn't stop me thinking about Josh. What a shock that had to have been. I suspected he was more upset with himself than he was letting on. All I could do was keep reassuring him and supporting him. I just hoped that his dad wouldn't push him away next week although that voicemail message he'd left for Josh gave me hope. When he left it, it must have taken Paul a lot of willpower not to blurt out that he was ill. Presumably he wanted any sort of father/son reunion to be because Josh wanted to try and repair their broken relationship and not because he felt obligated to do so because Paul was ill.

My phone rang and Dave's name flashed up on the screen.

'Hi Dave, how's it going?'

'Really good. Guess where Rich and I are?'

I could hear the clink of glasses and the chatter in the background. 'The Black Swan?'

'How could you possibly have guessed?' he said, laughter in his voice. 'It's a real quickie as our food could arrive at any moment. My Uncle Alex just rang. He drove past yours about fifteen minutes ago and it looked as though somebody had knocked over the donation bins at the end of the farm track. I thought I'd better give you a call in case you weren't aware.'

'No, I wasn't. I'll go down and have a look now. Thanks for the heads up.'

'No worries. That's our food arriving so I'll speak to you later.'

I said goodbye and hung up. Could that nurse have driven into them in her rush to get to work? Surely not. The entrance was really wide and they weren't even on the track.

My heart sank when I stopped my car at the end of the track a few minutes later. 'No!' I cried, yanking on the handbrake and jumping out.

Not only had the donation bins been pushed over but somebody had destroyed the contents. A large bag of biscuits had been emptied all over the paving slabs and pouches of food had been emptied over them, the empty pouches strewn all around. The contents of a couple of bottles of washing up liquid appeared to have been poured on top of the mess and squirted all over the donation bins along with...

'No way! That's disgusting.' I'd thought it was dog food at first but it was dog faeces instead, smeared all over the lids and the sides. Or at least I hoped it was from a dog rather than a human.

Sighing, I snapped several photos on my phone to send to the police then drove back up to the farmhouse to collect a shovel, gloves, binbags and disinfectant wipes.

As I held my breath and began scraping off the excrement ten minutes later, I refused to cry. I wasn't going to let them destroy me but why couldn't they just leave me alone?

Mum looked surprised as she opened the door to Primrose Cottage. 'Josh! That's four days running I've seen you.'

I gave her a weak smile before gratefully stepping into her hug. 'I've got some news that I wanted to give you face to face.'

'Bad news, I take it?' she said, releasing me. 'Of course it is with that sad face.' She nodded slowly. 'Lemonade in the garden?'

'Sounds good.'

I followed her to the back of the cottage and into the kitchen where she removed a jug of her special home-made lemonade from the fridge while I grabbed a couple of glasses.

The garden wasn't very wide but it was long. At the far end, there was a summerhouse with a patio in front of it where we settled onto a pair of metal chairs. She poured the drinks while I grappled with what to say.

'Beth rang and asked me to meet her this afternoon so I did.' There was no way to soften the news. I just needed to say it. 'The reason she's been trying to get hold of me is to tell me that Dad has Hodgkin lymphoma, the first round of chemo hasn't worked, and he might need a stem cell transplant.'

Mum's mouth dropped open and her eyes widened. 'Wow! I wasn't expecting you to say that. Poor Paul.'

We sipped on our drinks while I repeated the same information I'd given Sammie earlier.

'How do you feel?' I asked her when I'd finished.

She pondered for a moment then shrugged. 'In all the years we were together, I can count on one hand the number of times your dad was ill which was just as well because he was a terrible patient. I can't imagine him with cancer and it breaks my heart to think of him suffering like that but he's a strong man. Mentally and emotionally, he'll be positive and optimistic about beating it. Physically, he'll fight it with every ounce of strength he has. I'm actually more concerned for Beth. That's such a lot for her to deal with at such a young age with a baby and another on the way too.'

I raised my eyebrows at her. 'She destroyed your marriage and you're worried about her?' Disbelief made my voice higher than normal.

'I can't help it. Don't forget I spent lots of time with her when we thought she was only your girlfriend and not your dad's. I liked her. For all the confidence and bravado, there was a scared and vulnerable girl beneath the surface and I'll bet she's terrified right now.' Mum smiled weakly. 'What about you? How do you feel?'

'Slightly stunned at what you've just said about Beth but, that aside, I'm all over the place. I'm annoyed with him for not telling me himself when he first found out but then I feel guilty because I'm the one who told him I wanted nothing more to do with him ever so he was only respecting my wishes. I feel like a hypocrite that I'm planning to visit him because, if he hadn't been ill, I wouldn't have done that.'

'You're *not* a hypocrite. You're a caring son who has heard some devastating news about his estranged father and is doing the right thing.'

'What if it's for the wrong reasons?'

'Does it matter what the reasons are?' She reached across the table and squeezed my hand. 'Let me ask you a question. When Beth first said your dad had cancer, what was your immediate gut reaction?'

'To sort things out.'

'I rest my case. Trust your gut, Josh. The first instinct is usually the right one. Do you know what my gut's telling me? That I need to see him too.'

I widened my eyes. 'You *really* want to see him again?'

'It's something I've been thinking about for a while. I think he needs to know that, much as it hurt at the time, what happened changed my life for the better and I'm not angry with him anymore. Obviously I won't visit with you. I think that would be a bit much having a delegation turning up. But if you feel it's appropriate, could you mention that I'd like to catch-up and perhaps give him some closure? If he needs it, that is. He might have found his own peace but, knowing your dad as well as I do – or used to do – I don't think that will be the case.'

We sat in silence for a couple of minutes and I gazed round the garden. There was a bag of compost and a trowel laid on the patio alongside a couple of trays of bedding plants and some freshly potted tubs of flowers. Mum had done an amazing job in turning a long lawn into a beautiful cottage garden. I didn't remember her ever showing an interest in gardening when I'd been younger. Another life change since things had ended with *him*.

'Sammie said I should speak to you because there's something I'm not aware of that you need to tell me. She wouldn't say more than that. Does that make any sense?'

'It does,' Mum replied. 'Did you think your dad and I were happy together?'

'Most of the time.'

'We weren't.' She shook her head. 'No, that's not true. We were at first and for a long time. Not being able to have the big family we'd hoped for could have broken us but it didn't. We were happy and very much in love. When you were ten, your dad turned thirty and your granddad's birthday gift to him was the partnership in the practice.'

'I remember that,' I said, a memory from the past flashing into my mind. I could picture Mum driving us to the practice to pick up Grandma and Granddad ready to go out for a celebratory birthday meal. The practice staff were lined up outside, either side of my grandparents, and they were all holding balloons. We'd bundled out of the car and I noticed that the sign above the entrance was covered in a white cloth. Suddenly everyone yelled, 'Happy Birthday!' and my grandparents each pulled on a ribbon. The cloth fell to the ground revealing a brand new sign: Alderson & Son Veterinary Practice. Dad had always known he'd become a partner at some point in the future but hadn't expected it that day. He was ecstatic.

'At that point, we had everything we'd ever wanted', Mum said. 'We had each other, we had you and he had the partnership with his dad. But that's when things started to go wrong. As he settled into his new role, spending more time at the practice, I started feeling envious and perhaps a bit resentful that he had this amazing career and all I'd done since leaving school was part-time waitressing roles. Don't get me wrong, I enjoyed waitressing, but it wasn't a career like your dad had. It never bothered me at first because the plan was always that I'd be a stay-at-home mum and, by the time our four or five children were old enough not to need my full-time care, your dad would have a partnership and we could afford for me to train to be whatever I wanted to be.'

'But the big family never came...' I prompted when she fell silent.

'Exactly. Once you started secondary school, I tried to speak to your dad about career ideas but he kept saying there was no rush to make any decisions and that, financially, we were secure with the partnership so I didn't need to work. He was missing the point. I *wanted* to work and I wanted his help in sussing out what that might look like. I didn't want to be a lady who lunches. I didn't want to have no income of my own. I'd got good grades at school and I wanted to use my brain again but every time I tried to explain that, we ended up arguing.'

I frowned. 'I don't ever remember the two of you arguing.'

'That's because we never argued in front of you but, by the time you hit your teens, arguments were a pretty regular thing. And then they weren't.'

'What do you mean?'

'People argue when they're passionate about something and, somewhere along the way, all the passion had gone out of our relationship. I got a job in a shop. Still not a career at the time but I enjoyed it, I liked my colleagues and I felt like I was something more than a mum and a wife. I started going out with the girls from work and your dad saw his friends. Your Auntie Lauren went through her first divorce so I spent more time with her too and, before we knew it, your dad and I each had our own interests and our own lives. The thing is, the separate lives thing then gave us more to talk about. The laughter returned, the chatter returned and I thought we'd found our way back to a happy place after a bit of a blip.' She shook her head. 'We weren't happy, Josh. We still loved each other and probably always will but we're talking a nostalgic love. We both changed so much and became different people. Us being together only worked because we had our separate lives and the laughter and chatter only returned because it was like two old friends having a catch-up. That's not a marriage.'

'I had no idea.'

'Of course you didn't. And that's the way we wanted it to stay.'

I stayed for another hour or so, talking more about their marriage falling apart, Dad's cancer diagnosis and how Sammie was getting on. As a chill fell and Mum suggested we move indoors, I took that as my cue to head back to Hedgehog Hollow.

We carried the empty glasses and the jug into the kitchen and I gave Mum a hug. 'Thanks for sharing all of that with me. I know it can't have been easy.'

'Don't worry about me. Any hurt or rawness has already been dealt with as part of my counselling training. It was hard when it first came out but so much started to make sense including things I'd never even articulated in my own mind, like my resentment at your dad for having his dream career and me not having one.'

'He surprises me about that. I didn't have him pinned down as a chauvinist.'

She grabbed my arm. 'Oh, Josh, he isn't. Please don't think that for one moment. My career choice from a very young age was that I wanted to be a mum and I don't regret a single moment of being a full-time mum to you. Your dad would have supported me in any career I chose but he interpreted my indecision about what to do as a sign that I didn't want to work instead of what it really was – me needing direction on what path to take. It was a breakdown in communication. One of many.'

I drove back to Hedgehog Hollow, my mind swimming with new information. How had I lived with them for all those years with no idea there was anything wrong? Yet now that I knew, the signs had been there. Family time as a three had become pairs time instead or a boys-only trip with Lewis and Danny but they'd said it was because Dad was often on call or Mum had to work weekends in the shop. It was plausible – factual, even. But it wasn't the truth. The truth was that they'd grown apart and either nobody had wanted to call time on the marriage or neither of them felt it was broken beyond repair.

For the first time ever, I could see why Dad had let Beth in. I didn't like it and I certainly didn't condone it but I felt I now had an inkling of understanding as to how it had happened. A little more of that red mist of anger evaporated.

If I was a good son, I'd have driven straight over to see Dad, hugged him and forgiven him. Clearly I wasn't a good son. After eighteen months, I couldn't just flick a switch and stop being angry. I couldn't erase those memories of finding Mum in my old bedroom at death's door. I needed to get my head together before I saw him again to avoid an altercation like in the hospital.

My commitments to the practice, the hedgehogs and Sammie didn't suddenly disappear because Dad was ill. Sammie was adamant that she was feeling herself again but I didn't want to risk a relapse so Jonathan and I organised a rota with some of the team to look after the hoglets overnight. As expected, Sammie initially objected but then admitted that a week of undisturbed sleep would be welcome.

Time was not on my side so I rang Beth on Tuesday and arranged to visit on Wednesday after work. Which had now arrived.

✉ From Sammie
I know it's going to be hard but you've got
this. Fresh start. Clean slate. The hogs and I

are rooting for you. We're sending lots of love
and hugs for tonight xx

⊠ To Sammie
Thank you … although the hugs from the hogs were
a bit prickly! ;-) Leaving in ten mins. Nervous,
especially as he's no idea I'm coming or that I
know xx

⊠ From Sammie
I'm nervous for you! But remember that he wants
you back in his life. Did you keep his voicemail? You might want to listen to that when you
get there to give you some reassurance xx

⊠ To Sammie
Great idea. What would I do without you? xx

⊠ From Sammie
You'll never be without me. Now stop texting me,
finish your work, and get to your dad's!!!! xx

I smiled as I put my phone down and turned back to my
computer screen. Even by text, Sammie always knew what to say.
Just like Mum. What a surprising conversation that had been on
Sunday. I had no idea I'd been looking at their relationship through
rose-tinted glasses. Mum had openly admitted that she'd inadver-
tently played a part in Dad's relationship with Beth by not making
any effort to work on their marriage, making a naïve assumption
that they were meant to be together and nothing would get in the
way of that; even something as significant as them both changing so
much that their only common ground was their memories and me.

I swiftly finished off the email I was typing and approved a couple of medicine orders then logged off. It was time to face... What was he now? I'd thought of him as the enemy for so long. Could things go back to how they'd been before? No. It could never be the same. Far too much had happened. Could we wipe the slate clean as Sammie suggested and rebuild a new father/son relationship? Only time would tell. But if chemo wasn't working, did we have time?

* * *

Beth's flat in Wilbersgate – a market town roughly halfway between Reddfield and Hull – was a forty-five-minute drive south from the practice. I spent the journey trying to decide what to say but nothing seemed appropriate.

As I entered the outskirts of Wilbersgate, my shoulders tensed. My grip tightened on the steering wheel and I had to fight hard against the urge to pull a U-turn and race back to Hedgehog Hollow.

Beth's flat was on the top floor of a 1960s-built three-storey block, five minutes' walk from the town centre. In the two years we were together, I'd picked her up outside a handful of times but she'd always made an excuse not to invite me in. She said it was messy, we didn't have time, a friend was sleeping on the sofa bed and she didn't want to make her uncomfortable – excuses that seemed plausible at the time but were clearly a cover-up to keep me away from the evidence that Dad was a regular guest. I'd never dreamed that the first time I'd venture inside would be to confront my dad for having an affair with my girlfriend and almost killing my mum.

I parked in the public car park behind the flats and dialled into

Dad's voicemail, just as Sammie suggested. I listened to it three times before exiting the car, feeling stronger. *Here goes...*

There were three blocks of a similar size on three sides of a grassy area containing two shabby benches, each with broken slats. Patches of grass were overgrown and others were bare. Two trees looked as though they were either dead or dying. Music was blaring out of a couple of open windows, a painful blend of garage music and 1970s rock over which I could just make out a baby screaming and a couple of men shouting at each other, ever other word an expletive.

Beth's block – Juniper House – was on my left. I pressed the buzzer to number twenty-two and waited.

'Hello?' Beth's voice sounded tinny over the intercom.

'Beth? It's Josh.'

'Come up and don't beat the door down this time.'

* * *

'I wasn't sure if you'd come.' Beth looked at me uncertainly when she opened the door.

'I nearly turned round a few times. Is he here?'

'He usually gets home around six.'

I glanced at my watch. Five more minutes. 'Am I allowed in?'

'Sorry. Yes.' She stepped back so I could pass her. 'I'd give you a tour but it would literally take ten seconds. You saw most of it last time. Bathroom's on the right, bedroom's on the left and everything else is straight ahead of you.'

I had no desire to see their bedroom so I moved forward into the lounge. I'd barely glanced at it before but could now see that it was a compact open-plan room consisting of a small kitchen and dining area at one end overlooking the car park, and an L-shaped lounge.

'It's... erm...'

'Tiny?' she suggested, sighing. 'But it was cheap and it's handy for town.'

I thought back to the heated phone conversation I'd had with her a few months back about them moving into Alder Lea and cringed. It must have taken some guts for her to make that request but no wonder. One person would be snug in here but two adults and a baby, not to mention another on the way?

'Did you just say one bedroom?' I asked.

She nodded. 'It's not a bad size. We can squeeze a cot in there although Archie will have to move into the lounge when this one arrives.' She stroked her hand over her stomach.

I bit my lip as I gazed round the room. Where the hell would they fit Archie's cot? There was barely room for basic furniture as it was. Plastic crates were piled high against the far wall, seemingly providing the storage solution for Dad's books and journals and Archie's clothes and toys.

'Where is Archie?' I asked, suddenly aware of his absence.

'He's asleep which isn't ideal when—'

She didn't get to finish what she was saying because a key turned in the lock, my dad stepped into the hall, and stopped dead, mouth open, as he clocked me standing in the middle of the lounge. 'Josh? What are you doing here?' He sounded surprised rather than angry. Then he frowned and looked towards Beth. 'You told him,' he added in a flat tone.

'He needed to know.'

'Beth!' He took a couple of steps closer until he was framed in the doorway. 'We talked about this.' I'd expected him to be angry with her for going against his wishes but his expression and tone came across as hurt instead.

Beth shuffled over to him and placed her hand on his arm. 'Yes, but you know I didn't agree with your decision.' She rested her head against his shoulder. 'I'm not going to apologise.'

He kissed the top of her head. I wanted to look away from what seemed like such an intimate moment, yet I found myself glued to them. Mum and Dad had never been touchy-feely and neither had Beth and me. I hadn't wanted to believe that Dad and Beth could really be in love. It had been easier to imagine that she'd been using him for his money and he was just a middle-aged man whose head was turned by a young, beautiful girl but I could feel the electricity crackling between them.

Dad looked at me. 'You'd better sit down.'

There was a two-seater sofa and a mismatched armchair so I sat in the chair. Dad adjusted a couple of blue cushions then sat down on the sofa and looked at me expectantly. I grappled for a conversation starter and noticed a name badge attached to his shirt bearing the branding of a veterinary practice in Wilbersgate.

'You're a vet at Langton's?' I asked.

'Veterinary nurse.'

'Oh. I'm sorry.'

He shrugged. 'No need to be sorry. I'm still working with animals and still using my skills. There weren't any local vacancies for vets and beggars can't be choosers. How's the practice going?'

'Good. Busy.' I wasn't sure what else to say. The practice was thriving but I didn't want him to think that I was either boasting – especially when he'd taken a backstep in his career – or suggesting that it hadn't thrived while he'd been there because it had, although he had taken his eye off the ball during his last couple of years there, no doubt distracted by my presence in his girlfriend's life. With nothing else in *my* life, I'd thrown myself into the business and worked crazy hours looking at ways to improve the service and operate more efficiently which had now paid dividends.

'I hear you took on a new vet from Whitsborough Bay.' He could have sounded bitter – Sammie's dad was *his* replacement after all – but instead he sounded interested. His relaxed attitude kept surprising me and, even though it shouldn't have, it made me feel uncomfortable.

'Yes. Jonathan Wishaw. He's my girlfriend Sammie's dad and he's a brilliant vet.'

'Good. I'm glad to hear it.'

We sat in silence for a few moments. I glanced towards the kitchen where Beth was spooning instant coffee into mugs. I searched for another conversation starter. What would Sammie say? She'd compliment them on the décor or the furniture but what could I say without sounding sarcastic or as though I was judging them?

'Beth tells me you're living on a farm now,' Dad said.

'Yes. Hedgehog Hollow in Huggleswick. Sammie inherited it at the start of the year. It needed some work but we moved in when that was complete.

'I'm glad you've found someone special.' He sounded like he genuinely meant it. 'Hedgehog Hollow sounds familiar but I don't think the previous owners were clients.'

I smiled ruefully, remembering the second unsuccessful encounter I'd had with Sammie when she'd wanted me to honour the arrangement Dad had made with the Micklebys and I bit her head off for mentioning Dad's name. 'It was owned by a couple called Thomas and Gwendoline Mickleby. They wanted to run a hedgehog rescue centre there and spoke to you about providing treatment.'

'A hedgehog rescue centre?' Dad looked thoughtful. 'Yes! I remember that. I think it was just before or just after I got the partnership so we're talking roughly twenty years ago. I only met Gwendoline and we had a good conversation but she never returned.'

'She died. Probably not long after she'd visited you.'

'Oh. That's a shame. I presume her husband didn't set up the centre.'

I shook my head. 'It had been Gwendoline's dream and he couldn't bear the thought of doing it without her. Sammie's done it, though. We've got sixteen hedgehogs and two hoglets at the moment.'

'I love hedgehogs.' Beth handed me a coffee. 'I've never seen one round here, though.'

'It's mainly concrete and limited greenery so there won't be enough food.' I inwardly cringed. Did it sound like a criticism of where they lived?

I took a sip of my coffee as a distraction from the silence and tried not to react as it burned my mouth. *Can't keep putting it off.*

'So, you have Hodgkin lymphoma...' It was more of a prompt than a question.

Dad nodded. 'I found out last year and the chemo didn't work so we're exploring next steps.'

'Which might include a stem cell transplant,' Beth said.

Dad gave her a look that suggested she was not meant to have revealed that but, of course, I already knew.

'That's just one of a number of options,' Dad said, turning back to me. 'Nothing's definite yet.'

'The only reason it's not definite is because they need to find a suitable donor,' Beth said.

'Beth!' Dad's voice was sharp this time as he stared at her. 'We talked about this too.'

He turned to me once more, a forced smile on his face. 'A hedgehog rescue centre sounds like a great project. Do you remember when we found a nest of abandoned hoglets at the bottom of the garden at Alder Lea?'

Beth dug him in the ribs. Dad flinched but continued talking.

'They were so tiny. You were about twelve at the time and you could hold them all in the palm of your hand.'

'Paul!' Beth hissed, but Dad ignored her and carried on talking about hedgehogs.

'Paul!' A bit louder this time but he continued talking. I looked from one to the other wondering what was going on. Beth looked close to tears.

'Ask him!' she cried and then I realised.

'I'll be your donor,' I said, cutting Dad short. 'If I'm a match, that is.'

A sob escaped from Beth and the tears tumbled down her cheeks.

'No!' Dad stood up. 'You'll do no such thing.'

'Paul! He could be your only chance.'

Dad walked over to the window and stood with his back to us. 'They're still looking. They're hopeful. And there's an option to use the stem cells from the umbilical cord when the baby arrives.'

'You know that's not an option for you,' Beth wailed. '*I'm* not a match for you so my umbilical cord won't be either. Family are the best chance.'

Dad still didn't turn round. 'Siblings are but not usually children. You heard what the consultant said.'

'Surely it's worth a try. Please, Paul!'

He spun round. 'Stop it, Beth,' he snapped. Then he added in a gentler tone, 'It's not happening. Sorry, Josh, but this is the exact reason why I didn't let you know because I knew you'd volunteer, despite everything I've done to you, and I cannot and will not ask you to do that. Beth knew that.'

A wail from the bedroom indicated that Archie was awake. Beth pushed herself up from the sofa, wiped her eyes and stomped towards the corridor. Then she stopped and turned to Dad. 'That's your baby son in there and your daughter will arrive soon. I know the guilt eats away at you every day but are you really going to risk leaving them without a father because of it?'

'It's not going to come to that,' he said gently.

'How do you know?' she cried as Archie's wails intensified.

'I want to get tested,' I insisted.

'No, Josh. That's not why—'

'I know it's not but, if you've been eaten away at guilt for the past eighteen months, imagine how guilty I'll feel for the rest of my life if I don't try to help now.' I grimaced. 'That sounded better in my head.'

Dad gave me a shaky smile.

Beth returned to the room, holding a whimpering, sleepy Archie against her shoulder. 'Has stubborn dad accepted stubborn son's help?' she challenged.

I raised my eyebrows in Dad's direction and he sighed. 'Okay. Yes, if you're sure you don't mind. But don't get your hopes up, either of you.'

Archie reached out his arms towards Dad who took him from Beth, held him close and kissed his messy hair.

'Thank you, Josh,' Beth said. 'I can't tell you how grateful I am.' She pressed against Dad's side and kissed his cheek and suddenly the scene of family devotion was too much for me.

'I'd better head back home,' I said.

Beth frowned. 'But you've only just got here.'

'I know but Sammie needs help with the hoglets and you've got Archie to see to.'

Dad passed Archie back to Beth. 'I'll walk you to your car.'

'There's no need.'

'I want to.'

We walked down the two flights in uncomfortable silence. Every footstep and every breath echoed off the grubby walls. Why had he been so insistent on accompanying me to the car? Possibilities raced through my mind. Was he going to tell me he'd been lying on his voicemail and he didn't really want me back in his life? Was he going to tell me that the cancer was terminal and he hadn't told Beth the truth? My heart thumped and my stomach churned in anticipation.

'How's your mum?' Dad asked as soon as we stepped outside the building.

I stopped, a little astonished that it was the first thing he'd asked. 'She's doing well. She told me to pass on her best wishes to you both.'

It was Dad's turn to look astonished. 'She actually said that?'

I nodded. 'She's in a really good place right now. She asked if you want to meet up for a coffee at some point. She's keen for you both to get closure.'

Dad stared at me open-mouthed for a moment or two then seemed to gather himself together. 'That would be amazing. I'd really like that. Tell her yes.'

We set off walking.

'And what about you?' Dad asked. 'Are you in a good place?'

I chose my words carefully. 'It hasn't been easy but I'm getting there.'

Silence fell once more.

'This is me.' I jangled my car keys.

'I'm sorry for my reaction at the hospital.' Dad thrust his hands into his pockets. 'I was bang out of order.'

'Yeah, well, the first time we saw each other was never going to be easy after what happened. I gave as good as I got.' I couldn't bring myself to apologise in return because I'd meant what I said.

He nodded. 'I know. Where do we go from here?'

His expression was so hopeful but I couldn't do it. I couldn't pretend that him being ill obliterated all the hurt because it didn't.

'I don't know.' I shrugged. 'I'm still pissed off with you.'

He flinched. 'So why did you come tonight?'

'Because it's the right thing to do.' The words spilled out without any thought and, even though the pain in his eyes made me wince, he needed to know that the impact of his actions had been deep and lasting.

'You know what, son. If I could turn back the clock, I'd still choose Beth, but I'd have been honest about that choice right from the start. We're not time-travellers, though, and life's about learning to live with the decisions we make and the impact of those decisions. Beth and I both know that the things we did were unforgiveable and that's why I begged her not to tell you I was ill. When the truth first came out, all I could think about was how I could rebuild a relationship with you. I knew it would need time but then I got this diagnosis and I vowed that, when I was better, I'd make it happen. But I didn't get better and I was stuck. If we were to patch things up, it had to be because you were ready, not because you'd discovered I had cancer and felt some sense of duty to give it a go. That's why I begged Beth not to tell you.' He sighed and shook his head. 'It was great to see you tonight and to have a conversation. Yes, it was awkward and stilted and uncomfortable but it wasn't raised voices and insults. I'm thrilled you've found someone special and that the practice is thriving. You deserve those things. You don't deserve what I did to you and I don't deserve your forgiveness for it so let's say goodbye and forget about the stem cell test. It's a long shot anyway.' His voice cracked and tears glistened in his eyes. 'Send my love to your mum and tell her... tell her to be happy.'

He turned and walked away.

I should have shouted. I should have run after him. But my feet wouldn't work and my voice caught in my throat. Why couldn't I let go? My dad had cancer. He could be dying. Yet I was still clinging on to all my anger and hate. Why?

When he'd returned from Wilbersgate last night, Josh had been in a dark mood. He'd eagerly accepted my hug but was adamant he wasn't ready to talk about it so I didn't push. I figured he'd process things overnight and then he'd let me in.

Sure enough, when he arrived home from work tonight, he strode purposely down the barn, hugged me tightly and suggested we take drinks to Thomas's bench so he could tell me what had happened.

'I've got you a gift to say sorry for being a grump.'

'You weren't a grump. You just had a lot to process.'

'Thank you, but I know I was a grump.'

He handed me a gift bag and I smiled at the collection of four hedgehog mugs inside.

'They're not the same as the one that got broken but I thought you'd like them.'

'They're gorgeous. Thank you. I'm going to need to make my tea in one of these.'

* * *

We'd no sooner sat down with drinks in my new mugs than Misty-Blue launched herself at the bench then clambered onto my shoulder.

Josh ran his fingers through his hair and shook his head. 'I'm sorry I didn't tell you everything last night. I wanted to but I couldn't bring myself to say it.'

'Why? What was stopping you?'

'I messed it up.' His shoulders slumped. 'I hate myself and I didn't want you to hate me too. I couldn't bear to lose you.'

He looked so defeated and I gave his arm a gentle squeeze. 'You're not going to lose me,' I said keeping my tone calm and reassuring. 'It's pretty obvious things didn't go well but you're not going to turn me against you for telling me what happened, no matter how badly behaved you think you might have been.'

I listened intently as he ran through the evening. It hurt to see how much he was beating himself up about what he'd said in the car park and how badly it had ended.

'Have you called him today?' I asked.

'I've tried a couple of times but he hasn't answered. I've tried Beth too but she's not answering her phone either. I haven't left voicemails. I don't want to apologise to a machine.'

'But you do want to apologise?'

He nodded. 'It's funny that he talked about turning back time because I'd love to do that and change everything about last night.'

'If you *could* do it again, what would you say to your dad?'

'I'd ask him how he is. I didn't even do that. I'd ask if he was in pain or if he needed anything. And I wouldn't tell him I'd visited because it was the right thing to do.'

'So why did you visit?'

'Because he's ill.'

'That doesn't sound much better than what you actually said.'

Josh sighed. 'Because he's my dad.'

I wrinkled my nose. 'Getting warmer. Try again.'

'Because I was worried about him.'

'Ooh, that's a much better lukewarm sentiment. Come on, Josh, you can do better than that. *I* know the real reason and I know you know it too and I think you need to acknowledge it out loud. Why did you visit your dad?'

'Because I don't want him to die,' he cried.

'Because...?'

'Because I still care about him.'

I raised my eyebrows, determined he'd admit it.

'Okay. You've got me. I still love him and I miss him being in my life.'

I didn't say anything; I just held him.

Josh released a long, slow breath as he pulled away. 'If you get bored of the hedgehogs, you could have a great career as a lawyer or in the police. That was one heck of an interrogation.'

'Sorry for pushing but—'

'No, you were right to push. I guess it's true what they say about love and hate being close together.'

'They certainly are.' *Look at me and my mum. Oh, except I love her and she hates me.* 'What now?'

'I'll keep trying to call.'

'I've got a better suggestion. Why don't you go there after work tomorrow and say what you've just said to me? I can come with you if you like. Dad's already scheduled to have the hoglets. I'm sure he wouldn't mind seeing to the adults too. What do you think?'

'I think I should probably have taken you last night. Then I might not be in this mess.'

37

My stomach churned with nerves as I pulled my jeep into the car park behind Juniper House. The rain battered against the windscreen.

'We'll have to make a run for it and hope they're in,' I said.

Sammie pulled the hood up on her jacket but I didn't have one with me and shivered as the cold rain trickled down my neck.

I was about to press the intercom when the door opened outwards and a couple of teenaged kids sprinted out of the building, rudely shoving past us. I grabbed the door and we stepped into the lobby, shaking the rain off our arms.

'That was lucky,' Sammie said.

I looked up the stairs. 'It's the top floor. Stairs only.'

'How does Beth manage with the buggy?' she asked as we reached the first floor.

'I never thought about that.' Guilt stabbed me again for refusing to let them have Alder Lea.

We continued up to the top floor and stopped outside number twenty-two.

'You can do it,' Sammie whispered when I hesitated.

I rapped on the door and waited. Silence. I gave it twenty seconds and rapped again even louder. Nothing. 'They must have gone out.'

'Try ringing them.'

I tried Dad's phone, then Beth's, but both tripped straight to voicemail. I knocked again. Moments later, a young woman holding a screaming baby to her hip poked her head out of number twenty-three.

'Will you quit banging on that bloody door? You woke our Courtney up.'

'Sorry,' I said. 'I was trying to get hold of my... erm... Paul.'

'You could wake the dead with that racket. Ain't it obvious there's no bugger in?'

'You don't know where they might be, do you?'

'What do you think I am? Their bloody social secretary?'

'No, it's just that I—'

'Jesus! The racket from the ambulance was bad enough and now you're giving me earache,' she snapped.

My stomach lurched. 'Ambulance?'

'Are you dense or summat? Ain't that what I just said? He's gone to hospital, if you must know. Now sod off and bother someone else.'

'Which hospital?'

'Hull.' With a curl of her lip, she slammed the door shut making baby Courtney screech even louder.

I raced down the stairs and out into the rain. When I made it to the jeep, I beat my fists on the roof then sank down onto my haunches, fighting the rising nausea. Too late!

Sammie caught up with me, crouched down and gripped my head between her hands. 'We don't know that it's cancer-related,' she said. 'Don't assume the worst. You need to stay strong. Come on.'

She pulled me to my feet and thrust her hand out. 'I'm driving.'

I handed over the keys without debate. My arms and legs felt like jelly and I wasn't sure I'd be safe behind the wheel.

* * *

The journey through to Hull Royal Infirmary was agonising, the traffic being stop-start all the way because of flooded roads.

I kept trying Beth's phone. No luck. 'I should probably call Mum.'

'And tell her what? Why don't you wait until we get to the hospital and know more? The last thing you want is your mum racing to Hull in this horrific weather only to find that it's nothing to do with the cancer and your dad's stubbed and broken his toe.'

I nodded. She was right. I needed to stop speculating. Although who was to say their neighbour's information was reliable. Talk about hostile. In fact, hospital could even be a wild goose chase although my gut told me it wasn't.

* * *

'I'm looking for my dad, Paul Alderson,' I said to the receptionist. 'I've been told he came here by ambulance but I don't know when or why.'

The man gave me a gentle smile and tapped at his keyboard. 'I'll just check for you. Paul Alderson, you say?'

'Yes. Paul Patrick Alderson.'

He shook his head. 'I'm sorry. We've got nobody of that name registered here.'

'What about Archie Alderson?' Sammie asked. I looked at her frowning and she shrugged. 'Worth a try.'

'And Archie is...?'

'My brother,' I said, the words feeling alien on my lips.

'No. No Archie either.'

There was only one more person to try and I was going to have to tell a whopper of a lie to get the information from him. 'My mum? Beth Giddings?'

'Giddings.'

'Archie Giddings or Beth Giddings?' Sammie asked.

'Yes! Maternity has a Bethany-Jade Giddings.'

'The baby.' I pressed my hand to my mouth. 'She's early.' The relief I felt that it hadn't been Dad whisked away in an ambulance was swiftly replaced by worry for my baby half-sister.

We thanked the receptionist and Sammie slipped her hand in mine as we left the reception and hurried towards the separate Women and Children's Hospital.

'Remember what I said about not assuming the worst,' Sammie said as we dodged a large puddle.

To the left of the covered entrance, a man was resting his back against the wall, holding his head in his hands. Broken. My breath caught as I grabbed Sammie's arm and pulled her towards him. 'Dad?'

He looked up. He seemed to have aged in two days, his face grey and his eyes bloodshot. He squinted as though not convinced I was really there. 'Josh?'

'Is it the baby?'

Dad rubbed his eyes. 'And Beth. She had a fall. She's in surgery. It's not good. Oh my God, Josh, I could lose them both.' His voice cracked as he spoke and the last few words were barely audible.

I held out my arms to him – not because it was the right thing to do this time, but because I wanted to. There was no more anger. All I could feel was love and compassion for the man who was battling for his life himself and terrified that he might lose his girlfriend and unborn baby.

Dad clung onto me, his body shaking.

Several minutes later, with a deep intake of air, he stepped back and nodded at me. He didn't need to speak. I knew he was grateful I was there. He glanced towards Sammie.

'This is my girlfriend, Sammie,' I said. 'And my dad, Paul.'

He hesitated, as though he wasn't sure whether to just say 'hello', shake her hand or give her a hug. She took the decision out of his hands by putting her arms round him. 'It's good to meet you. I'm sorry about the circumstances.'

'Thank you. And you.' He sighed. 'I'd better go back in and see if there's any update. Can you both stay?'

I nodded. 'As long as you need us. Where's Archie?'

'In the hospital. He's asleep. One of the nurses said she'd mind him for five minutes while I got some air.'

We followed Dad into the building and into a waiting room where a nurse handed over the changing bag and Archie in his carrier. His eyes started to flicker open and Dad looked at the nurse in panic. 'I don't know if I've got any food. It was all such a rush.'

'Let me check.' I took the changing bag from him and searched through the various compartments. I found a bottle of juice but no sign of food.

'We've got some formula but no food here,' the nurse said apologetically. 'There's a shop in the main building. It'll still be open.'

'I'll go,' Sammie offered. 'What does he eat?'

Dad ran through a few suggestions and Sammie headed off.

The nurse left us and we made our way over to some seats. Dad released Archie from his straps and held him against his shoulder.

'What happened?' I asked.

'The stairs at the flat. They're a damn hazard when it's been raining and she slipped and tumbled down about half a flight right in front of me. Scariest thing I've ever seen.' He tightened his hold on Archie. 'Luckily I had hold of this one or it could have been even worse.'

'What have the doctors said?'

'Not much yet. She hit her head and kept drifting in and out of consciousness in the ambulance. They believe she's got a broken arm and a dislocated shoulder. She's covered in bruises and cuts as you'd expect but the biggest worry is the internal damage and that's what they're trying to assess now.'

I hardly dared ask. 'And the baby?'

'Lottie's in distress. They might need to do a C-section.'

'You've called her Lottie?' I asked, swallowing on the lump in my throat. 'After Grandma?' Dad's mum was called Charlotte but Granddad had always affectionately called her Lottie.

Dad nodded. 'Officially Charlotte but she'll always be Lottie to us. If she makes it. Oh, God, she has to make it. They both have to.'

I thought about what Sammie had said on the way over. 'Try not to think the worst, Dad. How many times have you operated on an animal with horrific injuries and it has pulled through? Keep believing.'

His eyes held mine. 'I'm glad you're here.' His voice cracked again as tears clouded his eyes.

'Me too.' I had to be strong for Dad but it was hard. Nobody should have to go through so much at one time.

38

SAMANTHA

Charlotte 'Lottie' Maeve Alderson was born by caesarean at 8.48 p.m. Six weeks early, she weighed in at 4lb 11oz and, despite the fall and the distress of the delivery, she gave the medical team little cause for concern. Beth, on the other hand, was not doing so well. She'd lost a lot of blood and needed a transfusion. The next twenty-four hours would be critical. The decision to deliver Lottie had been made so quickly that Paul hadn't been able to gown up and go in but he was now with his daughter in the transitional care unit while Josh and I minded Archie.

Josh had phoned his mum about half an hour before Lottie was born to let her know what had happened, then texted her with the news of Lottie's safe arrival. Twenty minutes passed but she hadn't responded.

'I hope Mum's okay,' Josh said, checking his phone for the umpteenth time. 'I thought she'd have replied.'

'I wouldn't read anything into it. She could have gone out.'

He nodded but I could tell he was still worried.

I linked my arms through his. 'Talk to me.'

'What about?'

'Anything. How you feel about having a new half-sister perhaps? Or we can talk about something completely mundane like if you really do like the hedgehog duvets I ordered or whether you were just being diplomatic.'

For the first time since we'd arrived at the hospital, Josh laughed.

'I really do like the hedgehog duvets. They're right for the rescue centre but I'd prefer it if you didn't order a duplicate set for our bedroom.'

'Damn! I'll have to cancel the order,' I said, winking at him.

'As for how I feel about everything else, I honestly don't know.' He glanced down at Archie, fast asleep in his carrier by our feet. 'I'm relieved Lottie's okay and I love that they've named her after Grandma although slightly gutted they've bagged the name. I always thought that, if I had a daughter, I'd like to call her Lottie. Couldn't name a boy after Granddad, though. I'm not convinced the name Raymond will ever make a comeback.'

I stiffened as nervous butterflies swooped in my stomach. 'It sounds like you've given this a lot of consideration.'

'Not really.' He shrugged. 'Just a passing thought. Besides, it would depend on what—'

'Josh!'

'Mum!' Josh jumped up. 'What are you doing here?'

'Oh, sweetheart, I had to come and see if there was anything I could do.' She hugged him. 'That poor family.'

I stood up when Connie released him and she hugged me too.

'Oh my word, is this little Archie?' She bent down and pressed her fingers to her lips as she gasped. 'He's the spitting image of you as a baby, Josh.' She lightly stroked his cheek. 'What a precious little angel. No wonder you're smitten. Wait till you have one of your own.'

I reeled at her last words and those butterflies took flight again as the conversation I'd overheard between Connie and Josh vividly returned to my mind. So much had happened since then, I hadn't given it another moment's thought. I looked at Josh smiling down at Archie with clear adoration. Was he thinking about me being pregnant? Was he thinking about us having a family? My pulse raced and I felt suddenly nauseous.

Connie straightened up and indicated that we should all take a seat. 'What's the latest news?'

As Josh updated her, I tuned out. Could I be pregnant? The thought that I could be filled me with dread.

'... Sammie?'

Hearing my name, I looked up at Josh. 'Sorry, what?'

He smiled. 'I was telling Mum how brilliant you were at feeding Archie.'

'You realise that, if you two have kids, you'll be on permanent nappy duty, Josh, while Samantha is chief-feeder. Best get practising.'

Looking from one smiling face to the other, I leapt to my feet, desperate to get out of there. 'I could do with a drink. Anyone else want one? No? Back shortly.'

I strode down the corridor as quickly as I could without breaking into a run then, as soon as I was outside, I ran across to the main building.

My eyes burned as I scanned the hospital shop shelves for a pregnancy testing kit.

* * *

I sat on the lowered toilet lid, staring at the words on the white stick held in my shaking hands. Not pregnant. Not. Definitely not. My body sagged as a feeling of relief swept through me. I pressed my other hand across my mouth and closed my eyes for a moment.

Why relief? That made no sense! I'd never been ridiculously gooey or obsessed about babies like Chloe, but I'd always wanted a family. Hadn't I? I loved babies and was really comfortable around them which was why I'd found it easy to feed Archie. I'd held loads of babies during my nursing career. I loved spending time with Amelia and had been close to tears when Hannah had asked me to be godmother. I craved snuggles with baby Samuel. But none of those babies were mine. Was that the difference? But that made no sense either. Josh and I loved each other, we lived together, he was my forever.

I wrapped my arms across my stomach and bent over, a wave of nausea hitting me along with a scary realisation. I didn't want children. That was the problem. Kids had never been an option before. Harry hated them and had always made it clear that he had no plans to be a father and James hadn't seen me in his future so they'd been ruled out there too. But now that they were a real possibility, I had to face the truth. I didn't see children in *my* future.

I started at the results again, my stomach churning. What was I going to tell Josh? I pictured the adoration on his face as he'd held Archie earlier. Okay, so Archie was his half-brother so there was a family connection there like I had with Samuel. But what about at the Family Fun Day? He'd been in his element playing with the kids while dressed as Mickleby. He'd loved it so much that he'd stayed in that sweltering costume for four hours. He was gentle and caring. He'd make such an amazing dad but I couldn't do it. I couldn't be a mum. Josh was my forever but could we really last forever if we disagreed on something so fundamental? This wasn't a difference of opinion on paint colour or where to go on holiday. This was a life decision. Look at his parents. Look at the choice his dad had made as soon as he'd had another chance at fatherhood. If Josh really wanted children, I was going to have to let him go so he could find someone who wanted a family too because, no matter how much I loved him and longed to make him happy, motherhood was something I absolutely couldn't do.

I could scarcely catch my breath at the scary thought of life without Josh. But the thought of being a mum was even more terrifying.

39

JOSH

I could have murdered a coffee but Sammie had already dashed off before I had a chance to ask. I turned to Mum. 'Did that seem strange to you?'

'A bit. Although in fairness, the whole thing is probably quite strange to her. Bear in mind that Beth's not just your dad's partner. She's *your* ex-girlfriend. That can't be easy. I remember you telling me how much you were dreading meeting Samantha's ex but you knew you had to be on your best behaviour because he's family. James, is it?'

I nodded. 'That's a fair point. I couldn't stand the guy for what he'd put her through. Even now, I feel a bit awkward around him although I don't think it's easy for him either.' I rolled my stiff shoulders. 'Sammie's been amazing about Beth all the way through this and, you're right, it can't be easy for her. She once saw a photo of Beth at Wisteria Cottage and felt really threatened by her.'

Mum frowned. 'But Samantha's beautiful.'

'You're telling me but she doesn't see herself like that. Her cousin, Chloe – James's wife – is striking and she looks a lot like Beth. Growing up, Sammie was always in Chloe's shadow. Boys flocked round Chloe and ignored Sammie and her mum used to rub it in that Sammie would never find someone special because she was nothing special. She started to believe it.'

'Her mum sounds delightful.'

'That woman has a lot to answer for. Sammie doesn't like to talk about it. She mentions things from time to time but I think the situation with Dad has stirred it all up again. She's always been keen for me to reconnect with him, saying we stand a chance of working through things because we had a strong relationship before. She never had that with her mum.'

'Never?'

'Her mum never wanted her and she's made that clear all the way through Sammie's life.'

'The pair of you have certainly had more than your fair share of parental screw-ups.'

'You did nothing wrong, Mum.'

'As I told you on Sunday, I'm not completely innocent in all this. I did nothing about our marriage deteriorating and I did nothing to pacify your strong feelings towards your dad by telling you the truth. You might have reached out to him sooner if you'd known he wasn't completely to blame.'

'Did you have a seven-year secret affair that resulted in a child?'

She smiled. 'No. No affair and no secret love child. But I did once...' She gasped and clapped her hand across her mouth. 'Oh my word! That's it! *That's* how I know him.'

'Know who?'

'Alex.' Her eyes shone as she spoke the name.

I shrugged my shoulders in bewilderment. 'Alex who?'

'I don't know his surname. Scout leader. He's the uncle of one of Samantha's friends. Came to the barbeque on Saturday.' She smiled widely. 'Good-looking, great sense of humour.'

'Oh! Him.' She had completely lit up in a way I'd never seen.

Clearly there'd been something between them. 'Are you saying you had a fling with Alex?'

She laughed lightly. 'Good grief, Josh. I think we'd have recognised each other immediately if we'd had a fling. Besides, I'd *never* have done that to your dad, no matter how bad things were at home.' She cocked her head to one side and pursed her lips. 'Or at least I don't think I would. I guess you never really know until the opportunity presents itself.'

'Then what happened between you and Alex?'

She smiled widely again. 'We had a moment.'

I raised my eyebrows at her. 'I have no idea what that means. Do I want to?'

She nudged me. 'It's nothing smutty so drag your brain out the gutter. It was about four years ago. Your Auntie Lauren's—'

'Connie?' I twisted in my seat to see Dad in the middle of the waiting room, blinking.

Mum rushed to him, arms outstretched. 'I'm so sorry, Paul.'

He looked momentarily stunned as she hurled herself at him but then he wrapped his arms round her and sobbed. A lump constricted my throat as I watched Mum comforting him. Where did she find the strength to forgive him and to rush to his side in his hour of need like this? To stroke his sleeping baby? To ask how his girlfriend was? I was learning so much from her about the type of person I wanted to be and the type of parent I hoped to become. I was learning so much from Sammie too. I just wish I knew why she'd taken off earlier. It was so out of character.

* * *

Sammie re-appeared ten minutes later looking pale-faced and anxious.

'Are you okay?'

'Yeah, just felt a bit sick all of a sudden. Some fresh air helped.' She sat down beside me. 'Any news?'

'Lottie's fine and Beth's out of surgery now. They reckon it went well but she's still unconscious so they won't know for definite until she's awake.'

'That's a relief.' She nodded towards where Mum and Dad were deep in conversation at the other side of the waiting room. 'Looks like World War III hasn't broken out.'

'As soon as he appeared, Mum hugged him and he broke down. It was quite something to see. I feel like such an idiot for being stubborn for so long. You were right about me letting him back in. I should have done it way before I knew about the diagnosis. You have permission to make me sleep in the cow shed if I'm ever that stubborn again.'

Sammie gave me a weak smile. I reached for her hand but she didn't curl her fingers round mine like she normally would.

'Have I said something that's upset you?' I asked although I couldn't think what it might have been.

'Just tired again.' She certainly looked and sounded weary.

'You would tell me if I did or if there's something on your mind, wouldn't you?'

'I'm fine. You focus on your family.'

'But you're my family and, right now, I'm focusing on you.'

Worryingly, tears shone in her eyes and I saw her swallow hard. 'Honestly, I'm fine. As I said, I just felt a bit sick earlier.'

She held my eyes and I could sense her willing me to believe her. I smiled and nodded but she didn't fool me. Something had upset her but she clearly wanted me to leave it so I would. For now.

40

About half an hour after I returned to the waiting room, Josh suggested I head back to Hedgehog Hollow but he wanted to stay at the hospital to keep his dad company.

'I'll call you a taxi,' he said, giving me a gentle smile. 'I don't want you falling asleep at the wheel.'

'I can drive. I'll be fine. Although that would leave you without a car.'

'I can take you back,' Connie said. 'Saves you money, leaves Josh with a car and gives me company on the way home.'

I couldn't argue with her logic so I picked up my bag and hoisted it wearily onto my shoulder.

Connie crouched down beside Archie then looked up towards Paul. 'What's he like round strangers?'

'Pretty good,' Paul said. 'Why?'

'Any allergies?'

'No.'

She nodded thoughtfully. 'How about I take Archie home to mine tonight? My next-door neighbour, Sian, has a baby about the same age as him. I'm sure she'll be happy to lend me anything you don't have in the changing bag.'

Paul shook his head. 'I couldn't ask you to do that. That's too much.'

She waved her hand dismissively. 'There's no need to worry about sleeping. I know Siân has a travel cot and I'm sure she'll have some spare bedding.'

'You'd really do that for me?' Paul asked, sounding as astonished as Josh looked.

'It's for all of you. You need to focus on Beth and Lottie right now. You can do that while this little one is sound asleep but it's not going to be so easy when he wakes up.'

'Thank you, Connie. It's... I... thank you.'

I hugged Paul goodbye. 'I'll be thinking of you all. Beth's got youth and good health on her side.'

'Thank you. And thank you for being there for my son.'

I bit my lip and swallowed hard. How much longer would I be there for his son? We couldn't talk about children now – not when he was facing so much turmoil – but we'd have to at some point. I was already dreading that day.

* * *

When Josh had finished strapping Archie into Connie's car, he stroked the little boy's cheek so tenderly that my heart melted. Then he closed the door, did the same to me and it melted even more. I could already feel the acute pain of potentially losing him.

'I don't know if I'll make it back to the farm tonight,' he said. 'It depends what happens with Beth. We might stay here or maybe drive back to the flat and return in the morning.'

I nodded. 'Text me and let me know.'

He drew me to his chest and whispered 'I love you' into my ear and I whispered it back, somehow managing to keep my emotions steady. I had to remain strong for now. He had enough to deal with. We'd talk when we were through the latest drama.

* * *

'Are you okay?' Connie asked for what must have been the sixth time since we'd left the hospital. I could feel her glancing at me but I kept my focus out the window on the dark shapes of the hedgerows and the silhouettes of trees.

'I'm fine. Just tired. It's been a long couple of weeks. Lots of change and lots of drama.'

Concerned I might be coming across as aloof, I turned away from the window. 'That was a really good thing that you did with Archie.'

I could see her smiling in the moonlight that gently lit the car. 'It's been a while since I've looked after a baby but I couldn't leave him at the hospital. Paul needs to focus on Beth and Josh needs to focus on Paul.'

We continued in silence for a while. The radio was on low, each track barely discernible. Some loud cheerful music would take the edge off. My hand twitched but I couldn't risk turning up the volume and waking Archie.

'I was talking to Josh while you were gone…' Connie started.

I bit my lip and tensed. *Here we go. She's going to ask questions to which I don't have answers…*

'You know at your barbeque when Alex and I thought we knew each other? I've remembered the connection.'

I relaxed back into the seat. She wasn't going to quiz me. 'Oh yes? What was it?'

'I didn't get to tell Josh the story because Paul appeared. I only got as far as telling him that Alex and I had had a moment about four years ago. Two moments actually.'

'Moments?' I adjusted my position so I could see her expression better. She was grinning. 'That sounds intriguing. Tell me more.'

'You know that Lauren's twice-divorced? Her second marriage was an unmitigated disaster and should never have happened. Story for another time. Anyway, when the divorce came through, she announced that it was a major cause for celebration which it absolutely was. She wanted to drink cocktails and go clubbing. Cocktails? Lovely. Clubbing? Not for me. But she'd had a rough time so I let her have her way and drag me out with a few of her friends. Lauren downed the cocktails like they were water. When we left the bar, she bashed into a group of men making one of them spill his drink. I stopped to apologise and that's when we had our first moment. Honestly, Samantha, I've never felt anything like it before. I found myself looking into this stranger's eyes and it felt like a thunderbolt had just hit me. I swear he felt it too. He had the kindest eyes and the warmest smile but, next minute, I was dragged away and the moment was gone.'

'This is Alex, I presume?'

'Yes, although I never knew his name. While we walked – or staggered in Lauren's case – to the club, I couldn't stop thinking about him which was ridiculous because it had been seconds. We'd only exchanged four words – me saying "I'm sorry" and him saying "That's okay" – but I couldn't shake that intense feeling that I'd just found my true north.'

I gasped. 'Your true north? Oh my gosh, that's so romantic. Could you not have gone back to the bar?'

'I wanted to. Every step I took away from that bar, I felt like there was a magnet pulling me back but doubt kicked in. What would I say if I let that magnet pull me? "Hello, my name's Connie, did you feel that thunderbolt too?"' She laughed lightly. 'Paul and I were friends at school and one day we kissed and that was that. No flirting. No dating. I didn't know how to do any of those things and, besides, I was married. Things might have lost their shine but I still loved my husband.

'Lauren started to feel a bit queasy in the club so one of her friends took her to the toilets while I went to the bar for some water. There was a huge queue and it took me ages to get to the front. I turned round with the drink and who should be behind me but Alex? The thunderbolt struck again. He smiled at me and said something like, "We meet again," and I could tell from his smile and the sparkle in his eyes that he was as pleased as me. And then one of Lauren's friends appeared and instructed me to hurry up with the water because Lauren had been sick.'

'Ooh, bad timing.'

Connie sighed. 'Tell me about it! I apologised again and Alex said, "Maybe I could buy you a drink later." I nodded and dashed off but there was no later. Throwing up had a sobering effect on my sister and melancholy hit. With Lauren so upset, I had no choice but to leave without seeing Alex again.'

'It's a shame you didn't know his name. You could have looked for him on social media.'

'True, although it's probably just as well I didn't. I wasn't about to call time on my marriage and I wasn't going to be unfaithful to Paul. I thought about the stranger with the kind eyes and the cornflower-blue shirt a lot after that day, wondering what if... but then I resigned it to just a couple of lost moments in time. I got to the point where I couldn't even picture him anymore and then, when the truth about Paul and Beth came out, my world turned upside down and my 'moment-man' went completely out of my mind.'

'That's why you didn't recognise him at the farm.'

'Exactly. Plus we both looked different back then. He didn't have a beard or any grey hair and I had long hair like Lauren and I wore glasses. It was four years ago. It was dark. Both encounters combined would have added up to less than a minute. It's no wonder neither of us could remember how we knew each other but it's funny how the recognition was still there.'

'And the thunderbolt?' I asked.

She was silent for a moment, then she sighed. 'Yes, and the thunderbolt.'

'What are you going to do about it?'

'I'm going to let those magnets do their work and see if he really is my true north.'

'Oh my gosh, Connie! Really?'

'You only get one shot at life and you can spend it regretting the past and getting angry or bitter about the wrong decisions you've made or the hurt caused by others or you can learn from the past and embrace the future instead. It would be easy for me to say I've been hurt before, it's too soon and I'm scared of taking a chance but that would just be another regret to add to the pile. My ex-husband has cancer, his girlfriend is fighting for her life after falling down the stairs, and that little baby girl could have died tonight. When Josh called with that news, any residual hurt just flew out the window and I had to be there for Paul. I'll always love that man but I've come to realise that he was my north west. Almost perfect but not perfect enough to last forever. Alex Williams could be my true north and I owe it to both of us to explore that.'

I could hear the smile in her voice and tears pricked my eyes at the conviction in her words. 'Did you swap numbers at the barbeque?'

'No. It never entered my head and, of course, I didn't realise who he was.'

'Would you like me to get his number from Dave or pass on yours?'

'Can you get his for me? I think it would kill me waiting around for him to call me. I want to be the one to make it happen.'

We'd reached Hedgehog Hollow and Connie turned her car onto the farm track.

'I'll get his number from Dave tomorrow,' I said.

'Thank you.'

Silence fell as she drove along the track. I loved the thought of a true north. Gramps had found his true north in Nanna, and Thomas had in Gwendoline. Hannah and Toby were a perfect match too, as were Rich and Dave. As for Josh and me...

Connie pulled up outside the barn. 'Talk to him,' she said, gently.

'Who?'

She applied the handbrake and turned to face me, the security light illuminating her face.

'Josh. Something's bothering you and it's none of my business to ask what it is but I've seen you together so many times and my heart has been bursting with joy at how happy you are.' Her tone was gentle. Understanding. 'Tonight, at the hospital, there was a shadow that I haven't seen before. I know my son comes with a lot of baggage and complications and currently they're all playing out like a soap opera, but don't we all have a past?'

'It's nothing to do with Paul or Beth.' I sighed and shook my head. 'It's maybe nothing at all.'

'Nothing has a way of growing into something. Talk to him. Tell him what's bothering you, no matter how uncomfortable it may feel or how trivial it might seem because, believe me, the trivial stuff can soon grow and destroy an incredible relationship. Paul and I are living, breathing proof of that.' She reached over and squeezed my hand. 'He's your true north and you're his. It's so obvious to anyone who's seen you together.'

I couldn't respond. If I opened my mouth, I was likely to start crying.

Connie gave my hand another squeeze then let go. 'I'm his mum so maybe talking it over with me isn't the easiest but what about one of your friends from the barbeque?'

I nodded and swallowed hard. 'I'll be in touch with Alex's number. Thank you.' I blew Archie a kiss then exited the car.

After waving her off, I slowly walked towards the barn. She was right. I needed to talk to Josh instead of creating a problem that might not exist. He was my true north, my forever, and he hadn't categorically announced that he wanted children and could not live without them. But before I spoke to him, I needed to get things straight in my mind and the best person to help me do that was Hannah. It was nearly midnight so I'd have to contact her in the morning. For now, I needed to check on Dad and the hedgehogs.

* * *

Dad took one look at me and offered to stay all night in the barn but I wouldn't let him and I insisted he leave the hoglets with me too. He was working the Saturday shift at the practice and had been on call on Thursday night so had to catch up on some sleep.

We exchanged updates then I had to pretty much push him out of the barn and send him home. A hot shower in the farmhouse revitalised me and I returned to the barn with a mug of strong coffee.

A couple of hours later, I lay down on the airbed that Josh had bought while we waited for the sofa bed to be delivered. My eyes were heavy and my body felt weary but I couldn't switch my brain off. I couldn't help but worry for Beth and Paul. Josh had sent a text at about 1 a.m. to let me know that he'd checked himself and Paul into a local hotel. Beth was still unconscious but stable and the doctor had said that the best thing Paul and Josh could do was get some rest, especially given Paul's health. At least they were nearby if Beth's condition deteriorated. Hopefully it wouldn't. That poor family already had enough to contend with.

On a cheerier note, Connie's tale of her 'moment' with Alex had warmed my heart. It certainly felt like destiny was at play, placing them back into each other's lives once more. I'd get hold of Alex's number in the morning and I couldn't wait to hear how that love story played out.

I was still awake an hour later when the hoglets squeaked for their feed. As I settled down on the airbed afterwards, I wondered whether Hannah would be free to come over to the farm later. When exhaustion took hold and I finally drifted off to sleep, my last thought was that I'd instantly thought of Hannah to confide in. This time last year, I'd have reached out to Chloe instead yet it never even entered my head to contact her. In fact, we'd had no contact since that disastrous visit to Whitsborough Bay two weeks ago. Had she been waiting for me to apologise? For what? I'd done nothing wrong. But I could have reached out and tried to recover things. She didn't know I'd been ill or that I'd left teaching. By excluding her from my life like that – albeit not intentionally or maliciously – could I have stalled the peace process?

41

JOSH

Dad and I both somehow managed to get a few hours' sleep. When we'd checked into the hotel, they'd only had one twin room left. It was probably for the best because, although it felt strange being in such close proximity to him after eighteen months estranged, I'd have worried about him if he'd been alone.

There'd been no calls from the hospital, which meant no deterioration but also meant Beth hadn't regained consciousness. Had they said something yesterday about inducing the coma? It had all started to become a blur.

While Dad was showering, a text came through from Mum to say that Archie was up and dressed and didn't seem fazed by waking up in unfamiliar surroundings with a complete stranger. I called her back.

'He's gorgeous, Josh,' she gushed. 'Such a content, happy little boy, full of smiles and cuddles. I sent some photos to your Auntie Lauren and she couldn't believe how much he looks like you. She wants to meet him now but I thought I'd better check with you and your dad first.'

'I can't see Dad having a problem with it. Go ahead.'

'Tell your dad that I'm happy to look after Archie for as long as he needs. Sian's little boy is in the next size clothes so she's got a stack of stuff in Archie's size she can lend me. I can buy food and nappies and some toys to keep him entertained.'

'Let me know what it costs and I'll pay you back. You shouldn't be out of pocket.'

'You'll do no such thing,' she said, laughter in her voice. 'Your dad walked away from our marriage with nothing and, on reflection, it wasn't fair of me to let him do that. A few bits and bobs for his baby is the least I can do.'

We said goodbye and I was about to FaceTime Sammie when Dad emerged from the bathroom with a towel swathed round his hips. I did a double-take at his ribcage showing and his shoulder blades protruding when he turned round – a stark reminder of how ill he actually was.

'I'm going to get dressed then head straight over to the hospital.' He reached for his shirt draped over the back of the chair. 'You don't mind if I don't wait for you, do you?'

'You don't want any breakfast?'

'I'm never very hungry first thing these days. If you could grab me a banana or something, that would be great.'

I probably wouldn't have felt much like breakfast myself but I hadn't eaten last night. I wasn't convinced Dad had either. I'd overheard snippets of his conversation with Mum, before Sammie returned, and I could have sworn he'd told her that they'd been on their way out for a meal when Beth slipped.

* * *

Forty minutes later, I left the hotel with a banana and a bacon sandwich wrapped in a napkin.

Walking across the hotel car park, the air felt fresh and cool following yesterday's downpour. I tried Sammie on FaceTime but she didn't answer. I tried her again when I reached the hospital but still nothing so I sent her a text:

✉ To Sammie
Just arrived at hospital. No more news yet. Mum had a good night with Archie. Let me know when's good to catch you. Missing you loads xx

I put my phone in my pocket and went inside but I had a niggling feeling in the pit of my stomach that Sammie was upset about something and I hated that I couldn't be there to comfort her.

42

I felt sick as I stared at my phone vibrating on the treatment table in the barn with Josh's FaceTime request. I might have been able to fudge my way through a call but there was no way I could manage looking at him. Not until I'd spoken to Hannah and got my emotions in check. Knowing she was always up by about seven at the latest, I'd sent her a text first thing to see if she was free and was relieved when she replied immediately to say she could come over with Amelia at about ten.

I'd been up since 5 a.m. and had decided that the best plan for the rest of the day was to keep busy. I scribbled down a to-do list and steadily worked through it, feeling a tremendous sense of achievement as I crossed each task out.

There'd been a few submissions for the logo design competition and, while there was clearly some talent on display, nothing tugged at my heart like I'd hoped – although the hedgehog wearing leather lederhosen, carrying a whip and wearing a gimp-mask did give me a good laugh. The closing date wasn't for another fortnight so there was still time.

* * *

Hannah arrived and settled Amelia on her playmat in the lounge with some building blocks while I made drinks.

'Right you, out with it,' she said, when I handed her a mug of tea. 'You've been on such a high since you met Josh and moved in here and now you look like you've won the lottery jackpot but lost your ticket.'

I took a deep breath. Might as well just get straight to the point. 'You know how I said Josh's mum, Connie, brought me home when I fainted at work? I overheard her asking Josh whether I might be pregnant and it got me thinking that it could be a possibility so I took a test last night.'

Hannah kept a straight face but her eyes were shining and I knew she'd be excited about the prospect of me having a baby, especially while Amelia was still so young. 'And...?'

'And it was negative.'

'Aw, I'm sorry, Sam.'

'Thank you, but there's no need to be sorry because I'm not.'

She nodded. 'I suppose it would have been a little soon. Plenty of time for kids later.'

I grimaced. 'I'm not sorry because I don't want children.'

Her eyes widened. 'You always said you did.'

'I know I did but it was never a possibility until now. Harry couldn't stand kids and James wanted them but not with me and I've only realised now that it didn't bother me. But Josh does want them and—'

'He's categorically said that?'

'Not directly. We haven't actually had a conversation about it but he sounded happy when Connie asked if I might be pregnant. He's brilliant with Archie and he loved playing with the kids when he was dressed as Mickleby...' I tailed off as Hannah held her hand in the air in a stop gesture.

'Wait a minute. So you're fretting that you don't want kids yet you haven't actually spoken to Josh about what he wants? You're making an assumption that he does because he didn't have a hissy fit at the idea of the woman he loves being pregnant and because he's good with kids?'

It sounded very lame when she put it like that. 'I'm worried about losing him.'

'Then you have to talk to him. None of those things are the same as him categorically declaring that he wants you to spawn a hundred babies. Plenty of people adore kids but don't want their own. I think you're creating a problem that might not exist.' Her eyebrows knitted. 'Why are you so adamant you don't want kids?'

I shrugged. 'I just don't.'

'But there has to be a reason.'

Colour flooded my cheeks and I shrugged again.

'You know I'm not someone who thinks that having kids is every woman's destiny but those who make a conscious decision not to have children usually have a reason.'

'I don't think I'm cut out to be a mum.'

'What? Why would you say that?'

Amelia knocked her building blocks down and started whining. Hannah swiftly re-built the tower then rummaged in her changing bag. She unwrapped a rice cake and handed it to Amelia then fixed her eyes square on me, clearly waiting for a response.

'I've never been gooey over babies like our Chloe.'

'So? That's not what makes a good mum. I'd like to think I'm a good mum but I've never been gooey. My mum wasn't either and she's an amazing m...' Hannah gasped. 'Oh my God! That's it, isn't it?'

I held my breath.

'It's because of your mum. You're worried you'll be like her.'

The tears I'd held back all night broke free and trickled down my cheeks.

Instantly, Hannah was by my side, her arms round me. 'Hey, it's alright. You're nothing like your mum, Sam. *Nothing*.'

'Maybe not at the moment but she wasn't like that until I came along.' I scarcely managed to get the words out between sobs.

'Perhaps not, but your mum was a special case. She obviously needed help after she lost your sister and she also needed time to grieve for her but she didn't get it. She then needed help when you were born and she didn't get that either. If you ask me, she still needs it now because what that woman did to you is...' She shook her head, her eyes flashing with anger. 'Don't get me started.'

Feeling so much better for getting it out in the open, I grabbed a tissue and wiped my eyes then curled up on the sofa and gave Hannah a grateful smile.

'Is that the *only* reason you don't want children. I'm not saying it's not a significant reason because it absolutely is, but is there anything else?'

I shook my head. 'Isn't that enough?'

'I'm just trying to establish if there's anything else so we can address it.'

'There's nothing else. I just couldn't put a child through what my mum put me through.'

'But you wouldn't do that.' Amelia cried out and Hannah swiftly scooped her up onto her knee and kissed the top of her head. 'You know how shitty it feels. It's not in your nature to be cruel like your mum. You are the kindest person I've ever known and you'd be a wonderful mum.'

'Do you know what my dad thought of my mum before I came along?'

Hannah grimaced. 'The same?'

'*Exactly* the same. He said she was the kindest, sweetest woman he'd ever met.'

'I still maintain you're nothing like her.'

We sat in silence for a moment. I wanted to believe her but there were no guarantees in life. Mum changed when she had me and I couldn't risk doing the same.

'I'm going to have to nip to the loo.' Hannah stood up with Amelia. 'Are you okay to look after her while I'm gone? You won't morph into your mum and accuse her of making too much noise or mess?'

I rolled my eyes at her. 'Hand her over.'

'Are you going to be a good girl?' Hannah swooped Amelia into my arms, making her giggle. 'Back soon.'

I cuddled Amelia to me. 'You have rice cake in your hair. You smell like popcorn. Can I gobble you up?' She squealed with laughter as I made chomping sounds and pretended to eat her.

'Should we go and see the baby in the mirror?' I stood up and carried her over to the mirror on the wall in the dining room. 'Who's that, Amelia? Is that the baby in the mirror?' I turned her to face her reflection and she giggled as we moved closer, then I turned away. 'Where's she gone? Where's that baby?' I turned back to the mirror. 'There she is!'

We repeated it several times, each as funny as the time before. She got the hiccups which made her giggle even more.

'You're so beautiful.' I stroked her hair then kissed her soft cheek. 'Although that baby in the mirror might be more beautiful. What do you think?' She giggled helplessly as we returned to the mirror. 'You're both beautiful and I love you very, very much.'

'How can you possibly think you wouldn't be an amazing mum?'

I spun round to see Hannah leaning against the doorframe. 'How long have you been there?'

'The whole time. You're a natural, Sam. If you don't want children, that's fair enough. That's your choice. But don't remain childless because of your mother. I know five minutes with Amelia is hardly the same as twenty-four hours with your own baby but if you can feel and demonstrate that much love for a baby not connected to you by blood, imagine how you'd feel towards your own child.'

'But my mum—'

'Was a poorly woman who needed help as we've already established.'

Amelia pulled at a lock of my hair and tried to stuff it into her mouth. As I extricated it from her hand, she wrapped her fingers round mine and I felt a rush of love for her. Could Hannah be right? My heart said she was but my head was buzzing with memories of the past – the harsh words, the hateful looks, the indifference and rejection – and they seemed so much stronger than the sliver of self-belief that I could rise above it and do things differently.

43

JOSH

Lottie looked so tiny lying in her incubator. There was a tube up her nose and she was attached to a multitude of wires and cables.

'It's not as scary as it looks,' said a nurse checking on a baby in the next incubator. 'The tube up her nose is for feeding her and the rest of the wires are for monitoring things like heartrate. She's small and she's early but she's doing great.'

'Thank you.'

The nurse left the room. I felt a bit helpless just standing there so I only stayed a few more minutes then returned to the waiting room.

Dad was hunched over in his seat, his hands between his legs nursing a half-drunk paper cup of coffee. He looked up as I approached. 'Did you see her?'

I nodded. 'She's beautiful. Any more news on Beth?'

'Still waiting.'

'How are you holding up?'

'Honestly? Never been more scared in my life. Beth thought my cancer was our punishment for what we did to you and your mum. Now this. Makes you wonder if she could be right.'

'No! Oh, Dad, you can't think like that. The cancer and Beth's accident are *not* the universe's way of judging you.'

'I'm not so sure anymore.'

'Well, I am. Good things happen to bad people and bad things happen to good people and, despite everything we've gone through, you still reside in the good person camp. You just detoured a bit on the way back from the shower block.'

Dad's shoulders shook as he laughed. 'That sounds like something your granddad would have said.' He sat up straight and drained the last of his coffee. 'It was good to see your mum yesterday. I still can't believe she was willing to look after Archie like that. She's an impressive woman.'

'She is and she surprises me every day with it. Do you know what the strange thing is? What you did turned out to be the making of her. I've never seen her as strong or as happy.'

Dad smiled. 'Has she met anyone else?' His voice sounded hopeful.

I shook my head but then thought of her eyes shining when she'd started to tell me about how she knew Alex. I pictured them laughing together at the barbeque. 'No. Nobody since you but I think there may be a possibility.'

'I hope he appreciates her more than I did. I took her for granted. I know that now. I did love her, though. I still do.'

'She knows. And she'll be fine. I don't think she'd put up with another man for long if he didn't appreciate her.'

We sat in silence for a few minutes.

'Is your oncologist based here?' I asked.

'He's in the main building. Why?'

'You're scared of losing Beth but she's just as scared of losing you. We can't lose sight of what you're going through. We should make an appointment for me to get tested for a stem cell match while we're here.'

'We've already talked about this. You're not likely to be a match.'

'We won't know that for certain unless we try.'

He sighed then nodded slowly. 'I've got an appointment with him on Tuesday morning. You'll be working, though.'

'I'll have a word with the boss.'

Dad smiled and the relief was obvious in his expression. 'Thank you.'

Shortly after Hannah left, I was called out to rescue a hedgehog stuck down a drain. My first ever rescue! It all went smoothly and I was able to reach him fairly easily. We'd had another six new arrivals across the week so Barnum – named after the lead in my favourite film, *The Greatest Showman* – became our thirty-fifth adult patient.

My heart leapt when I returned to Hedgehog Hollow and spotted Josh's jeep parked in the farmyard. I needed to get Barnum cleaned up so I texted him after I'd opened the barn:

✉ To Josh
Great to see you back. I've been out rescuing a hog from a drain. In the barn cleaning him up xx

Fifteen minutes later, Josh appeared. 'So the badass hedgehog saviour was called out on her first rescue mission, was she?'

I smiled as he approached the treatment table. 'This is Barnum who took a tumble down a drain on Adlington Row. He was covered in cooking fat so I've cleaned that off and I've just finished cleaning up his wounds.'

'Deep ones?'

'Superficial. Give me thirty seconds and you have my full attention. You can add him to the Happy Hog Board if you want.'

Josh busied himself doing that while I finished with Barnum then placed him in a fresh crate to heal.

'How's everyone?' I asked as I washed my hands.

'I'll tell you in a minute but there's something I have to do first.'

I didn't get a chance to pick up the towel before Josh took my face in his hands and kissed me with longing. I snaked my arms round his neck. His hair was damp from the shower and I breathed in the scent of lime from his shower gel.

I was out of breath when he stepped back, smiling.

'What was that for?' I asked. 'Not that I'm objecting.'

'I missed you and I wanted you to know how much I love you. I know I stayed at the hospital but that was for dad. It's not because I still have feelings for Beth.'

I stroked his cheek and gave him a gentle kiss. 'I know you don't. I'm not worried about that.'

'Then what are you worried about because I know something upset you yesterday?'

I gazed into his eyes and felt the love emanating from him. I owed him the truth but it wasn't going to be a quick conversation. 'Are you home now or did you just pop back to get changed?'

'I said I'd meet Dad at the hospital this evening so I'm all yours for a few hours.'

'Okay. We'll go over to the house and I'll tell you what's on my mind but I need a full update first. How's Beth?'

* * *

We took mugs of tea out to Thomas's bench and sipped on them while Josh filled me in on Beth's progress. She'd regained consciousness late morning and was coherent but she needed significant pain management and kept drifting in and out of sleep.

'Dad phoned Mum while I drove him back to the flat to freshen up. She's on her way to the hospital now with Archie so that Dad and Beth can see him but she's going to look after him for a bit longer. Dad was going to pack some stuff for Archie which he can give to Mum.'

'Your mum's amazing.'

'Isn't she just? I don't think many women would step in and do what she's done. Really puts my behaviour to shame.'

'Hey, don't beat yourself up about it. What's important is that you're there for your dad and his family now when they really need you.'

'I can't help thinking it's too little too late.'

'No, Josh, it's never too late to start over.'

He looked at me thoughtfully. 'If your mum turned up and asked you to start over, would you?'

I didn't even need to think about it. 'Yes. I must be a glutton for punishment but I'd grab the chance. It wouldn't be easy. I'd probably be setting myself up to get hurt all over again but I'd give it a go.'

'Why?'

'Because I don't want to live a life full of regrets.' I looked towards the meadow. 'Thomas gave up on life the day Gwendoline died and he regretted it. He used to talk about how disappointed she'd have been that he cut himself off from the world, let the farm decay around him, and didn't fulfil their dream of running the rescue centre. He left me this place so I could do what he wasn't able to. I know Thomas was an extreme case of what grief can do to a person but it's a valuable lesson around how important it is to accept that bad things happen and move on instead of letting the bad stuff eat away at you.'

'But wouldn't letting your mum back in be a bad thing?'

I shrugged. 'Potentially but the difference here is that she'd be the one who initiated it which would mean she's finally made the decision that she wants me in her life. Previously, it's been me pushing against a closed door.' I gave him a wry smile. 'And the door has been a foot thick, made from reinforced steel and someone's lost the twenty keys needed to unlock it.'

Misty-Blue jumped up onto my knee and I stroked her warm back. 'I've done my bit and I'm not going to try again but, if she approaches me, I'd hear her out. I wouldn't want to get a phone call from my dad or Auntie Louise one day to say something's happened to Mum and I have to live with the regret that she offered an olive branch and I didn't take it.'

Josh shuffled along the bench and drew me into a gentle hug. 'That's why you were so keen I reach out to Dad.'

'The regrets would have been far greater than the discomfort of tackling the hurt and betrayal.'

'You're not wrong there. I'm already feeling that because of Dad's cancer. I feel so helpless and wish I could do more but I've arranged to get tested to see if I'm a stem cell match. He's got an appointment on Tuesday and I'm going with him.'

'That's brilliant news.' I twisted to look at him and frowned. 'Why the anxious face?'

'Dad said that children aren't often a match and I thought he was just saying that so I wouldn't get my hopes up but I Googled it and he's right. Siblings are more likely to be a match but Dad hasn't got any.'

'I'm sorry. It's worth trying, though.' I squeezed his hand, feeling his worry. 'Could I get tested? Could my dad? Your mum? Lauren?'

'You'd really do that?'

'Without hesitation. Surely the more people we can get tested, the more likely we are to find a match.'

'The website I was looking at said the best matches are aged sixteen to thirty.'

'Then we can ask our friends and get them to ask their friends. Put a poster up in the practice. Hedgehog Hollow is online now so I could put out a plea there. We haven't got many followers yet but it'll grow. Look at how the community pulled together to rebuild the barn. They're kind people. They'd respond to this.'

Tears glistened in Josh's eyes as he leaned forward and tenderly brushed his lips against mine. 'Your mum's missing out on so much by cutting you out of her life. She should be so proud of you.'

We sat in contented silence for a while listening to the relaxing sounds of the countryside accompanied by Misty-Blue's gentle purr. Was I disillusioned to keep hoping that Mum would change her mind about me one day? I sometimes wondered if all I needed was to hear her saying 'well done' one time, her voice warm with pride, a gentle smile on her lips. Would that be enough? Or did I need an apology?

I placed my empty mug on the bench beside me. 'You haven't mentioned Lottie so I'm assuming she's doing well.'

'I got to see her this morning. She's tiny but she's so cute...'

His eyes shone as he spoke about his first glimpse of his baby half-sister and how he'd been able to reach into the incubator and stroke her hand. It warmed my heart to hear him talk about his new family like that – the family he'd been adamant he wanted nothing to do with. He'd made incredible progress in such a short time. I knew he'd regret that it had taken a potential tragedy to let them into his life but I'd help him focus on the positives instead of the regrets. As a district nurse, how many family feuds had I seen cast aside when illness or injury struck and everyone rallied together?

Equally, I'd seen families destroyed by siblings squabbling over decisions around care.

Josh's family scenario had shown a family pulling together whereas mine... I could have died and Mum hadn't come to say goodbye. I should hate her for that. I should be able to cast all thoughts of her completely out of my mind. Yet I felt empathy for her. She'd been ill and things could have been so different between us if she'd had some professional help.

'Are you ready to tell me what you're worried about?' Josh's gentle voice cut across my thoughts.

I lifted up my mug. 'I think so, but only if you make me another cuppa.'

He took my mug with a smile. 'Your wish is my command.'

Misty-Blue jumped down off the bench and trotted after him, presumably hoping she could wheedle a few treats out of him.

'I have to tell Josh I don't want children,' I said, looking towards the meadow. 'I'm scared of being like Mum. What do you think about that?'

I could imagine Thomas's response: 'Nonsense. And this place is perfect for kids. Should be teeming with them.'

After I'd found Thomas collapsed and he was taken away by ambulance, I'd searched the farmhouse for pets. It felt tired and unloved and I remembered thinking what amazing potential it had to be a happy family home.

Thomas had told me over Christmas dinner – our final meal together – that he and Gwendoline had longed for a family but she'd been unable to carry a baby to term. With a boy and girl stillborn at eight and seven months respectively, he'd said, 'I sometimes feel comforted knowing those babies have their mum back.' If the Micklebys had been able to have children, they'd have been in their late teens or twenties by the time they moved to Hedgehog Hollow but, within a few years, there could have been grandchildren running round the grounds.

'Are you okay? You look confused.'

I turned to see Josh standing to my left, a mug in each hand.

'Sorry. Miles away.'

'Talking to Thomas?'

I nodded and smiled.

Josh sat beside me and passed me my drink and we both gazed out across the meadow.

Despite my doubts about whether I was the right person for the job, I'd found the strength to set up the rescue centre. Could I cast aside my doubts about motherhood and let the farm ring with the sound of children laughing? *My* children? Could I fulfil another of Thomas and Gwendoline's dreams?

I'd talked to Josh earlier about not having regrets. What if I said no to children out of fear of being like Mum then regretted it when I was older? What if Josh stuck with me and we bumbled round that enormous house on our own, torn apart by our regrets?

I was going to have to let him in. *Deep breath. Out with it.* 'I'm not pregnant.'

'Okay. Where did that come from?' He sounded puzzled and no wonder. It was a random way to start a conversation.

'I was in the office last week when your mum asked if I could be but I'm not. I've taken a test.'

'Oh. When did you do that?'

'At the hospital yesterday. It went out of my mind after your mum questioned you but it came rushing back to me when the conversation was all about babies. Suddenly I had to know.'

'So that's why you rushed out. I was worried about you.'

'You want kids, don't you?'

'At some point in the future perhaps.' There was hesitation in his voice. 'But only if it's what you want.'

I took another deep breath and slowly shook my head. 'It isn't. I didn't realise it until the pregnancy test was negative. I was so relieved but I had this huge panic that you wouldn't want to be with me if we didn't have children and the thought of you letting me go so you can be with someone who *does* want children terrifies me.'

Josh put his arm round me and kissed my forehead. 'Do you really think I'd let go of what we have because you don't want children?' His voice was filled with so much love and sincerity. 'You're my forever. I can live with a future without children. I can't live with a future without you.'

Tears rushed to my eyes. 'You really mean that?'

'Of course I do. I love you, Sammie. All I ever needed to make my life complete was a badass hedgehog saviour and it just so happens that one knocked on my door, demanded I move my jeep and called me an idiot.'

I laughed at the memory of our cringeworthy first encounter.

'Is there a reason you don't want children?'

'It's because of my mum.' My voice cracked as I said the words.

'How?'

'I can't shift this fear that I'll be like her.'

Josh twisted so he could see me better, a frown creasing his brow. 'Straight off the top of your head, give me three words to describe your mum.'

I smiled at him. Dave had got me to do the same thing about Chloe after pointing out that he thought we had a toxic relationship. 'Cold, bitter, angry, selfish, sarcastic... That may have been more than three.'

'It was five. So here's five words off the top of my head to describe you. Kind, warm, loving, selfless, generous and I could easily reel off a whole load more. Think about those lists. Two completely different people.'

I grimaced. 'I talked to Hannah about it this morning and she made the same point but, before I came along, that second list of words would have applied to my mum. People change. Sometimes for the worse.'

Josh sighed. 'Yes, but I don't think that would be the case here. I'm reluctant to debate it because that will seem like I'm putting pressure on you to change your mind when I'm not. I stand by what I say. You're the future that I want.'

I bit my lip. 'Cards on the table. Would you like a family? Please be honest.'

He paused for a moment. 'I honestly hadn't given it much thought but, if you wanted children and were asking me if I wanted them or not, I'd say yes. But you don't want them so I say yes to that too because I say yes to you. I know there are people – like my mum and dad and your cousin, Chloe – who are desperate to have kids and can't contemplate a future without them. I'm not one of those people, Sammie. I swear it. And do you know what you're not?'

'What?'

'You're not your mum. Again, I emphasise that this is *nothing* to do with trying to persuade you to have children but I don't think it's healthy for you to compare yourself to your mum so I'm going to play teacher and set you some homework.' He winked at me. 'I want you to write a list of all the ways you're different to your mum. From what I already know about her, I think you'll be surprised at how long that list is.'

I was touched by the passion in his voice. 'And when's my deadline, sir?'

'The end of next week.' He smiled and shook his head. 'In all seriousness, I'm not going to chase you. It's something you need to do in your own time. I'll be here for you when you're ready to share but I promise I won't pester you for it.'

'Okay. It's a good idea.'

'I do, however, have an assignment that needs submitting right now.' He stood up. 'Put your tea down and give me the biggest hug you've ever given.'

As we clung onto each other, I felt light with relief at how well he'd reacted to the conversation. I felt convinced it wasn't one of those awful situations where he'd said one thing but meant another. But I thought about the Micklebys and how perfect Hedgehog Hollow was for a family and doubt set in once more. Would having a child be the best way to exorcise my ghosts and prove to myself that I was nothing like Mum? Or would taking that risk be playing with a child's life?

45

Sammie's revelation about not wanting kids hadn't floored me but I definitely hadn't seen it coming. She loved spending time with Amelia and Samuel and, at the Family Fun Day, she'd been so engaging with all the kids.

I couldn't shake the feeling that, deep down, she longed for children of her own and, if we could address her legitimate concerns about being like her mum, she'd reconsider. The comment that kept circling round in my mind was about her mum being just like Sammie before Sammie was born. What if she hadn't been? What if she'd misheard or latched onto some untruths? The only person who'd know for sure was Jonathan. After dinner, on my way back to the hospital, I'd make a detour via Auntie Lauren's to investigate further. If it turned out to be true about her mum and Sammie still didn't want children after that, fair enough. I meant what I said about wanting to be with her forever, with or without kids. I just hated the thought of her making a decision that she might regret later based on inaccurate information.

'That was delicious, thank you.' Sammie put her knife and fork down and pushed her plate away. It was good to see her eating properly at last. 'I've been thinking. You know you said earlier that you feel a bit helpless and wish you could do more for your dad? I've thought of something that would be a massive help.'

I raised my eyebrows, my curiosity piqued.

'When she's discharged, Beth's going to need loads of time to recover. Imagine those stairs at her flat with a broken arm, broken collar bone and two babies. She'll be trapped indoors. I have no idea how your dad found the energy to manage two steep flights when he was going through chemo. And you said yourself that the flat is small.'

I pictured the cramped living space and the plastic crates piled high. 'It's tiny. You think they should move into Alder Lea?' I'd been adamant that they couldn't but that had been before. Now it seemed churlish.

'That was my first thought but what about them moving in here instead?'

I dropped my fork with a clatter. 'Into the farmhouse?'

She smiled. 'They couldn't exactly take up residence in the cow shed.'

'But having my ex in our house? Wouldn't that be strange for you?'

'No stranger than being bridesmaid while my cousin married my ex and having them name their baby after me. No stranger than Thomas leaving his farm and his dreams to me. No stranger than me giving up my entire nursing career to care for injured hedgehogs. Or me moving in with a rude, stubborn vet who I argued with the first four times we met. I've come to the conclusion that life is pretty strange and sometimes we just have to roll with it.'

I ran my fingers through my hair. 'You just keep astonishing me. Are you sure? It wouldn't just be having another four people living here. It would be babies crying at all hours and two poorly adults needing lots of care and attention. That's a huge ask of anyone.'

'Yeah, you're right. It would probably be better if they moved in with a trained nurse. Hmm. If only we knew one of those...' She assumed a deep-thought pose.

I laughed. 'Good point.'

'Seriously, though. I can't think of a better place for them to convalesce. If they were at Alder Lea, they'd be there alone at night and they'd effectively be there alone during the day too because you'd have a job to do. Here, I'm going to be around all the time. They can have the bedroom that Dad would have had which is ideal because it's en-suite. One of the empty bedrooms can be converted into a nursery. Then, when all's well, perhaps you could consider Alder Lea for their future home.'

I moved round the table and hugged her. 'I'll speak to Dad tonight and see what he thinks. Thank you.'

* * *

When I kissed Sammie goodbye a little later and set off down the farm track, I couldn't stop marvelling at how strong the two women in my life were. Where did they find this ability to care so much and put others first all the time? I needed to be more like that.

My stomach churned when I pulled up outside Auntie Lauren's cottage. It felt deceitful, like I was going behind Sammie's back, but I had to do something. Even if the outcome remained no children, I couldn't let her go on thinking she was anything like her mum when she couldn't be more different.

46

After Josh left, I cleared away the dinner dishes then locked up the farmhouse and took my laptop over to the barn. If I was going to be on my own all night, I might as well continue working through my to-do list.

I checked my emails and spotted a reply from Jeanette Kingston, the community leader in Terry's village, saying she was on holiday over half-term but could visit the farm late the following week. I confirmed a time, pleased at the positive response. There'd also been another logo submission and, while skilfully drawn, the expression on Mickleby's face was more psycho hedgehog than cute. The closing date was the end of half-term next week so hopefully somebody would get creative during the holidays and come up trumps.

The next few hours flew by as I worked through my tasks, only pausing to make a drink or feed the hoglets. Shortly before ten, I stretched and wandered round the barn. I paused in front of a display of drawings from the children who'd visited the activities tent Chloe and Auntie Louise ran at the Family Fun Day and tutted. Still no contact from Chloe. It was too late to call her now but it looked like I was going to have to be the bigger person and make contact tomorrow. I'd best be prepared for some sarcastic comment about forgetting who she was – a bit ironic for someone who'd cut me out of her life for months.

I made a hot chocolate then returned to my laptop, opened a spreadsheet and created two columns headed 'Mum' and 'Me'. 'Right, let's impress the teacher and do this before he gets back tomorrow.'

* * *

I sat back in my chair and scanned my eyes down the two columns that I'd feverishly populated for the past forty minutes or so. That had certainly been enlightening. Josh was right and Hannah was right. I really was nothing like how Mum was now. I'd never behave in the way she did or say the cruel things she did. The niggle was that, if I'd done this exercise on Mum pre-pregnancy, the 'Mum' column would have read like the 'Me' column and that's what scared me.

My phone rang with an unknown mobile number, making me jump.

'Hello, Hedgehog Hollow Rescue Centre.'

'Hi there. My name's Fizz Kinsella. I know it's really late to call but my cat has just returned from her night-time neighbourhood prowl with one of her special precious gifts for me and I'm not really sure what to do with it. It's a baby hedgehog.'

'Is it still alive?' *Please say yes.*

'Oh yes. Jinks is always super gentle with what she catches although it's usually mice which I end up chasing round the cottage. A hoglet's a first.' Her voice was full of energy and I instantly warmed to her.

'Where are you?'

'I'm in Great Tilbury but there's no need for you to come out. I can bring it to you. It's the least I can do.'

'That would be really helpful if you don't mind. Could you do me a favour first? Do you have a garden?'

'Yes.'

'Could you check it to see whether there are any other hoglets out there? They could be on the lawn or under some shrubs or they might be in a nest which is more likely to be hidden under a log pile or compost heap. If Jinks has disturbed a nest, their mum won't return or she might return and eat them, grim as that sounds.' I kept my voice gentle, not wanting her to think I was angry at her cat for potentially disturbing their nest. It was natural behaviour for a cat and hardly the owner's fault.

'That's gross. Poor things. I've got some palettes piled up that my furniture was delivered on. I'll grab my torch and investigate under those. What if I find them?'

'Can you bring them all in? Or they'll be at the mercy of predators who aren't quite as gentle as Jinks – or their mum.'

I gave her some guidance on keeping hoglets warm but not smothered. When we'd hung up, I plugged in a couple of heat pads in case there was a litter and prepared a crate and some formula. I wasn't sure how I'd manage on my own if there were several mouths to feed but I'd cross that bridge if it came to it. Maybe I could convince Fizz to help. I didn't want to have to call on Dad again. He'd done so much recently.

* * *

As soon as I heard a car engine, I stepped outside and waved at the driver of the brand new electric-blue convertible Mini Cooper. She skidded the car to a halt near the barn and jumped out.

'You must be Fizz. I'm Samantha.'

Dressed in a sparkly unicorn T-shirt and with pink hair piled on the top of her head in two messy buns, Fizz looked a lot younger than she'd sounded on the phone although large round glasses added a look of maturity.

'Oh my God, I've so been dying to meet you,' she gushed. 'I adore hedgehogs and really wanted to come to your opening day but I had to go to a christening so I missed out.' She opened the passenger side door. 'It was just as well you got me to check the garden.' She lifted out a washing up bowl with a pile of kitchen roll scrunched up in it.

'How many did you find?'

'There's four including the one Jinks had. You were right about her disturbing the nest. I found one on the grass, another near the palettes and another one in some leaves under them.'

'You did well. Thanks so much for bringing them in. Do you need to rush home because I could use some help if you don't?'

'Yes!' She grinned and punched the air. 'I was hoping you'd ask me that.'

She handed me the bowl and followed me into the barn, gasping every few steps and commenting on how much she loved something she saw. Her enthusiasm was infectious and gave me a boost of energy.

'This is so exciting!' she said as I placed the bowl on the treatment table. 'You have made my evening!'

I pulled on some gloves and peeled back the kitchen paper. 'Hello, little hoglets.' I turned to Fizz. 'I don't suppose you know which one your cat had?'

She leaned over and peered into the bowl. 'That one. It has darker prickles at the back than the other three.'

'So it does. Thank you.' I picked it up and ran my finger over its soft tummy. 'I'm going to start by giving this one a once-over to check for wounds. I know you said Jinks is careful but their skin is still delicate at this stage so it's best to make absolutely sure.'

'What can I do?'

'If you could wash your hands in the sink over there, I'll get you to help me feed them.'

Fizz was right about Jinks being gentle. There was no sign of scratches or puncture wounds on the one she'd pointed out and, as I placed the others on the heat pad, I gave them a check just in case she'd got them mixed up but they all seemed fine. They were a similar size and stage of development to Leia and Solo so were probably the same age as our first orphans.

'I'm surprised your cat managed to pick one of them up without it prickling her,' I said to Fizz when she joined me at the table.

'I think she was holding it by the belly rather than the spikes. I tell you what, it gave me ever such a fright. I thought it was a hair-brush or something but then it grew legs and moved!'

I laughed at the thought. 'That would scare the life out of me too.' I swept my hand across the four hoglets. 'The main thing we have to do now is keep these four warm and fed. There are heat pads under these fleeces which means that the ones not being fed can stay warm. Are you happy to have a go at feeding?'

Her eyes shone with excitement. 'A dream come true. I've fed kittens, puppies, piglets, calves, foals and ducklings before but it's my first time feeding a hoglet. I'm a super quick learner.'

She was. As soon as I'd shown her the best way to handle the hoglets, she capably handled and fed two of them while I worked on the others. They all seemed fairly active, snuffling round on the heat pad without much stimulation from us, so hopefully they were made of sturdy stuff and would all survive. I didn't feel the same sense of dread that I'd felt with Leia and Solo's litter.

'Do you know what sex they are?' Fizz placed the second hoglet back on the heat pad and lightly stroked her finger along its spines.

'They're both female on your heat pad and, on this pad, I've got one of each.'

'How can you tell?'

I lifted up a girl in one hand and a boy in the other and pointed out the difference. 'We need names for them. We're working through book and movie characters at the moment. Would you like to do the honours?'

'Ooh, yes!' She beamed at me. 'Can we do Disney? How about Belle, Aurora and Ariel?' She pointed to each of the girls as she christened them. 'And Charming for the boy.'

'All great names. Speaking of which, I love the name Fizz. Is it your actual name or a nickname?'

'My real name's Felicity.' She opened her mouth, pointed to the back of her throat and made a gagging sound. 'I'm so not a Felicity. I couldn't say my name when I was little and it came out sounding like 'Fizz' instead so that stuck, thank God! At twenty-five, I don't think I could get away with hair like this or a wardrobe full of sparkly unicorn T-shirts if I was called Felicity, could I?'

I laughed. 'Possibly not. It suits you. The name and the hair.'

Aurora made a sudden bid for freedom so Fizz scooped her up and placed her back on the heat pad with Belle.

'You said you've fed various baby animals before. How come?'

'My grandparents on my mum's side had a farm so I spent loads of time there when I was younger and got the animal bug. They're retired now and my brother runs it. I studied animal care at college and got a job at a cat rescue centre afterwards but I left there because I won the lottery last year.'

I gasped. 'Oh my gosh! That's amazing!'

She laughed. 'It is but there were a few winners that week so we're not talking millions. It was enough to buy a little cottage, my car and to pay to get qualified as a veterinary nurse. I started studying full-time in September and, oh my God, it's awesome. Best thing I ever did.'

'Congratulations! And if you're ever looking for somewhere to do some work experience, you should... Hang on a second.' I cocked my head to one side. 'Did you hear a car just now?'

Fizz narrowed her eyes and cocked her head to one side too. 'I don't think so.'

I shrugged. 'Must be me imagining things. Where was I? Oh yeah, my boyfriend owns—'

We both screamed as something hit the window above the sink.

'What the hell was that?' I ran towards it and squealed again as more objects hit the glass. 'Eggs!' Trails of thick yellow yolk trickled down the pane and chunks of shell clung to the window in among the sticky whites. I peered through the mess but it was too dark to see anyone.

I turned to Fizz. 'Can you put the hoglets in a crate and put them under the table then move back from the windows?' I didn't trust the Grimes boys – or whoever it was – not to lob a brick through the glass. 'And can you call the police?'

While Fizz followed my instructions quickly and calmly, I ran upstairs with a notepad and pen. A knackered old beige Ford Escort with both front doors wide open was parked near Fizz's Mini. I scribbled down the registration number and ran back downstairs to Fizz who relayed the information to the emergency services operator.

'They say to stay inside and away from any windows,' she said. 'The police are at an address nearby so they'll be here in minutes. I'm to stay on the line.'

I nodded and mouthed 'thanks', my heart racing as I listened for sounds outside.

'What do you think they're doing?' Fizz whispered.

I pictured the previous message painted on the stones. 'Graffiti.

It's not the first time.'

'There's a moggie here,' shouted a man from outside.

I gasped. 'Misty-Blue!'

'Give it a kicking,' called the other.

I heard Misty-Blue howl and rage propelled me towards the door.

'Shit! I missed.'

'There it is! Get it!'

Not on my watch. I flung the door open and yelled into the night, 'Kick my cat and it's the last thing you will ever do!' I have no idea where the threat came from or the power in my voice but I meant it. Brandishing a heavy torch in my hand, I ran round to the back of the barn. 'Now get the hell off my farm!'

I could hear the rustling of running through the tall grasses but couldn't see anyone when I shone my torch. They must have legged it round the other side. Moments later, a car door slammed and the engine started. I dashed back towards the farmyard to see a hooded figure sprinting towards the passenger side.

'Don't you dare come back!' Then I screamed as something heavy hit me on the side of my face before the car screeched across the gravel towards the farm track. The pain was acute, causing spots to swim before my eyes. I pressed the palm of my hand against my cheek and, for a moment, I thought I might faint again but the dizziness ceased. I trembled as I looked down. A box of a half-dozen broken eggs lay by my feet and eggs dripped down my T-shirt. Removing my hand from my face, I looked at my egg and blood-covered fingers. Crap. But that would have to wait.

'Misty-Blue!' I called. 'Where are you, sweetheart?'

'Have they gone?' Fizz rushed to my side. 'Oh my God! You're bleeding.'

'I know but I need to find my cat and make sure they haven't hurt her.' My voice was shaking.

'You're bleeding pretty bad. Let's get you inside and patch you up then I promise I'll look for her.'

The adrenaline had left me and I sagged against Fizz as she put her arm round my waist and led me into the barn.

She pulled one of the chairs over to the sink and lowered me down onto it.

'I know it might sound gruesome but can I take some photos? Might be useful evidence.'

'My phone's on the table.'

'What should I use to clean your face?' she asked after taking some photos.

I indicated a drawer containing fresh tea towels. She wet one and gently cleaned the egg and blood off my face with it, tutting and muttering under her breath about 'cowardly scum'.

'How's it looking?' I asked when she stepped back.

'You're going to need stitches.'

'I'm a nurse. I've got some Steri-strips in the house.'

Fizz shook her head. 'It's deep. I don't think they're gonna do the trick.'

'No! I could do without a trip to A&E tonight.'

She wet a fresh tea towel which I held against my cheek while she went to look for Misty-Blue. Her howl echoed in my mind and I felt sick with fear that they might have hurt her. They'd certainly hurt me. My cheek throbbed and my eye felt painful too.

Feeling some strength return to my legs now the initial shock had worn off, I shuffled into the toilets. One look in the mirror confirmed that Fizz was right about needing stitches. I'd no idea a box of eggs could inflict so much damage but I suppose anything thrown with force could be a weapon.

I returned to the main room and felt weak with relief when I spotted flashing blue lights reflecting in the windows followed by a knock on the door. 'Hello? Police.'

I recognised the police constable as one of the ones who'd given me the news about them originally catching the Grimes boys.

'PC Sunning? Come in.'

'You're bleeding.'

'One of them threw a box of eggs at me.' I lifted the towel away from my cheek. 'As you can see, he had a pretty good aim.'

'That looks painful.' He shook his head. 'We've caught them. Bear with me a moment. I just need to tell my sarge you were assaulted. Back shortly.'

I sank down into the chair by the sink. They'd caught them? Thank goodness for that.

The barn door opened again. 'Is this her?' Fizz called.

I pressed my fingers to my lips at the sight of Misty-Blue cradled in Fizz's arms, feeling light-headed with relief. 'Yes. Is she okay?'

'A little jittery but it doesn't look like they've hurt her.' She brought the cat over to me.

'Thank goodness.'

'She's so beautiful.' She tickled her behind the ears and Misty-Blue's purrs instantly soothed me. 'Did you see the police are outside?'

I nodded. 'One of them came in just now but he saw my cheek and went to tell his sergeant. Apparently they've caught them.'

'Awesome.'

PC Sunning returned. 'Fizz! What are you doing here?'

'Hi, Mike. I was helping feed some baby hedgehogs I'd brought in. Are you on with my dad tonight? Is he outside?'

'He's calling for a van. Does he know you're here?'

She shook her head. 'He'll find out soon enough.'

'Small world,' I muttered as PC Sunning turned to me. If Fizz's dad was a police sergeant, it explained why she'd been so calm and why she'd thought to take photos for evidence.

'I need to take a statement,' PC Sunning said, 'but you might need to get that gash seen to first.'

'I'll be fine to give a statement now but I will need to get to A&E straight after. Would you mind if I call my dad? I'm going to need him to look after the hedgehogs while I'm gone.' So much for not disturbing him tonight but, with six hoglets to feed now, I couldn't risk being held up too long at hospital.

'Go ahead.'

I rang Dad and quickly explained what had happened. It pained me to hear the panic in his voice. He'd be feeling guilty for me being alone at the barn and I suspected we'd be having another conversation about him staying when Josh was away or on call but he couldn't keep trying to protect me like that. The perpetrators had been caught and hopefully this would be the end. If it was the Grimes boys, surely they had to get locked up now. I couldn't understand why they hadn't been already.

'My dad's on his way. Have a seat.' I picked up the crate from under the table and gently placed the hoglets back on the heat pads. I smiled weakly at him. 'They'd give you a statement but they were hiding under the table for protection in case a window got put through which it thankfully didn't.'

'Erm, I hate to say this but it did.' Fizz shrugged apologetically. 'I heard glass smashing upstairs when you went outside.'

I closed my eyes for a moment and shook my head. It just kept getting worse.

PC Sunning took out his notepad. 'I know it's little comfort when your property has been damaged but every charge adds up to a stronger case against them.'

'Is it the Grimes boys?' I asked.

'No. They're currently serving at Her Majesty's Pleasure. Did nobody tell you?'

I sighed and shook my head. 'No. And I've had several of your colleagues here about other incidents but nobody ever came back to me with an update so I had no idea if it was them or someone new.'

'I'm really sorry. Not that it's a good enough excuse but we've had a few staffing changes. You should have been told about their sentencing. I'll make sure someone gets in touch early next week with the details.'

'Thank you. So if it's not Brynn and Cody Grimes, who have you got outside?'

'A couple of young lads who aren't giving their names. They *are* connected to the Grimes boys because the car they're in is registered to one Cody Grimes. I think it's too much of a coincidence to suggest that they happen to have stolen his car to attack the same farm he attacked. They're not saying how they're connected – they're not saying much of anything – but we'll find out down at the station.'

'Scum. I bet the car isn't taxed or insured,' Fizz muttered.

'Fizz Kinsella, what could possibly make you jump to such an assumption about a fine upstanding member of our community?' PC Sunning rolled his eyes and shook his head. 'Needless to say, the recovery truck is on its way too, not that Mr Grimes needs his car where he is.'

PC Sunning asked me to run through the full events of the evening with Fizz chipping in extra detail like the windows smashing. He took photos of my face for his records and asked me to email him the ones Fizz had taken, then he went upstairs to check out the damage and take photos up there. When he came back down, he reported that there were two broken windows and two bricks on the floor. A note was wrapped round one of them containing two words: GOLD DIGGER.

'Exactly what they painted on the wall a fortnight ago.' I filled him in on the three other incidents – the faeces on the donation bins, the graffiti on the barn and the box of roadkill – just in case they hadn't been properly connected. He asked me to email him those photos too, saying he'd make it his personal mission to ensure everything was looked at together and he'd rather have the evidence twice than not at all.

'If the Grimes boys are in prison and you've caught their partners in crime too, do you think it will finally be over?' I felt so weary, I could barely string the sentence together.

'They're certainly in a whole heap of trouble, especially as there's an assault involved.'

'Good.'

'I think you should send someone round to their house, pelt it with eggs, smear it with dog crap and put a few windows through,' Fizz declared. 'See how they like it.'

PC Sunning smiled ruefully. 'Nothing would give me greater pleasure but, oddly enough, that sort of behaviour is not part of our police training.'

'It should be.'

The barn door burst open. 'Sammie! Are you okay?' Dad rushed towards me, closely followed by Lauren. 'Oh, poppet! What have they done to you now?'

'They egged me.'

Lauren and Dad both winced when I took the tea towel away to show them the damage. 'That looks painful,' Lauren said.

'It is. Needs stitches so looks like I'm off to A&E.'

She placed her hand gently on my shoulder. 'I'll take you while your dad looks after things here.'

I still felt pretty shaky so the offer was very welcome.

PC Sunning flipped his pad closed. 'I've got everything I need for now so I'll let you get to hospital while I check the building perimeter to see whether they've painted or sprayed on it like you suspect.'

Seconds later, PC Sunning's radio buzzed. He listened on his earpiece and nodded. 'The tow-truck's just arrived. Are you heading home now, Fizz?'

She turned to me. 'Can I stay and help your dad?'

'Aren't you tired?'

'I'm a night owl. Far too much energy. I only need about four hours' sleep.'

'I can vouch for that.' PC Sunning smiled fondly at her. 'I've known this one since she was knee-high to a grasshopper and she's always been a bundle of positive energy.'

I did the introductions and explained to Dad who Fizz was and how helpful and capable she'd been earlier. 'He's a vet, Fizz, so you might be able to bag yourself a work experience opportunity if you impress him.'

Her eyes lit up and she clapped her hands together excitedly.

Dad smiled. 'I'm happy to have the help and the company.'

'Thanks for everything, Fizz. I'm so sorry about what happened.'

She grinned. 'Not your fault. I loved feeding the hoglets and I loved cuddles with your cat. The other stuff wasn't quite so much fun but it *was* exciting. Can I come back and help again some time?'

'You haven't been put off for life?' I nodded. 'It would be a pleasure to have your help. Drop me a message on the Facebook page and we'll sort something out.'

'Yay!' She drew me into a hug, taking care not to brush against my wounded cheek. 'Thank you.'

* * *

'What a lovely girl,' Lauren said as we set off down the farm track. 'New friend?'

'I think she might be. We had fun before the barn came under attack again. She seems keen to help and, if she's happy to do that on a voluntary basis every so often, it could make a real difference. Imagine if I could find a whole team of volunteers who'd be willing to help out or collect donations or educate the community...' My mind was whirring again with possibilities. 'Just think how much we could achieve.'

'I bet there'll be a lot of willing volunteers out there.'

Lauren pulled off the farm track and steered her car in the direction of Reddfield Hospital. 'Does Josh know what's happened?'

'Not yet. He'd insist on driving straight back here and he's barely had any sleep recently. It's not like he could do anything to help if he came back. I'll let him know tomorrow but he's got enough on his plate at the moment without having to deal with this.'

'You're not having the best May, are you?'

'You're telling me! The start of it was amazing but it's gone on a downward trajectory since then. What doesn't kill you makes you stronger. If a barn collapsing on top of me didn't kill me, a drive-by egging certainly isn't going to.'

'That's the spirit.' She laughed. 'Drive-by egging. What are you like?'

'Tonight wasn't all bad either. I met Fizz, we rescued four hoglets, I found out that the Grimes boys *did* get locked up and the police caught the baddies from tonight.'

Lauren laughed again. 'Baddies? What are you? Six?'

'Don't make me laugh. It hurts too much.' I pressed the tea towel against my wound. It had been a hell of an evening but there'd been lots of chinks of light in the darkness and, throughout my life, I'd naturally gravitated towards the light. When Mum was unkind, I turned to Nanna and Gramps, Dad and even Chloe because, despite what happened with James, she had been my best friend and I missed the moments where it was just the two of us cracking up with laughter. Would that love and friendship ever return?

47

Mum was at the hospital with Archie when I returned on Saturday evening. He was wide awake and full of beans, becoming especially animated when I handed him a soft toy penguin I'd picked up from a supermarket on the way. She wanted Archie to fall asleep in the car on the way home so she could transfer him straight into the travel cot and suggested I change his nappy and dress him for bed. I was all fingers and thumbs having never dressed a baby before but she gave me tips and encouragement and, other than a popper-alignment disaster, it went fairly smoothly.

When I settled him in my arms with his bottle, Mum beamed at me. 'Already a pro for when you have your own.'

As my parents both smiled proudly at me feeding my half-brother, the expectation that fatherhood would be imminent for me hung in the room. Little did they know. Although what Jonathan had told me was enlightening and might help change Sammie's mind.

Archie snuggled against me after finishing his bottle, his eyelids drooping, his hand wrapped round Waddles the penguin. I couldn't deny a tug of longing to have my own child but it would only feel special if they were also Sammie's child. She meant more to me than anything in the world. I only had to think about those bleak days while she was in hospital fighting for her life and the same fear I'd felt when she'd been ill recently to know that I'd be lost without her. If a combination of her homework, a conversation with Jonathan, and time didn't change her mind then I would focus on being the best big brother possible to Archie and Lottie. If it was a choice between Sammie and no babies or babies and no Sammie, it was an easy decision. Sammie every time.

I walked Mum and Archie out to the car park and told her Sammie's proposal for Dad's living arrangements.

'That's a wonderful idea, sweetheart. Samantha's such a kind girl.'

'It wouldn't bother you if they accept?'

She glanced down at Archie. 'I think we're beyond anything about this situation bothering me. Besides, I may have a potential love interest of my own.'

I stopped and stared at her, surprised. 'Who?'

'Alex, from the barbeque. I told you about him... actually, no, I didn't get to explain but I will. Or you can ask Samantha. She knows the full story and she sent me his number this afternoon.' She unlocked the car and secured Archie's car seat in the back.

'And you've already organised a date?'

'Too right I have.' She finished fastening Archie in then stood up straight and gently closed the door. 'There's no point putting these things off. I met him four years ago and didn't seize the moment then. I'm not going to make that mistake again. Life's too short and we have to live our best life every day because you never know when that will be in jeopardy as several people close to you have proved recently.' She smiled then gave me a quick squeeze and kissed my cheek. 'Take care, sweetheart.'

I stood back and waved as she drove off. She kept delivering surprise after surprise. A date? And one that she'd initiated? I'd sat beside her hospital bed, clutching her limp hand two years ago this October, terrified I'd lost her forever. My emotions had swirled into a ball of rage towards Dad and Beth yet look at her now. Who knew something so positive could come out of something so dire?

* * *

When I returned to the waiting room, Dad's pallor was grey and I could see he was fighting to keep his eyes open.

'We're going back to the hotel. You're going to have something to eat and then you're getting an early night.'

'No, I need to—'

'You need to listen to me and, if you won't, I'll find a doctor who you *will* listen to. You're no use to Beth or Lottie like this.'

He stood up and followed me without further objection.

Back at the hotel, he insisted he didn't need any dinner but I physically shoved him in the direction of the restaurant and said we wouldn't leave until he'd eaten.

For a man who allegedly wasn't hungry, he devoured his soup before I'd even put away two of the five potato skins I'd ordered so I requested another soup.

'Sammie and I have a proposal for you,' I said when it arrived. 'We want you to move into the farm with us. All four of you.'

He dropped his bread into his soup as his head shot up and he stared at me with disbelief. 'You can't mean that.'

'We do. I thought about you moving into Alder Lea but Sammie suggested you'd be better off at the farm as she'll be there 24/7. Could be handy to have a nurse around.' I nodded towards his soup. 'And you might want to rescue that bread.'

He looked down and swiftly fished it out. 'You'd really do that for us? After everything we did?'

'We're drawing a line in the sand. Your family needs some space which is at a premium in your flat and you're going to need some help. We can offer both. And, before you say anything, the offer isn't because you're ill and Beth's injured and I feel it's the right thing to do. It's because I *want* to do it.'

Dad pressed his hand over his mouth and slowly shook his head. Tears glistened in his eyes and he took a couple of deep shaky breaths. 'Thank you, son. That means a lot. I wasn't sure how Beth was going to manage on those stairs back at the flat.'

'There's stairs at the farmhouse but the difference is we'll be around to help.'

'I want to say yes but—'

'I know. You need to check with Beth first but, assuming she's happy with it, we can move your things over whenever you're ready.'

It must have been a big weight off his mind because the colour returned to Dad's cheeks and he tucked into his second bowl of soup with gusto and even managed a portion of apple crumble with custard afterwards. He was suddenly talkative too. Wanted to know all about Sammie and Hedgehog Hollow so I told him how we'd met, Thomas's legacy and how the Grimes boys had done their best to destroy it. I even told him about Sammie being ill but I didn't mention anything about babies. It felt far too personal to be sharing that level of detail and we didn't have that relationship back yet. We probably never would. One step at a time, though.

* * *

An hour after we'd finished eating, Dad was sound asleep and lightly snoring. I kept picturing the grateful expression on his face earlier and, for the first time, I considered everything he'd lost. It was actually greater than what Mum or I had lost: his practice, career, home, financial security, son, surrogate sons and his best friend since school, not to mention his reputation and dignity. It was testament to the strength of his relationship with Beth that they'd survived what had to have been a tough time with both of them unemployed and a baby on the way. He obviously loved her very much and, having seen them together, it was definitely mutual.

I still would never have put them together as a couple yet it seemed to work. They were so different. Or were they? Did I really know Beth? I'd never have believed she could have kept up such a pretence. We'd been together about eight months when I finally admitted to my parents that I had a girlfriend. After that, Beth had Sunday lunch at our family home several times and even spent Christmas there. She'd been my plus one at a wedding and the four of us had gone on a weekend break to Berlin. What had they both been playing at? Had they nipped off for a quickie on those occasions, laughing at Mum and me for being so clueless that we'd facilitated time for them to be together.

Staring at Dad's silhouette in the darkness, I had to quash the rising anger again. It was done and I needed to stop focusing on it. When they were better, maybe I'd question them or maybe I'd leave it. I probably wouldn't like the answers anyway.

I turned over and closed my eyes. Enough. The past was in the past and, as Mum said earlier, life was short and we needed to live our best life every day. Stewing on the choices Beth and Dad had made was not living my best life. Not at all.

48

'Are you okay?' Dad stepped out of the en-suite as I was frantically stuffing my belongings into my bag the following morning.

'There was another attack on the farm last night. I need to get home.' I could hear the panic in my voice.

His mouth dropped open. 'What happened? Is Samantha okay?'

'They threw a box of eggs at her and split her cheek open.' I yanked the zip closed. 'She had to go to A&E for stitches. She's playing it down but I can tell she's really shaken.'

'She's bound to be. That's awful. Can I do anything?'

'I don't think so.' I looked round me. 'I think I've got everything that's mine and the room's already paid for. Will you be alright today without me?'

'I'll be fine. Don't worry about me.'

'I'll try to make it back later.' I hoisted my bag onto my shoulder. 'Although I'm not sure about leaving Sammie on her own.'

'Don't even think about coming back. There's no need. Beth's through the worst now and I'm feeling a lot better after a good night's sleep. We've got the appointment with my oncologist on Tuesday so I'll see you then.'

'Okay. Good. I'll pick you up for that.' I'd completely lost the ability to do the simple maths around what time I'd need to collect him. 'We'll make arrangements later. Sorry. My head's all over the place.'

'Go! Send Samantha my love.'

With an apologetic shrug, I closed the door and power-walked along the corridor and out to the car park, feeling sick with worry. What was wrong with people? Who drove up to a remote property at the dead of night and did something like that? The only comfort was Sammie's assurances that they'd caught the perpetrators and that the Grimes boys were already behind bars where they belonged and that she hadn't been alone when it happened. I was a bit confused as to who Fizz was and what she'd been doing at the barn but thank God she had been. Sammie must have been terrified.

* * *

My eyes widened as the farmyard came into view over the hill. I recognised Jonathan's car and Dave's van but who did all the other vehicles belong to?

As I drove closer, I could see that the barn was a hive of activity with a group of people lined up along the wall scrubbing off graffiti. Sammie was in the middle of the farmyard talking to a woman with pink hair. She waved when she spotted me and they both moved aside so I could park.

'I told you there was no need to rush back. I'm fine.' Her tight grip round my waist suggested otherwise.

'I knew you'd be fine. You're a badass. It was the hedgehogs I was worried about.' I stepped back and winced at her face. A track of neat stitches ran along her swollen left cheekbone and there was bruising beneath her eye. She still had the remnants of bruising on her arm from when she'd fainted and now she was in the wars again. I gently stroked her other cheek with my thumb. 'I had to make sure you were okay. I'm so sorry.'

Her eyes glistened. 'It was pretty scary but it's over now. Hopefully properly over.'

'Who are all these people?'

'Friends of Fizz's. 'Come on. I need to introduce you to her. She turned up an hour ago with an army of helpers and they're doing a great job. Dave's inside boarding up the windows until we can get some glass cut and Dad's on hoglet duty.' She took my hand.

* * *

By mid-afternoon, the stonework on the barn was scrubbed clean. The graffiti had been spray-painted this time rather than painted. The words 'gold digger', 'get out' and 'leave' were on the back wall but, more disturbingly, 'all hedgehogs must die' had been sprayed in large letters across the front. Sammie told me that, despite the fear and pain, she'd managed to hold back the tears last night but it had been too dark to see the graffiti then. Seeing those vicious words in the daylight was too much. It broke my heart as she described how she'd sunk to the ground sobbing. Fortunately Jonathan had stayed all night and was able to comfort her and assure her they were just words and the hedgehogs were safe.

Fizz's army of volunteers – a mix of friends and students from the veterinary nursing course she was taking – had been amazing. As for Fizz herself, if her performance across the day had been a job interview, she'd have aced it. Not only had she rounded up everyone off her own back to save Sammie the distress of sorting it out, but she'd driven off with a couple of them at around II a.m. and returned with disposable barbeques and a mountain of food.

She seemed to have an endless pool of ideas around promoting our work and gathering support from the local community. She had connections everywhere from the women's institute to the young farmers and was keen to do anything she could to help us. I was so impressed with her that when Jonathan said she'd mooted the idea last night of work experience at the practice, it was a no-brainer. When did she want to start?

It had been good to hear so much chatter and laughter after such a tough couple of days but, by the time Fizz and her friends said goodbye with enthusiastic waves and offers to call on them anytime, I was craving some quiet time with Sammie.

'The Disney Quads are fed and settled for a bit.' Jonathan stood up and stretched. 'Why don't you two take a mug of tea out to the garden while I feed Leia and Solo?'

Sammie looked up from the chart she'd been filling in. 'Are you sure you don't mind, Dad? You've been up all night.'

'Not *all* night. I had a couple of naps. You've barely seen each other so grab some time together and we can all have a catch-up later.' He gave me a meaningful nod when Sammie wasn't looking. Good. So we were still on for what I'd asked him yesterday. I wasn't sure if the timing would be appropriate but he clearly thought it was okay.

* * *

'It doesn't matter how chaotic things are, I feel so peaceful the minute I sit down on Thomas's bench.' Sammie tilted her head towards the sun and closed her eyes, breathing in long, slow lungfuls of air.

'And life is certainly chaotic at the moment. How's the cheek?'

'Painful but it could have been worse. It hurts most when I smile or laugh and there's been a lot of smiling and laughing today which is unexpected in the circumstances.'

'You really like Fizz, don't you?'

'Oh, Josh, she's amazing. She was so calm last night and then to do all of that off her own back this morning...' She shook her head. 'Talk about experiencing the best and worst of human behaviour in the space of twelve hours. Fizz is going to call round one night during the week to feed the hoglets and discuss how we can best use her. She knows we can't pay but she's eager to help and, given how valuable she's been so far, I think I might be seriously indebted to her cat, Jinks, for bringing her into my life.'

'You sound so positive.'

'I feel it. The vandals have been caught, I'm back to full strength, I've recruited a brilliant volunteer and I'm living Thomas and Gwendoline's dream properly now.' She took my hand in hers. 'And I've found my forever.'

I lifted her hand to my lips and lightly kissed it. 'Speaking of finding forevers, Mum has a date lined up with Alex.'

'She's rung him? That's brilliant news.' She beamed at me then winced. 'Ow! Smiling hurts.'

'She said you could tell me their story because she never got a chance to.'

'And you need to tell me about your dad. Did you ask him about moving in?'

We sipped on our drinks while we brought each other up to speed. Dad had texted to say he hoped Sammie was okay and that Beth couldn't thank us both enough for the kind offer so yes please to moving in.

'I wondered if your dad might be a bit stubborn about it, like a certain person I know.' Sammie gave me a gentle prod. 'I'm really pleased they've accepted. Do they have any idea how long Beth and Lottie will be in hospital?'

'Not sure. Dad was hoping for some guidance later today.'

'I was thinking about your dad's job and him having to

commute to Wilbersgate each day when your practice is so close...'
She raised her eyebrows at me and I had to smile. Always thinking
about others.

'I'd rather he didn't do the commute every day either but having
him back at the practice?' I shrugged. 'I'm not sure. I *do* have a
vacancy for a veterinary nurse but wouldn't it be humiliating for
him to step into that role at the same place where he was a partner?'

'I never thought of it like that. Yeah, could be awkward.'

'It's probably best to see what his oncologist says on Tuesday. He
might be out of action for some time and work will be the last thing
on his mind.'

As we walked hand in hand towards the barn, my stomach
tightened into a knot. We'd had such an uplifting half hour on
Thomas's bench just now. I hoped me involving Jonathan wasn't
about to undo that positivity.

49

'What are you two scheming?' I looked from Dad to Josh and back to Dad again. They were acting really weird. With all the hoglets fed, Dad had suggested we move over to the farmhouse for a change of scenery. It was fine at first. Josh gave him an update from the hospital and Dad told him about a couple of emergency cases at the practice yesterday. Then it fell silent and they kept exchanging meaningful looks across the lounge as though they wanted to say something but each wanted the other to start the conversation.

'We're not scheming anything,' Dad insisted.

'You are such a liar. Something's up and, if one of you doesn't spill it soon, I'll go over to the barn and ask the hedgehogs if they know what's going on. I'll probably get more sense out of them.'

'Okay.' Josh nodded his head. 'You know how I thought that my parents had a good marriage and you discovered that wasn't quite the truth so you suggested I have a word with my mum?'

'Yes...?'

'When we were talking about your mum yesterday, you said that she'd been a lovely person before you came along and I wondered whether it could be a similar situation where you haven't quite had the full picture so I went to see your dad on the way to hospital...'

I stared at him, wide-eyed with disbelief. I was really close to my dad and Josh knew it but this wasn't something I wanted Dad to know about. Not yet anyway. He was still consumed with guilt that he hadn't done more to stop Mum's abhorrent behaviour despite my recollection of him constantly being my shield. The last thing I'd ever want was for him to think that his perceived lack of action had contributed to me not wanting children.

'I didn't say why I was asking,' Josh added quickly, placing a calming hand on my leg. He looked over to my Dad. 'Will you tell Sammie what you told me?'

Dad sat forward and clasped his hands between his legs. 'When I met your mum at her cousin's wedding, I'd finished college and was preparing to leave Whitsborough Bay to train as a vet. The last thing I was looking for was a girlfriend but love has a habit of turning up when you're not expecting it or looking for it. We had two months before I left and spent every minute together. Those two months were amazing and, by the end, I knew I wanted to be with her forever so I asked her to marry me before I left for university.'

He smiled wistfully. 'As I told Josh, she was a lot like you back then – kind, sensitive, always putting others first. I actually got cold feet about going away and leaving her but she insisted I didn't give up on my dreams saying it was only four years and then we'd have a lifetime together.

'When I was qualified and got a job, we rented a small two-bedroom terrace in town but going from a long-distance relationship to living together was tough. Your mum had built a life for herself in Whitsborough Bay without me. She had friends and a routine and it was hard for both of us to adjust. Your mum liked things done a certain way. She had a quick temper which I'd never seen before and she could be really moody but it's not like I was perfect either. I hated arguing so I'd go quiet and sulky which wound her up even more.'

I didn't say anything but this was unexpected detail. Josh had been right to question their relationship before I came along. It sounded like things hadn't been quite so rosy between them after all. I nodded encouragingly for Dad to continue.

'Most of the time it was really good and, despite the challenges, I never doubted that your mum was the one. But there were bad times. Way before we got married, I saw flashes of how she is now.'

'See!' Josh took my hand in his. 'You're *nothing* like your mum. You don't need to worry about that.'

'Why would you think you were?' Dad asked.

I looked at his bewildered expression and squirmed. I couldn't keep it from him. 'The subject of having children has cropped up recently and I told Josh I didn't want any and the reason for that is...' I paused and bit my lip, hating how much my revelation was likely to hurt him. 'The reason is because I'm worried I'll be like Mum. I thought she'd been just like me then changed after she had me. I know it sounds stupid when I say it out loud but the idea of the same thing happening to me is terrifying.'

Dad's cheeks paled and he shook his head. 'Oh, God, Sammie. I never dreamed you might feel like that. I should have been clearer about how things were. You absolutely will *not* become your mum if you have children.'

'How do you know? You just said you only saw flashes of bad temper and moods but, after I was born, that's all we ever saw.'

Dad winced. 'There's a reason why your mum turned on you.'

'I know. She never wanted me.'

He covered his face with his hands and shook his head. 'There's something else. I should have told you this a long time ago but it wasn't... I promised your mum but...' He shook his head again then removed his hands and looked at me, his eyes full of pain. 'I think it's time you knew everything.'

'There's more?' My stomach felt in knots. What more could there possibly be that Mum hadn't already blurted out in anger?

'Your mum was really excited about the wedding and, while we were planning that, things were the best they'd ever been. My best mate from university, Lee, came to stay one weekend. Your mum had met him several times and they'd got on well so the three of us went on a pub crawl. Your mum wasn't a big drinker but Lee was and we all got a bit carried away. I know my limits and drew the line at the tequila shots but they both kept going. By the time we got to the club, your mum was behaving strangely. She was aggressive towards me but flirty towards Lee and, when we were on the dance floor, she kept pushing me aside and giving him all her attention. He wasn't encouraging it. He wasn't the sort to try anything. Inevitably we had an argument and she stormed off to the toilets. She'd said some cutting things and I was seething. Lee felt bad because he'd been the one plying her with drink so he suggested I go home to calm down and he'd wait for her, let her sober up then walk her home.'

He ran his hands down his face and steepled them under his chin, his eyes downcast.

'Lee didn't walk her home. He couldn't find her so he assumed she'd left with me in the end. He met a woman and went back to her place.' His eyes filled with tears and he released a shuddery breath. 'I got a call from the hospital at about half three in the morning to say your mum needed collecting. I wasn't prepared for what I saw. She had a black eye, a bust lip, loads of cuts and bruises. She claimed she'd fallen down some steps then passed out in the alleyway where she was found.'

'Claimed?' The word came out as a whisper and I shuddered. *Please don't say it!* But my thumping heart told me he was going to.

'I came home from work about six weeks later to find her curled up in a ball on the bathroom floor with a positive pregnancy test kit in her hand. She never heard him approaching. She never saw his face but she could still feel the knife against her throat and smell his sweat.'

He rubbed at his eyes as he fought to contain his emotions but I could hear it all in his voice and see it in his face – the guilt and the pain and the loss.

'She told me that the nurses at the hospital believed she'd been attacked but she'd been adamant she'd fallen. I asked her why she hadn't let them call the police and I still remember the exact words she said to me. "An extremely drunk female wearing a short skirt and flimsy top who walks home alone after flirting with another man and arguing with her boyfriend about it is asking to be raped, isn't she?" And suddenly I understood. I hope things have changed now but, back then, she'd have been poked and prodded and made to feel like the guilty party so she'd buried it deep and hoped it would go away. Only it wasn't going to go away.'

'She had the baby?' Josh asked.

Dad shook his head. 'She couldn't. She thought about adoption but she hated the idea of the baby growing up and discovering their origins and maybe coming in search of her.'

I moved to the other end of the sofa and reached across for Dad's hand. 'I'm so sorry.'

'Your mum was never the same after that. She told me I didn't have to marry her now that she was "soiled goods". I was never going to stop loving her because some bastard had violated her. I also had this desperate need to protect her because I blamed myself for leaving her. I knew how drunk she was. It was my responsibility to make sure she got home safely – not Lee's – and I'd let her down. The only way she'd agree to getting married was if we eloped. She couldn't bear the thought of everyone looking at her, convinced they'd somehow all know. All those big plans she'd been so excited about were shelved. We went away for a weekend with Louise and Simon and came back as Mr and Mrs Wishaw.'

'Did they know?' I asked.

'Louise did but, to this day, Simon doesn't. Chloe doesn't. Your grandparents never knew. They were really hurt by us eloping. That's what started the deterioration in her relationship with them.'

'So it wasn't just because they hated how she treated me?'

'No. That didn't help but the decline was way before that. They didn't understand why we'd changed our minds and married without them. They asked questions that she didn't want to answer so she started to push them away, stopped visiting so often, was aloof when she did.'

'That's awful. Poor Mum.'

'When she fell pregnant with your sister, she was so excited. Perhaps overly so. Being pregnant and preparing for motherhood was like a project for her – a focus on something pure for the future that had nothing to do with what happened that night. She pored over baby books, practised making her own baby food, knitted and sewed loads of clothes. And then we lost the baby and she became convinced it was her punishment for not going through with the previous pregnancy.' He slumped back in the chair and shook his head. 'You know the rest.'

'I can't believe she went through that.' I smoothed the pile on one of the scatter cushions beside me, trying to get my head round it. How horrific! It explained so much. Mum claimed she hadn't wanted me because she hadn't wanted another baby after losing my sister at seven months but it clearly ran so much deeper than that. She'd thought my sister had been taken away from her because she was unworthy and couldn't face it happening again so she completely shut herself off to me. No wonder she'd fallen apart.

'She was a good woman, Sammie. She still is somewhere deep

down but we're talking over thirty years ago when this happened. Mental health was barely a thing. Counselling wasn't commonplace. When people lost their way either the support wasn't there, or it was and we didn't know about it or how to access it. As for going to the police, she saw no point and kept saying it was her fault.'

'I still think she needs help.'

'So do I, poppet. I actually think she has post-traumatic stress disorder but I've lost count of how many times I've had conversations with her about it over the years. She claims she's dealt with it and that her relationship with you was nothing to do with what happened. I say it has everything to do with it.'

'I agree.'

He sighed. 'If we bring this all back to the starting point and Josh's conversation with me about whether you're like your mum, it's an answer of two halves. You have your mum's best qualities. You're like the Debs I remember from our early years. One spring evening a sequence of events fundamentally changed her. It scarred her physically and it scarred her mentally and the Debs who became your mother... she's what *he* did to her. And what I did to her because I failed her every step of the way.' His voice cracked as tears rolled down his cheeks.

I rushed to his side and flung my arms round his neck. 'No, Dad. You tried but you can't save someone who doesn't want to be saved.'

It was just as well that I hadn't promised Dad I'd be back at the hospital on Sunday night or even see him on Monday. After Jonathan's unexpected revelation, there was no way I could leave Sammie on her own.

'I'm struggling to take it all in,' she said as we fed the Disney Quads. 'I can't believe she went through all that. I'm not surprised Dad thinks she has PTSD. It doesn't sound she ever dealt with the rape or any of the fallout from it.'

'Do you think she ever will?'

Sammie shrugged. 'I'd like to think so but she's tried to bury it for thirty-two years already so I don't hold out much hope.' She ran her finger over Belle's tummy as the hoglet greedily sucked from the syringe. 'It explains so many things, though. Not just about her behaviour towards Dad and me but other comments she's made over time.'

'Such as?'

'You know how I've always said she idolises Chloe? Never had a bad word to say about her or to her but now I'm remembering that, when we teenagers, she used to obsess about Chloe wearing short skirts for a night out. She'd go on about it sending out "the wrong message" and beg Chloe to go home and change but, of course, nobody tells my cousin what to do. I remember them having a few heated debates about it but I just put it down to Mum being all adult-y on her.'

'She never lectured you about it?'

Sammie rolled her eyes. 'Have you *ever* seen me wear a short skirt? Not my style at all. She used to lecture us both about knowing our drinking limits and never walking home alone. Parents say these things to their kids but, now that I'm thinking about it, there was an intensity to the way Mum said it that clearly came from personal experience.'

'Did she only say that when you were going out with Chloe?'

She scrunched her forehead up as she pondered the question. 'Do you know what? She didn't. I still got the warnings when Chloe wasn't with me although it was always like a barked order from a military sergeant rather than given with genuine motherly concern.'

'But she still said it so maybe there was some motherly concern there.'

Sammie laughed and rolled her eyes at me.

The logical next step – what Sammie would probably do if our positions were reversed – would be to make more of the chink in her mum's armour. The downside was that it might send Sammie scurrying back to Whitsborough Bay, hoping to start over. I hated the thought of her getting hurt again so I remained silent and left her to mull it over, hoping that was the kinder thing to do.

51

SAMANTHA

Bank holiday Monday dawned and the first thing on my mind when I woke up was Dad's revelation about Mum. I could hardly believe it. Yesterday, my heart breaking for her, I'd wanted to drive straight over to Whitsborough Bay but what good would it do anyone? It might make me feel better to try to give comfort but, if she knew Dad had shared her secret, it would likely drive a wedge between them. She could turn an amicable divorce process into something ugly and I couldn't risk that. Dad had enough stress without me adding to it.

I kept recalling more things she'd said and done over the years that clearly stemmed from what had happened that fateful evening. If only she'd talked to someone about it, our relationship could have been so different. Yet she'd never wanted to talk about it. When I'd gone across to Whitsborough Bay in March to see whether we could find a way to move forward, she'd accused me of ambushing her and said, 'What's the obsession with talking? Why does everything need to be dissected and analysed?' At the time, I'd assumed they were just words thrown out in anger but now I knew differently. Dad and Auntie Louise had tried so many times to get her to open up and address the past but she'd refused to do so. Had she been afraid that it would all come out if she talked to me?

She'd accused me of turning her parents against her and taking her husband away from her but now I knew she'd pushed them away herself. Had it been easier for her to project the hate and blame for everything onto me? I did, after all, have a name and a face. Her attacker didn't.

* * *

Josh spoke to his dad once we were up and organised but Paul insisted he was fine and Josh should stay at the farm with me. I was glad he did because we had a lovely, relaxing day together, tending to the hogs but also walking round the farm, hand in hand, talking about everything that had happened over recent weeks.

He was worried that he'd interfered by going to Dad but I assured him it was the best thing he could have done because now I knew everything. I was devastated for Mum for what she'd been through and for Dad too but, the more I talked it over with Josh, the more positive I felt about my relationship with her. It filled in gaps. It made me feel like Mum's behaviour towards me was not as personal as I'd previously believed.

* * *

In the evening, PC Sunning and Fizz's dad, Sergeant Kinsella, visited Hedgehog Hollow with a full update. As soon as they'd got my attackers back to the station, they'd been able to confirm who they were because they were both in the system. The driver turned out to be Cody Grimes's younger brother, Connor, and the other degenerate – the one who'd thrown the egg box – was one of his mates. Both were on parole – Connor from prison and his friend from a youth detention centre – so they'd been sent straight back. They'd admitted responsibility for all the incidents so I didn't need to worry there was someone else at large.

I asked about other family members picking up the mantle and there never being an end to the harassment. Sergeant Kinsella assured us that they'd already spoken to the immediate family and there would be visits to the extended family over the next few days. The message was loud and clear about what the repercussions would be if they so much as sneezed in the direction of the farm.

'It's finally over,' I said to Josh when they'd gone. 'I honestly couldn't have coped with any more.'

He hugged me close and I closed my eyes. No more attacks, no more trying to work two full-time jobs and no more believing I'd caused all Mum's problems. Things were looking more positive than they ever had.

On Tuesday morning I drove to Wilbersgate to collect Dad for his hospital appointment and reflected on the police visit. Sammie seemed comforted by what Sergeant Kinsella said but I wasn't convinced it was over. I'd read the letters Gwendoline's loathsome family had bombarded her and then Thomas with over the past four decades. Hate like that passed down from generation to generation wasn't going to disappear just like that. If anything, they were the sort of family who'd blame Sammie for Brynn, Cody and Connor being in prison. I wouldn't say anything to worry her but I'd certainly be extra vigilant about security.

Dad's oncologist, Dr Burrows, confirmed a date in June for the second round of chemotherapy but anticipated that a stem cell transplant would also be needed. I heard Dad's sharp intake of breath at those words. He kept a poker face but I knew that, like me, he'd been hoping it wasn't going to go that far.

Dr Burrows turned to me. 'I understand you want to be tested?'

'Yes, please.'

'Okay. Before we do that, let me explain what we're looking for. We need a donor who matches or closely matches your dad's tissue type. When someone needs blood, there are lots of donor matches because there are only eight blood groups. With tissue type, there are significantly more variations. Each person's tissue is made up of five genes, each of which has two variations, one inherited from the mother and one from the father. Biological siblings are therefore usually the best match for donation because they have the same parents but children are not. We don't need it to be a ten out of ten match but it needs to be closer than a child is likely to be.'

He opened a drawer on a wall unit and removed a package. 'I'm very happy to test you today, Josh, but I need to know first that you understand how unlikely it is that you'll be a match for your dad.'

'I understand.' Didn't mean I wouldn't get my hopes up. I couldn't help it. I was going to be on tenterhooks waiting for the results.

'Would you be prepared to go on the register in case you're a match for someone else? Testing you for your dad is not conditional on your answer, by the way.'

'Erm, yes. Definitely. I hadn't thought of that.'

'Thank you. We're desperately short of donors and especially male ones. Let's get you tested then.' He washed his hands then ripped open the package. 'Simple cheek swab. Mouth open... and all done. I'll get it over to the lab and you'll get a text with the results tomorrow.'

'Great. I'm assuming you've got no matches for Dad's tissue type in your database?' I knew it was a silly question but I felt I needed the spoken confirmation so that I didn't hold out false hope there too.

Dr Burrows removed his glasses and gave me a weak smile. 'I'm sorry. It's the first thing we check but there simply aren't anywhere near enough donors. Only 2 per cent of the UK population are registered.'

'My girlfriend wants to get tested and we have a few friends who'd probably be willing too. Do they all need to make appointments?'

'It's quick and easy through the post. Here.' He opened a cupboard and removed a box. 'There are twenty testing kits in here, all to be sent back to the lab individually. Do what you can and all I'd ask is you return any kits you don't use.' He opened another drawer and grabbed some flyers. 'They can specifically be tested for a match for your dad but I'd appreciate it if you can encourage them to join the register. You've seen how quick and painless testing is. Contrary to the myth, collection is perhaps a little uncomfortable rather than painful. It's all in the leaflets. Have a read.'

We stayed a little longer exploring more about plans for Dad. After the appointment, he wanted to stay at the hospital and said that Mum had arranged to bring Archie through again so she'd drop him back at the flat on her way home.

As I drove back towards the practice, I rang Sammie.

'I'll meet you in the practice car park,' she said after I'd updated her about the appointment. 'You can do my swab and we'll get it straight in the post. We can spend some time ringing round friends tonight then one of us can go for a drive to deliver the kits. The sooner they're done, the sooner we'll know the results.'

* * *

Between hoglet feeds that evening, we were both pretty much welded to our phones, ringing any local friends we could think of to ask if they'd be willing to be tested, then I hit the road delivering kits. At thirty-three and thirty-five respectively, Rich and Dave were above the ideal age category but we decided it was worth a try and made thirty-five our cut-off point. Hannah and Toby were willing and several of my mates confirmed they were happy to be tested too.

'I can't believe it, mate,' Lewis said when I called him. 'I know what your dad did to you was shitty but nobody deserves this.'

'I know. It was a hell of a shock.'

'I bet! It's good you're back in touch, though. I'm in, no question. How about you drop off a kit for me at work and one for our lad cos he'll be up for it. Bring some of those leaflets too and I'll have a word with my manager. We have loads of staff in that age bracket so I'm confident we could drum up volunteers if you can get some more testing kits.'

'Lewis, you absolute legend. Cheers, mate. I'll drop them off later.'

* * *

Spurred on by Lewis's offer to look into a testing programme at Aversford Manor, I called a special staff meeting on Wednesday morning.

Looking round the curious gazes was reminiscent of the last time I'd called a special meeting – after *the incident*. I hadn't wanted to share the very personal reason for Dad's departure but Beth had friends on the team so I knew there'd be gossip and rumours. I'd therefore prepared a basic statement and hoped I could deliver it with confidence and my dignity intact: 'With immediate effect Paul Alderson is no longer a partner at this veterinary practice. His long-term girlfriend, Beth Giddings, has also left.' I'd winced at the gasps but the shocked expressions suggested that most of them hadn't known about our sordid little love triangle. 'I have no plans to change the practice name as that's my granddad's legacy. I was *not* aware of the relationship between Beth and my father and that's all I'm going to say about the matter. I'd appreciate it if you could respect what a difficult time this is for my mum and me and refrain from discussing it.'

Facing the team again now, I recalled how excruciatingly uncomfortable that meeting had been. This one was uncomfortable too but for different reasons. I cleared my throat and glanced towards Jonathan who gave me an encouraging nod.

'Most of you here worked with my dad, Paul, and those who joined the practice after he left will likely have heard about his legacy.' I noticed a couple of smirks but it was understandable; it *was* a major piece of gossip.

'My dad is ill. He has Hodgkin lymphoma which is a type of blood cancer and his chemotherapy treatment hasn't been working so it's fairly certain he'll need a stem cell transplant...' I finished explaining what that meant and the age bracket needed for donors. 'I'm going to leave some leaflets in the staffroom for anyone who wants to read more and there's information online. I have some testing kits in my office. There is no expectation on any of you and I can assure you that there will be no change in how anyone is treated whether they volunteer or not, but if anyone aged thirty-five or under would be willing to be tested, please come and see me today or later this week.'

* * *

I'd only been back in my office five minutes when the first staff member appeared requesting a kit. Across the morning, there were further requests. Those who'd worked with Dad expressed their shock and asked me to pass on their best wishes and those who'd never met him said they'd heard good things about his ability as a vet and were keen to help if they could.

Then came the text I'd been both longing for and dreading in equal measures. My hands shook as I opened it.

Not a strong enough match.

Numbly, I sank back into my chair staring at it, willing for the

words to change. I'd been warned. I knew the odds. But I'd dared to
hope.

I'm not sure how long I sat there but I suddenly felt quite claus-
trophobic, desperate for space to breathe. I grabbed my keys and
headed for Alder Lea and this time I managed to unlock the door
and step inside.

It felt strange being in the house. It had that distinctive smell of
somewhere that hadn't been lived in – a foisty aroma that screamed
for fresh air.

I perched on the edge of the sofa, feeling guilty that I'd abandoned the home that my grandparents had designed and built
themselves and had loved so much. I'd let them down, not only for
walking out on their home, but also for walking out on their son.
They'd have been disappointed in what Dad had done but they'd
also have been disappointed in my reaction.

Sadness overcame me as I wandered round the rest of the shell
of a house. It had once been a happy family home and it would be
again. I'd get it refurbished and, when Beth and Dad were suffi-
ciently recovered, they could have it. If the worst happened and
Dad didn't recover – I shuddered at the thought – it would be Beth's
home if she wanted it and I'd do everything I could to help her,
Archie and Lottie.

As for the more immediate future, the reaction of my team had
inspired me. So many of them had expressed how much they loved
my dad and missed working with him. Even though I'd told
Sammie it could be embarrassing for him to accept a more junior
position at the practice, it was obvious now that I'd been protecting
myself. I'd been embarrassed and humiliated by his actions and it
had taken a lot to walk tall at work again. But this was about him,
not me.

Dad had returned to work today in Wilbersgate. He hadn't
wanted to leave Beth but she'd insisted. He was going to need a

significant amount of time off for his next round of chemo and I got the impression money was tight; hardly surprising considering he'd walked out of his marriage with nothing and had taken a massive salary drop.

When he was settled at Hedgehog Hollow, I'd offer him the position of veterinary nurse at my practice. If he accepted, his role would be different from before and it might be a little strange for both of us at first, but what hadn't changed was the admiration and respect the team had for him. Having Dad surrounded by people who cared and understood was more important than any discomfort I might feel.

53

SAMANTHA

The sofa bed arrived on Thursday afternoon and I was in the process of ripping the plastic covering off it when a text came through from the hospital. My heart sank. I wasn't a match either. I sank down onto the plastic, staring at my phone.

'Hello? Samantha?' Connie's voice from the barn doorway brought me out of my trance.

'Sorry. I didn't even hear you arrive.'

'Everything okay?' she asked coming closer, holding a squirming Archie in her arms. With Paul at the hospital every non-working hour, it seemed easier on everyone – and less disruptive – if Archie stayed with Connie until they were ready to move into Hedgehog Hollow.

'I've just had my text through from the hospital and I'm not a match for Paul.'

'Aw, sweetheart. I'm sorry.'

'We both tried so hard not to get our hopes up but Josh was crushed yesterday and now I have to give him more bad news.'

'Don't give up. Someone somewhere will be a match. I'm sure of it.'

'Hopefully. Is this a fleeting visit or do you have time for a cuppa?'

'A cuppa would be great.'

'Why don't you take Archie round to the garden and I'll bring the drinks out?'

* * *

Connie was strapping Archie into his buggy by Thomas's bench when I approached with the drinks.

She passed him a cup of juice and placed a tub of chopped fruit on the tray. 'I thought this might be the best way for us to have a drink in peace.'

I handed her a mug and we both sat down.

'I'd ask if you're missing teaching but so much has happened, I bet you've barely had a chance to think about it.'

I smiled. 'Teaching seems a lifetime ago now, even though it has only been a fortnight. I loved that job but I love the hedgehogs more and it was the right decision to leave. Not that I actually made that decision. Your sister did that but I'm glad she did.'

She laughed. 'So very Lauren but it was for the best.'

'Definitely.' I took a sip of my tea. 'Josh tells me you're going on a date with Alex. Presumably the phone call went well.'

Her eyes twinkled. 'I was so nervous about ringing him but it couldn't have gone better. I'd thought he might say, "Connie who?" but he said he was thrilled to hear from me and had been kicking himself for not asking for my number because he'd love to take me out for dinner some time. Lauren's coming round to look after Archie tonight and Alex is taking me out to The Silver Birch.'

'How lovely. Josh and I had our first proper date there.'

'And look at you two now. I'm hoping it will work its magic on Alex and me.'

'I have a feeling it will. Although I think the magic happened when you had your moment with him four years ago and destiny has simply been waiting for the right time to bring you two together.'

'I think you could be right. It wouldn't have worked back then. I wouldn't have thought I was ready to let anyone in again now but this is Alex we're talking about. I'm so excited! I've already planned what to wear and how to do my hair.' She shook her head and laughed. 'Listen to me. I sound like a fourteen-year-old heading out on my first ever date.'

'It's sweet. It shows how much you care. Are you going to tell him where you know him from?'

She picked up Archie's cup which he'd dropped onto the ground and gave it a wipe before handing it back to him. 'Yes. It'll be hard not to blurt it straight out but I want to see his reaction properly so I'm going to have to try to control myself and wait until we get to the restaurant.'

'He might have already worked it out for himself.'

'I'd love it if he has. I guess I'll know either way in a few hours.'

* * *

Fizz had arranged to come round to help feed the hoglets. 'We've had another three adults admitted this week and I've just had another arrive,' I told her. 'You probably passed the person who brought him on your way up the track.'

'Perfect timing! What have we got?'

The hog was curled up in a bowl on the scales as I'd been weighing him when Fizz arrived, ready to prepare his painkillers and antibiotics. I scribbled his weight down on his chart.

'This is Neo. Large adult male, seriously dehydrated and in a pretty bad way. He's got several cuts on his head, probably caused by a dog or a fox, and a bad case of flystrike. Bit smelly as a result.' I pointed to his head. 'You see these scabs?'

'Oh my God! They're moving!'

I nodded. 'Maggots. Poor thing must be in a lot of pain so I want to get some painkillers into him as a priority then get him cleaned up as quickly as I can.' I started filling the syringes as I spoke. 'I won't be able to let you work on him as speed is of the essence to minimise stress and pain but I'll explain what I'm doing. Would you be my photographer?'

The woman who dropped him off had only just found him in her garden but I'd read of cases where people spotted injured hogs and did nothing until the following day. It takes about four hours from flies laying eggs to maggots hatching, quicker in hotter weather. Although the photos would make for gruesome viewing, I wanted to show how bad things could get if injured hogs weren't tended to quickly.

Fizz picked up my phone and started snapping from various angles. 'It looks sore.'

'Sore. Itchy. And he'll have been trying to scratch it which will have made it even worse.' I administered the injections. 'We'll make you better, little one. Hang on in there.'

I opened up a fishing tackle box and lifted out a head torch. 'I need to clean the wounds and, because they're infested, I need to ensure I've got everything out so the torch helps. This box is full of all sorts of useful things for cleaning out wounds like cotton buds, pads, tweezers...' I placed a pile of cotton wool pads on the table.

'Are those mascara brushes?'

I smiled. 'I picked up the idea from another rescue centre. They're great for cleaning round the spines.'

I lifted Neo from his bowl and placed him on the layers of blue paper towel then lifted a small knife. 'This is going to be messy. I'll start with cutting away the scabs because we need to get all the maggots and any yucky stuff out of those.'

'This is so gross but so fascinating.'

When I'd removed the scabs, I picked up a can of special spray and shook it. 'This part is magic. Watch!'

'Oh. My. God! That is super awesome!'

The spray drew all the maggots out of the wound and it was astonishing how many there were which, even with my extra-bright head torch, I could never have seen and removed myself.

I worked with the various items in my toolkit, cleaning out the wounds before a thorough flushing with saline solution and a special wound cleanser. I attended to a couple of small patches of flystrike further down his body where he had grazes rather than cuts, then settled Neo into his crate with a fresh bowl of water.

'Wow! That was so amazing to watch.' Fizz scrolled through the photos on my phone. 'You've just saved his life.'

I removed the head torch and smiled at her. 'He wouldn't have survived without this treatment but we're not out the woods yet. You know yourself from being around animals that they can go downhill fast. The shock and stress can be too much for them. Hopefully that won't be the case for Neo and we'll be releasing him when he's healed and hydrated.'

'Can he be released in my garden when he's better?'

'I don't see why not. We prefer to release where they came from if it's a suitable environment but the woman who dropped Neo off said she's moving house next week so it's not an option. They need releasing where hedgehogs are known to be as that suggests there aren't many predators, particularly badgers. Seeing as the hoglets were from your garden, releasing Neo there is as good a place as any.'

She clapped her hands together and grinned. 'Yay! So what's next?'

'We need to clean out the crates and put out fresh food and water for all the adults and the hoglets will be ready for feeding any minute.'

Josh arrived at the barn at that point. 'Sorry I'm so late. A couple of complications during surgery but all sorted now. Hi, Fizz, how are you?'

'Brilliant. I've been watching Sam with Neo and she was awesome.'

Josh raised an eyebrow at me. 'Neo?'

'New arrival. I'll fill you in later. Erm... I got my text.' I grimaced.

'No match?' He sighed. 'It was a long shot. They're all a long shot – Dr Burrows was very clear on that – but someone's surely going to come close.'

I turned to Fizz. 'Josh's dad has blood cancer and very likely needs a stem cell transplant. Josh and I have both been tested but we're not matches.'

'What does being a donor involve?'

I cleared away the equipment and wiped down the table while Josh started to explain. The hoglets had started squeaking so, with the heat pads plugged in and covered in fleecy blankets once more, I took them out their crates and conversation paused while Fizz squealed with excitement at how much they'd grown since the weekend.

'Sorry,' she said to Josh. 'You have my attention again now. Please continue.'

When he'd finished, she nodded her head solemnly. 'Sign me up. How many tests can you get hold of?'

'Probably quite a lot. Why?'

'I reckon I can get you a hundred volunteers. Easily.'

I nearly dropped Aurora as I stared at her in disbelief. 'Where from?'

'Friends. Young farmers. University. Most of the people I mix with regularly are in that age bracket. I'll have a word with my dad and I reckon the police would be up for it. Ooh, and you could spread the word round the TEC and the sixth form. I bet there's loads of students who have no idea what's involved and would sign up when they do. Someone from the hospital might even come and do a mass testing session which will probably have a better hit rate because some numpties would be bound to take the kit home then never get round to doing it or they'd do it and not post it.' She rolled her eyes. 'If you email me some details and your contact at the hospital, I'm happy to arrange it all.'

Josh and I exchanged astonished looks. 'You'd really do all of that?' he asked.

She grinned. 'You want to ask why, don't you?'

He looked sheepish. 'Yes, but it sounds rude. The thing is, we've only just met you and you don't even know my dad. It's a big undertaking and so generous.'

'When I was little, I was *that* kid. You know the weird, quirky one who talks to themselves and approaches life a little differently? I never really fit in. I wasn't bullied but I didn't have friends either. I didn't mind because my grandparents had this amazing farm so I spent loads of time there. My grandma would often ask whether I wanted to invite friends to the farm, particularly when it was lambing season because they could help feed them. I'd make excuses but then I admitted that I didn't have any friends I could ask. She said to me, "You know how to get lots of friends, don't you? Always be kind." It went way over my head at first but I watched the other kids and started to work out what she meant. They often said nasty things and fell out with each other and I could see how much hurt it caused so I looked for things I could do that would be kind instead. If somebody fell over and scraped their knee, I'd be the one to clean them up. If somebody didn't have a snack, I shared mine. I didn't make a big deal out of it. I didn't expect anything back but, by the time I finished primary school, I had more friends than I knew what to do with. I think it helped that I was nice to everyone, even the class bully. I was never in a gang and never had a best friend and I've stuck to that throughout life. Kindness and friendship attracts kindness and friendship and makes everyone happy, including me.'

I smiled at her. 'That's so lovely.'

Josh looked from me to Fizz and back again. 'The pair of you are like kindred spirits.' He turned to Fizz. 'Sammie's the kindest person I've ever met. What was that saying your Gramps had, Sam? Something about giving roses and keeping the fragrance.'

'The fragrance always stays in the hand that gives the rose. It was apparently something Nanna used to say.'

'No way!' Fizz cried. 'That's what my grandma always says and I've *never* come across anyone who's heard it before.'

Josh laughed. '*Definitely* kindred spirits.'

'That is so weird,' Fizz said. 'Wouldn't it be strange if our grand-parents knew each other and that's why they both knew that phrase?'

'It's certainly possible. Mine aren't with us anymore but they were both Wolds born and bred. They lived in Little Tilbury for most of their married life.'

'I'll have to ask Grandma. What were their names?'

'Elizabeth and William Danby. They'd have both been coming up to seventy-seven.'

'About the same age as mine. I'm seeing them at the weekend so I'll check.'

We continued chatting about Fizz's childhood as we fed the hoglets then moved onto the adults. It turned out that she and Josh knew a lot of the same people although that was hardly surprising because Fizz seemed to know everyone.

Josh went over to the farmhouse to prepare a meal and invited

Fizz to stay. Over dinner, she wanted to know how the setting up of the rescue centre had come about so I told her the full story including my uncertainty as to whether I was the right person to fulfil Thomas and Gwendoline's dreams.

Fizz widened her eyes in surprise. 'You really had doubts?'

I nodded. 'It was huge. I knew very little about hedgehogs at the time and I knew nothing about running a charity. It's been one heck of a learning curve.'

'After seeing you with Neo earlier, you are absolutely the perfect person, and you seemed as though you'd been handling hedgehogs for years rather than months.'

'Thank you, Fizz. That means a lot.'

Fizz had to leave to meet a friend after dinner so I walked her to her car. 'I've just realised that we haven't discussed what volunteering here on a more regular basis might involve.'

'It's fine. I decided it could wait.' She smiled. 'As soon as you said about Josh's dad, I knew you'd have had too much on your plate to think about it and, actually, you probably need more time to settle into the full-time role before you decide how you could best use me. So how about we leave it that I'll come and help with the hoglets a couple of nights a week but I'm at your disposal whenever you're ready to have something more structured?'

'That would be great. I've got so many ideas about what we could do but, you're right, there is so much else going on up here at the moment.' I tapped my forehead.

Fizz gave me a quick hug. 'Thanks for letting me be part of something so special.'

'Thank you for wanting to be part of it.'

As I waved her goodbye, I couldn't stop smiling. I went round to the back of the house. The security light lit the garden but the meadow beyond it was in darkness.

'Did you send her to us?' I asked. 'I think you did. Thank you so

much.' I pressed my fingers to my lips and blew my kiss in the direction of the meadow. 'Goodnight, both of you.' The gentle breeze
kissed my cheek and I knew they were there, looking out for me as
always, doing what they could to help the centre thrive.

It had been a month of ups and downs but, as we moved into
June next week, things were looking very promising. Fizz had
sparkled into our life, Josh was rebuilding his relationship with his
dad, Connie had found her 'moment-man' and there'd be no more
visits from the Grimes family. All we needed now was to find a
donor for Paul and for Mum to find a way to start to heal. The odds
of finding a stem cell donor match for Paul were not good but I
favoured them over the odds of Mum addressing the past. If only
there was something I could say or do.

I opened my eyes on Saturday morning and gazed down at Sammie asleep beside me, her dark hair fanned round her on the pillow. Her left cheek held little reminder of the assault a week ago. The bruising had faded to beige and yellow and, with the stitches now out, there was a faint red line which would be barely visible over time.

'Mmm, that was a good sleep.' Without opening her eyes, she reached out towards me and I clasped her hand in mine. 'My dad's a saint for doing the full nightshift.'

'He certainly is, especially as this weekend is going to be manic.'

Beth had been discharged on Wednesday afternoon. She'd be on strong painkillers for some time and needed to avoid heavy lifting – not that she could do much with a broken arm and collar bone – but was making good progress otherwise. She'd been staying in a room at the hospital since then for easy access to Lottie who would hopefully be discharged tomorrow or on Monday at which point they'd officially move in.

I'd always thought Beth rented her flat but it turned out that

Dad actually owned it, having bought it for Beth to live in about a year after they met. He'd managed to let it out to a work colleague with immediate effect so Dave had stepped in yet again and offered his van today for moving their personal belongings out. Rich had swapped a shift so he could help too. Three pairs of hands should make speedy work of it.

'What time is it?' Sammie asked.

'Half seven.'

She opened her eyes and gave me a sleepy smile. 'You realise that this could be one of the last times we're alone in the house for a long time?' She shimmied closer and lightly kissed me. 'Better make the most of it.'

'Dave will be here in fifteen minutes.' My objection wasn't very convincing as I surrendered to her touch.

* * *

'We've had our test results back,' Dave said as we headed down the farm track a little later. I knew from his regretful tone that it was a no before he even said it. 'Sorry, mate.'

I sighed. 'Not to worry. It was a long shot but worth trying.'

'Hang in there,' Rich said. 'I'm sure somebody will be a match. Or the chemo will work.'

'Yeah, hopefully.' There were no matches from work so far although not all the results had come back yet. Hannah had phoned last night to say neither she nor Toby were matches. Each negative result filled me with panic that I could lose Dad, followed by guilt that my stubbornness had kept us apart for so long. Sammie had been such a tower of strength, trying to keep me focused on the time I had with Dad now – however long or short that might be – instead of regretting the wasted months.

'What have you both been up to this week?' I asked, keen to change the subject.

'Good week for me. Lots of saves and no fatalities.' Rich was an ambulance paramedic. It was how he'd met Sammie after she found Thomas collapsed.

'Big barn conversion over at the coast near Roxborough Cliffs for me,' Dave said. 'It's a bloke I do quite a bit of work for. He buys up old buildings like barns, churches and schools and gets us to sympathetically convert them into holiday cottages.'

As Dave chatted about his current project, I pictured the outbuildings at Hedgehog Hollow. It seemed such a waste not to use them. They needed a lot of work but the structures themselves were solid. Was there potential to convert them into holiday cottages? Hedgehog Hollow was a stunning setting and not too far from the coast so would be an attractive place to stay. Could there be a way to connect it to the charity and offer hedgehog handling experiences? I quickly dismissed the thought. It would be too stressful for the hogs but there would be nothing stopping visitors finding out about the work Sammie did.

'Is there much money left from what Thomas set aside for the renovations?' I asked Dave.

'Quite a bit. I was hoping to find a quiet moment with Sam to ask what she wants me to do with it but there's not been a quiet moment since she moved in.'

'Is there enough to turn one of the barns into a holiday cottage?'

'Definitely. Maybe two. Why? Is that what you're thinking of?'

I shrugged. 'We've not really discussed what to do with the outbuildings but hearing you talk about holiday cottages has got me thinking.'

'I bet he'd love to be let loose on that cow shed,' Rich said.

Dave laughed. 'And the stables. The more unusual and quirkier the property, the better.'

The cogs were whirring. 'Don't say anything to Sammie. She's got enough on her mind with my dad's family about to descend on us but I'll talk to her about it when everyone's settled in and, who knows, we might have a future project for you at the farm.'

I was on my way over to the barn to relieve Dad when I spotted a car driving extremely slowly along the farm track. My heart started racing. Why were they going so slowly? *Please don't say it's more of the Grimes family trying to creep in unnoticed. Surely they wouldn't be so stupid after the police warning.*

I opened the barn door. Dad was at the treatment table with the hoglets. 'Morning, Dad. There's a car approaching so I'll be in shortly.'

'Okay. Shout if you need me.'

I hoped I wouldn't but it was good to know he was there, just in case.

When Dave picked up Josh, he'd handed over a bag full of wooden hedgehog platforms to help hogs escape from water that his joiner friend had made from off-cuts. I placed the bag on the floor then waited in the doorway as the car pulled into the yard, my heartrate steadying as I spotted wedding ribbons tied across the bonnet.

I'd placed a pair of thick gloves and a crate near the door in case anyone needed to make a speedy drop-off so I grabbed them and walked over to the car as a middle-aged woman wearing a beautiful pale lemon dress and matching fascinator exited the driver's side.

'Good morning. Can I help you?'

She smiled. 'We're on our way to a wedding as you can probably tell by the outfit but we've found a hedgehog.' She opened the back passenger door to reveal a suited man with a red tartan picnic blanket on his knee and a hedgehog laid across it.

'It was in the middle of the road about a mile back.' He gently lifted the blanket towards me. 'We thought it had been hit by a car but there's no blood and I can't see any obvious injuries.'

I pulled on my gloves, bent down and placed the crate beside me. The poor thing didn't look good. Hedgehogs should look nice and round but this one was clearly very emaciated, giving it more of a wedge-shaped appearance.

'I'm afraid we didn't have anything to put it in,' the man said, 'but it's just laid here as good as gold. Will it be alright?'

I lifted the hog off the rug and turned it over in my hands. It didn't even attempt to curl into a protective ball suggesting it was completely devoid of energy. They were right about the lack of obvious injuries. 'I can't promise that but I'll do my best. It's a girl, by the way.' I gently placed her in the crate. 'Hopefully she's just hungry and thirsty but I'll give her a thorough check-over inside. Thanks for bringing her in.'

'You're a charity, aren't you?' the woman asked nodding towards her husband who was clambering out of the car.

'Yes, so there's no charge.'

The man pressed a twenty-pound note into my hand. 'Hopefully this will cover some food and medicine.'

'That's very generous of you. Much appreciated.'

The woman handed the car keys to him and pointed to her strappy sandals as she caught my eye. 'I can barely drive in these but I was scared of messing up my dress if the hedgehog rolled off the blanket.'

So that's why the car was crawling along the track. Nothing sinister at all. I hated that the Grimes family had done this to me, making me suspicious of all visitors. I said goodbye and made my way into the barn to examine our latest patient. Thursday's new arrival had been christened Neo so it made sense to stick with *The Matrix* and call her Trinity.

'More hoglets?' Dad looked up from feeding.

'No. Adult female – Trinity – extremely dehydrated.' I put the crate down. The heat pads were set up on the table but there weren't any hoglets on them. 'Where're the others?'

'They're really feisty this morning. I decided it was easier to keep them in their crates and only feed one at a time or it would have been like lemmings in here. Ariel's my last one then I'm done.'

'Thanks, Dad. I really appreciate the night off. Best sleep in ages.'

I cleared a couple of the heat pads away, wiped down the table and weighed Trinity. As expected, she was underweight. Her skin felt loose and she'd lost a few spines but a closer inspection didn't reveal any cuts or any sign of flystrike. It was likely that she'd struggled to find food and water in the warm weather and it had taken its toll on her. We'd had a few hours of torrential rain the day Beth fell down the stairs but nothing in the week since then.

'We'll get some fluids into you, little one, and fatten you up a bit.'

I placed her on the heat pad I'd left out as I prepared a dish of food and another of water. I positioned them close to the pad and felt reassured when her nose started twitching. Moments later, she slowly shuffled towards the food. Another sniff of the air and she dived in, eagerly slurping and smacking her lips together. Hedgehogs are phenomenally noisy eaters but I love the sound knowing that each mouthful is helping them to recover.

'There's certainly nothing wrong with Trinity's appetite,' Dad said as he returned Ariel to her siblings.

'That's a relief. Do you think she could have had a litter and abandoned them somewhere?'

'Possibly. But if she has, they're not likely to have survived. If she's been struggling to feed herself, she's not going to have managed to feed babies.'

'That makes me sad.'

'I know, poppet, but we...'

'Can't save them all,' we chorused together.

I gave him a weak smile. 'I wish we could.'

After she'd finished her food, I settled Trinity in her crate and cleared the table. Dad put the kettle on while he tidied the bedding and folded away the sofa bed.

'Speaking of saving people,' I said as we sat down on the sofa bed with mugs of tea five minutes later, 'how are you feeling now after what you told me about Mum?'

Dad pondered for a moment. 'Conflicted. I think it's right that you know and I can imagine it's explained a few things. But, for me, the guilt is worse than ever.'

'It wasn't your fault, Dad. Or Mum's or your friend's. The only person to blame is the man who raped her. Him and him only. You *do* know that?' I took in his hunched shoulders and downcast eyes. 'Unless... did Mum blame you?'

He didn't meet my eyes but I could tell from the way his shoulders tensed that I'd hit the nail on the head.

'She was hurting, Dad. People lash out at the ones they love the most when they're in pain.' As I said the words, it struck me that she'd lashed out at me all my life. I knew now it was because of how hurt she was but did that meant that, deep down she loved me? It certainly didn't feel like it. But she had loved Dad and he had to hold onto that.

He finally looked up. 'What have you got planned for today?'

'Busy day. Connie's coming for a cuppa at some point, I have a handful of hedgehog releases and a stack of emails to go through.'

Dad stood up. 'I'd better let you crack on. Don't worry about me. Lots of thoughts and memories swirling round at the moment but I'm fine and, believe it or not, your mum's doing okay. I spoke to her last night.'

I stood up too and followed him over to the sink with the mugs. 'You phoned her?'

'She rang me actually. There were a couple of financial things she wanted to discuss but we were on the phone for about half an hour. She sounds happy and settled. The move seems to have done her good. She even asked after you.'

'Very funny.'

'I'm serious. She asked how you were and whether you were enjoying running the rescue centre. No word of a lie.'

'Was she drunk?'

He smiled. 'I don't think so. She also asked if you'd spoken to Chloe recently but I said I wasn't sure. You haven't mentioned anything to me.'

I shook my head. 'Not since I went across and it all went wrong. I keep meaning to get in touch but never seem to find time. What made Mum ask after me? She was so rude when I saw her.'

He shrugged. 'I honestly don't know. Maybe her new start has made her reflect on things.'

'Maybe.' I shook my head, bewildered. Mum asking after me? That was new and most unexpected.

* * *

Dad had scarcely been gone ten minutes before Connie arrived with Archie so we took coffees round to Thomas's bench. Archie was dozing in his buggy which I was secretly pleased about because I could hear about her date with Alex without interruptions.

'I am dying to hear how it went.'

She looked at me with a solemn expression on her face. 'It was awful. It was so...' She started laughing. 'Nope. I can't do it. I can't wind you up. Truth is it was incredible. You know when you imagine the best possible scenario and then, when it happens, it's even better than that?'

'I'm so pleased for you.' I wished Josh was with us to see how alive his mum appeared. Her cheeks glowed, her eyes sparkled and her smile made my heart melt.

'I opened the door to him and it was like stepping back in time. The beard was gone and he was wearing a cornflower-blue shirt, just like he'd done that night. He told me later that it was obvious from my reaction that I'd remembered too which gave him the courage to go on. "It's not the same shirt," he said, "but it's a close match. You had long hair back then and glasses and you're more beautiful now than I remembered".'

'Oh my gosh, that's so romantic!'

'The whole evening was so romantic. We talked non-stop. He'd felt exactly the same as me about our moment. He'd wanted to run after me when we left the bar but chickened out for the same reasons I did. He couldn't believe it when he saw me in the club and was determined to speak to me but, of course, I got pulled away. He'd recently separated from his wife and they were going through a divorce. It was amicable but there was baggage and he thinks that the timing would have been wrong for him too.'

'And now...?'

'Both baggage-free and going out for dinner again tomorrow night.' Tears glistened in her eyes. 'I'm so happy, I could cry.

Meeting a new man was the last thing I wanted to do right now yet it couldn't feel more right.'

'He's not a new man, though. He's your "moment-man" and your one true north.'

Tears spilled down her cheeks at that point and she laughed as she swiped at them. 'What an emotional mess I am!'

At the sound of a car in the farmyard, I left Connie to compose herself. It was the collection for Ron, the hedgehog who'd been found in a pond. The family had been keen to have him back and release him in their garden as he'd been a regular visitor and they even had a hedgehog house for him. We'd discussed the pond situation over the phone and they'd loved the idea of installing one of the hedgehog platforms. It gave me comfort that, if Ron took a tumble again, he'd have the means of escape.

With Ron handed over and a generous financial contribution gratefully accepted for the platform and his 'board and lodgings', I returned to Connie. Archie had woken up and was sitting on the grass chewing on a teething toy.

'This place is magical,' Connie said gazing over at the meadow as I sat down beside her once more. 'It feels as though it's the sort of place where miracles happen.'

'That's because they do.'

She turned to me and smiled. 'Josh would think we've been on the wine if he could hear us.'

'Actually, he feels it too. He might not choose the word "magical" but he does think it's pretty special.'

Connie squeezed my hand. 'Thank you so much for everything you've done for him. I've been so worried about him but not anymore. I've got my boy back and I think he might just be kinder and wiser than he's ever been.'

Archie flung Waddles the penguin behind him with a squawk then tumbled over backwards as he tried to retrieve it. I leapt up to right him and was rewarded with a slobbery grin when I handed back Waddles. Sitting cross-legged beside him on the grass, I wondered whether I could push down my anxiety and have children. Right here in this magical setting, could there be any more perfect a place for raising a family?

'You look very thoughtful,' Connie said.

'In your course, have you explored post-traumatic stress disorder?'

'PTSD?' She nodded. 'It's an area that particularly interests me so I've done a lot of extra research into it. That's an unusual question for a sunny Saturday morning.'

'It's possible my mum has PTSD from a traumatic incident that happened a couple of years before I was born. It hasn't been diagnosed so I could be way off the mark. She's never sought help and I think she should.'

Connie sighed. 'I'm sorry to hear that your mum has had a trauma. PTSD is a huge area. Not everyone who has a trauma experiences it and the symptoms of those who do can massively vary in both type and extremity. As for seeking help, if it is PTSD, it can be treated years after a trauma so it's never too late, but...' She paused and I knew what she was going to say next.

'It has to be your mum's choice. I know that can be frustrating for a friend or family member who cares and wants to help or even try to fix things but it's not that simple.'

'I thought you'd say that. I just feel a bit helpless.'

'I understand that. When you're on the outside of a situation, it can sometimes appear straightforward but, when you're inside it, it's often full of complexities. Family can encourage treatment but they can't force it. If and when your mum is ready, she'll address it and you can be there for her when she does.'

* * *

Connie left and I returned to the barn thinking about what she'd said. I was definitely going to have to leave it. What else could I do? Turn up with a gift voucher for ten pre-paid counselling sessions? She'd probably rip it up in front of my face.

My thoughts turned to my conversation with Dad. How strange was it that she'd asked after me? Was he right and her new start had given her a fresh perspective on things? If it had, she wouldn't have been so rude when I saw her at Chloe's. Unless she'd reflected on her behaviour since then and decided it was time to make an effort. Was she reaching out to me? Should I respond? I shook myself. I had to stop overthinking things. She'd chosen to sever all ties with me so I wasn't going to build up my hopes and drive over to Whitsborough Bay only to have her crush me again. She'd asked three questions about me in a short phone conversation with Dad. It didn't mean anything.

'And one of those questions was actually about Chloe,' I muttered, pulling my phone out of my pocket. 'Who I *must* call now before I get distracted again.'

I waited for the FaceTime call to connect but it was cut off. I tried again. Also cut off. I bit my lip, hoping she wasn't screening her calls because she was in a mood with me. It was a very Chloe thing to do if she was. No. I had to think more positively about her and not instantly assume she'd defaulted back to spoilt-Chloe mode. She was probably feeding Samuel and it was inconvenient to speak. I'd try again later.

My stomach grumbled and I glanced at the time on my phone. Already 1 p.m.? No wonder I was hungry. Over in the farmhouse, I made a sandwich and took it out to Thomas's bench. Misty-Blue bounded out from the meadow and circled round my legs. I'd been worried she'd be skittish after last weekend but she'd seemed as affectionate as ever which reassured me the thugs hadn't laid a finger on her.

Terry was due around mid-afternoon to collect the two hogs he'd brought in – Arwen who'd been tangled in the goalpost netting and Dumbledore who'd had the elastic band round him. I was therefore surprised to see him pulling into the farmyard as I returned to the barn after lunch.

'I know I'm early but it's an emergency.' He opened the back door of his car. 'Our Wilbur started going crazy by the front door earlier. I opened it and there was nobody there but there was this box.'

He thrust a cardboard box towards me. It was filled with toilet paper but curled together in one corner was a litter of tiny hoglets.

'This was dumped on your doorstep?'

He nodded. 'Bloody idiots. What if I hadn't been in or our Wilbur hadn't barked? They'd have died.'

'I need to get them inside and warm. Do you need to rush back?'

'No. Why?'

'I could do with your help.'

He locked his car and followed me into the barn.

'There was no note?' I asked.

'Nothing. I've spoken to loads of people about this place so presumably that's why they were dumped on my doorstep. They didn't even ring the bell.'

'Can you wash your hands while I set up the heat pads? Did you check how many there are?'

'No. There's at least four in the pile but there could be some underneath or in another corner. I saw them moving and drove straight here.'

'You did the right thing, Terry. Speed is so important.'

I swiftly lifted the hoglets out of the box one at a time. There were eight of them – an unusually large litter – but two were already dead and one looked beyond saving. It was a tough call. In theory that one was the priority but we could invest time and energy trying to save it to the detriment of the others... and we might still lose it anyway.

'We need to get them warm and build some energy...' We held them between our hands, blew on them and pushed them around on the heat pads. All the while, I explained what we were doing and why. Terry followed my instructions to the letter and didn't speak other than the occasional encouragement to the hoglets to move, breathe, live. It took me back to my first hoglets delivery from Alex nearly three weeks ago. These tiny babies were a similar size to Leia and Solo's litter when they'd been brought in.

After about fifteen minutes, there was a knock on the barn door and it burst open. 'You're not going to believe what my grandma—' Fizz started.

'Hoglet emergency!' I called, so relieved to see her.

She ran down the barn, tossed her bag to one side, washed her hands, and was by my side in a flash. 'What do you need?'

'Can you work on these ones while I prepare some formula?'

* * *

The next couple of hours were intense. A couple of the hoglets were visibly bigger than the others and responded well to stimulation. They were able to take some formula quickly so I was reasonably confident they'd both go the distance. Fizz was determined to do her best for the weakest one and, with three pairs of hands, she could give it extra attention but, sadly, it wasn't to be.

'That was tough,' she said, blinking back tears as she laid its limp body in the box beside its two deceased siblings.

'Worst part of the job,' I agreed, swallowing on the lump in my throat. 'How are you holding up, Terry?' I was very conscious that he hadn't signed up to this and I kept thinking about Dave's reaction when we lost the first hoglet. Fizz had chosen a career with animals and knew what to expect but Terry was just a lover of wildlife who happened to have had a box of hoglets dumped on his doorstep.

'Humbled and privileged to be part of this.' He sounded really choked up. 'What you do here... the lives you save... it's incredible.'

I smiled at him. 'And you're part of that. I may have done the medical stuff but you're the one who gave Arwen and Dumbledore a chance by bringing them here. You've done the same for these hoglets and, however misguided it was to dump them on your doorstep, it's better that somebody did that rather than leave them to die in a garden or field or wherever. I just hope that they didn't remove them from a nest that their mum was actually looking after but I guess we'll never know.' I didn't want to dwell on it. The thought of their mum roaming around, wondering where her babies were and the idea that the three deceased hoglets might not have been deceased if they'd been left with her was too horrible to contemplate.

* * *

Josh, Rich and Dave returned shortly after four. Hearing them talking in the farmyard, I rang Josh to ask him to come into the barn. Terry hadn't specifically said he wanted to leave but he'd mentioned his dog being home alone on a couple of occasions so I knew he was keen to head off.

'Where are you calling me from?' Josh asked, sounding bemused.

'The barn. We've got five more hoglets. We need help.'

Moments later, the three of them appeared and I explained what had happened. Terry seemed relieved when I said he was free to go.

'Can you spare five more minutes while I get Arwen and Dumbledore ready?'

'How about I come for them tomorrow? You focus on the little'uns for now.'

I walked him to the door, checked he was definitely okay and thanked him again for all his help. I'd already warned him that we may lose others across the evening while reassuring him all would have been lost if he hadn't acted fast. He seemed so genuinely touched by my words that he reminded me of Thomas – initial gruff exterior but chip away to reveal a heart of gold. I nearly hugged him goodbye but thought that might be a bit much.

* * *

Five people for five hoglets – two girls and three boys – was overkill so Rich and Dave unpacked the van while Josh, Fizz and I stayed in the barn. It was lucky Paul's family weren't moving in tonight because I'd have felt bad having to leave them to just get on with it.

Fizz decided to stick with the Disney theme but moved away from fairy tales and christened them Minnie, Mickey, Donald, Daisy and Pluto.

'You do realise that Pluto is a dog and that the dog is actually one of their biggest predators?' Josh asked her.

She had such an infectious laugh-snort combination that soon we were laughing with her. It felt good to enjoy a moment of lightness.

We rang for pizzas and took it in turns to eat and see to the hoglets then I insisted on Rich and Dave heading home as they had evening plans. They'd been such a huge help all day and there was no way I was going to keep them from drinks with friends. The hoglets were all doing well. It felt as though we were over the worst already and, even if Fizz left, Josh and I could manage five between us.

'So, I saw my grandparents today...' Fizz said while Josh fed the adult hedgehogs.

'Oh, gosh, yes! I'm sorry. You started saying that when you arrived.'

'I need to show you something. Am I okay to put the hoglets down for a minute?'

'They'll be fine.'

She retrieved an envelope from her bag, removed some photos and placed them face down on the table.

'These are my grandparents, Mary and Frank Dodds.' She handed me the first one. 'This was taken at their farm about twenty-five years ago.'

I smiled. 'That's a great photo.' Mary was sitting on a shiny blue tractor and Frank was beside it on a quad bike with a pair of border collies in a basket on the back.

'It's my favourite. I've got it enlarged at home.'

She handed me the next photo and her eyes sparkled with excitement. 'Who's this with my grandparents?'

'That's Nanna and Gramps!' The four of them were sitting on hay bales at what looked to be a village fête.

'They met your grandparents several times because they had a mutual friend.'

She passed me the next photo which had obviously been taken at the same event. This one showed her grandma, Nanna and another woman. I gasped as I studied it more closely. 'That's Gwendoline!'

'I know! Isn't that amazing? Grandma says she knew Gwendoline from school. Grandma was four years younger so they weren't friends but they kept seeing each other around over the years and always chatted. Then, when Gwendoline started rescuing hedgehogs, she sometimes released them at the farm and they became good friends. They were gutted when she died.'

'I can't believe it! That's so amazing.' I handed the photo back.

She grinned. 'I've got one more.' She handed me a picture of Gwendoline holding a toddler in her arms.

'Oh my gosh! Is that you?' I gazed from the photo to Fizz then back again.

'It is! I was three at the time. Too young to remember her but Grandma says I met her lots of times. She used to joke with her that Gwendoline was more interested in seeing me than her.'

I could well believe it. As we continued to tend to the hoglets, I told Fizz about the Micklebys being unable to have children and how Gwendoline had had a similar relationship with me when I was little as she'd had with Fizz. The discovery that I was the Sammie that his wife had adored had softened Thomas's attitude towards me and turned us into friends.

'Oh my God!' Fizz declared when I'd finished the story. 'I don't know whether you believe in this sort of stuff but it's like you and I were always meant to be here to fulfil the hedgehog lady's dreams.'

I smiled at her, a lump in my throat. 'I do believe that. They sowed the wildflower meadow out the back and, when I'm out there, I always feel so close to them. I talk to them sometimes – tell them about the hedgehogs and ask their advice – and I swear they send me messages.'

'I've got goose bumps.' Fizz thrust out her arm.

I looked down and so did I.

56

JOSH

I rolled over in bed and frowned, momentarily confused as to where I was and why Sammie wasn't beside me. I blinked a few times in the dim light. Of course! I was on the sofa bed in the barn.

'Have you been up long?' I asked, seeing Sammie at the treatment table.

'About half an hour.'

'What time is it?'

'Half seven.'

I rubbed my eyes. 'Why's it so dark?'

She cocked her head to one side. 'Listen.'

Rain.

'It started at about five,' she said. 'Hasn't let up since but I quite like it. I feel all warm and cosy tucked away in here.'

Adjusting position so I was sat on the side of the sofa bed, I rolled my shoulders. They were aching from all the carrying yesterday. Every spare inch of space in Dad and Beth's flat had been stowed out with plastic storage crates – under the bed and cot, on top of the wardrobe and kitchen units as well as all the ones I'd spotted in the lounge. And most of them had been heavy. As I stood up, I felt my calves and thighs twinge too from the stairs. I really needed to get back into the habit of going for a run. I'd taken it up after cutting Dad out of my life as a way to alleviate my frustration. Pounding the pavements was a great stress release but, since meeting Sammie, I hadn't felt that same need to burn off my anger so the running had stopped.

I ambled over to Sammie and nuzzled her neck. 'How are the hoglets?'

'The good news is there's still five of them.'

'And the bad news?'

She kissed my cheek. 'There isn't any. Why don't you grab a shower? I'm nearly done with the feeds.'

'Then why don't you come and join me?' I gently kissed her neck. 'Very last opportunity to be alone in the house.'

'Give me ten minutes.'

* * *

'Best shower I've ever had,' I said as we sat at the kitchen table later with tea and toast.

She gave me a coy smile. 'I'd love to say it could be repeated soon but your dad's about to move in and...' She gave a shudder.

I laughed at the face she pulled. 'At least their bedroom isn't next to ours.'

She shuddered again. 'How are you feeling about everyone moving in?'

'Okay. I think. Spending so much time with Dad at the hospital has broken the ice. We haven't discussed *the incident* but we've talked about plenty of other stuff and that awkwardness has gone. It's occasionally felt like old times.'

'That's encouraging.' She bit her lip. 'Are you going to talk to them about the past? Get it all out in the open?'

I shrugged. 'I don't know. I wonder if it would be better for everyone if we just forget about it and move on.'

She raised her eyebrows doubtfully. 'I'm all for moving on but this isn't something you can just forget about, not when it had such big repercussions. I really think you need to talk it through because it's going to be the elephant in the room and that elephant's going to keep growing if you don't pay any attention to it.'

I smiled at her analogy.

She brushed the toast crumbs off her fingers and pushed her plate aside. 'If they were sat at this table right now, what's the first thing you'd ask them?'

That was easy. It was the one thing I absolutely couldn't get my head round. 'I'd ask why Beth cheated on Dad with me. I'm his son! Who does that? And, for that matter, who accepts that? He knew yet he never stopped it. It turns my stomach when I think about it all.'

'There you go, then. You *have* to ask them. Living under the same roof for the next few months will be intense. I can pretty much guarantee there'll be tensions and arguments and I think it would be best for everyone if you get it all on the table in a civilised discussion early on instead of it being blurted out in anger at some point down the line and any progress you've made in recovering your relationship being destroyed.'

'You're right. This isn't something I can push aside. I need some answers.'

'Once they're settled in, though. They've been through a lot.'

I nodded. 'Don't worry. I'll pick my moment. I promise. Maybe once they've unpacked.'

I left Josh to clear away after breakfast and run the vacuum cleaner round the house while I dealt with my emails.

Terry arrived mid-morning to collect Arwen and Dumbledore. The hoglets had just been fed but he had a peek in their crate and looked like a proud father gazing down on them.

'Can't tell you how happy I am to see them all still alive,' he said. 'When that first one went...'

'I know. I was worried too but we did it and they're doing brilliantly thanks to you bringing them in so quickly. You'll have to give Wilbur a hug from me because, if he hadn't barked and alerted you, it would have been a different story.'

'I'll kill the stupid bugger who left them on my doorstep.'

I shook my head. 'I wouldn't even try to find out who it was, Terry. They probably thought they were doing the right thing. Focus on the fact that a combination of their actions and yours mean there are five hoglets alive right now who wouldn't be otherwise. Promise me you'll do that?'

He stared at me, brow furrowed, then his face softened. 'Aye, lass. I'll do it for you.'

'And I'm meeting Jeanette Kingston on Thursday so I'll be talking to her about the goalpost netting and other things that can be done around the village to help hedgehogs. Elastic bands will be my priority after that.'

Terry smiled. 'You're a good lass. Gwendoline would have been proud of you.'

'You knew her?'

'I went to school with her. One day this little bird flew into the classroom window. Knocked itself out. She ignored the teacher telling her to sit down and went outside to rescue it. I can still picture her, sat cross-legged in the middle of the yard, stroking this bird until it came round and could fly off again. Magical, it were.'

'That's such a lovely story.'

'She always had animals with her. I called her Snow White. Have you seen the film when the animals help her clean up? I told her I imagined her house was like that. She said that was really funny, especially because it was true.'

When Terry left, I couldn't stop smiling. The thought of Gwendoline as Snow White filled my heart with so much joy. As I got to know more people in the community, there'd hopefully be more stories about her. Clearly she was known and loved by many of the locals. I already adored her from the brief encounters I remembered from childhood and how lovingly Thomas had spoken about her but these memories from Fizz's grandparents and now from Terry were extra special.

* * *

Shortly before lunchtime, Hannah rang.

'Hi Mrs Full-Time Hedgehog Whisperer Guest House Owner. Have they moved in yet?'

I laughed. 'We've just heard from Paul. The hospital has

confirmed Lottie will get discharged today so we're expecting them this afternoon.'

'Wow! Good luck with that. Look, I know things are hectic so I won't keep you long. We're on our way to Toby's parents' for lunch and he's just been filling me in on his catch-up with James last night. Have you spoken to Chloe recently?' Toby and James were best mates; it was through Hannah and Toby that we'd been introduced and it was at their wedding that he admitted that he didn't see me as his future wife.

'No. I tried to FaceTime her yesterday but couldn't get hold of her. Why? What's happened?'

'Maybe nothing but Toby said James looked knackered which isn't surprising. The guy's in remission and he's got a new baby. James told him that Chloe's always biting his head off and he feels he can't do anything right. When he gets home from work, she's usually still in her PJs and looks like she's been crying. You know she's not exactly my favourite person so I can't help feeling that, if she's having a nightmare with Samuel, it's a spot of karma, but I know you still care so I thought you'd want to know.'

My stomach churned. Staying in her PJs didn't sound alarm bells – new mums on their own often struggled for time to shower and change – but the crying part *did* sound worrying. I thought about how dishevelled she'd looked when I visited – very unlike Chloe – and how unfriendly she'd been. Was it all getting on top of her?

'I'll try her again now. Thanks for the heads up.'

'You're welcome. I'll give you a shout tomorrow and arrange to come across one day in the week.'

'Brilliant. Enjoy your lunch.'

As soon as I'd hung up, I tried Chloe on FaceTime. It rang several times and I thought it wasn't going to connect but, just as I was about to give up, Chloe's make-up free face appeared on the screen.

'Hi, Chloe! How's it going?'

She didn't smile. 'Oh. So you've remembered I exist. How kind of you.'

I winced at the sharp edge in her voice but tried not to let my smile slip. 'I'm sorry. I have no idea where the past three weeks have gone.'

There was a stony silence and I panicked. 'How's the gorgeous Samuel?' *Argh! Why did you ask about him instead of her?*

'Do you want me to put him on so you can talk to him instead?'

'Chloe! Don't be like that.'

'Like what?'

'All sarcastic. Can we start again? How are you?'

'I'm just peachy, thanks. How are you?' She said it in a sickly sweet voice and flashed me a fake smile at the end. 'Is that better for you?'

My thumb twitched with a strong urge to disconnect the call. *Deep breath. Try again.* But my mind went blank. I had so much to tell her but everything seemed so huge and I couldn't think where to start without eliciting accusations of keeping her out the loop. I wanted to quiz her about what Hannah had said but couldn't think of a lead-in without dropping James in it. She'd probably be mad that he'd spoken to Toby about her. I glanced towards the window and blurted out the first thing that came into my head – the most stupid typically British thing I could possibly say – 'It's bucketing it down here. They say it's meant to stop by lunchtime but I can't see it myself. What's the weather like over there?'

She shook her head, her expression conveying unmistakable disgust, then the screen went blank.

* * *

Josh laughed when he joined me in the barn and I told him about my pitiful attempt at a conversation with Chloe.

'Don't laugh!' I gently shoved him. 'It's not funny!'

'Believe me, it is! I'd love to have seen Chloe's face.'

'I did and she wasn't impressed. Epic fail. I should try again later but I don't know if I can face it.'

'Then don't. Why don't you send her one of those "HOT TIP" texts the two of you used to send each other instead?'

I smiled at him. 'Genius. I'll do it now.'

'But don't get upset if she doesn't respond. She probably won't. Far more high-maintenance that way.'

'If she doesn't respond, it says more about her than it does about me.'

'Too right! And remember staying in touch works both ways. She could have called you at any point after your visit and, let's face it, she should have done to say sorry. I know she's a new mum but so are you – to eleven hoglets and...' He glanced towards the Happy Hog Board, '...twenty-three adults. It's not fair of her to throw a strop. Again.'

In the past, if anyone said anything against Chloe, I would bristle and jump to her defence, but Hannah had made a dig earlier and Josh had just now and I hadn't reacted to either. It could be that I had bigger things on my mind or it could be that I was just tired of all the drama that surrounded my cousin. I'd send her a text and put the ball in her court. As Josh said, I had thirty-four hedgehogs in my care now, we were moving into the height of babies' season, and I was about to add two human babies and two adults into the mix. Life was not about to slow down any time soon and I didn't have time to keep calling Chloe and apologising when I wasn't the one who'd done anything wrong.

✉ To Chloe

HOT TIP! There's a woman on a farm in the Wolds who sometimes asks silly questions but she's a good listener. You know where to find her if you want to talk … about something other than the weather! She still loves you and is always here for you xx

The rain *did* stop around lunchtime, as predicted and Chloe *didn't* respond to my text, as predicted.

✉ From Beth
Leaving the hospital now. Thank you doesn't seem
big enough to express how grateful we are to you
and Samantha for everything you've done and
continue to do for us but THANK YOU THANK YOU
THANK YOU!!!!

It was mid-afternoon and we were sitting on Thomas's bench having a break from feeding hoglets when Beth's text came through. I showed Sammie and she smiled. 'I think they might be grateful.'

I took her hand in mine. 'And so am I. Have I told you lately how amazing you are?'

'Yes, but you can tell me again.'

I cupped her face and gently kissed her. 'You, Samantha Wishaw, are amazing. Looking after poorly hedgehogs is impressive enough but I don't think many people would also take in a poorly ex-girlfriend, an estranged dad about to undergo chemo and a couple of babies.'

'What can I say? I'm a sucker for the needy and damaged.

Which is probably why I can't seem to let go of Mum or Chloe. I have this inherent need to make things better.'

'Well, I love you for it.'

I cuddled her against my side and we sat there together, watching Misty-Blue pouncing across the lawn. The grass and flowers smelled so fresh after the storm and the colours of the meadow were so vibrant but I couldn't help thinking that we were relaxing in the calm before our own personal storm.

* * *

An hour later, they arrived and the peace was shattered. She might be tiny but Lottie could make a hell of a racket. Beth looked exhausted after the journey and Sammie instantly jumped into nurse mode, ordering her upstairs for bed rest and telling her that we could look after Lottie between us. With Beth being on strong painkillers, Lottie was being bottle-fed which made it easier for us to help.

We'd arranged for Mum to bring Archie across for early evening to give them a chance to settle in first. She hadn't seen Beth since *the incident* and, although she'd expressed sympathy for her, I was a little apprehensive about them seeing each other again. It would take impressive dignity and strength for her not to show any sort of hostility. Yet, when she stopped by that evening, she managed it.

Beth tried to get to her feet as I stepped into the lounge with Mum, Archie snuggled into her shoulder.

'Please don't try to get up,' Mum said gently.

Beth nodded and stayed put, worry lines creasing her forehead.

'There's your mummy!' Mum exclaimed, turning Archie round in her arms. 'You've missed her, haven't you?'

Archie's face lit up as he spotted Beth. He bounced up and down excitedly in Mum's arms and dropped Waddles the penguin.

'Somebody wants a cuddle.' Mum gently settled Archie onto Beth's lap.

'Thank you,' Beth whispered, cuddling him tightly with her good arm.

Mum smiled. 'I'm glad you're okay. We were all worried about you.'

Beth promptly burst into tears and whispered 'sorry' over and over.

'It's done,' Mum said. 'It's in the past and you've got an exciting future ahead of you with your lovely family. Focus on that. And speaking of family, where's that little princess? I have gifts.'

Dad appeared from upstairs with Lottie. Mum hugged him then took Lottie from him and cooed over her before handing over a bag of presents then settling into an armchair for Lottie hugs.

When Mum left an hour later, Beth turned to me. 'Your mum's amazing.' She then looked up at Dad. 'No wonder you struggled to leave her. I didn't realise she...' She sighed. 'I'm feeling sleepy again but do you think we could talk tomorrow, Josh, when you and Paul are back from work? The three of us probably need to discuss what happened and clear the air, don't you think?'

I looked across at Sammie and she gave me an encouraging nod.

'That would be a good idea.' And even better that she wanted to get it out of the way sooner rather than later.

'Good luck.' Sammie gave me a tight squeeze on Monday evening. 'I might not be with you in body but I will be in spirit.' She stepped out the front door onto the gravel. 'Remember to stay calm and listen.'

'I will. See you in the barn later.'

I took a deep breath of fresh countryside air then closed the door. Truth time.

Beth had said that Sammie was welcome to join us but Sammie was unsure. She wondered if, despite the invite, Beth and Dad might feel more comfortable if it was just the three of us. A surprise arrival of hoglets late last night made the decision for her. Trinity – the emaciated hog who'd been dropped off on Saturday by the couple on their way to a wedding – gave birth to healthy triplets. Two girls and a boy. None of us could have called that! How those little ones survived when she was in such a bad way herself was one of nature's many miracles.

I grabbed my mug of tea from the kitchen and pushed open the lounge door. Beth was half-lying on the sofa with a throw over her legs, Lottie asleep on her lap, and Dad was on the floor playing with

Archie. It was the perfect scene of family bliss. I had a fleeting moment of regret that I might never have that with Sammie, which swiftly passed at the thought of having that scene of family life but without Sammie in it. She hadn't said anything to me about finishing her homework and, as promised, I hadn't chased. I had wondered whether she'd done it and what she'd concluded but I'd pushed the thought out of my mind. She'd talk to me about it when the time was right.

I settled into the armchair by the front window and looked up expectantly.

Beth shuffled to a more upright position, taking care not to awaken Lottie. 'I wanted to start by saying a huge thank you to you and Samantha for everything you've done for us this month.' She shook her head and sighed. 'Thank you doesn't seem enough. You've shown us so much kindness and been there for us when we both know we don't deserve it.'

She looked towards Dad who gave a gentle smile and a nod.

'I don't think I'll ever find the words to show our gratitude but I think the least we can do is try to offer some sort of explanation for the appalling way we treated you and give you a chance to do what you want to do – shout, swear, laugh. We deserve it all. I'm sure you've got questions. I would if I was you. We thought we'd be best to get it out in the open now rather than have it hanging over us.'

I nodded. 'I have loads of questions but the main one is why? Why me? Why both of us at the same time? That's pretty si...' Sammie's words rang in my ears – *stay calm and listen* – and I stopped myself but not quite in time.

'Pretty sick?' Beth suggested. 'If someone I knew told me our little tale, I'd be all like "ew, that's gross" so I hear you. Why you?' She shrugged. 'When you found me crying that day, it wasn't a set-up. I wasn't trying to snare you or anything like that. What I told you was the truth. Paul and I *had* split up. I *had* given him an ultimatum to leave Connie to be with me and he wouldn't do it so it was over and I was devastated. I'd lost the love of my life and I'd lost my way. My friends didn't approve and they'd gradually pulled away from me so I was all alone after five years in a relationship that seemed like it was never going to go anywhere.'

Dad shuffled over to the sofa and took her hand in his, presumably feeling the pain he'd caused.

'You were so kind to me when I needed a friend,' Beth continued. 'I never meant for anything to happen, especially with you being Paul's son. I kept thinking that, now that I'd carried out my threat and ended our relationship, Paul would see sense and end things with your mum. But he didn't.'

'So you figured what the heck?'

She lowered her eyes. 'Something like that but you have to know that, as far as I was concerned, it was over with Paul when you and I got together.'

'So when did things start up again?'

They exchanged looks. 'We bumped into each other a couple of weeks before Christmas,' Dad said. 'We went for a drink and admitted our feelings hadn't changed but absolutely nothing happened. Beth told me she was seeing someone else and she wasn't willing to end that while I was still with your mum but I still couldn't bring myself to leave your mum.'

I frowned. 'I'm confused. Beth dumped me two weeks before Christmas because her married man was back on the scene. Are you seriously telling me you didn't get back together then?'

Beth nodded. 'As Paul says, he was still with Connie. I couldn't put myself through that once more but, seeing him again, I realised how much I still loved him. It wasn't fair to you so I ended it with you but I didn't get back with Paul at that point.'

It was a surprise to hear that. Not that it gave me much comfort because they had got back together eventually and Beth had definitely been two-timing us. 'So what happened next? When did it start up again?'

'I kept thinking of Beth all alone in that flat over Christmas,' Dad said. 'I went to see her between Christmas and New Year. She told me to get lost but I turned up on New Year's Eve and promised to end it with your mum that week. I meant it.'

'But it didn't happen,' I said flatly.

Dad sighed. 'Your mum came down with the flu and then her Auntie Sonya died and there was never a right time.'

'It felt like excuse after excuse,' Beth said. 'I'd had enough and I wasn't going to let him do that to me again. Besides...' Her cheeks coloured as she looked at Dad. 'Being apart from you over Christmas, I realised I'd fallen in love with you as well. I told Paul we were never going to be able to try again – not while Connie was still on the scene – and I came to see you.'

I thought back to that January evening in the torrential rain. I'd assumed that it had all been lies. Another move in her twisted game. I fixed my eyes on Beth's. 'So the first few months you didn't two-time us but how long was it before you started seeing us both?'

'I never saw you both at the same time.'

'Bullshit!'

'I didn't. I swear.'

'BULLSHIT!' *Stay calm. Listen.* I lowered my voice again. 'So what was Archie? An immaculate conception? I know we split up several times but we were together the whole of that summer.' The words were low but they were still angry, bitter.

'You and I had an on-off relationship but so did Paul and I.'

My gaze flew from one to the other. 'So you're telling me that every time you pulled away and ended it with me, you were shagging my dad?' The volume was back again but I couldn't help it.

'It wasn't like that!' she cried. 'We didn't go back to how things were before between us. We never...'

'You never what?'

'We didn't...'

'Didn't what?' I yelled.

'We weren't sleeping together,' Dad shouted. Archie let out a wail and Dad quickly picked him up and hugged him. He lowered his voice. 'Obviously we were before but this time it was different. I knew it was you who Beth was seeing by then and I couldn't do it to you.'

'But you were still together?'

'Yes.'

'Just not having sex?'

'Yes.'

I ran my hands across my face and shook my head, trying to squash down the mounting rage at their blatant lies. 'Your honour, I'd like to present exhibit A.' I pointed to Archie and glared at them both, my expression matching my sarcasm.

Beth sighed. 'It was one time. It was—'

'It was my dad's seventieth birthday,' Dad interrupted, his voice soft. 'Or it would have been if he'd still been with us. I had a couple of drinks and reflected on the mess my life was in. I thought about how disappointed Mum and Dad would have been in me for lying to Connie and to you and for not pulling my weight at the practice. I worked myself up into a bit of a state and Beth was there to pick up the pieces. We never meant for it to happen.'

Beth took his hand and they exchanged a look full of love and understanding. I knew how much Granddad meant to Dad. I could imagine the pain he'd have felt at Granddad not being around for that milestone birthday and remembered feeling low about it myself. But that one night of passion didn't excuse all the other times they'd been together while Beth was still my girlfriend, albeit an on-off one. I wasn't sure whether or not I believed their no sex claim but did it make any difference if they had abstained from full-on sex when there were other things they could have been doing?

'Okay. So let's say I believe you about it being on with you two when it was off with us two. And let's say I even believe the abstinence thing until Granddad's seventieth. What's your excuse for you seeing us both, Beth?' I then pointed to Dad. 'And what's your excuse for going along with that?'

Beth lowered her eyes. 'You're not going to like the answer.'

'I don't like any of this so you might as well tell me.'

She glanced towards Dad but he had his head lowered. 'Because Paul still wouldn't leave your mum so I wouldn't leave you.'

'You used me as a bargaining chip?'

'No! Yes.' She shrugged. 'Maybe.'

'Oh my God! That's it, isn't it? You were seeing who'd break first and me and Mum were stuck in the middle.' I pointed to Beth. 'You wouldn't have sex with him again until he left Mum but he wouldn't leave Mum until you left me.'

Tears tracked down Beth's cheeks. 'It sounds so bad when you say it like that.'

'But that's how it was.'

Dad exhaled loudly. 'I'm so sorry, son. Yes, you're right. If we strip it back to the basics, that's what it was. I loved Beth but I still loved your mum. We'd been together since we were thirteen. It was so hard to walk away and I know how weak that makes me when I look back. We can't undo what happened, though. We can only give you the truth.'

'You *really* didn't have sex the whole time I was with Beth? Even when Beth and I were on a break?'

'I swear we didn't. The one and only time was the night...' He nodded towards Archie.

'It's true.' Beth sniffed and wiped her cheeks. 'You have no idea how confusing it was for both of us. I'd never understood Paul when he said he loved me and Connie. I didn't believe it was possible to love two people at the same time. Until it happened to me.'

* * *

Sammie looked up from the hoglets as I entered the barn half an hour later feeling a mixture of exhaustion and relief. It was all out in the open now. No more secrets. No more speculation.

'How was it?' she asked, concern creasing her brow.

I dropped onto the chair beside her and sighed. 'Awkward. Emotional. Frustrating. But you'd be proud of me. I managed to stay calm, even when I felt anything but that. Well, most of the time. And I listened.'

She gave me a warm smile. 'Even if you had lost it, I'd still be proud of you because it took guts to sit down with them and have that conversation. Could you use a hug?'

'More than ever.'

'Can you hold that thought for two minutes while I finish feeding? Then I promise you the biggest hug ever.'

'That sounds like something worth waiting for.'

I wandered over to the Happy Hog Board and spotted that she'd named the triplets. A lump formed in my throat as I clocked their names: Ray, Charlotte and Lottie.

She must have followed my gaze. 'I didn't see why you should miss out just because Beth bagged your grandma's names first. And Ray may not be great for a baby but it's not a bad name for a hoglet, don't you think?'

'It's perfect.' My words came out husky. 'Thank you.'

A smile, a touch, a few words from Sammie and she could instantly lift me, no matter how low I was feeling. I glanced at the triplets' names again and smiled, thinking about my grandparents and the positive influence they'd been throughout my life. They'd have loved Sammie so much, especially Grandma. I turned back to look at her whispering to the hoglets about how much she loved them before she settled them back in their crate. I knew what I had to do – what Grandma would have wanted for me.

'Enormous hug on its way,' Sammie warned, rushing over to me, arms outstretched. As she held me, the discomfort of the past hour or so ebbed away and all I could think about was the amazing woman in my arms who didn't play games and didn't let people down. I suspected there weren't many people who'd open up their home to their boyfriend's ex, bounce back after being attacked twice, and still feel kindness and empathy towards a parent who'd treated them with such cruelty. She made me laugh, she made me feel again – a full spectrum of emotions instead of only anger – and she filled me with excitement for the future.

We sat on the sofa bed and, over coffees, I relayed the conversation. 'I don't know what I expected,' I told her when I'd finished. 'I suppose I was hoping for some lightbulb moment where I could go "yes, that makes sense" but it never came.'

'So you're no further forward?'

I shrugged. 'Yes and no. I suppose I am in that it's now out in the open. Some gaps are filled in but was I ever going to understand the scenario? Doubtful. They were adults who made bad choices and continued to make those bad choices with absolute disregard for anyone but themselves. Even if I believe everything they said about being apart when Beth was with me and abstaining from sex until Archie's conception, it's still not right is it? He was my dad and she was my girlfriend and they lied.'

Sammie sighed and stroked my arm. 'I'm sorry, Josh. I'm disappointed for you. I hoped there'd be something more than that although I'm not sure what it could have been.'

'Towards the end, Beth started wittering on about her dad

walking out when she was two and her mum paying more attention to a string of no-good boyfriends than she did to Beth but it all sounded a bit psycho-babbly.' I shrugged. 'I don't know. There could be something in it but it felt like an excuse thrown in there when I wasn't appeased by the rest of it. Probably makes Beth feel better to be able to blame someone else for her bad behaviour.'

'Where have I heard that before?' Sammie rolled her eyes at me. 'You said her mum's in Crete. Is Beth in touch with her now?'

'I think they text each other once in a blue moon. Dad said she's never met Archie and it's pretty telling that she never flew across when Beth was in hospital. What sort of mother does that?' I winced when I realised what I'd said. 'Sorry.'

'Don't be. Not a very good mother is the answer to that. At least Beth's mum had the excuse of living in another country. Mine was even offered a lift to the hospital.' She sighed. 'So how have you left it with them? Is there an atmosphere?'

'It was all very civilised. My shouting days are behind me. I told them there was a lot to take in and I might have further questions but I want to take the same attitude as Mum – it's done, it's in the past and we need to draw a line and start afresh.'

'If you do need to shout and scream, there are plenty of fields and outbuildings where you can vent. I bet there's a brilliant echo in the cow shed.'

I hugged her. 'I might do that. Or I might come and find you for hugs. You always know what to say and do to calm me down.'

'That's because I've been let down. Hurt recognises hurt.'

I cupped her face in my hand and gently kissed her. 'You're not still hurting, are you?'

She smiled. 'Not since I met my forever.'

The next few days were busy at the rescue centre with three new arrivals – Morpheus, Forrest and Moneypenny – all with various stages of flystrike. We had four releases too. Frodo was collected and Hermione, Barnum and Snoop Hoggy Hog were released on the farm. I still felt sad at each goodbye because I couldn't help but become attached to all our patients, but it was easing. After all, the whole point of what we did was to get them ready to return to a normal life in the wild.

There were no more new hoglet admissions but fourteen was more than enough to keep me occupied for the moment while I was in and out of the farmhouse checking on Beth. She was pretty much confined to staying upstairs during the day as she couldn't manage babies on the stairs with her injuries. They'd unpacked their kettle and mugs and Josh's office had become a makeshift kitchen with a mini fridge and their bottle steriliser. She could probably have struggled through the day on her own but I could tell she appreciated the help and the company.

I was surprised to find that I enjoyed being around her and could even see us becoming friends which was perhaps unexpected under the circumstances. That vulnerability that I'd detected the first time she turned up at the farm was definitely there and it was endearing.

* * *

On Thursday morning, I met with Jeanette Kingston from Terry's village. I showed her the pictures of Arwen tangled in the netting and she was shocked. She claimed that Terry always had a bee in his bonnet about something so she'd assumed that this was his latest crusade and he was making it up. No convincing was needed and she vowed to have the nets removed immediately. She was keen to learn more and asked if more members of the committee could visit later in the month to explore what they could do in the village to make it more hedgehog-friendly.

Hannah visited at lunchtime that day and we sat in the garden with Amelia, Archie and Lottie to give Beth a break. Amelia and Archie were so cute together. They kept prodding each other which sent them into fits of giggles.

'How are you finding it with a house full of babies?' Hannah asked. 'Any more thoughts on what we discussed?'

'A massive tangle of them. I've been rushed off my feet but it's always there at the back of my mind.'

'It's bound to be. It's a big thing.'

'Archie and Lottie are adorable and watching Josh with them tugs on my heart so much. He'd make such an amazing dad and I can't help thinking it would be unfair of me to take that opportunity away from him.'

She gave me a stern look. 'And it would be unfair of him to have a partner who agrees to having babies when she doesn't want them. Unless you've accepted that I'm right about you being sod all like your mum.' She raised her eyebrows in question.

I couldn't share what Dad had revealed about Mum's past. I didn't like keeping secrets from Hannah but it wasn't my secret so I needed to pick my words carefully. 'My head's still in a mess about that. A combination of what you said, something my Dad told me about Mum before they were married, and a bit of homework from Josh all scream at me that I really am nothing like her. But I just can't seem to shake the fear.'

'Are you saying you want kids?'

I looked towards Amelia and Archie still giggling at each other and at Lottie fast asleep in the Moses basket beside them. I thought about the past few days when I'd helped bathe and feed the siblings, and how wonderful it felt to give them sleepy hugs. I couldn't deny the pull.

'I do,' I whispered. 'It's just...'

'I know,' she said, gently. 'It's been tough. But remember you have time on your side. You're not even thirty yet. It's not like your baby-bearing years are nearly behind you. Why don't you spend some time working on your fear instead of feeling you have to make a decision right now? And keep talking to Josh. He needs to know where your head's at.'

I nodded. He'd been so brilliant. He'd kept his promise and not chased me about the 'homework' he'd set. Even when we'd talked in depth about what Dad revealed and how I felt about it, he hadn't taken that as an opportunity to push the baby agenda. He said he chose me whatever my decision, and I believed him.

* * *

On Friday morning, a winning hedgehog logo arrived by email. Finally! A first year called Devansh Chandra had designed a delightfully happy cartoon hedgehog with grey eyes and glasses – a tribute I wanted to Thomas – and had taken it a step further by also designing a wife and four hoglets.

'Thomas, Gwendoline and the four babies they lost,' I whispered, tears clouding my eyes as I scrolled through the images of each character and then scenes of them together in the wild. They were simply perfect.

I sat back in my chair, smiling. Life was pretty close to perfect at that point. Long may it continue.

SAMANTHA

Saturday arrived and, as I worked, a feeling of melancholy settled over me. This evening we were going to release Mr Snuffles.

I'd known the day would come eventually but I'd been dreading it. He'd been our second admission before we'd opened for business, before I'd even moved into the farmhouse, before the fire. Brought in with a broken leg, he'd been the first patient to need an operation and, as a result, had become our longest-staying guest.

For me, Mr Snuffles had also signified a new beginning. He'd arrived a few days after Mum told me she'd never wanted me and chose to cut me out of her life. His arrival had lifted me and given me focus. But now he was fully healed and it was time to set him free.

As dusk fell, Josh and I took the carry crate to Thomas's bench and sat for a moment. The sun was sinking over the fields to the west but wouldn't disappear for another hour or so. The light was beautiful, bathing everything in a golden glow.

'Big moment.' Josh patted the crate.

'Huge. I know it's a good thing but...'

'He's been with us since the start. It was always going to be harder saying goodbye to Mr Snuffles. You'll probably be the same when Gollum has to leave, although he won't be going anywhere if those spines don't grow back.'

Gollum had rapidly become another favourite. He was such a character and the thought of him leaving made me feel sad too.

'Do you think we'll see Mr Snuffles again?'

Josh laughed lightly and indicated the collection of hedgehog houses and feeding stations positioned round the garden. 'If you were a hedgehog and had five-star accommodation on hand like this, would you go far?'

I smiled. 'Probably not.' *Deep breath. It's time to let go.* 'Okay. Let's do it.'

I carried the crate across to the fence between the garden and meadow, lay it gently on the ground, pulled on my gloves and lifted Mr Snuffles out.

'Goodbye, little one,' I said, my voice catching in my throat. 'Stay safe out there.'

I placed him on the grass pointing towards the meadow. He raised his nose in the air and sniffed. He explored the immediate garden for a few moments, then shuffled along the side of the meadow, suddenly ducking between the stems. And that was it. The last of the original admissions was back in the wild where he belonged.

I didn't need to say anything. Josh reached out and pulled me into his arms while silent tears rained down my cheeks which quickly turned to sobs.

'He'll be fine,' he whispered. 'He's exactly where he should be.'

When the sobs finally eased and my body stopped shaking, he gently pulled me to my feet and led me over to the bench where we had a couple of cold bottles of lager waiting to toast the occasion.

'To the second hedgehog the badass hedgehog saviour rescued. May he have a long and happy future.'

I clinked my bottle against his. 'To Mr Snuffles.' Then I raised it towards the meadow. 'And to Quilly, Ripley, Luke and the other hoglets who crossed the rainbow bridge to be with Thomas and Gwendoline.'

The tears started again and Josh cuddled me to his side.

'I love it out here,' he said after I'd composed myself.

'Your mum thinks it feels magical.'

'My mum's probably right. Especially when you're here.' He tilted my face towards his and kissed my damp cheeks before his lips met mine.

'Definitely magical,' I whispered when we pulled apart, my heart racing and butterflies swooping and soaring in my stomach.

I cuddled into his side again and looked towards the meadow, straining my eyes in the hope of a last glimpse of Mr Snuffles.

'Oh my gosh!' I jumped up. 'Look!'

I crept to the edge of the garden, captivated by two adult hedgehogs and four hoglets who'd emerged from the meadow and were scurrying towards one of the feeding stations. It was like a scene from Devansh's winning logo entry and most unexpected as hedgehogs were solitary creatures so it was unusual to see adults together.

'Thomas, Gwendoline and their lost babies,' I whispered. My heart melted as the hoglets clambered over each other in an effort to get to the food and one of them tumbled over another, face-planting the bowl before quickly righting itself.

'Isn't this amazing?' I realised Josh wasn't beside me and turned to face the bench. My stomach did the most enormous backflip as he smiled and lowered himself onto one knee.

Oh my gosh! Is he...?

'I've been carrying something round all week trying to find the right moment and I can't think of a better one than right here in our favourite place at sunset, overlooking the Micklebys' meadow with one of our original hedgehogs returning to the wild. I love you, Sammie. I love you more than I ever thought it was possible to love another human being.' He smiled. 'You met an angry, stubborn man and you turned him into someone who cries saying goodbye to a hedgehog.'

'You were crying too? You big softie. That's so sweet.'

'I told you. You've changed me. I didn't like the person I'd become. It wasn't me and you helped me find the way back to the real me. I'm so proud of everything you've done here, how quickly you've learned, how caring you are. I'd always planned the future for the practice but never for my own life because I'd never found someone I wanted a future with. Then this crazy brunette banged on my door and accused me of being an idiot for parking too close.'

He reached into his pocket and removed a ring which he held out towards me. 'This was my grandma's and the man who gave her it made her so happy. I'd like to do the same for you. Will you marry me?'

I thrust out my left hand towards him, barely able to speak. 'Yes,' I squeaked. 'Yes I will!'

He slipped the ring on my finger then caught me in the most tender heart-melting kiss.

'You've made me cry again,' he said, wiping his cheeks as he pulled away. 'What have you done to me?'

'It's not me. It's this place. Magical.'

We stood in front of the bench, arms round each other, looking towards the meadow. I held my hand in front of me and twisted it from side to side to catch the fading light on the trio of diamonds.

'Do you like it?'

'It's exquisite.' I bit my lip, feeling the need to confess. 'I thought that the first time I saw it.' The morning after Josh and I got together, he'd been called out, leaving me alone at Wisteria Cottage. Not wanting to get a taxi back to Rich and Dave's in my party dress,

I'd raided his drawers for some suitable clothes and found a framed photo of Beth and the box containing the engagement ring. He knew I'd seen the photo because I'd had a wobble about how beautiful Beth was compared to me, but I'd never mentioned seeing the ring.

Josh stepped back, eyes wide with surprise. 'When have you seen it before?'

'When I was looking for some clothes to come home in the morning after we got together. That photo of Beth wasn't the only thing I found in your drawers. I know it was in a box but I couldn't help peeking. I'm sorry.'

He smiled and drew me to my side. 'It was obviously calling to you. You do realise that it was coincidence that the ring was with Beth's photo? Even when I discovered she was pregnant and, for the briefest of moments, thought the baby could be mine. Even when I could hear my granddad's voice in my head telling me I should "do the right thing", I could never have given Beth my grandma's ring. It was always meant for you because I was always meant for you just like this farm and the hedgehogs were always meant for you.' He kissed me again and my body felt like one with his.

We returned to Thomas's bench and Misty-Blue jumped up beside us and laid half on Josh's knee and half across mine, demanding attention. We both tickled her tummy as we watched the hedgehogs, chuckling at the hoglets. 'Oh my gosh!'

I leaned forward, squinting my eyes, as one of the adult hogs turned to face the other direction, revealing her left side. 'Look at her spines. I'm sure that's Mrs Tiggy Winkle!'

Another of the four hedgehogs I'd rescued from the fire, Mrs Tiggy Winkle had been our third patient brought in with a small cut on her face. She'd been easily distinguished from the others by a wiggly band of blonde spines – like a worm – on her right side.

Her cut had healed quickly so Josh had released her on the farm while I was still in hospital.

'I think you're right. She certainly didn't waste any time after she was released.'

'How lovely that she's had babies and brought them back here.'

Lottie's cry from the nursery filled the air and echoed across the fields. I glanced up at her window, across to Mrs Tiggy Winkle and her family, then at my beautiful engagement ring. Josh had proposed to me without an answer about having a family. He'd committed his future to me, accepting that the only babies we might have were prickly ones that couldn't stick around. I pictured him on the Family Fun Day dressed as Mickleby telling me that, if ever I doubted how he felt, I should picture him in that costume because that was true love. I never had doubted him. I felt it emanating from him every single day.

I looked back to the hedgehogs and across to the meadow and smiled. *You sent them, didn't you? It's a sign. And I hear the message loud and clear.*

I took Josh's hand in mine. 'How many babies do we have on the farm at the moment?'

'Lots of babies,' he said, laughing.

'I make it fourteen in the barn, two upstairs, four in the garden and goodness knows how many others on our land.'

'It's pretty special, isn't it?' He stroked his thumb gently over the back of my hand, sending tingles up my arm.

'It is. Babies make the place feel alive. New life, fresh starts, and I think it's time I made my own fresh start. You know that homework you set me? I did it.'

Josh squeezed my hand. 'What did you discover?'

'Exactly what you thought I'd discover. What Dad said. What Hannah said. What I know deep down but am fighting to accept. So I'm going to ask your mum to put me in touch with a good counsellor. The truth is that I *do* want a family. It's not because I'm a bit broody being surrounded by babies at the moment or because Thomas and Gwendoline would have wished for the farm to be filled with children. And it's not because, even though you are the most incredible man in the world for putting me first, I know you long for children too. It's because *I* want them. For me. But I'm scared. Mum never reached out for help but, as you've all said, I'm not my mum so I'm reaching out. I'm asking for help because I want this for us.'

Josh's eyes glistened. 'Whatever you decide and whenever you decide it, I'll help and support you every step of the way.'

I knew he would. He was the man who'd sat by my bedside while I was in a coma, held me when we lost hedgehogs and cried when we released them. He was the man who loved me so unconditionally that he was willing to cast aside his own hopes for fatherhood to be with me. He was the man who Thomas and Gwendoline chose for me and for Hedgehog Hollow. And, boy, did they choose well.

EPILOGUE
ONE WEEK LATER

I sat on Thomas's bench with a mug of tea in one hand, the other hand stroking Misty-Blue's warm belly as she lay sprawled across my lap.

'Listen to that,' I said to her, cocking my head to one side. 'Isn't it so peaceful?' The only sounds were the chirp of birds, the buzz of insects and Misty-Blue's gentle purrs.

'No babies crying for once,' I added, not that I really minded.

Closing my eyes, I tilted my head back towards the sun. It was a bright, warm Sunday in the middle of June so Paul and Beth had taken advantage of the gorgeous weather and driven Archie and Lottie to the coast. Josh had been called out to a goat emergency an hour ago so I was on my own at Hedgehog Hollow enjoying a rare and precious moment of tranquillity.

After a few minutes, I opened my eyes and sipped contentedly on my tea. My heart fluttered as the diamonds on my engagement ring sparkled in the sun. We hadn't made any plans for when we'd marry yet. It didn't feel right to set the date until Paul had been through the next round of chemotherapy later this month and we were, of course, still hoping a stem cell donor would be found.

Everyone had been thrilled at the announcement of our engagement. We'd invited Dad, Connie and Lauren to join Paul and Beth for afternoon tea last Sunday so we could share the news. After that I'd called Hannah who'd squealed down the phone, delighted for me but extra excited because she'd always longed to be a bridesmaid.

I tried my cousin Chloe next but she didn't answer. Loyalty towards her after years of close friendship meant it didn't feel right for Auntie Louise to hear first so I held off phoning her, trying Chloe repeatedly over the next few days but without success. On Thursday, fed up that messages and texts to get in touch urgently had seemingly been ignored, I phoned Auntie Louise who was also delighted. Then I texted Chloe:

✉ To Chloe
Josh asked me to marry him! I'm so excited. I've been trying to get hold of you all week as I ideally didn't want to tell you my big news by text but you haven't responded to my messages and I'm worried. I hope you're OK. HOT TIP! There's a woman on a farm in Huggleswick who is always here for you. You know where she is if you ever need her xxx

So far, she hadn't responded and I was determined not to let it dampen my excitement. If Chloe had decided to have an epic strop, I wasn't going to bend over backwards this time. I'd waved the white flag plenty of times and now it was her move.

I'd also sent a quick text to Mum:

✉ To Mum
I hope all's well with you. Just letting you

know that Josh asked me to marry him and I said
yes. Not planning to set a date yet. Sam x

She hadn't responded but I hadn't expected her to although I had hoped she might, even if it was just one word: 'congratulations'. I wasn't going to let her dampen my excitement either.

I swallowed my last mouthful of tea. 'Right, Misty-Blue, it's back to the hoglets for me.' She leapt off the bench and bounded towards the meadow to chase butterflies and I headed for the kitchen.

As I rinsed my mug in the sink, I gazed out of the window and spotted a car driving at speed along the farm track. Hedgehog emergency? I wiped my hands and rushed to the farmyard to help, then stopped dead, heart thumping. *Hang on! That's Chloe's car!*

She screeched to a halt with a spray of gravel beside me, yanked on the handbrake and leapt out. 'Did you mean your "HOT TIP"?' she cried.

'What?'

'You said you were always here for me. Is that true?'

'Of course. What...?'

She removed her sunglasses, revealing red, swollen eyes. 'Good, because Samuel and I need to stay here. I've left James.'

ACKNOWLEDGMENTS

Thank you so much for reading *New Arrivals at Hedgehog Hollow* – the second book in my Hedgehog Hollow series and my eleventh novel. Eleven! Eek!

I usually end my acknowledgements by thanking my readers for their support, reviews and kind messages but I'm going to start with that because the outpouring of love I've received for the first book in the series – *Finding Love at Hedgehog Hollow* – has been phenomenal. I'd worried about how readers might react to a move away from my usual Whitsborough Bay coastal setting but they have welcomed the farm, the meadow and the cast of characters – human and hedgehog – into their hearts. *Finding Love...* was released while I was writing *New Arrivals...* and the reaction to it gave me such a boost, especially as I was writing during strange and unusual times. Yes, *New Arrivals at Hedgehog Hollow* was written during the spring and summer of 2020 when the world as we all knew it changed beyond recognition.

You'll have noticed that, despite following a 2020 calendar (dictated by the first book – written pre-Covid – being set in 2019-20), *New Arrivals...* is set in a world without Covid-19. I've had so many messages from readers and read so many reviews expressing gratitude to me for writing uplifting novels that have provided much-needed escapism. It is therefore a conscious decision on my part to continue to provide this escapism with a book that isn't set in a socially distanced world.

My dedication for this book is to my brother-in-law, Richard Fisher, who passed away suddenly and unexpectedly in June 2020 at the young age of fifty. The loss was devastating and lockdown restrictions meant reaching out to his wife – my husband's sister – and two sons was challenging. At times like this, all you want to do is rush round and give your loved ones a hug and my heart breaks for anyone who lost someone they care for during this pandemic, whether that's been Covid-related or, like in Richard's case, completely unconnected. Restrictions and social distancing made an already challenging and emotional time even more difficult.

I wanted to dedicate this book to Richard – a fun-loving, gentle man who I always picture with a big smile on his face – and it felt particularly appropriate to do so because I was writing Book 1 the last time I saw him in February and writing my first draft of Book 2 when he left us. Rest in peace, Richard xx

My continued appreciation goes to my Auntie Gwen who rescues hedgehogs and who provided the original inspiration for writing a book set in a rescue centre. One of my favourite prickly characters, Gollum, is inspired by one of Auntie Gwen's permanent patients, Baldy, and I've used some of her treatment knowledge too.

Thank you to my brother, Chris Williams, for his pharmaceutical expertise and advice and to Tracy Underwood for her expertise on counselling. I also researched Hodgkin lymphoma in depth and am grateful to the valuable information available online from the NHS and various cancer charities including Anthony Nolan, Cancer Research UK, Macmillan Cancer Support and DKMS. I needed to make specific decisions, based on my research, about

Paul's treatment and his response to this. Each cancer patient's journey is unique to them so Paul's experiences may differ to others who have been diagnosed with the same type of cancer.

This is the first book of mine that hasn't been read by my beta readers. It's not that I didn't want them to, but more that I finished it at the eleventh hour and had no time to seek their advice. Mum, Liz and Sharon – hope you enjoy discovering one of my stories in its final format for once rather than an early draft!

Of the eleven books I've written, this has been the hardest. I think of writing series as being my thing but it only struck me when I was a little way into *New Arrivals...* that this is the first time I've written a series or connected book using the same main character. All of my other books have a new heroine each time. And, suddenly, I was thrown. There was more of Samantha's story I wanted to tell but much of the plot revolved round Josh and his family situation and it wasn't working telling this purely through Samantha's eyes. I sent a frantic email to my amazing editor, Nia Beynon, asking her how she felt about me writing from both Samantha's and Josh's perspectives. She was very happy to go for that and, thankfully, the story began flowing much more freely.

As well as being the hardest to write, this book became the hardest to edit. Although Nia loved the story, she felt the timescale needed adjusting. She was right. She always is. But doing that had a massive knock-on effect on so many parts of the story and I effectively had to unpick it and sew it back together in a completely different way including writing a host of brand new scenes. It nearly broke me. I spent days on end, staring at my computer, wondering if I was capable of doing it but Nia was there with ideas, support and encouragement and it got there in the end. Nia – you are absolutely the best.

As always, thank you to Dushi Horti and Sue Lamprell for their expertise in copy editing and proofreading and to Debbie Clement for this stunning cover. Isn't it just gorgeous? And, of course, thanks to the whole of the team at Boldwood Books who are the most supportive, friendly, professional publisher with whom it is an absolute pleasure to work. Boldwood – I'm thrilled to have signed another contract with you – a whopping 12-book one – meaning lots more stories are on the way! Thanks also to my fellow Boldwood authors who read and promote my work. You're all so amazing.

Thank you also to the fabulous Emma Swan for bringing the characters to life on the audio version of *New Arrivals at Hedgehog Hollow*. It sounds incredible. And thanks to ISIS Audio for producing the recording and Ulverscroft for distributing it.

In among the challenges of lockdown and the sadness of losing Richard, summer 2020 brought me something pretty amazing. Since becoming a published author in 2015, I've dreamed of being able to write full-time. Thanks to Boldwood Books and my amazing readers, I've now achieved that dream and I still can't believe I get to spend my days chatting to my imaginary friends and making stuff up. Most of the time, it doesn't feel like work and I cannot thank you all enough for making this possible.

The other two people who made my dream possible are my incredible husband and daughter who support me, champion me and understand me – even when imposter syndrome takes hold and I feel like a fraud pretending to be a real author. Mark and Ashleigh, I love you both so much xx

Thank you to Rachel Gilbey for organising a fabulous blog tour and to all the bloggers/reviewers who give their time for free, reading and reviewing my books, then promoting them to their followers. I felt so much love from this community for *Finding Love at Hedgehog Hollow* and hope *New Arrivals...* is loved just as much. There are so many bloggers I would love to name but it would be a pretty long list so, to all those who have given a lovely review for one, two or all of my books, you are superstars and I am so grateful for everything you do.

Last, but not least, we ran a competition in the summer. Subscribers to my newsletter were put into a draw and the winner was asked to name a hedgehog which would appear in this book. I hoped that the chosen name would be an exciting one and I couldn't have been more thrilled when the winner, Sarah Rothman, suggested Snoop Hoggy Hog. I laughed out loud when I heard it and couldn't wait to include it. I hope it gave you a laugh too. Thank you, Sarah. That was inspired. I hope you enjoy your copy of *New Arrivals at Hedgehog Hollow* with Snoop Hoggy Hog making his debut appearance in Chapter 33.

If you've loved this second trip to Hedgehog Hollow, I'd be ever so grateful for a review – a sentence is enough – and a recommendation to friends and family. I'm off to write the third instalment now!

Love and hugs

Jessica xx

HEDGEHOG TRUE/FALSE

Hedgehogs are born with spines

FALSE - Imagine poor mum giving birth if they had spines! Ouch! When hoglets are born, their skin is covered in fluid and, after a few hours, this is reabsorbed and soft white spines erupt from the skin

Hedgehogs are good swimmers

TRUE - They're really good swimmers and, perhaps even more surprisingly, can climb trees. They do sometimes drown, though. It's not the swimming that's the problem; it's the getting out again and they can perish due to the exhaustion of trying to escape. It's therefore important that ponds have the means for a hedgehog to get out if they accidentally fall in

Baby hedgehogs are called hoglets

TRUE - Isn't it cute? They're sometimes known as piglets, pups or kittens but the official term is hoglets

Hedgehogs are nocturnal

TRUE AND FALSE – We tend to think of hedgehogs as being nocturnal which would suggest they're only out at night but, while they are most active at night time, the technical term for hedgehogs is 'crepuscular' which means they can be active at twilight too. We often see hedgehogs moving around in summer when it's still light because the days are longer and they need to search for food

Hedgehogs can run in short bursts at speeds of up to 3mph

FALSE - They're even faster than that. They are surprisingly nippy and can reach top speeds of 5.5mph in short bursts. Go hedgehogs!

Hedgehogs lose half their body weight during hibernation

FALSE - It's actually just over a third but that's still a significant amount and hedgehogs fresh from hibernation are going to need some major feasts to build up their strength quickly

Hedgehogs got their name in the Middle Ages from the word 'hygehoge' which translates today as 'hedge' and 'pig' combined

TRUE - The name does what it says on the tin! They snuffle round hedges for their foot and this snuffling/grunting is just like a pig

Hedgehogs have good eyesight

FALSE – Eyesight is the weakest of the hedgehog's senses and they are very susceptible to visual conditions. They have a keen sense of smell, taste and hearing and it's these senses they will use far more than their eyesight so one-eyed hedgehogs and even blind ones can survive in the wild thanks to their other senses

Hedgehogs are quiet eaters

FALSE - They're very noisy when they eat. They love their food and will slurp, crunch and lip-smack with their mouths open. Not the ideal dinner guest!

HEDGEHOG DOS AND DONT'S

Food and Drink

DO NOT give hedgehogs milk to drink. They are lactose intolerant. Dairy products will give them diarrhoea which will dehydrate them and can kill them

DO give hedgehogs water but please have this in a shallow dish. If it's in a deep dish, the risk is that they'll fall in and be unable to get out again

DO give hedgehogs dog or cat food - tin, pouch or biscuit format - they can eat both meaty and fishy varieties. It's a myth that they can't have fishy varieties of food but they may prefer meaty varieties because they prefer the smell

DO try to create a feeding station for a hedgehog so that other garden visitors (including cats) don't beat the hedgehog to it. You don't need to buy anything expensive. There are loads of tutorials and factsheets online around creating your own simple station

Your Garden

DO avoid having fences with no gaps under them. Hedgehogs can travel a long way in an evening and they rely on being able to move from one garden to the next. Or you can create a hedgehog highway in your fence

DO place a ramp by a pond so that, if a hedgehog falls, it can easily get out

DO NOT let your dog out into your garden without checking it's hedgehog-free. This is especially important during babies season (May/June and Sept/Oct) when there may be hoglets out there

DO build a bug hotel and DO plant bug-friendly plants. It will attract all sorts of delicious food for your hedgehogs

DO NOT use slug pellets. Hedgehogs love to eat slugs so pellets reduce their food supply and/or poison hedgehogs

DO have a compost heap or a messy part in your garden. If you can have some sticks/wood piled up in a safe corner, this makes a perfect habitat for hibernating

DO check your garden before strimming or mowing. Garden machinery can cause horrific accidents or fatalities

DO NOT leave netting out as hedgehogs can become trapped in it. If you have football goals in your garden, lift the netting up overnight and secure it safely to avoid injury or fatalities

DO always check bonfires before lighting as there may well be hogs nestling in there

Finding Hogs

DO NOT assume that a hedgehog out in the daylight is in danger. They usually are but watch first. It could be a mum nesting. If it's moving quickly and appears to be gathering food or nesting materials, leave it alone. If this isn't the case, then something is likely to wrong. Seek help

DO handle hedgehogs with gardening glove - those spines are there to protect the hogs and hurt predators - but keep handling to a minimum. Stay calm and quiet and be gentle with them. Transfer them into a high-sided box or crate with a towel, fleecy blanket or shredded newspaper (and a thick layer of paper on the bottom to soak up their many toilet visits). This will help keep them warm and give them somewhere to hide. Make sure there are plenty of air holes

DO NOT move hoglets if you accidentally uncover a nest but, if mum isn't there, do keep an eye on the nest and seek help if mum doesn't return. Hoglets won't survive long without their mother's milk. Put some water and food nearby so mum (assuming she returns) doesn't have far to travel for sustenance. If the hoglets are squeaking, this means they are hungry and you may need to call help if this continues and there's no sign of mum

MORE FROM JESSICA REDLAND

We hope you enjoyed reading *New Arrivals at Hedgehog Hollow*. If you did, please leave a review.

If you'd like to gift a copy, this book is also available as an ebook, digital audio download and audiobook CD.

Sign up to Jessica Redland's mailing list for news, competitions and updates on future books.

http://bit.ly/JessicaRedlandNewsletter

ABOUT THE AUTHOR

Jessica Redland writes uplifting stories of love, friendship, family and community set in Yorkshire where she lives. Her Whitsborough Bay books transport readers to the stunning North Yorkshire Coast and her Hedgehog Hollow series takes them into beautiful countryside of the Yorkshire Wolds.

Visit Jessica's website: https://www.jessicaredland.com/

Follow Jessica on social media:

- facebook.com/JessicaRedlandWriter
- twitter.com/JessicaRedland
- instagram.com/JessicaRedlandWriter
- bookbub.com/authors/jessica-redland

ALSO BY JESSICA REDLAND

ABOUT BOLDWOOD BOOKS

Boldwood Books is a fiction publishing company seeking out the best stories from around the world.

Find out more at www.boldwoodbooks.com

Sign up to the Book and Tonic newsletter for news, offers and competitions from Boldwood Books!

http://www.bit.ly/bookandtonic

We'd love to hear from you, follow us on social media:

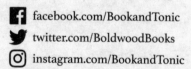

facebook.com/BookandTonic
twitter.com/BoldwoodBooks
instagram.com/BookandTonic